SLAUGHTER BY THE WABASH

The brightening sky revealed a gory, horrifying tableau on the bloody hill so close to the Wabash. Hundreds of men were down. Hundreds of others, their eyes wide and haunted, continued to fire wildly at faint shapes in the mist or shadows among the distant trees.

The soldiers had a little more elbow room now, because so many men were dead or wounded. General St. Clair, sick as he was, strode fearlessly among his men, exhorting them to fight, praying for a miracle.

Through the unspeakable, murderous horror of this battle came an impulse to survive. Since the soldiers could not win, they could at least escape to fight another day—if they made their move right now.

St. Clair's surviving officers organized one last, massive, desperate bayonet charge . . .

The First Frontier Series
by Mike Roarke
from St. Martin's Paperbacks

THUNDER IN THE EAST
SILENT DRUMS
SHADOWS ON THE LONGHOUSE
BLOOD RIVER

BLOOD RIVER

MIKE ROARKE

SMP
ST. MARTIN'S PAPERBACKS

BLOOD RIVER

ISBN: 0-312-95420-4

Printed in the United States of America

St. Martin's Paperbacks edition / April 1995

10 9 8 7 6 5 4 3 2 1

For Quay Grigg

1

HE WASN'T A YOUNG LIEUTENANT. HE WAS AN old lieutenant. And he was shabby. Seth Collins smothered a laugh. Old lieutenants were always shabby. Maybe that was why they stayed lieutenants. This one was riding a horse so wide-bodied that Seth was sure the old lieutenant must have requisitioned it from the barn of the last farmer he had visited with his indolent drunken contingent of soldiers.

But he did have the power of the government, such as it was, behind him. That meant he could commit murder and claim that it was in the line of duty. Seth knew he would have to be careful.

"What can I do to help you, sir?" he asked the old lieutenant. He almost gagged on the *sir*.

The lieutenant looked down from his swaybacked brown plow horse. His face was drawn. Was there a trace of pain there? Were his legs and backside on fire from the agony of spending the day spread-eagled across the back of his stolen animal? Seth sincerely hoped so. He hated this man on sight. He knew that the lieutenant had been sent by Congress to throw him and other Ohio settlers off their lands. That was reason enough.

The lieutenant looked around him and took in Seth's homestead with a mixture of distaste and envy. This was not one of your hack-a-little-clearing-and-grow-corn-between-the-stumps homesteads. The cabin was well-built and spacious, as cabins go, and there were several outbuildings that apparently housed people. There was a nice little barn, probably full of horses, at least forty acres of fine, cleared land, and forty more that had been somewhat cleared. There was corn growing in straight green rows. Someone must have done some powerful work to get all that seed in the ground and keep the weeds down.

The lieutenant smiled. It would be a pleasure to take this would-be country squire down a peg. "You," he said. "I need to talk to you."

"The name is Collins," Seth replied. "And you're on my land."

"Your land? This is Indian land." The old lieutenant dismounted and walked over to the frontiersman to face him down with all the authority that the Congress of the confederation had vested in him. Unfortunately, once he was down off the back of his horse, he found himself looking up into the eyes of the frontiersman, who was nearly a head taller than the sawed-off lieutenant.

Collins's wife appeared at the door of their cabin. The lieutenant frowned when he saw that this was not the big, rawboned brood mare he had seen in other frontier cabins. She was tall and slender, wore a blue cotton dress and had a stubborn, angry set to her face. The lieutenant suppressed a sneer. The woman was not high-bred, she only pretended —looked at her husband's clear acres and imagined them a vast domain. Their humble log cabin was her plantation house, no doubt. Beside her stood a young girl, maybe twelve years old. The girl did not cling to her mother's skirts. Her proud, strong chin showed that she was not intimidated by the lieutenant and his men in their threadbare uniforms. Nothing he hated more than fake fine people, he thought maliciously. But he had some news for them that would make them considerably less fine.

"Sir," he said with a sarcastic slur on the end of the word, "you have until noon the day after tomorrow to pack your belongings and leave this property. Failure to do so will place you in violation of both the statutes of Congress and peace treaties of these United States."

He saw the woman suck in her breath, and he took an almost obscene pleasure in her distress. Seth studied the face of this lieutenant. He was a ne'er-do-well, that was for certain, and so were the dozen soldiers who stood behind him, at ease in formation, their dusty muskets barely gleaming in the summer sunshine. Few men of any substance or character were serving in the ranks these days. After the war had ended, Congress had rapidly dismantled the Continental army. The people had suffered enough at the hands of soldiers over the past decade. They didn't trust soldiers. What use did the new nation have for a standing army? In times of dire need they could simply call out the local militia.

But things had changed quickly. All along the frontier, restless Americans had been crossing the mountains to homestead in Indian territories. The Congress had no desire to irritate the various tribes of the West. It needed to drive the settlers back to the east side of the mountains before the intermittent massacres turned into a general firestorm. To this end they had raised a small army and sent it west to persuade the settlers to desert their new settlements before the Indians did them in.

Seth looked down at the wretched lieutenant and felt the man's self-satisfaction oozing from him like infection from a suppurating sore. He could see the lieutenant's wretched outfit fingering their muskets. It had been a long, boring march along the Ohio, and they were itching for action, especially action that did not entail much risk to themselves. He did not want to give them an excuse to exercise their superiority. Best not to irritate them much. But neither did he want to make them suspicious by being too obsequious. Best to irritate them a little.

"Where's your commission?" Seth asked testily. From the corner of his eye he could see his hired man, Mose Johnson, standing in the barn, concealed by shadow to the lieutenant, who had the sun to contend with.

"This is my commission," the lieutenant answered, gesturing toward the men behind him.

"You'll have to do better than that, sir. If I'm going to vacate my property."

The lieutenant was angry but he did have a set of orders, which he retrieved from his pack and smugly handed over to Seth.

"This is it?" asked Seth, amused, as he unfolded the parchment. "I can't read a thing on here."

"Hell, mister," the lieutenant replied, unconsciously slipping into a respectful mode and resenting Seth for making him do it. "We were fording a creek down in Virginia and I slipped and the parchment got soaked and the ink washed off. You look at it closer and you'll see some words on it—look here." He pointed out a couple of squiggles. "Lieutenant John Worley, you see?"

Seth did see, barely. He had never doubted the lieutenant and his mission. He was merely wondering what the lieutenant would do with it. The next actions of the lieutenant and his men opened up many possibilities.

"Get the animals out of your barn," he said.

"Why?" Seth asked.

"Never you mind, you. Just do as I say." Now that Seth

had acknowledged his authority, the lieutenant's manner lost all deference. He was the petty tyrant of his wretched domain. "Get the animals out of your barn or I will shoot you now."

Seth walked into the barn, followed by a large lout the lieutenant called "Sergeant." He began to lead from the barn the first of the two horses, two mules, and two milk cows that were inside because it was still morning and they had not yet been turned out to pasture. Johnson was hiding, Seth did not know where.

The sergeant led out the second horse, and two privates entered the barn to help him finish the job. The lieutenant now entered the barn. He was checking the priming of the huge pistol he held in his hand.

"You're gonna fire my barn, Lieutenant?" Seth asked, his voice somehow remaining calm.

"In two days I'm gonna fire every building you've got standing on this place. It's in my orders, the ones you claim you can't read." Seth wanted so badly to smash the smirk that the lieutenant did not try to hide. "You people have got to learn that the United States has laws and that you've got to obey them."

"I know about the United States, sir," said Seth. "I fought in the war of independence and killed a few of its enemies."

The lieutenant missed the sarcasm in Seth's voice and assumed that the *sir* denoted respect. That pleased the lieutenant and made him all the more eager to intimidate Seth. The two privates had by now led the cows from the barn. The lieutenant held the gun to a bed of straw and pulled the trigger. The straw caught quickly.

"You men!" he hollered to the remaining soldiers, who had been standing around in various postures of lazy ease, picking their noses and scratching their lice. "Pile on some more straw and some wood and let's see if we can make this woodpile burn fast."

It had taken Seth, Johnson, and another hired man a week to put up the barn. By noon it would be ashes.

As the flames began to rise along the walls, Seth wondered why Johnson had not come out of hiding. He was contemplating running into the barn and doing a last moment search for his longtime friend, but something told him that Johnson was all right and that he had a reason for not making an appearance.

The lieutenant stood, hands on hips, watching the barn burn. Seth stood next to him, his mind at work planning his next move. He had put several backbreaking years into his farm, and had no desire to abandon it because a feeble central government could not make up its mind whether or not it wanted pioneers.

Suddenly the lieutenant had a whim. "Shoot the cows," he shouted toward the two privates closest to them.

Seth took hold of the lieutenant's wrist. "Where does it say that you have the right to kill our livestock?" he asked.

The lieutenant pulled his arm away. "The same place it says that I can put you up against a wall and shoot you if you stand in my way."

Abruptly, a scream emerged from one of the outbuildings not far from the main cabin. A door opened and a woman flew out, head first, and tumbled down the stairs onto the dry earth.

"Lord, if it ain't a nigger wench," said the lieutenant. "Ain't you the high-blown one to own a nigger wench."

"I don't 'own' nobody, lieutenant. She's a free woman and she works for me." You're going too far now, Seth started to say, but he clamped his mouth shut, because he had made his plans, and they were dependent upon his staying alive.

"Ralston!" shouted the lieutenant. "Leave the wench alone and help Heath 'n' McReynolds shoot them two cows. Then we'll carve out some beef and take it with us. Hurry up. We've got more homesteaders to visit today!"

Seth Collins was a hard man. He had experienced plenty of war and hardship in his thirty-six years, but his heart nearly broke when he saw the two privates walk up to his milk cows and shoot them between the eyes. "You will pay, you sonofabitch," he muttered silently, turning his back so he would not have to watch the butchering. "And if anything happened to Johnson, you'll live to roast."

Seth walked over to where the woman lay writhing in the dust. Two children had run from the house and were on their knees crying, hugging her and trying to make her feel better.

"You!" the lieutenant shouted at him. "What is your name?"

Seth did not reply until he had ascertained that the woman, whose name was Millie, was all right. Then he turned around and walked back to the lieutenant. "Collins," Seth replied.

"Collins what?" the lieutenant asked, so contemptuously that Seth could not bear to give him the courtesy of a proper answer.

"Zeb Collins," he said.

"Two days," the lieutenant reminded him. "Thanks for the horses."

Now, the contingent was much better mounted than they had been. The lieutenant was especially well-mounted, having taken Seth's best horse for his own. "Let's go, men," he ordered. His sergeant, who had taken Seth's other good riding horse and rescued a saddle from the burning barn, rode up to the lieutenant and started whispering something to him, meanwhile pointing to some of the privates who stood sulking nearby.

The lieutenant replied in low spoken tones that Seth picked up with his keen woodsman's hearing. "Don't worry, when these people leave, on foot, they'll leave a lot behind. Tell the men that's when they can pick and choose."

The roof of the barn fell in on itself in a shower of sparks and a black curtain of smoke. Seth stood silently in the yard, his head hanging, as the U.S. military contingent rode and marched out to the road and headed south. Once the army was out of sight, the door to his house opened and the tall woman stomped down the stairs. The dignity was gone, replaced by raw anger.

"You just let 'em burn down the barn. Just let 'em burn it down!" she growled. "Let 'em shoot our cows! How are we gonna make butter?"

"Don't worry about the butter," he replied, abruptly shifting his anger from the lieutenant to his wife. "They're gonna come back and burn down everything else."

"I told you not to move us out here, but oh no, the farm in Pennsylvania wasn't good enough. Now what are we gonna do?"

It was the nasty, accusing tone in her voice that made him want to hit her. Sometimes he did. Sometimes she hit him back. Then their daughter would have to slip out and hide in the barn for safety.

There were three homes to the south, those of Walker, St. Jean, and Elberton. As soon as the lieutenant and his men had disappeared down the road, Johnson emerged from the cornfield behind the barn with Jake, the other hired man, beside him. Both of them were filled with silent fury, but both, like Seth, knew how to control their emotions and turn them into useful tools.

"Walker is three miles down the road. Johnson, you take the short trail and find him. Jake, you get Elberton and his sons, and I'll grab a hold of St. Jean. I believe if we hurry, we can make it to the sunken road just north of Walker's farm before those lazy bastards."

The three farms to the south were pretty close to each other. Collins and his two workers had grabbed their weapons and ammunition and were about to head for the neighbors, when Seth had another idea. "Your wife's handy," he said. "Why not have her come with us?"

Johnson nodded. While he headed for his cabin, Seth and Jake set out at a swift lope down the old trace beyond the hill. It was a shorter run, but impossible for a wagon to move on, so it had fallen into disuse. Now it made the difference for the men of Walker Valley.

Hughie Elberton was a short, stocky man who had been an overage sergeant in the war of independence. He had two squat sons and one tall one, all in their late teens or early twenties, all redheaded, all good with a gun, and all present when Seth left the trace and headed up their road to the front of the house.

Elberton walked slowly down his road to meet Collins. "I saw the smoke," he said. "Indians?"

"Much worse," Seth answered. "Government men."

"Burned your house?" the old sergeant asked in a hissing tone.

"My barn. Shot my cows. He aims to burn us all out!"

"What can we do?"

"There's about a dozen of 'em. Either we give in and get out, or we take care of them."

"Army troops?" Elberton mused. "I don't know about that."

"You gonna give up and let your family starve this winter? Come on, man. Get your boys out. "We're goin' huntin'!"

Elberton thought for a moment. Once he had made up his mind, he wasted no time assembling his three boys and taking them down the trace to the cutoff that led to the sunken road.

There was a stand of hickory trees just east of their destination. It was here that the frontier farmers met, four men who had headed west after the war and with their strong arms hacked a bare living out of the forest. There were a few others close by, but not close enough to help out. Anyway, Seth reasoned, there would be nine of them, not including Johnson's wife, Sally, and that should be enough.

The sunken road was a place where the road ducked into a defile seven feet deep, with sides too sheer to climb, though a truly desperate man might somehow claw his way up to the top and make his escape. Here Seth would set up his ambush. His plan was simple and deadly.

2

THE MEN WHO SET UP THE AMBUSH OF THE shabby lieutenant and his soldiers did not think of themselves as rebels. They were Americans, desperate Americans who could scarcely believe that their own government would make war on them. They had in their lifetimes seen the English do the same, but the English were foreigners. Was it possible that the Virginians and New Englanders who led their new nation were also foreigners to the families who struggled on the western frontier? These men thought maybe so, and so they armed themselves and went to the woods to fight for their homes, even as they had years before against the English.

At the end of the defile the road took a sharp turn to the left. Seth stationed four men there—Johnson and the three Elberton boys, Luke, Charles, and Dan—plus Johnson's wife Sally. The men were armed with straight-shooting rifles, and Sally, a big, rawboned woman, favored a musket loaded with small shot.

Seth and Jake were concealed on the right side overlooking the road. Hugh Elberton, St. Jean, and Walker lay at the bend behind the defile, to cut off any possible retreat. They would not appear until the first shots were fired. "Please, gentlemen," Seth begged them as he led them all into position, "aim for the men, not the stock. I need my horses and my mules. And whatever you do, don't let a one escape."

They waited. Some were veterans of one or two wars. To them this was a turkey shoot. It was the first big fight for the three young Elbertons, but Seth had seen them hunt in the woods and he trusted their shooting eyes. What he could not imagine was how they struggled to control their excitement. They took deep breaths and licked their dry lips with dry tongues. They took practice aim down the road and nodded their heads when Johnson reminded them not to fire until he had, but that when they pulled the trigger they must kill their man.

Then there was silence. But only for a moment. Deep in the woods, up the road, they heard a sharp whinny. It was Hex, Seth's favorite horse, giving the lieutenant the very devil of a ride, just as Seth knew he would. Why did every man who had ever ridden a horse think he was man enough to control a spirited charger? Seth wondered. In fact, few men could, and the rest generally rode in quiet desperation, clinging tightly to anything that was handy. The lieutenant would be useless in this fight.

Soon they could hear the sound of voices, men quarreling about something or other and the lieutenant telling them to shut their yaps, or traps. Then came the clip-clop of hooves on the dry, hard-packed dirt road, and the booted footfalls. There was not a woodsman in the bunch, Seth thought, but still he looked behind him on the off chance that the lieutenant had thrown a flanker or two out. But no, the lieutenant could not imagine that a miserable settler might dare to attack the mighty army of the United States. They were just out on a Sunday ride to throw somebody out of his house and burn it down. No cause for care or alarm.

Seth could hear them up close now. His ears told him that if he looked over the edge into the defile, they would be below them, but he did not dare look until he knew they were past him. Thanks to his horses and mules, most of the men were now mounted. Kind of irregular, he thought, to just mount infantry on any animals they happened to come across. There was a lot that was irregular about this group.

A shot rang out ahead, followed by a volley, and finally, a single shotgun blast. Seth stuck his head up in time to see three of his animals, their saddles or blankets empty, go galloping off down the trail. Hex had reared up at the first shot and flung the lieutenant back over his tail, probably saving his life. The soldiers on foot turned and fled in the direction they had come from, moving extra fast to avoid being trampled by the two men behind them on the mules. Seth took aim with his pistols and brought down first one, then another, of the terrified men as they tried to flee past him. Jake fired his rifle and brought down a third.

Meanwhile Elberton, St. Jean, and Walker had moved to the middle of the road, cutting off the retreat of the survivors. Like the veterans they were, they took cool aim and shot down the two remaining foot soldiers and one of the mule riders. The lone remaining rider then fell off his mount and lay quivering in the roadway, certain that his end had come.

The men and woman on either end of the defile reloaded and walked toward the carnage, their senses tensed for more action. The two men who had been thrown from their mounts were on the ground waiting for their senses to return. The lieutenant appeared unhurt, but the other man was flexing his arm and checking it for breaks. As the numbness wore off he began to groan.

Eight of the men lay still, and two others were curled up in pain, gut-shot and only a few agonized minutes from death. Seth and the others moved from body to body. It turned out that one of the eight was not wounded, though unconscious. Johnson studied him, brought him around with some water, and told him he would live if they let him. Another man, it was discovered, was playing possum. Seth gave him a kick in the ribs that made him go "Oof!" and then hauled him to his feet by his hair. While the others wore some kind of Continental blue that showed they were government soldiers, this one dared to travel in an old, frazzled green tunic like those the Tories had worn during the war.

With a sour look on his face Seth rubbed the fabric with his fingers.

"I got it off a dead Tory at King's Mountain," whined the soldier, his eyes wide with fear.

"I'll bet you did," Seth responded with such a fierce look that the man took a step back. Unconsciously, Seth put his hand on the head of the hatchet he had stuck in his belt, and the man's knees buckled.

Johnson laughed. "This man will die of fright if you don't leave him alone, Seth."

"All right, we've got 'em, what in hell are we gonna do with 'em?" the senior Elberton asked. Two of the privates and the lieutenant were on their feet in a group, their hands tied behind them, the fourth survivor standing by himself. The privates stared at the twigs and dead leaves on the forest floor, one silent, the other moaning from the pain in his broken arm. But the lieutenant was salty.

"What in hell do you think you've done, damn you!" he exploded, once he understood the full extent of his disaster. "You've gone to war against the United States, that's what you've done!"

Their conquerors stood in a circle surrounding their prisoners, contemplating the enormity of their deed. They had indeed taken on the army of the United States and effortlessly defeated them.

"You men are all as good as dead. You might as well give up your weapons and come back with me, or the next time there'll be a bigger army and they'll just come in and wipe you out!" The lieutenant spoke with the arrogant wrath of a man who knew he was in the right.

Walker spoke up. Of them all, he was the most easily bullied. "We've done it now, boys," he said.

Seth threw him a look of contempt. "Done what, Walker?" he hissed. "They were fixin' to throw us out and burn us down. What would've happened to you and your family if we'd let 'em do that?"

"We could've waited for them to leave and then rebuilt somewhere else."

"Oh? With what? They took my livestock, remember? Killed my cows. They'd have done the same to you. It's too late to get another crop in, and you don't think they would've left without destroyin' our corn, do you?"

"We shouldn't have done it," Walker insisted.

"Yes we should have," interjected St. Jean, the half Abnaki son of a French Courier de Bois.

"We've done it," said Seth calmly.

"Well, what'll we do now?" asked Elberton. "There's four of 'em still alive. We set 'em loose, they'll have the whole American army down on us. We can't kill 'em all."

Seth looked around at the bodies, and the prisoners, and his allies.

"I don't know if you men can understand what you got

yourselves into when we moved out here. We are beyond the proclamation line of settlement."

"That's an old British law. Who'da thought our government would honor it?" asked Walker.

"They do," replied Seth. "Maybe because there's politicians who have land companies that want this land. Well, we're here and we can't go back. Every year there's more 'n' more settlers pourin' over the mountains and flatboatin' down the rivers, and there ain't no government on earth gonna hold 'em back. Sooner or later the government'll give in. Meanwhile we have to fight off the Indians, and the army, and whatever fools come out with a piece of skin sayin' that your land belongs to them. And we—"

"All right, I get your point!" Elberton said. "But what about them? We let them go back, they'll have the army on us. But we can't just kill 'em."

"They'll kill us if we don't kill them," said St. Jean, a pragmatic man whose knife still held bloodstains from long ago in the higher nicks on his blade and handle.

"But they were just doin' their duty, weren't they?" Elberton stood close to Seth, his eyes like bullets.

Seth was not intimidated by the older man. "Their duty? See these mules? These horses? They belong to me. Lieutenant, did you give me any vouchers promising to pay me for these 'requisitions'? Did you even say anything like, 'Sorry, but I need your animals. I'll bring 'em back when I can'? Or did you just steal 'em?"

Frightened as he was, the lieutenant knew where these questions were heading.

"Sure I did," he answered. "Yeah, that's what I did."

"What did you do?"

"I, uh—yeah, I wrote you vouchers all right."

"You men—you!" Seth pointed to the two privates. "Did

you see him write out vouchers? Did you see him hand them to me?"

They looked at their lieutenant, then spoke up. "Yeah, that's what he did," said one. "You prob'ly threw them away all right," said the other.

"Threw them away? Would I throw away the only legitimate claim I had to my animals?" He pointed at the possum player in the Tory green tunic. "Did your lieutenant write out a voucher and hand it to me? You were close enough to see him do it."

The man in green saw that Seth had a hanging look in his eye. There was no saving the lieutenant, that was for sure. He spat in the lieutenant's direction. "Nah, he never did nothin' like that," he said.

"Damn your eyes, Thrasher!" hollered the lieutenant.

"All right, we got a horse-thief lieutenant and two horse-thief privates ready to lie for him." Elberton had made up his mind. "We can hang them. But what about this one?"

"That one," Seth declared, "is a Tory. He should have been hung when the war was over."

The four survivors had been in such a state of shock over the sudden massacre of their contingent that their thoughts had been reduced to confusion. All this talk about hanging them brought their world into sharp focus.

"You can't just hang us!" complained the lieutenant. "Where's the justice?"

"What kind of justice were you gonna give us?" Elberton asked.

"We were just doin' our duty. Doin' what Congress ordered us to do."

"Now that's the nub of it," said Elberton. "Every man of us fought for the United States. We got paid in worthless dollars and come home with nothin'. We go out to western Pennsylvania, and who owns all the land out there? General Washington and his friends. So we cross the Ohio to settle in the territory of Injuns that fought against the United States, and what do we get? We get you out here tellin' us we got to go back the other side of the line where there ain't no land for us to stretch out on.

"Them smart lawyers in the Congress don't fool me a bit. When they feel like it, they'll erase that line, only then they'll be the ones that own the land we're on now. And then we'd have to buy it from them if we want to live here. Only we wouldn't have the money to buy it with 'cause you will have burned us out."

The lieutenant looked down at the ground. "That ain't my business," he said. "They give me orders and I'm supposed to carry them out. Don't blame me. Them's the ones passed the laws."

"I'm not blamin' you for the laws, I'm just tellin' you why we're hangin' you for stealin' Collins's stock. We let you go, and you'll be back with half an army and you'd probably hang us on the spot. Say, how stupid do you think we are?"

The lieutenant did not answer. His thoughts were on his own mortality. Two of Elberton's boys raced back to their farm and returned in a few minutes with a mattock and two shovels. They found some soft dirt near a creek and put three of the prisoners to work digging graves. The lieutenant tried to argue some more, and did not notice that meanwhile Johnson had disappeared. It took the rest of the afternoon to dig the graves. When the number of graves had reached eight, Seth stopped the digging. The three gratefully discontinued their labors. They looked around and counted the graves, and when they realized that they had only dug enough to accommodate their fallen comrades, they began to think complimentary thoughts about Seth Collins.

"Thank you, gentlemen," he said to the three diggers as

he walked down the two rows of graves they had dug. "Now, if you'll just take your friends and drop 'em in them holes—help 'em please, Lieutenant—and then cover them up, I'll be real pleased."

They did as they were told. Even the lieutenant obeyed. He too had been counting graves. These men were not savages, after all, he thought. They would make a deal. He would promise them anything, and they would agree. Then, when he got the chance, he would find a way to escape and someday bring back a big enough army to squash these sons of the devil like a bug.

The graves were covered up. The privates were wiping the sweat off their faces on their sleeves. It had been hard to cover up their comrades so unceremoniously, but at least they had survived. Now, finished with their labors, they looked toward Seth for approval.

"Nice work, men," he said. "Now, Johnson, did you find us some rope?"

Johnson had returned with a lot of rope. The four men looked on, unbelieving, as Elberton and St. Jean cut the ropes into four lengths and threw them over the boughs of two different trees.

The quietest private, a short, squat fellow with a bulbous nose, snapped his head toward Seth.

"You're still gonna hang us?" he rasped. "After we did everything you asked of us?"

"And I thanked you, if you remember," Seth reminded him. "Now it's your turn, and before we let you dangle, we'll give you plenty of time to square things with your maker." St. Jean made passable nooses. Then he swung from the ropes to see if the boughs were strong enough to hold them.

"I think you won't feel too bad. Happen quick," St. Jean said with pride.

"You can't do this to us," said the man in the Tory tunic.

Seth looked around the clearing, at the defile where they had executed their ambush, at the eight neat graves by the creek—they'd be overgrown with brambles in a year or two—at the four frightened men standing before him and his neighbors. "And if we let you go," he said, "you'd be back in a month with an army and we'd be the ones stretchin' rope."

"No, no! I give you my word."

"And their words? Even if you wanted to keep it quiet, you couldn't. Why, one of you'd tell a drinkin' buddy, and then the drinkin' buddy'd get drunk and tell a whole tavern full of his drinkin' buddies, and then you'd all be in trouble for not tellin' your commander in the first place. No, you'd have to report it to save your necks in your own army."

Elberton sneered. "So I'm sure you'll understand."

By that he meant for the doomed men to mount their animals for their final ride, but the four men stood rooted. "If you think we're gonna help you kill us, you must be pretty deep into your rum," said the lieutenant.

He had hit on something there. All four settlers had had a tot before the ambush and were still feeling some of the glow, though not enough to have affected their aim during the ambush. The lieutenant, for that matter, had been drinking steadily on the trail before he had found Seth Collins's place, and he had taken a bracing gulp or two in the defile just before the ambush. The valley of the Spay-Lay-Wi-Theepi had that effect on many of the white men who tarried long in its wilderness.

Elberton nodded toward his three boys. One after another they lifted their prisoners onto Collins's animals, not without a struggle. First the lieutenant objected because they tried to seat him atop a mule. An officer, he protested, deserved a good horse, anyway. Seth compromised by having him seated on the broad plow horse he had first ridden onto Seth's farm. The privates struggled fiercely in spite of their bonds. Seth pacified each one with a blow to the head from one of his pistol butts. Only the man in Tory green, to their surprise, allowed himself to be mounted without a struggle.

The three boys and Elberton led the men to the oak trees where their nooses stood waiting. Just before they were settled under the big old hanging limbs, the man in the green tunic kicked his horse and whistled shrilly. The horse bolted forward, and here the old Tory ran into a fatal bit of bad luck. Had one of the boys been leading him, his horse might have bolted loose, but Elberton was leading him, and Elberton had the reins wound around his wrist. The horse jerked him off his feet, but Elberton clung tight and the horse reared up, then settled down.

"Okay, boys," Elberton muttered, climbing stiffly to his feet. "Fun's fun, but we got work to do and you might as well cooperate."

St. Jean mounted behind the man in the green tunic and pulled a noose down over the man's head. He tightened it around his neck and placed the knot behind his right ear.

"You look like you done this before," Elberton remarked.

"Seen it done once or twice. Hope I'm doin' it right," said the Frenchman, sliding back down off the horse and climbing atop the mule that carried one of the privates. "I'd hate to do a bad job. Want to give these boys a fast trip, so it won't hurt 'em too bad."

The private was breathing hard and sweating furiously as St. Jean adjusted his knot. "Please don't," he said weakly, but he did not resist. All the settlers except Elberton felt a moment of regret. This private was by far the youngest. But the job had to be done. The four settlers arranged themselves behind the horses and the mule. At a signal from Seth, they all delivered a solid smack to the rumps of the animals and hollered loud. Three of the animals surged forward, and three bodies hung twitching and dancing from the limbs of the oak tree.

Only the young private remained alive, astride the mule, which had not budged.

Walker looked around at his neighbors. "What do we do now?" he asked.

"We finish the job," growled Elberton. "If you'd hit that animal harder, it would be over." He fetched the mule a titanic whack on the animal's flank, and then another. Still the mule didn't move.

The young man had tears on his face. His eyes were closed. His lips were moving in prayer. Seth seized Elberton's arm. "Let him alone," he said. "Gettin' hung once in a day is enough.

"Come on, son." Seth helped the private down from the mule. "Boys," he said to Elberton's three sons. "Would you cut down these soldiers and plant 'em next to the others?"

Three young men nodded and grabbed their tools. The private stood by his mule, his head down, trying to keep his legs from caving in under him.

And meanwhile, in the deep shadows of the woods, three pairs of eyes were watching the entire story as it unfolded.

3

THEY WEREN'T EXACTLY UNITED. TO BE A WARrior of the Twightwee was to have an abiding distrust of the six nations of the Iroquois Confederacy. In some ways the Iroquois were like white men, conquerors who gloried in their contempt for other people. For generations the warriors of the Longhouse had dared to war against the people to their west and south, making slaves of free men, stealing women, weapons, food and horses, and boasting that they owned their neighbors and the land they lived on —yes, even that, like a white man.

And when the people who lived around the lakes rebelled against the English, the Iroquois folded their arms, wrinkled their noses and refused to join. Had they joined, the people might have pushed the white men back to Albany or maybe even across the Hudson River. But no, they would not join. And now the men of the Longhouse were sorry. Most of them had lost their lands along the Mohawk, the Genesee, the Unadilla and Susquehanna, Lake Ontario and Lake Erie, the latter named for a tribe that had been related to them but whom they nevertheless had wiped out. Now their hearts had been hardened to the English alongside whom they had fought against the surrounding tribes. But it was too late. They were too weak to make a difference. And the lake tribes, who had feared them so much for so long, no longer respected them or their battle prowess.

The old Shawnee called Hidden Heart did not know the entire history of the Longhouse and the tribes of the lakes, but he knew enough. Over the past decade, the hated English had become his friends. The English, like him and the other Indians along the lakes, hated the settlers. Furthermore, they were willing to help the Indians get rid of the settlers.

With English food in their bellies, and English lead in their pouches, Hidden Heart and others were combing the woods of Ohio in search of frontier settlers. They had been five miles away, sitting on a hilltop, when they spotted the black smoke where Seth Collins's barn burned. They sent one of their number to round up the other warriors who were scouting in the area, while the remainder headed for the smoke. Painted for war in red and black, they loped along the old trace until they sensed the commotion, then they paused and listened. Above the wind-rustled leaves they could hear the movement of men and horses. They followed their ears until they could see the bluecoats on the road. Ahead was the defile. Beyond it, with their keen vision and the woods sense they possessed from birth, they spotted among the shifting shadows of the woods a couple of the unnatural straight lines that had to be rifle barrels.

This was fine, thought Hidden Heart. Bluecoats about to die, and the Twightwees did not have to lift a hand to make it happen. All they had to do was watch. But how could the fools in blue not sense their peril? How like a white man to blunder into such a clumsy trap, he thought. Above one side of the defile he spotted ill-concealed ambushers, and in the woods between him and the road were others. Prone, concealed by tree trunks and the debris of the forest floor, the three warriors watched the first puffs of smoke, watched the bodies fall, watched as the settlers rounded up the survivors. They had hoped that the soldiers might put up enough of a fight to weaken the settlers' group, but they supposed it did not matter all that much.

They followed the settlers and their prisoners to the clearing and witnessed the first burials and then the hangings. Hidden Heart and the Twightwees had been fortunate over the years at not having to deal much with white men. This was Hidden Heart's first hanging. How strange these white men were. If they wanted to kill them, quickly and easily, why not just chop open the tops of their heads? On the other hand, if they wanted to torture, then why so quick? This thing with the knotted rope, a little torture and a lot of death. It didn't make any sense. But then, they had heard that the white men did not make a whole lot of sense.

While the three hanging victims were being buried, Hidden Heart and the other two warriors retreated to the old trace to wait for their friends. They did not have to wait long. A dozen painted braves arrived, more than enough to do the job. While the three Elberton brothers were laying their victims to rest and covering them with creek dirt, fifteen warriors of the Twightwee and Shawnee nations silently surrounded them. Scalp locks blowing in the breeze, they knelt hidden in the wilderness for the signal that would set their attack in motion. Their enemy stood by the graves, carelessly discussing their future, leaning on the barrels of their rifles.

"I think we'd better level the tops of those graves and pack 'em down and see that wild things are growin' over them," Elberton was telling Seth. "And not a one of us should ever tell a soul about this, not even Hetherly or McAllister down the road there."

Seth nodded, but Walker was only now beginning to feel the impact of what they had done. "Tell you what, boys," he said. "I'm not so sure I can stay around after that. How can I risk it with my family, if somebody gets drunk and lets it out? You know how St. Jean here is—you know how you are, Jean. Then what'll happen to us?"

A bit of movement over Elberton's shoulder caught Seth's attention. He squinted to focus but did not quite believe what he saw. A whistle blew and the thing he saw move belched fire. Elberton's forehead exploded into a red shower. He heard the barrage of shots and saw all three of Elberton's sons crumple and fall. So did Johnson and his wife.

Seth and St. Jean immediately dropped to the floor of the forest and found a tree trunk to hide behind. They could only hope that they were not surrounded and exposed from behind. While the Indians were reloading, St. Jean crawled over to where Walker stood paralyzed beside a skinny little ironwood tree. He grabbed the frightened squatter by his ankle and jerked him to the floor of the clearing. Walker grunted but otherwise didn't object as St. Jean dragged him into a small depression between two trees. There, St. Jean and Collins lay facing in opposite directions, staring toward the woods that surrounded them, but seeing nothing. Both checked their priming. Both could scarcely swallow, their mouths were so dry.

The moments passed like hours as they waited. In front of them nothing moved except the leaves on the trees. But Collins and St. Jean knew they were out there, and very close. The shots were too deadly to have come from more than fifty yards away. Except for the summer breeze, the forest was silent. Collins looked around at the still bodies and decided he was glad St. Jean had survived. He was a good man to have in a fight.

A voice echoed through the forest. "White man, no shoot."

"We no shoot. You come out," St. Jean answered. Collins saw movement to his front. A lone painted figure separated itself from the underbrush and walked toward them. A brave man, thought Seth, but he noted that the man stayed half concealed among the trees as he approached. Then he stopped, maybe thirty feet away from where Seth lay. He pointed to Seth. "You." He beckoned to Seth to come forward.

From his hiding place Hidden Heart watched the old Seneca Skoiyasi as he coaxed the settlers out.

"I am Skoiyasi of the people of the Western Door. If you . . ." Long years away from the English had caused him to forget the word surrender. He made the sign with his hands. Seth had seen the sign before.

"Give up?" he asked.

"Give up," Skoiyasi repeated. "We take your weapons, we burn your farm, but we let you live if you will leave this place forever, go back to—" His voice almost faltered. "Go back to the Te-non-an-at-che." Go back to the Mohawk River in New York, on the other side of the proclamation line. The Indians were offering him, Walker, and St. Jean the same deal as the lieutenant had, but given their circumstance, the Indians' deal seemed so much better.

"Let me talk to the others."

"You be quick," Skoiyasi replied.

"What do you think?" Seth asked St. Jean.

But it was Walker who found his voice first. "We better do what he says," he said, his voice shaking.

St. Jean shrugged his shoulders. "Don't see as we have a choice," he agreed. "I don't trust 'em, for sure, but maybe the English have persuaded them to be civilized today. If we didn't have families, I'd say fight to the death. But we have to think of them. If we don't surrender, we haven't a chance."

Seth nodded. The two stood up. St. Jean gave Walker a push ahead of them and the three men walked out to where Skoiyasi stood.

"Here are our weapons," Seth said.

"Lay them on the ground in front of me," Skoiyasi responded. The three men did as they were told, first their rifles, then their powder horns and bullet pouches.

"Knives too?" Walker asked, and Collins could have strangled the fool.

"All of your knives."

The men obeyed.

The woods had come alive with fiercely painted redmen. Seth and St. Jean watched with fear and fascination as the warriors approached, warily, their eyes scanning the clearing from one side to the other, suspecting that the whites might have a trap set. Suddenly the three men felt their arms being grabbed from behind, ropes slipped around their wrists and tightened.

Quietly the Twightwee warriors went from body to body, picking up rifles and stripping each body of anything that possibly could be of use. There were braves very close to them. Too close, Seth thought. Almost as if he were conjuring up the scenario himself, he saw the men closest to them draw their tomahawks from their belts. Again, strong arms grabbed them from behind. Oh damn! Seth thought as the braves in front of them raised their tomahawks high and brought them down hard on the last three male settlers of Walker Valley. The blood boiled from their heads as they fell, and only then did the Twightwees, the Shawnees, and their Seneca ally Skoiyasi begin to whoop and screech. But they were not through yet. Crawling away into some thick brush, almost making it, was the young private who had barely escaped being hanged. Had he made his move a few seconds sooner, he might have escaped death a second time that day. But one of the young warriors spotted him moving. The Twightwee took a dozen quick running steps, drawing his knife from his waistband as he ran. Then he flew through the air and landed with his knees on the private's back, grabbed the private's hair, jerked his head up and drew the knife across his neck. The blood poured out and the private died quickly. Then the rest of the war party drew their scalping knives from their belts.

David Watley took immense pride in the flatboat he was steering down the deep channel of the Spay-Lay-Wi-Theepi. He had laid down cash in Pittsburgh then waited in line for six weeks before Thomas Caine, the best boat builder in town, had finally gotten to it. But the wait was worth it. The planks were seasoned, the seams were tight, and the design was exactly what he needed.

Of all the Watleys, David was the most restless. Called Jinja by his grandfather, after an old Mohawk friend who had died fighting the French many years before, he had grown up in Albany, fought in the war of independence, and worked in his family's trading business for more than a decade. Through his father's mother he bore the blood of Seneca chiefs. Unlike his father, who had shed the blanket long ago, Jinja longed for the wilderness. For years he had made the risky trade runs along the Susquehanna and Genesee rivers, but every year it took longer to find the lands of the Ganonsyoni and Lenni Lenape, so rapidly were they being pushed west. And then, when the trading was done, there was always the need to return to the crowded, fetid streets of Albany.

He had decided to found a trading post on the north bank of the Spay-Lay-Wi-Theepi. To do so he would need funding from the firm of Wendel and Watley, Wendel being his maternal grandfather and Watley being the name of his other grandfather and his father. He had called a meeting of his elders in order to sell them on the concept.

"By heavens," said Big Oak, as his father's father was called, "if I were twenty years younger, I would go with you—no, if I were ten years younger. That's a real good proposition."

"Come with me anyway, Grandpa. Your name is great even in the Ohio River valley."

"No, no. My time is long past. I never thought it would happen to me, my boy, but my pipe and my fishing pole are now my best friends, after my wife. It is almost summer, and I am ready for a shady spot by the pond, to dream about the days when my legs could carry me from one end of New York to the other in less than a week. In my dreams my body is light as a feather, but in real life it is as if I had to carry a canoe on my shoulders wherever I go."

Now his mother's father, the old Dutch storekeeper Dieter Wendel, spoke. "When I was younger, David," he said, "all that mattered was to build the company. I was a gambler. Sometimes I gambled on other people's lives. But now that there is peace in New York, and easier money to be made, I do not like to gamble. Especially I do not like to gamble on the life of my only grandson. Do not do this thing. We are not supposed to be on the other side of the mountains. I hear that the Indians attack everyone, and I hear that the *verdammt* English help them. That is the English for you. They lose a country and they shake your hand and leave, but then they sneak back in and try to win by sneakiness what they could not win by manly arms. Do not do this thing. I would miss you, and I cannot bear to lose you."

"Pa?" Jinja peered anxiously toward his father. "You have not spoken."

Thad looked long and hard at his son through the shadowed eye sockets of his Seneca forebears.

"You know my feelings, Jinja," he said. "I was raised to be a Seneca, but educated to be a white man. I was allowed to choose between the wilderness and the town. I chose the town, and I believe I made the right choice. It is not good to raise your children in the shadow of the tomahawk. A child should be able to grow up without the fear that an enemy will come, kill his family, and carry him away into the night. There is a part of your spirit that makes you not fear for your life. When the war of independence came, I was afraid you would be reckless in battle. I would have liked to lock you up in your room for the duration of the war. Instead I watched over you in battle when I was with you and prayed for you when I was not.

"After the war it was my dream that we could trade in peace with my brothers the Ganonsyoni. It was not to be. Many of them went off to Canada. At least New York is now at peace. So you want to go west, where the Shawnees, and the Twightwees, and the Wyandots still crave the scalps of Americans. If it is space you long for, then there are fields and forests in New York where a man can raise a family without listening for the war whoop in the wind at night. And yet you would go where the Mingoes would seek your scalp. I must tell you, Henri recently came back from trading with the Delawares. They told him that their brothers in the West have been getting fine new muskets and rifles from somewhere."

Big Oak smiled grimly. "That can only be the English, up to their old mischief," he said.

Thad nodded. "Last year the Twightwees and the Shawnees defeated an American army sent west. I believe the English are betting that they can do the same again this year."

Dieter shook his head. "Not this time," he said. "We will have a bigger army. Better men. Better guns. More cannons. And when the Indians are defeated, they will turn away from the English. Then the trading will be good, yah." The old Dutchman puffed on his pipe and nodded approvingly toward Jinja. "This one is a smart one," he said. "He wants to be first. We have been first before, and we are still profiting because we were first."

"I thought you didn't want him to go," Thad growled at his father-in-law.

Dieter shrugged his shoulders. "A father's son never grows up. I have seen you and Sam take bigger risks. We have seen Jinja survive great battles. I have great faith in this man. He is strong and wise in the woods. I would trust him with my life. I would trust him with the goods of Wendel and Watley."

"I'm not worried about Wendel and Watley, I'm worried about my son."

"As I worried about you in battle, so many times," Big Oak reminded Thad. "There was a time when you would have seized this opportunity for yourself, and called us old maids for worrying about you. If you had your way, Jinja would be clerking in the store for the rest of his life."

Thad gave in. "You would be very careful?" he asked.

"I will take nothing for granted," his son answered. "In the wilderness, I will trust no one but my companions."

They agreed to back his venture. But they insisted that he take along his longtime friend James Derontyan, an experienced Oneida trader, and a free black man called Obie Weeks.

So here they were, drifting with the current of the Spay-Lay-Wi-Theepi through miles and miles of the most beautiful country Jinja had ever seen, on the biggest flatboat he had ever imagined.

Sixteen feet wide by sixty feet long, it had a small stable near the stern with a platform on the roof where he manned the sweep that kept the boat in the middle of the river. He insisted on keeping it in the middle, even though the boat had such a shallow draft that there was little chance of her grounding on a sandbar unless he took her close to the shore. But he felt exposed on the roof of the stable, and he wanted the boat as far from snipers on either shore as he could manage.

Builder Caine had constructed a barricade five logs high surrounding the tiller position for further security. Mounted on the front and rear of these barricades were two small swivel cannon, an unusual touch for an Ohio River flatboat.

As Jinja watched his flatboat drifting down the center of the Ohio, he felt relaxed, though his keen eyes scanned the trees and shores on both sides. He saw deer and water birds, pigeons and squirrels, but he saw no human beings. He was not surprised. If there were Indians along the shores, they had no desire to be seen. Indians regarded white men as unpredictable. They considered it risky to approach a strange white man. White men were filled with hates and fears that made them dangerous to Indians who failed to stay alert. Of course, white men thought similar things about the Indians. Jinja's opinion was that they were both right.

Forward of the stable was the living quarters. In addition to Jinja there were six people on board, Obie and his wife

Mary, James and his wife Anna, Obie's two-year-old girl Dona and his eleven-year-old son Jack. Obie was the handiest man that Jinja had ever known. He could build a tight cabin and was a first-rate gunsmith. His wife Mary could sit down at a loom with flax and woolen thread and turn out fine cloth all day long. James spoke not only the Iroquois dialects, but could understand several of the Algonquian tongues spoken by the western lake tribes. Anna, his wife, was a magician with a hoe. She could tell the best soil by its taste, and grow enough corn, beans, and squash on an acre to feed a lodge through the winter.

Thad and Big Oak had encouraged Jinja to marry before he went West, but he knew no girls in Albany who shared his lust for adventure. In fact he didn't know any girls in Albany whom he liked even a little. "If I can't find one out there," he told his father, "keep a lookout for one back here. I'll come and get 'er when we're settled in."

Jinja brought some skills of his own to this party. Besides his years clerking for his grandfather, he had spent many days with James or his father on the trails and rivers of New York and Pennsylvania trading with the Delawares, Caughnawagas, and, in times of relative peace, the six nations of the Longhouse. Like Big Oak and Thad before him, he was a deadly shot, and James believed Jinja to be nearly as good a woodsman as he was. Considering the motley assortment of drunks, slobs, and ne'er-do-wells so often found on the frontier, Jinja's group had a lot going for them.

Stowed in low compartments toward the front of the flatboat were massive quantities of trade goods and living implements. There were hoes and hatchets, ammunition and strouds—coarse woolen blankets—glass beads and face paints, shirts and shoes, nails and carpenter's tools, kettles and ladles, all the goods most in demand on the frontier by men and women, red and white.

Jinja heard the soft steps of moccasins on the ladder, then quiet footfalls across the deck. James was standing beside him, tall and straight, two inches shorter than Jinja's six-foot-three. They said nothing to each other and let the minutes stretch by as the scenery slowly changed. It was April and the trees bore early foliage like bright green feathers, rippling softly in the breeze. The breeze was blowing against the flatboat, but the current was stronger, so the boat made its quiet headway on waters that could take them all the way down the Mississippi River if they would let it.

The two longtime friends did not need to speak. Silence between them was like a third welcome companion. Their eyes saw many of the same things and their minds thought many of the same thoughts. No need to share them without purpose. Jinja applied the gentlest pressure to the sweep and felt the clumsy craft respond as it made its way through a bend in the river. He could feel the boat wanting to go sideways. His sensitive hands pressed on the sweep the other way and the boat squared itself. All this he did without compromising his vigilance. Left, right, forward, his eyes swept the horizon, and then the shores, in ceaseless motion.

And then, suddenly, they stopped.

"You saw it too?" James's voice did not sound concerned, yet there it was, something at the edge of the woods that ought not have been there.

"Saw him," Jinja replied.

They were being observed, as they knew they would. Sooner or later, whoever was watching would either show himself or not show himself. They still had a hundred miles to go and had no desire to drop anchor and go searching for stray customers. Their idea was that if they set up a little trading post and stockade, their customers would come to them. The swivel guns mounted atop the stable had not been brought along so much to defend their boat as to defend their stockade, once they had built it.

The following day dawned misty and wet. Jinja and James stood by the tiller and decided not to risk their boat by testing the visibility. They took advantage of their idle time to help Obie rig a canvas awning over the tiller handle, so it would be possible for whomever was steersman to drift down the river on a rainy day and still stay dry. By the time the position had been roofed, the visibility had improved to a quarter mile, and all three agreed that it would be safe to weigh anchor.

Obie went back to the cabin, where he checked the little group's weapons, which included a dozen rifles, half that number of pistols, and assorted knives and hatchets. The blades were to be sharpened and the firearms disassembled, cleaned, oiled, and reassembled. Obie enjoyed the work, and took great pride in doing a fine job. He worked slowly and methodically, yet so dexterous were the movements of his fingers that he could accomplish a great deal in a short time. Soon there were rows of blades, keen and gleaming where they had met stone. Now for the rifles.

As the day passed and the mist lifted, Jinja and James kept a careful eye on the banks of the Spay-Lay-Wi-Theepi. Before them numberless waterfowl of many colors and sizes announced their approach. Both Jinja and James imagined sharp dark eyes like their own peeping out from the deep woods that sometimes crept up to the banks of the river and sometimes receded beyond broad flood plains. But they had to admit to each other that they could see no one.

"They will attack us sooner or later, don't you agree?" Jinja asked.

"It is impossible to know," answered the Oneida. "But there is no way for us to get away from them without giving up the flatboat." He was talking about the two canoes stowed on the low roof of the cabin. Presumably, if they felt the odds were too great, they could abandon the flatboat in the middle of the night and paddle back upstream to civilization. "Imagine what old Dieter would say if we came crawling back to Albany and told him we'd left a flatboat full of his trade goods for the improvement of the Indians down on the Ohio."

"Imagine what my father would say!" exclaimed Jinja. "He says that I have no sense. The only reason he agreed to this mission was because it was the first time I wanted to try something like this on my own."

James nodded. "Your father is right, you know. You have no sense. The sting of battle makes you crazy. Surely the Lord protects men who lose their senses in battle, or you would not have seen daylight past the age of eighteen. I do not understand why your father—wough, what is this?"

There was a bend in the river perhaps a mile down from where the boat was, and on that bend a sand spit projecting fifty yards into the water. From beyond the sand spit, around the bend, they could see a line of canoes emerging from shore and making their way up the river toward the flatboat. There were nine canoes, each bristling with painted, scalp-locked, bare-chested warriors. The late afternoon sun glinted off the paddles as they rose and fell, and off the barrels of rifles and muskets held by those who were not paddling.

"Obie!" Jinja shouted. "Canoes comin' your way."

"Right!" came the response from within the cabin, and they could hear him throw open the two shutters facing forward. Along with Obie, the two women would be aiming their weapons downstream. While Jinja clung to the tiller, James climbed down and flung out an anchor, which dragged along the bottom of the river for several moments, then caught.

Fascinated, they watched the canoes as they made their way up the river, a row of four up front, followed by a half-dozen more in no particular formation. Two of the canoes lagged considerably behind the others, as if their occupants were content to let the others test the strength of the flatboat first.

James squinted as he studied the canoes that surged over the gray water toward the flatboat.

"Shigapo!" he muttered.

"What?"

"You call them Kickapoo. Kickapoo might do anything. They might shake your hand or they might cut it off. They might save your life today and roast you tomorrow. The other tribes try to steer clear of the Shigapo. For certain they aim to take this boat. They are not here to parley."

Almost as a response to James's words, puffs of smoke began to bloom from the first four canoes, followed by the dead-sounding pop of muskets and rifles in the open.

James smiled grimly. "They must be low on powder," he said, knowing the Kickapoos had undercharged their weapons and that if they hit anything but the river, it would be by chance.

Jinja wasted no time in loading the swivel gun with solid shot and pointing it toward the closest canoe, which was still nearly half a mile away. "James, could you bring up some of that old iron junk we loaded on just before we left Pittsburgh?" he asked.

The Oneida reached into one of the big boxes beside the cabin and hauled out a sack full of old rusty iron pieces, nails, spikes, pieces of old horseshoes and broken tools. He dragged the load up the ladder and parked it by the forward swivel gun. Jinja had ignited a pile of tinder with a spark from his flintlock and then lit a torch, with which he stood poised over the swivel gun while he waited for the Kickapoos to come closer. Now something was about to happen that both he and James had dreaded. Both men had done their share of killing in the late war. With the wisdom that comes from experience, they had hoped that the day of their bloodletting had ended, but there was no doubt in either's mind that they could save themselves and their people only by doing something very nasty to the people attacking them.

Jinja fired the swivel then, a single solid ball at relatively long range, that hit the water fifty feet in front of the closest canoe, skipped over the canoe, and landed in the river ten yards beyond. He was satisfied to see the canoe slow down and let the other three lead canoes compete for first coup.

He swabbed out the barrel and reloaded, this time with the iron scrap, and waited while they came closer. Puffs of smoke were beginning to appear from all the canoes, and inside the cabin Obie and the women had begun to return fire, although the range was still a little long. One of the canoes pulled out ahead of the others and decided that if they moved over to the left flank of the flatboat, they might avoid the fire from the swivel gun, as well as the rifle fire from the cabin. The idea would have been a good one had Jinja and James not seen to it that gun mounts were built into the left and right, as well as the front and rear barricades above the stable.

The first shot from the swivel had set the horses to misbehaving down below. Obie's son hurried into the stable to calm the animals, and almost immediately he quieted the racket. James and Jinja picked up the loaded swivel and remounted it on the left barricade. If the Kickapoos in the flanking canoe noticed, they ignored the movement. They were coming in close now, recklessly close. Jinja brought the swivel gun to bear on them. There were four warriors in the canoe, all paddling, their flank exposed to the flatboat. Now they began their turn and Jinja knew he could wait no longer. "Poor devils," he muttered to himself. And he fired.

4

THE SMOKE CLEARED AND THE SIGHT NEARLY made Jinja ill. All four men were writhing helplessly in the canoe, which drifted less than a hundred yards from the flatboat. The warlike screeches had been replaced by pathetic groans as the lifeblood of the Kickapoos drained into the bottom of the canoe. The other canoes came to a sudden stop and began to backwater quickly while the rest of the warriors watched in horror. Death by artillery was not the same as death by musket, or death by arrow, or knife or war club. There was a mighty fort floating in the river. They wanted nothing to do with a weapon that could do *that* to a human body.

All eyes were on the decimated canoe. Two of the occupants were seriously wounded and moving, two of them unmoving, perhaps dead. All of them were visible, draped over the sides or each other. All of them were covered with blood. One of them paddled feebly for a few strokes, trying to retreat from the flatboat, then the paddle slipped from his nerveless hands into the river and floated away. The scrap iron Jinja had fired at the Indians had also torn a hole in the side of the canoe. It was filling with water and nobody was bailing.

After a minute or two of watching the tragic scene, the closest canoe began to paddle toward the wounded men. James and Jinja would have liked to signal the Kickapoos to come on fast and rescue their braves, but there were too many rifles being pointed at them. So they watched the canoe approach, warily, while the canoe full of wounded rode lower and lower in the water. When the rescue canoe was still a hundred feet away, the shot-up canoe slipped beneath the surface of the river. Three of the Indians sank briefly with the canoe, then floated to the surface, motionless, surrounded by blood-colored water. The fourth tried to swim a few strokes, but he soon lost command of his arms and then sank beneath the ripples.

From the rescuing canoe came a cry of anger. One of the paddlers hollered a challenge to the rest of the canoes. Then there began a debate, carried on in shouts from the various canoes in a dialect nobody on the flatboat could understand. The canoes surged into motion, keeping as much water as possible between themselves and the flatboat while they surrounded it. James pulled the anchor and the flatboat began to move with the current.

For nearly an hour, like a convoy, the canoes matched the speed of the flatboat as it drifted down the river. While Obie and the women watched forward from the front windows of their cabin, Jinja and James stood atop the stable, watching port, starboard, and stern. Their eyes were so keen they could see distant feathers rippling in the breeze.

"What do you suppose they're up to?" Jinja asked.

"I'm not sure," James replied, "but they're not doing this because they want our company. I promise you they want revenge, and they have a plan for taking it."

Jinja did not reply for several minutes. He knew James was right. "Everything all right down there, Obie?" he shouted toward the cabin.

"All fine down here!" Obie answered in a steady voice. Once again they stood in silence, listening to the water lapping against the sides of the flatboat and the sounds of water birds in the distance. More minutes dragged by, and still the canoes kept pace with the flatboat as it drifted downriver, keeping their distance.

Or were they?

"Are they closing in on us, just a little?" Jinja asked.

"I think maybe yes," James said. "Why don't you pick out one and take a shot at it?"

Falling to one knee to conceal himself, Jinja pulled out a small brass telescope and took a closer look at the canoes nearest to them. He noted a figure in the bow of one of them. He was a fine, muscular specimen of a man who carried a rifle but no paddle. His eyes squinted steadily at the flatboat, as if he were staring directly into Jinja's telescope. Jinja peered at the other canoes. None of them had a man in the bow without a paddle. Surely this man must be a leader. Jinja once again peered through his telescope at the nearest canoe. Slowly it was coming closer, that was certain. The Indian was looking down at his rifle, maybe checking the priming. Then, once again, he fastened his eyes on the stern section of the flatboat.

There were firing loops in the barricade. Jinja rested the muzzle of the rifle in one of them but did not push the barrel through the opening. He did not want the rifleman in the canoe to discover that he was a target. It was a long shot, nearly three hundred yards, but Jinja felt confident that the moment he pulled the trigger, the life of a Kickapoo chief would end.

He pulled the rifle up to his shoulder and moved the barrel across the water until he found the man with the rifle in his sights. The warrior, or chief, had raised his weapon and was now pointing it at the flatboat. Jinja took a deep breath and let a little out. The head and shoulders of the Indian loomed steady in Jinja's sights. Jinja pulled back the hammer, took another breath, and took in what little slack there was on the trigger. He hated to stir up those hornets again, but James was convinced that they were bent on revenge, so he had no real choice.

He pulled the trigger. The pan flashed then with a sharp bang, the rifle kicked, and for a moment a cloud of gray smoke floated between his eyes and his target. When the smoke cleared the canoe was leaning toward the left, away from the flatboat, and the forward paddler was reaching down into the water. The paddler pulled his arms toward him and then Jinja's target came into view. His face was a red mask and the blood had dripped down over his chest. Another paddler moved forward to help the first pull the wounded rifleman into the canoe. The other paddler leaned as far to the right as he could to keep the canoe from tipping over. Once they pulled the wounded man back in the canoe, they rested his head on the chest of one of the others, trying to make him comfortable. Even from where Jinja stood he could see the wounded man's chest heaving. The man who was holding him grabbed a blanket and was wiping the blood off his face. Both James and Jinja doubted that he would survive his wound.

The canoes were all moving away from the flatboat. The Kickapoos realized that they had chosen a poor battlefield for themselves. Most flatboats held farmers, not deadly sharpshooters and artillerymen. Those in the canoes behind the flatboat paddled toward shore and pulled their canoes into the woods. The canoes to their left and right and their front paddled downriver and around a bend and disappeared.

"We've not seen the last of them," Jinja said.

"A bitter time for them," agreed James. "I believe we killed five of them, and they have nothing to show for it."

Jinja sighed. For several moments both were silent as they stared ahead and behind them. "I didn't want to kill that last man, James."

James nodded. "They were moving in on us. Your shooting him might have saved the flatboat. You made them feel like easy targets." He turned away from the river, toward Jinja. "I think, my brother, that you no longer long for battle as you once did."

Jinja looked abashed. "I don't know if I ever thought of it as *fun,*" he replied. "It made me feel more alive. Don't forget all those years when you were out on the trail and my grandfather had me standing behind the counter of his store, or in the warehouse taking inventory. I wanted to be on the trail with you and your father and Big Oak. Sometimes I had to stop whatever I was doing and run out the door into the air so I could breathe."

Neither wanted to talk about the rest of it: how Jinja finally proved to be a terror on the battlefield during the Revolution; how the sights and smells and sounds of battle made him lose his mild manner; how often his father had had to restrain him when he had wanted to pursue a fleeing enemy singlehandedly, and how he became even more deadly once he had learned to be a bit more careful. James had lived through most of it with Jinja. They did not need to talk about it.

They saw no more of the Kickapoo on that day or the next. Slowly the boat drifted with the current, steered through numerous bends and crosscurrents by the sure hands of James, Jinja, and Obie. At night they anchored as far from shore as they could, and never did they have the comfort of feeling alone on the river. The third day after they had fought the Kickapoos the rain came down like the falls of Niagara. Before noon the rain slackened to a grim drizzle and Obie threw in a few fishing lines over the barricade by the tiller. They were keeping a careful eye out for canoes, but all they saw was the gray-green of forest and rolling mist.

Obie wondered out loud if all the tribes in the Northwest would be hostile.

"All of 'em sometimes, some of them all the time," Jinja replied. "There's Mingoes, Kickapoos, Miamis, Shawnees, Wyandot, Weas, and a bunch of others, and all of them were told by the government that beyond the mountains was gonna be red-man country only."

"Then why is there all them new settlers we saw pullin' out of Pittsburgh when we were gettin' this boat built?" asked the black man.

Jinja pulled out a piece of jerky and took a bite. "There's two reasons," he said. "This government is too weak to stop people from crossing the mountains, and some of the militia got paid in land. They're comin', and there's no soldiers to stop 'em. And the Indians don't like it a bit."

"Can you blame us?" James asked.

"Certainly not," Jinja responded. "And don't forget, my redder brother, the blood of Seneca warriors runs through my veins."

James gave a little laugh. "Jinja, you're a white man and better off for it. If you run into white men in the forest, they're likely to invite you to dinner. If I run into red men, looking like I do, they're likely to serve me for dinner to the crows."

"Aye, and a good thing too," Jinja added. "If the Indians were to ever unite, they could make it awful hot for us in the forests."

"A good thing for you maybe," James said ruefully. "For me and my people, not so good."

One of the fishing lines stiffened and began to run around behind the boat. Obie grabbed the line and started to haul it in. Whatever the fish was on the other end, it was a big one, big enough to snap the line as if it were a piece of straw. He babied it to the edge of the boat and lifted it, ever so gently. It was a huge catfish. Halfway up the side of the boat the line broke and the wriggling catfish splashed back into the water.

"Hope he likes swimming around with a hook in his mouth," growled Obie as he reached down for a spare hook to tie to the line. Jinja had seized his arm with his left hand even as he pointed to the northern shore with his right. Obie finished tying the hook, then looked toward where Jinja was pointing.

"What does that look like to you?" Jinja asked both his companions. They stared in silence at a bulky object that lay half in the water and half on the shore. It was nearly black, almost shapeless, but regular enough to be a man-made something. Jinja pulled out his little telescope to get a better look. His grandfather Big Oak would have once snickered at the thought of using a telescope. With his peerless eyesight he could have afforded to snicker. Nowadays the old man was lucky to be able to spot a bird across his pond. Obie and James shook their heads.

Jinja squinted into the eyepiece and focused the telescope. There. No doubt about it.

"The remains of a flatboat," he concluded. "They must have taken off everything from the deck up, maybe some of the deck wood. But they left the hull. I'll bet they did it just in case they wanted to pull up stakes and head farther west. There's a real frontiersman for you. He probably figured to get restless after a spell and move on."

"Think we ought to take a look?" asked the Oneida.

"That hull has been there for several years," Jinja answered. "Maybe this is a good place. Anyway, if we're gonna trade, we want to be near people. Look at the woods just beyond the hull. There's an opening there, isn't it?"

"Looks like a trail head," James answered. "A little overgrown maybe, but somebody's moccasins have been there a time or two."

"What about the Kickapoo?" Obie was a practical man whose mind never strayed from practical things.

"We'll wait for nightfall," Jinja suggested. "James and I will take a canoe and see what we can find."

"How you gonna find anything in the dark?" asked the freedman.

"We'll miss a little, for sure," Jinja agreed. "But I'd rather sneak around in the dark and miss a little than land in broad daylight and run into a band of angry Kickapoos."

The quarter moon threw enough light on the river to give James a sure landfall near the old flatboat hull. There was no wind on the river. The water was like a sheet of black glass, broken only by the eddies of the paddles and the ripples made by the bow of their canoe. The smell of damp earth met their nostrils as the canoe touched land. Without a sound they picked it up and carried it into the woods, and placed it in a shallow ravine, as close to shore as secrecy allowed, just in case they felt the need to make a quick escape.

Both men were jumpy. If the Kickapoos had followed them down the river, if they stood waiting for them in the night, if they captured them, there would be no mercy, only a long painful death at a fiery stake. They waited in the ravine for several minutes, listening for the night sounds to tell them that all was well. Then they headed for the path.

They found it easily enough. Evidently, it was still getting some use. They followed it silently as it twisted and turned through the thick forest, first away from the river, then parallel to it, then away again. After about a fifteen-minute walk they found themselves in the flood plain of a creek more than twenty feet wide. Had they traveled down the Ohio another mile or so, they would have discovered the mouth of the creek.

No wonder the owners of the flatboat had stopped here. Even in the light of the quarter moon, Jinja could see what fine farmland this flood plain was. They turned north to follow the creek, studying the land as they walked. The plain varied from a few feet wide to a hundred yards, beyond which lay wooded hillsides. They said nothing, just walked and listened. What they heard, and what they didn't hear, convinced them that the Kickapoos had decided to give up their pursuit, at least for the present.

James tapped Jinja on the shoulder and pointed to a hillside at their right. Jinja thought he saw what James was pointing at, but he was not certain. Leaning his head forward as if to get an extra inch or two closer, and squinting, he perceived what he thought was a yellow glow. Now they ceased to follow the creek and made a beeline for the glow. As they came closer they saw that the glow was no illusion. The hillside turned out to be a plateau elevated about thirty feet above the plain. There was a cabin on that plateau—no, there were several buildings, including the cabin with the glow in the window.

Approaching a cabin in the wilderness at night could be risky business. At night, folks might be lying in bed, or doing a chore by candlelight, the children asleep and all quiet. That's when they would hear changes in the night. That's when they would grab their rifles and shoot into the night. That's when neighbors could get hurt.

They worked their way up the hill well away from the

cabin, onto the plateau, and approached it through a grove of oak trees. When they got to the edge of the grove, they found that they were no more than ten yards from the cabin. Only then could they clearly see that the three other buildings had been damaged by fire. There was also some evidence of fire damage to the cabin itself.

Jinja looked at James, who nodded.

"Hello, the cabin," said Jinja in a voice not much louder than a normal conversational voice. The candle inside immediately went out. "We're not here to hurt you," Jinja added.

Now they heard the sound of metal on wood, the sound of a gun barrel on a windowsill. "What do you want?" The voice was female.

"We need to talk to you."

"We? How many of you is there?"

"Two."

"White folks?"

Jinja hesitated. "One of us is."

"And the other?"

"He's an Oneida Indian."

"And you expect me to let a redskin in my cabin in the middle of the night? I know where you are. I got a gun pointed at you and I can blow you into the hereafter if I've a mind to."

"I hope you won't," Jinja said. "We're thinkin' of settlin' in these parts and we just want to be neighborly. I want to open a trading store."

"You do, hey? There ain't nobody much 'round here to trade with."

There was silence for a few moments. Then the woman in the cabin spoke. "Well, we ain't gonna get any sleep with you and that heathen skulkin' around out there. But I warn you, we can't keep you for the night."

"No need to," Jinja replied, stepping from the woods and walking toward the front door, followed by James, who walked five steps behind, just in case. "After we talk to you we'll go back to our flatboat."

They walked in and stood by the door, which she had closed and bolted. She did not invite them to sit down.

"My name is David Watley, and this is James Derontyan, my partner."

She was a tall woman, but still, she had to look up at them. About sixty years old, Jinja thought. No, younger, much younger. Hard life.

"Got a reg'lar name, hey?" she said, looking James in the eye. "That's good. Don't like those heathen names. 'Little Turtle.' *Chhhmmm!*" She gave a contemptuous snort. Jinja looked around the cabin, which was a little bigger than a typical frontier structure. There was a homemade table and chairs, but the bed had come from the East and there were a few other sticks of furniture that indicated that she had once known greater prosperity. She wore a homespun linsey-woolsey dress that had obviously known a lot of hard wear. Her mouth was turned down severely at the corners and her forehead was combed by deep furrows. Her hair was half gray, half dark brown, and done up in a utilitarian bun. Her eyes were gray and her gaze was sharp. She held a heavy musket effortlessly in her hands. Although she did not point it at them, neither did she put it down.

"I'm Ruth Collins. That's my daughter Joanna," she said. Only then, looking across the room to another bed, was Jinja aware of another being, this one tall, thin, long-legged and barefooted, sitting on the bed, her back braced up against the logs of the far wall. He looked again. Her long dark hair hung down straight and uncombed. In the dim light he could see that her face was not absolutely clean. He could also see that she was very pretty. His heart gave a little leap. She was more than that. Scarcely aware of what he was doing, he stepped toward her.

"Hello, Joanna," he said, regaining his composure and stopping halfway across the floor of the cabin.

"Hello, yourself," she said. Her voice was not friendly. With a lot of effort, Jinja turned away from the young girl and spoke again to her mother. He could see that some of the rafters were charred, as were some of the logs that formed the south side of the cabin.

Little observations were adding up to one sad fact. These two women were living alone in the middle of a wilderness.

"What happened here?" he asked the older woman. A few moments of silence made Jinja feel very uncomfortable, even wishing that they were back on the flatboat.

"I had a husband," she said simply.

Jinja looked at the woman and waited for her to say more. After a silent minute that seemed like an hour to Jinja, she did.

"We have been living alone, Joanna and me, for five years," she said. "Sometimes somebody comes by to visit. Sometimes a white man passing through. Sometimes Shawnees, sometimes Miamis, sometimes Mingoes. I am surprised that the Indians do not harm us. It was Indians that killed my husband and burned the house and the sheds.

"Have you ever had fam'ly that you found dead after the Injuns got through with him? White folks are mean, I'll tell you, but generally when they kill a man they leave his body to rest. When the Injuns came to the house after they killed my man, we hid in the secret basement that he had dug just in case something like this happened. They got tired of burnin' this place and they left and then the rains came before the house burned to the ground. Joanna and me come out about half a day after we'd heard the last of them heathens and we went out to search for Seth, which was the name my man was called. We found him, and all the other men in the valley."

There was no grief or horror in her voice as she recounted her story. There was no expression at all on her face, or in her words. But her daughter had grasped a corner of her ragged blanket and held it over her face.

"Wasn't just their scalp that they were missin'. It was fingers, and ears and arms, and their—"

"Mama!" the girl's voice was sharp and angry. She had put the blanket down. Her tan, dark-eyed face glowed in the candlelight. "Stop it, Mama. Stop it!"

"You know what I mean," she said to Jinja. Then she turned to James. "I know *you* know what I mean."

"I seen whites do the same to dead Indians," Jinja replied. "I'm sorry for what happened to your husband, ma'am," he said. "I really am."

"He wasn't like the rest of them folks in this valley," she continued, as if she hadn't heard him. "He was quality, Seth was. He worked hard, had himself a good farm goin' for him. Then they come and tell him to get off the land, that it didn't belong to him."

"Indians told him that?" Jinja was surprised to hear her say that, because out there, where there were few whites, he could not imagine any Indians who spoke fluent English.

She looked at him but did not speak. Jinja looked at Joanna, at the black anger on her small oval face. There was something not right about the story. He thought maybe the girl would add something to it that might make it right, but she had nothing to add. The girl distracted him, pulled at his feelings and made him want her to think well of him. This was a different experience for him. He wanted to talk to this girl. No, it was more than that. He wanted to hold her. He wanted to see that beautiful little face at peace.

He was not blessed with the gift of persuasive speech. "We will not harm you, ma'am," he said to the mother. "We're looking for a place to build a stand." He knew he had already told her that. But she only nodded, as if she didn't remember what he had said only a few minutes before. He turned to the girl. "I think you'll feel better about having us around. We'll build a stockade you can come to when there is danger. We have guns, cannon. We can protect you."

The mother eyed him suspiciously. "And once we're inside your stockade," she said, "who will there be to protect us from you?"

5

THE THREE YOUNG MEN WERE IN HIGH SPIRITS as they loped along the southern shore of Lake Erie. And yet they were wary. War was in the air again, and during wartime people often had the choice of paying attention, or losing their lives. So said their father Big Oak, and Big Oak, as most people knew, was the greatest woodsman of them all.

But Big Oak was a white man, and these three young men wore the scalp locks of the Tuscarora, the sixth nation of the great Iroquois Longhouse. The Tuscaroras were not at war with the United States, or the Fifteen Fires, as many of the tribes called the new republic. Members of this fortunate tribe, along with the Oneidas, had sided with the Americans against their fearful brethren, the Senecas, Cayugas, and Mohawks during the war of independence. Consequently, the Tuscaroras were not thrown out of New York like their hostile brothers. Instead they were squeezed by the Americans into small places, and made to know that, after all, they were still Indians, not Americans.

This did not sit well with the three young men, Caleb, Ken, and Joshua Big Oak. As they grew up they grew tired of hearing their half-brother Thad Watley, Big Oak's first son, tell them that they could be white men if they chose. After all, he said, he had a Seneca mother, and yet he was a prosperous merchant in Albany.

He could not understand that they did not wish to be white men. Their Longhouse mother had not died when they were little children. They could not pretend to be what they did not feel. Big Oak understood, of course, but he had told them that there was no future in clinging to the blanket. "My sons," he had said, "the whites will sweep west like a destroying wind, and when the wind passes, everything you hold dear will be gone. Do not let them do that to you."

But as much as they loved and respected their father, his deeds were more powerful than his words. He did not live on the stinking streets of Albany as did Thad. He lived in the woods, and hunted and fished and traded, and visited his friend Paul Derontyan in Oneida. He spoke three Iroquois dialects as if he had been born into the Longhouse. Much of his life was spent on the red side of the blanket, and they all knew it was the side he loved most.

Because of Big Oak's wisdom, they, more than most of their red brothers, knew that if they were to survive, they must stop thinking of themselves as Iroquois and start thinking of themselves as red men. They knew that in the West the white settlers were streaming across the mountains into the land that the whites had promised the Indians forever. They told their father that the time had come for them to go west and join their brothers. He grieved and begged them to consider another way, Grand River in Canada with Joseph Brant, for example. But no, they would go west, to fight, if necessary.

It never occurred to Big Oak to forbid his sons to go west. They would have been astonished if he had. They were grown men, and he had no power to forbid them. So he kissed them good-bye and told them he would pray for them. He also warned them that the time could come when they would be across the battlefield from Jinja and Thad, and that if such a thing happened, his heart would break.

"We will pray that this will not come to pass, my father," said the middle son, Ken, the responsible one.

And now they were loping west along the south shore of Lake Erie when they saw five canoes on the lake, single file. Twightwees, they were certain. In another era they would have vanished into the dense woods to the south, but this day it was the Twightwees whom they had hoped to encounter. They stood by the shore, leaning on their rifles, watching until they knew that at least one of the paddlers had spotted them. Caleb signaled for them to come ashore and talk with them. Two of the canoes paddled landward, while the other three drifted a few yards offshore, their warriors wary, fingers on triggers. Two men disembarked, leaving paddlers in the two canoes, in case of a trap.

"We are Tuscaroras," Caleb signed to one of them when they were close.

"I am a Mingo," replied one of them in the Seneca tongue, which all three of Big Oak's sons understood.

"We have come west to be with our brothers," Ken replied.

"The Tuscaroras are no longer brothers to us," said the Mingo. "You have fallen into the bed of the white men."

"Not all of us," Ken said.

"Would you fight against the white man?" the Mingo asked.

"We would fight any white man but our father," Joshua said.

"He is past seventy winters," Caleb added. "We are not likely to have to fight him."

"Then come with us, brothers. We will have a fight with them soon," said the Mingo. "We need your deadly rifles," he added, eyeing their long-barreled weapons.

Jinja and James let the flatboat drift downriver until they found the mouth of the creek. They were pleased to see that the creek was wide enough at that point for them to pole their boat upstream a ways, far enough to get it out of sight of canoe traffic on the river. Once they had secured it to their satisfaction, James and Jinja left Obie with the women and children and went scouting for an ideal spot to place their business.

What they intended was a combination trading store and "stand," or inn. They also planned to do some farming. They followed the creek until they were within a mile of the cabin of the Collins women, as they called it. The creek had made a sharp turn there, so that for a short time it ran nearly parallel to the river, which was less than a mile south. Between the creek and the river was a fertile, gentle slope, then a level plain, and finally a hill that rose about a hundred feet above the creek. They walked up the hill and found that on the other side it overlooked the river. They did not have to look any farther. They could farm down the hill on the gentle slope, plant a few apple trees where the slope grew steeper, and build the stand on the plain, far enough from the hill to be out of range of small arms. They would clear an area at the top of the hill as an observation point, and perhaps build a little shed where someone could stay when they were watching for river traffic.

The next few weeks the work was unrelenting, fourteen hours a day, transporting supplies, felling trees, and disassembling the flatboat to use the planking for one of the houses. They built the inn, the store, the stable, and a warehouse inside a tiny stockade. They set up their little swivel guns in strategic places and built an observation tower high on the nearby hill so that it overlooked both the stockade and the Spay-Lay-Wi-Theepi. They girdled trees to clear the slope in front of the stockade, down to the creek. The women did their share of the heavy work. Jinja had to admire the raw toughness of Mary and Anna Derontyan as they hammered nails and felled trees. They stood some guard duty too. One of the first things they did was to clear a patch on the hill west of the store and plant a number of seedlings they had brought with them, three dozen apple trees and a dozen plum trees. They found a place for some grapevines too. There would be cider and wine at their inn.

Jinja took extra care in planning the stockade. He put supply sheds at the corners, with overhanging second stories as blockhouses. He was pinning his hopes on the idea that people would settle in the area to be near a store, and that they would all come to the stockade during moments of Indian unrest, which he was sure would occur sometime between that day and the time when the whites would inevitably push the Indians west again. Jinja was a realist about Indians. "The life of a Longhouse brave," his father had told him, "is a noble one, but it is usually short and tragic. Count yourself lucky that you have a choice, and when you choose, do not choose the red road."

Jinja knew his father was right. After the Revolution most of the Mohawks who had been their friends had gone off to Canada, leaving their ancient lands to escape the retribution of the new American republic that they had opposed. They would never again see their beloved valley of the Te-non-an-at-che, the "River that Flows through Mountains." He was sad for them, because he felt that they loved that land as no white man ever could.

While he worked in the fading sun of the late summer,

his thoughts often turned to Joanna, the girl who lived in the cabin on the hill a mile away. He wondered if she had the strength and toughness of the women who toiled shoulder to shoulder in the stockade with their men. The night they had visited the cabin of her and her mother, she had stood up to say good night. He was surprised to see how tall she was, nearly six feet, and slender. He bet she could put in a long hard day's work. He had been able to see, even in the dim candlelight, that her face was sunburned. Both she and her mother were outdoor women. He could feel it in their callused hands when he took them and thanked the women for letting him and James visit.

Gradually the little stockade and the land surrounding it took shape. They had used some of the trees close to the stockade to build the walls. Now they cleared more trees to create fields of fire so that any attackers could not sneak too close. Fortunately, the trees close by were younger than most of those in the forests they had passed on the way west.

They chopped some of these felled trees into firewood and stacked the logs by the store in the stockade. Goods were piled in the warehouse and in the store. But the work was not done. They had brought food supplies with them, but with leaves due to start turning colors and winter not far away, they knew they'd better get some meat put away. So while the women scoured the woods for nuts, berries, and roots, the men hunted and fished.

Though a day did not pass without Jinja thinking about Joanna, he did not see her during the entire four months that they spent laboring to prepare their little community. There was just no time. In the course of their labors a number of people had stopped by. A wandering band of Delawares had visited and smoked with them, left with a few gifts and promised to be back in the spring with some furs. Several neighbors—people who lived within ten or twenty miles of them—had heard about the new post and bartered some vegetables and grain for a little ammunition. Jinja showed them a small pair of millstones he had brought along, and they told him about a place upstream on the creek where they thought the current ran fast enough to run a mill.

But neither Joanna nor her mother came to visit. So Jinja decided to call upon them. He climbed the hill to their cabin mid-morning on a Sunday, bringing with him a brace of ducks he had killed an hour earlier. The older woman was outside in front of the house, chopping firewood. At first she didn't notice him, so intent was she on making little pieces out of big ones. She was wearing boots, a loose-fitting wool dress, and a woolen kerchief around her head. By her side was a ragged blanket, as if she had been wearing it in the cool morning air until the chopping had warmed her enough that she could drop it on the grass.

In the bright October sun she looked older, her cheeks hollow, her body painfully angular, her eyes angry, as if the wood were her enemy.

"Hello Miz Collins," Jinja said, and the woman froze with her ax held over her head. For a moment Jinja imagined that she might decide to chop on him for a while. Her eyes left the wood she was splitting and rested on him.

"Hello, you."

"David," he said.

"I heard the Injun call you somethin' else when you was last here."

"He called me Jinja."

"That an Injun name?" she asked without any kindness in her voice.

"It's a nickname my grandfather give me."

"That ain't what I asked." Her eyes narrowed into snake-like slits.

"My grandfather gave me that name in memory of a Mohawk friend of his. Listen," he said, "there's Indians that are devils, all right, but I hope you don't think that way about James."

"Who's James?" came a voice from the front door. Jinja flinched at the sound. He looked up and saw that Joanna looked a lot younger in the light of day than she had by the glow of a candle.

"I brought you folks some ducks," he said, stepping forward until he was within ten feet of the both of them. Joanna walked down the stairs slowly, staring hard at Jinja.

"I asked you who is James." She was about as sweet as her mother, he thought. What do I want to get mixed up with a pair like this for?

"James is the man who was with me the night I came to visit," he told her.

"The Injun."

He was beginning to get annoyed. Everything about these two was rude and unsociable. "I'm a quarter Seneca myself," he said. Left unspoken but not misunderstood was, And what are you gonna do about it?

"Thought you might have some a that in you," said the girl.

"Well," he said, "do you want the ducks or don't you?" It made him feel better being rude back to them. "If you don't want 'em, I'll take them back with me, me and the Injuns'll eat 'em tonight and I'm sure we'll enjoy 'em."

The mother swung her ax one more time, and buried it deep in a stump. "Come on in, we still got some sassafras tea on the fire." Joanna vanished into the cabin. Jinja followed her mother up the stairs and through the front doorway.

"If you'd like to stay for Sunday lunch, I'll cook them birds for us. It was right nice for you to bring 'em, you know."

"Well, I come by to see if you were doing all right."

"Better'n we got a right to, I guess. Joanna, would you show this young man to the crick? He's strong, he can take the big bucket and carry it back for us."

"Ma!" The girl was offended. Clearly she was used to doing that chore herself.

"You mind me now," said the mother.

The girl also wore a wool dress, but she was still barefoot, although the morning was chilly. The dress came down only to her knees. "C'mon, you strong man, and take this bucket." Her voice was husky, not sweet. He followed her down to the creek. She stepped off the bank into the icy water and watched it swirl around her legs while he stooped down and filled the bucket.

"You know why she had me take you down here, don't you?" she asked in an annoyed tone of voice.

"I guess I don't," he said.

"Men are so stupid," she said.

"How would you know, you're only a girl."

"She told me men are stupid, and if you don't know why she had me take you down here, then she must be right. She wants me to have a man, you know."

"Even with Indian blood in me?"

"Shoot, you don't look no more like an Indian than I do," she said.

"Less, I would think," he replied, looking into her black eyes.

"You watch your mouth, you," she spat. "Who do you think you are, comin' into this country, roostin' on land my daddy helped to clear, with a Injun, yet."

He almost ignored her anger. Anger was just a part of

her. No, anger was her. Too bad, he thought. Such a pretty thing. Strong-looking, smarter than a lot of the frontier brats he'd met over the years. Seventeen was a good age. You could raise a girl that age into a good wife. But not this girl. The thought of waking up next to her made his scalp itch. He took off his beaver pelt cap and scratched his head.

"You gonna kiss me or something?" she asked.

"Not in my lifetime."

"Well, that's fine with me. I don't want nothin' to do with men, that's for sure."

Jinja didn't believe her. Not one bit. And he did not want a thing from her. If he could have run, he would have, but he had to be polite. After a few more moments of pointless small talk, he carried his rifle and her bucket up the hill and put it down inside the door.

"Miz Collins, I'm sorry I can't stay, but I have to get back and finish some work at the store," he told Joanna's mother.

For a moment he thought she wouldn't answer. Her eyes were blazing as they stared at Joanna.

A man had popped into their lives and she had figured out a way to get the two alone with each other. The girl had bungled her chance. What do you do with a girl like that? God gives her a pretty face and a nice body, and she can't even make a hungry man bite. Ruth Collins had seen the way Jinja had looked at Joanna the first night he had visited them. And now he was running off as fast as he could. What was the matter with that girl?

"Come and visit us down at the store soon as you can," he said. "Thanks for the tea." Then he remembered they hadn't even gotten to the tea, but it didn't matter much. He hoped that both the mother and the daughter would be infrequent customers. They got under his skin like a nasty rash. "Enjoy your ducks," he said just before he stepped on down the hill. He left them glaring at each other. They were probably on their best behavior when other people were around. He could imagine what went on when they were alone with each other, which was almost all the time.

He had to admit that he was disappointed. Like most men, he longed to be with a pretty woman, but he was too independent to put up with rudeness for the privilege. Still, he thought it was about time he found himself a woman, and women were scarce on the frontier, especially young girls who could speak English and were pretty to look at.

Well, he wasn't about to fret about it. In fact, now that he thought about it, he didn't like the idea that the mother was so fired up about her daughter snagging a man, especially him. That's all he needed. Move in with a girl and have to deal with her old bitter harridan of a mother. By the time he made it back to the stockade, he felt as if he had been released from purgatory.

By the middle of October the little trading community was doing a little business. Whites had continued to trickle in with farm produce, and one afternoon their first boarder arrived, an army captain on his way west.

Jinja was pleased to see him and his horses approaching the gate. A well-dressed, well-mounted army captain might have some hard money to spend, a little Spanish gold maybe. Jinja greeted him at the gate of the stockade, helped him down off his horse and led the horse and the captain's packhorse to the stable. While Jinja and the captain chatted about his journey, Obie removed the packs, uncinched the saddle and began to rub the horses down. The captain was impressed, but he was too worn out to say so. He stood beside Jinja, his face sagging with exhaustion. Jinja thought he might have to take hold of the man to keep him from collapsing.

"I'm sure you'd like to see your room," Jinja said.

"My room?" The captain, familiar with inns of the time, no doubt had expected a loft occupied by a half-dozen, louse-ridden wayfarers.

"You are our first guest, Captain. Your room is your own."

The captain needed the rest. A large man of about forty, his journey had been long and uncomfortable, he said. If Jinja did not mind, he would tumble into bed now. They could wake him in time for supper.

That would be in about four hours, Jinja replied, pointing to the place where the sun would be at the appointed time.

"Thank you," said the captain softly as he followed Jinja to an upstairs bedroom. The captain entered the room, but Jinja did not follow. "My name is Armstrong," said the captain just before Jinja closed the door behind him and listened to the sound of a very tired man falling into his bed.

The following morning Jinja was surprised to find Ruth and Joanna knocking on the gate of the stockade, wearing their newest old dresses. They needed some supplies, they said. They had a cow they were willing to trade. Could Jinja use a cow? How, he asked, had they managed to survive for the past five years?

The same way families with men had managed, they told him as he proudly gave them a tour of the stockade. Ruth's husband had cleared the land and built the cabin before his death, and like Indian squaws, they had grown a lot of corn. They had also made cheese from their cow milk and done some fishing and somehow made do with the clothes they had.

"You sure got a lot of work done these few months," Ruth said, and Joanna agreed that, yes, they must have worked very hard.

He took them into the store and let them walk around and look at the goods. The store was laid out, on a smaller scale, the same way his grandfather Dieter Wendel laid out his store in Albany. "You sure have plenty of goods," said Ruth, and Joanna agreed that for a frontier store there sure was a pleasing selection.

James took it all in as he stood behind the counter listening to the mother and daughter being impressed. James was not impressed. He had a good feel for straight talk, and theirs was not that. He wondered if Jinja understood what was going on.

"I'd like to see your hairbrushes if you have any," Joanna said.

"I'm sorry," Jinja replied. "The next time we go back East for more goods, we'll have a better idea of what folks need out here. And I promise then I'll get you your hairbrushes."

He saw her lip curl into a sneer and he reminded himself that there were other uses for hairbrushes. He saw Ruth give her daughter a stern look.

"What about material for a scarf?" Joanna asked.

"We have linen, we have wool, we have linsey-woolsey, we have a little silk. If it's something you can't make, Mary there can make it for you." He pointed to Mary, seated toward the back of the store, mending a shirt of Obie's.

"That's good," Joanna said simply, her dark eyes fastened on those of Jinja. They clung to him. They would not let go. Her mind was searching for flattering words, but she had gone as far as she could go with him. At that point Captain Armstrong walked into the store. Anna had brushed off his blue uniform with its buff facings when he had come downstairs for breakfast. Tall, straight, dignified in his uniform, he looked like a flower among weeds as he walked into the store. Jinja saw Joanna catch her breath at her first glimpse of the American captain. Quickly her eyes dropped their grip on Jinja. "I need to . . ." her voice faded into nothingness as she and her mother slowly drifted toward where the captain was looking at a pair of fleece-lined gloves.

They did not sidle up to him, but rather allowed him to discover them as they looked at the small assortment of iron kettles and caldrons close to where he stood. He felt the movement over to his left, turned to look, and found himself staring at the prettiest face he had seen since he left the tidewater country.

"Hello ladies," he said, not troubling to glance Ruth's way. His eyes were fixed on Joanna, who, with some effort, managed to tilt her head downward and stare modestly at the floor. She said nothing. It was up to her mother to speak.

"Good mornin', officer," she said.

"Captain Terrance Armstrong at your service," he replied.

"Mrs. Collins, widow," she said, attempting a more cultured speech. "And this is my daughter, Joanna."

"I *am* charmed," was his response. He took the widow's hand briefly, then reached for Joanna's, held it close to him and contemplated it for a moment, a rough and callused hand, but dainty in its way, and anyway, what did that matter, when the face held such beauty? Maybe it would be good to stay an extra day.

"What brings you here to us, Captain?" she asked, as if the stockade had suddenly become her community.

"The Indians are up in arms," he said. "Arthur St. Clair" —he saw that the name was strange to them—"the governor of Northwest Territory . . ." He saw that the place name did not ring a bell. "It's where you *live,* ma'am, he's raised a large army to put down the tribes."

"Where is all this happening, Captain?" Joanna's mother asked calmly.

"Somewhere west of here," he answered.

"Oh my," she said. "I hope he is successful."

At that moment an idea seized the captain. Long campaigns could be deadly dull without companionship. "Great heavens, ma'am," he said, "don't you understand that the territory is at war? That your beautiful daughter might be in danger if you stay here?"

Joanna's mother ignored the implication that her own undesirability put her beyond the threat of harm.

"Would you ladies care to dine with me?" the captain asked. Assuming their assent, he walked over to Jinja.

"Sir," he said, using the sir that was meant for condescension, rather than the sir that was meant for superior officers, "I know this might be an odd hour, but I wish to dine with the ladies."

"I will see to it," Jinja responded. "Stay and see if any of our goods meet your needs. I'll call you when your table is ready." He walked to the kitchen and told Anna there would be guests dining shortly. He had observed the older woman shifting her daughter's affections from himself to the captain. His disappointment quickly gave way to relief. The girl and her mother were nothing but trouble. Anna gave him a strange look as he left the kitchen. He was whistling a tune. She had never heard him, or anybody else, do that before.

6

IN THE GRAY MISTS OF THE OHIO RIVER VALLEY, three horses made their way west slowly, through the freezing rain and sleet that turned the faces of the riders red and raw. All three riders finally decided to swathe their faces in scarves, exposing only their eyes to the elements. Leading the party was the gallant captain, warm beneath his uniform tunic and a heavily lined cloak that covered him from his ears to his boot tops.

Second in line was his packhorse, a strong work animal equal to the task of carrying the captain's personal comforts. Third and lagging was another big farm animal, Seth Collins's old plow horse, now burdened with the long deceased frontiersman's widow, his daughter, and what few of their belongings had survived the first thirty miles.

During their late breakfast at Jinja's stand, Captain Armstrong had given them a news report. The countryside, he told them, was alive with bloodthirsty Shawnees, Miamis, Delawares, and Wyandots. These fools who had built the flimsy stockade would be dead men and women within six months, he said, and so would all the outlying frontier farmers and their families. They would be safer, he continued, if they went west with him to St. Clair's army, which was rumored to number more than three thousand and was prepared to wipe out the Indians in the Northwest Territory forever.

Ruth Collins needed little encouragement. To have her daughter pursuing the favors of a frontier trader who would soon be dead, when a live Virginia army captain with hard money in his pocket was available, was just plain stupid, she had decided. And so the very next morning they started west from the gate of the fort. Joanna was the only one who looked back as the gates closed behind them. She had come to like Jinja, sort of, and felt a slight twinge at having to leave. She wanted one last glimpse of him before she engaged in the serious task of winning over the Virginia captain. Jinja, as he watched the three of them disappear in the cold misty downpour, felt only relief. There was a good fire in the huge fireplace in the stand. That was the only warmth he sought.

Just about ten miles out, Joanna's mother began to complain that the motion of the horse was making her body ache. If she was expecting chivalry from the captain, his response must have caught her by surprise.

"We don't stop on this journey, you old sack," he said.

Joanna was also very uncomfortable. The horse had a wide body to start with, and she was astride behind her mother, where the horse's body was even wider. From her waist down she was a mass of aches and uncomfortable numbness. After another mile or so she told her mother to stop the horse and she half climbed down, half fell, to the cold wet floor of the forest.

"I'm not going any farther!" she yelled to the captain, who was a hundred yards ahead. Exasperated, the captain rode back to where the two women were standing beside the old horse.

The captain exhaled noisily, impatiently. "All right,

then," he said. "We'll stop here. I'll put up a tent and I want you ladies to find me some dry wood." Joanna and her mother looked at each other and did not move. The captain dismounted and walked up to the two women.

"Let there be no misunderstanding, starting now," he said sternly. The courtly and courteous captain who had dined with them the day before had vanished. "You are in the middle of a godforsaken country with Indians swarming all over the forests. You are with me. You will each do as you're told or I'll leave you here. You *will* do as you're told," he repeated.

They stood before him, quietly terrified.

"Go out and find me some wood, and it had better be dry," he said. "A dry stick is good for burning. A wet stick is good for beating," he said, smiling.

Each took a blanket and went out in search of wood. Once they were out of his hearing, Joanna grabbed her mother's arms with both hands. "What have you gotten us into?" she asked. "That man's a monster."

Angrily, the mother jerked her hands away from her daughter. "You've seen too little of men, girl, since your father was killed. All men are monsters. But it's real hard livin' without them. That's the way life is. A woman can't get comfortable without a man, she's got to live poor-like, like we've been livin' since your father died."

"So this is what we've got to live with?"

"You listen to me. I've been living a long time and I know what I'm talking about. It's your job to gentle him down. He thinks you're the prettiest creature in the world and he wants you in his bed. You be sweet to him. You make him want you, then you give him what he wants and he'll come around. Men are like that. You hear? This is your chance to get out of this horrible wilderness. You do right and he'll take us back to Virginia with him. You might even wind up bein' a lady. What do you think of that?"

Joanna did not know what to think of that. They went about their chore of looking for dry wood, searching in different directions. Joanna got lucky. She found a tree that had been blown down months before. Parts of its crown had fallen beneath a rock shelf. There the wood had seasoned, and remained dry through the current spell of bad weather. Joanna gathered as much wood as she could, wrapped it in a blanket and carried it back to the clearing where the captain had made camp. The captain had pitched his tent, which included an awninglike flap in front of it.

"Bring the wood in here!" he said from within the tent when she announced her presence.

She brought him the wood and unwrapped it. "Ah," he said. "That's fine. I'll make a woodsman of you." He smiled at her and she smiled back. The smile encouraged him to go further. "But first I'll make a companion of you. In the woods, in the army, officers of stature usually take a lady, of good breeding, of course, to be a companion, to keep him warm on cold nights, to make him comfortable so that by the morning he will feel refreshed and rested for battle. It is a most honorable calling. I'm considering choosing you."

Joanna thought about what her mother had said. She curtsied, and the captain nearly laughed aloud. She looked at him from beneath lowered eyelids.

My heavens, he thought, the wench fancies herself being courted. "Where is the old— Where is your mother?"

"She was looking for wood in a different direction," she said.

"For her sake," he said, "she'd better find some. Everybody pulls his own weight in an army camp. Come here and help me spread out this blanket. There."

A half hour later Joanna's mother returned, wet and sniffling, with an armload of wood wrapped in her blanket. "Joanna? Captain?" she shouted to the tent.

"Shut your mouth you miserable crone. Do you want to summon every Shawnee from here to the Cumberland River?"

Ruth was not about to put up with this insult. The captain was a lot like her dead husband. She didn't put up with Seth Collins's nastiness, she fought with him, year after year, until his untimely death. The captain had crawled out through the flap of the tent, which was barely tall enough for a short person to stand in, and he was not a short person. They faced each other under the awning. Behind him stood Joanna.

"You will not speak to me that way, Captain," she said, gathering the last shreds of dignity she would ever claim in this world. "My daughter and I are ladies and we expect to be treated like ladies."

"You? A lady? Why, you witch. Children run from you and lay awake all night. What! Grown men lose sleep. *I* wouldn't be able to sleep tonight if I didn't have your daughter to warm my bed."

"My daughter? My daughter goes where I go, Captain, if you want—" Her speech was interrupted by a backhanded slap across the face. The wood she was holding dropped to the ground with a wet clatter. The captain bent down and picked up a stick.

He glared at her. "You call this dry wood, you withered hag? If we could burn it we'd raise enough smoke to signal all the tribes west of the Monongahela. Your daughter brought *dry* wood." He reached into the tent and brought out an armful, then a kettle, then some provisions that he had purchased from Jinja. "Do you see that the rain has stopped? I want you to kindle a fire, cook some food, and bring it to us. I will be with your daughter in my tent. In my bed, in fact. She and I will be dining there. You will serve us. And then, if the food is good, and timely, you may sleep outside, under the awning, in case it should start to rain again."

The mother looked at her daughter. Joanna did not look back at her mother. Ruth suddenly realized that she was an older woman than she had been when her husband was alive, much older. She no longer had the heart or the strength to fight. She longed only for life. If this captain could help to preserve it during this time of troubles, she would have to submit. She had seen what the savages had done to the men of the valley. She would not let such a thing happen to her. The captain urged Joanna back into the tent, and Ruth began to carry wood to a sheltered area, to begin her chores.

This would be Skoiyasi's last warpath, of that he was certain. Fifty-two summers was a long time for a Seneca warrior to live. His body ached all over from arthritis and from old wounds that he had received in his years of fighting against the whites. And his soul ached with loneliness.

As a young man, nearly crippled, he and his wife, Kawia, had taken their two boys and moved west, away from the English. He was not the first of the Longhouse to do so. Hundreds of Senecas, known among the Iroquois as the Guardians of the Western Door, had moved west to flee from the endless stream of English land speculators and frontier farmers. It was hard to understand these people, the Senecas had thought after many years of dealing with them. They smile at you and give you a present and then a few days later they come back and tell you that the land your people have lived on for seven generations belongs to them.

These western Senecas were known as Mingoes. Skoiyasi's children had grown up as Mingoes. For many years they had found peace in the valley of the Spay-Lay-Wi-Theepi, the Ohio River. The whites had come, but not many, not so many that the Mingoes could not live as they wished to live.

But last summer Kawia had died, along with half the village. Another white disease, he was certain. The old ones had told him that such diseases had never occurred before the whites had come. He sat by her for two days while the old one made medicine until he got sick and died, before Kawia. She lingered on and babbled about her childhood. The last words she said he could not understand, but they were about Little Oak, the half-Seneca son of the white trader Big Oak. Little Oak had gone east and now lived like a white man, a rich white man. But Kawia had chosen Skoiyasi over Little Oak, and all these years, after they had moved so far west that they rarely saw a white man, all these years had been good.

How pleased he was that his sons had moved their families to a Munsey village farther west. Still, he had lost his mate of many years, and he felt lost. So when word came that the white chief St. Clair was leading an army west, and that Little Turtle was assembling a mighty force of red men to defeat him, Skoiyasi gained heart. Never mind that his grandfathers would have never considered being led by a chief of the Twightwees. Never mind that his grandfathers had disdained the idea of a red people that was made up of many nations. He had seen enough whites in his lifetime to last him forever. His sons had gone west, he expected never to see them again. He would die fighting whites. The thought filled him with a sense of purpose.

He rode an old dappled mare through the freezing rain, covered by two big old army strouds. There was once a time when he would have disdained such an animal, when his two good legs would have eaten up fifty miles of forest trail in a day. These days he walked with a heavy limp, when he could walk at all. He had no business on the warpath, except that he was still keen with a rifle, and had been since his childhood, when Big Oak had taught him how to shoot. It would be a fine joke if Big Oak could have known how many white men he had slain with his rifle. But Big Oak was probably dead, he thought. So many people dead. All the Senecas he had grown up with, dead. It would be fine to die in battle and join them. There had been a time when he thought he would live his life out with Kawia, in peace. He would have never left Kawia, but Kawia had left him, mumbling about Little Oak.

He sat straight up on the old, droop-necked nag, but as he rode, his head began to nod and he dreamed of the old days on the Genesee, when he and his family would paddle down the river to visit relatives among the Chenusios. It would be summer and the huge fields of corn would be tall with the promise of a wonderful harvest. Sometimes they would take with them gourds of strawberry juice, not sour and fermented like the white rum that burned the belly and made them silly, but sweetened with sugar from the sugar tree.

When their canoe would arrive at the village of his aunt, one of his cousins, playing in the river, would race for their longhouse shouting, and family would start to spill out of the longhouse, one after another, in an unending stream. They would wade into the river and pull the canoe to the shore, and that night all the old ones would tell stories that went back before the white man had ever come, stories of the early days of the Ganonsyoni, and the clan mother, and the good and evil twin, and then stories of great warriors and their battles against the Wendot, when a handful of Ganonsyoni caused the whole Wendot nation to flee before them.

It was almost dark when Skoiyasi's daydreams finally fled. Dreams did not make him sad, they gave him peace. Carefully he dismounted, led the horse to a shallow cave he knew, and tied her close by. Then he took his rain-soaked blankets and his pack into the cave. He chewed on a handful of corn and drank a few swallows of water. He had a little dry kindling and a white man's piece of iron. He struck a spark, then another, and another, and finally the kindling caught. He blew it into a flame, took a small dead branch and caught the fire, and used it to light his pipe. Puffing on his pipe, he took the bottom blanket, the dryer of the two, and wrapped himself in it. Then he sat back against the wall of the cave and drew in the rich smoke of the kinnikinnick. His face creased with pleasure.

The three riders continued their slow pace west for three days. The morning of the fourth day dawned crisp and bright, with only two mounted. A third walked behind the two on horseback and the packhorse. The terror of being killed by Indians made Joanna's mother keep up in spite of her fatigue. She did not suffer in silence. A torrent of abuse spilled from her mouth, but it came out in mumbles. She was too frightened of the captain to tell him what she thought of him and of her strumpet daughter.

Her daughter and the captain, it turned out, got along quite well, once the captain had showed Joanna what she was supposed to do. Since her father's death, her mother had been more like a drill sergeant than a mother, telling her what to do nearly every hour of the day. Captain Armstrong was surprised their first night together to discover that this beautiful girl had never before been with a man. He was not gentle with her, but Joanna had known little gentleness in her life, so a little more pain was not about to upset her. After the first night she learned that there was pleasure attached to the captain's attentions.

Now, Ruth could lay outside in the cold and listen to her daughter as she cuddled comfortably with her captain. But it was the whispering that went on between the bedded couple that really drove Ruth crazy. She was certain that they were whispering about her, that her daughter was telling Captain Armstrong how much sweeter it was knowing that her mother was out there shivering in the cold.

In truth, the daughter was trying to persuade her lover to let her mother into the tent, but he was not about to let the old lady inhibit his nightly romp with Joanna. When Joanna insisted, he got gruff and salty. She refused to back down, and he finally agreed to hang some blankets from the tent awning to shield her mother from the night wind and the blowing rain.

Suddenly, up ahead Ruth could see the captain raising his hand for them to halt. He had heard something, that was for sure, and now she heard it. It was not the crackle of skulkers in the bush, but the low buzz of conversation that grew louder as the talkers came closer. The closer they came, the more apparent it was that there were a lot of them, and that they were speaking English.

They had to be Americans, thought Captain Armstrong. Better holler before they come through the trees, see us, take us for some blasted Indians, and let loose a musket volley.

"Who goes there?" he shouted, not being able to remember a military phrase from the manual that would be right for the situation.

Immediately the trail grew silent.

"You tell us who goes *there!*" came the reply.

"Captain Terrance Armstrong!" he cried out, and almost immediately men in shoddy blue uniforms began to appear on the trail in front of him. "And who, may I ask, are you?" he asked.

The lead soldier was a sergeant. He walked up to the captain, studied his uniform, decided the man was who he said he was, and gave him a smart salute. "Sergeant William Judson," he said, "First Regiment, sir."

Armstrong returned the sergeant's salute. He had heard of the First Regiment, they were supposed to be the best troops St. Clair had. "What luck," he said to the sergeant. "Is the army coming this way?"

"I should say not, sir," the sergeant responded. "The army is busy building forts, sir. But the weather's been bad, there's been sickness, and the damn contractors have shorted us on supplies. Small wonder why we're getting so many desertions, sir."

"Is that what you're doing, Sergeant, deserting?"

"No sir," was the reply. "General St. Clair is stationing us along the trail to catch deserters and bring 'em back so's we can hang 'em. Have you seen any of the miscreants?"

"We haven't seen a soul since we left the new stand about forty miles back," Armstrong said.

"Well, we got one yesterday. Sent him back up the trail. I'd hate to be him when he gets into camp."

"Why? What can they do to him after they hang him?"

"Ain't what they do after they hang him, Captain. It's what they do before."

"Which is what?" The captain decided that he would be taking considerable interest in the army's treatment of deserters.

"What? Why, they flog all the skin off him first, that's what . . . sir."

The captain nodded. "I see. Sergeant, how far are we from General St. Clair?"

"Maybe fifty mile, maybe a little more, depends on if they've moved since we left 'em."

"Do you have someone who might be able to guide us there?"

"Don't see how you could miss 'em sir," the sergeant said, then deciding that later on he might need the goodwill of this captain, he said, "I'm sure I can spare a man for you, Captain." Now he spotted Joanna, and he removed his hat. At this time, her bedraggled mother appeared through the trees and struggled up to the group. The sergeant took one look at the mud-spattered woman and put his hat back on his head.

Fatigued though she was, Ruth Collins did not miss the insult. I'll fix you some day, she told herself. And you too, she thought, looking at Armstrong and her daughter. But there was no defiance left in her. How could she "fix" them? They were so young and powerful. And she was so old and powerless.

7

HIGH ON THE HILL BEYOND THE SOUTHWEST corner of the stockade was a tower that rose just high enough to command a glimpse of the Ohio River above the surrounding trees. It was not always manned, because it didn't seem all that important. On this day Obie's boy Jack was in the tower. Jack was a dreamy child who loved to go up there and watch the clouds chase each other from one horizon to the other. On this sunny autumn afternoon he snatched a piece of child's glory for himself when he spotted a pair of canoes filled with Indians moving unhurriedly down the river.

He continued to watch until he saw them veer right, then the trees and the contour of the hill obscured them. But he knew they had veered to enter the creek. He scampered down from the tower and ran down the hill, through the grounds to the store. "Indians," he said to Jinja. "On the creek, I think."

Maybe customers, Jinja thought. Maybe not. He ran around the stockade rousting the women from the kitchen, Obie from the stable, and James from the warehouse. The stockade wall was only about nine feet high, with a catwalk around it that stood less than five feet off the ground. The women and men drew rifles and headed for their designated posts on the catwalks, just in case. Jinja, meanwhile, placed himself on the catwalk by the gate, watching. After a few minutes he could see the first canoe on the creek. There were only two figures in the canoe. The other canoe was nowhere to be seen. Bad news. Peaceful traders did not hide in the bushes.

The two Indians hauled the canoe up on the bank of the creek in full view of the people on the catwalk. They pulled their blankets around them. Each took hold of a blanket-wrapped bundle and strode toward the fort. They were halfway up the path before Jinja realized that one of them was a woman, a very unfeminine, hard-looking woman.

Once they were close to the gate, the man dropped his bundle and cupped his hands around his mouth. "Trade!" he shouted, then repeated the word in an Indian tongue that nobody in the fort understood. "Might be Twightwee," James said, using the word with which the Iroquois described the Miamis. Both were wearing long buckskin jackets. They wore their hair long and parted down the middle. The man had two eagle feathers that lay down the right side of his face, between his ear and eye. "Trade!" he shouted again.

Neither was carrying a rifle, and Jinja mentioned that fact to James. The Oneida laughed. "I'll bet they've each got at least two knives and two tomahawks under all that deerskin," he said.

"Well, let 'em in," Jinja said. "Jack, as soon as they come in, you close the gates and bolt 'em, quick, understand?"

The boy nodded and proceeded to unbolt the gate. The two Miamis picked up their bundles and entered. The man wore a smile much too big to be genuine, while the woman looked grim as a Presbyterian. James walked toward them with an equally phony smile on his face and shook the hand of the man. From his place on the catwalk Jinja held his rifle on his hip, but the barrel was pointed at the Miami.

The Miami pointed to his chest. "Young Eagle Claw," he said, extending his hand again. In the middle of the second handshake the Miami brave heard the gates slam behind him and his smile froze, then disappeared.

Young Eagle Claw dropped his bundle and began to sign and speak. "Why do you shut the door behind us and make us prisoners?" he asked indignantly.

"My brother," James replied in sign and Seneca. "We do not shut you in. We saw some bad Shawnees prowling around the woods yesterday. We are worried about them. We would not want them to sneak in and harm you."

Both James and Jinja had heard stories from Big Oak of how during Pontiac's rebellion the Ottawas and others would visit the English forts, their faces gentle and peaceful. Once the English let them in, they would wait until the soldiers were careless and inattentive, and they would slaughter the entire garrison. Using this trick, the Indians nearly threw the English back across the Alleghenies.

"Guns and bullets," Young Eagle Claw said, meaning for Jinja to show them his stock of weapons.

"You stay here, my brother," James said. The Indians stood in the open space twenty yards inside the gate. They looked around at the catwalk and saw that from each wall someone stared down at them. Jinja, Obie, Jack, the two women—all were well-armed, and the guns were pointed casually in their general direction.

James emerged from the store with two muskets that were used but in excellent condition. Young Eagle Claw was smiling again as he grabbed hold of the best one and hefted it. But when he looked up the barrel he frowned. "Rifle," he said in English. "Need rifle."

James shook his head. "First we see furs," he said, pointing to the bundles.

The Miami started to say no, but he changed his mind and opened his bundle. The furs were old and had not been very good pelts even when they were new. These were somebody's rejects.

"No no," James said as soon as he saw the furs. "You go back to the woods and bring me good pelts if you want good rifles."

"Good," Young Eagle Claw replied, closing his bundle and turning back toward the gate.

James followed the two Miamis to the gate. Jack looked toward James, who gave another quick glance outside the stockade and nodded. The gates swung open and the Indians began to walk through. James and Jinja were almost ready to take an easy breath but the two Indians stopped in the gateway, looked back at James, and smiled as they dropped their bundles.

Jinja and James gave each other a quick look and wasted no time. Jinja jumped down from the catwalk and the two began to shove the gates closed, surprising the two Miamis. The woman fled, but Young Eagle Claw ran back through the gates, a tomahawk suddenly in his right hand. Things now happened very rapidly. Young Eagle Claw took three quick running steps toward Jinja, meaning to prevent him from completely closing his side of the double-doored gate. Jack, seeing this, ran to the gate and kept pushing it while Jinja gave his attention to the Miami. In the meantime, eight Indians sprinted from the woods toward the gate. Obie and his wife came running along the catwalk toward the gate, stopped and took aim. The Indians had about sixty yards to run to make it to the gate.

That was too far. Obie and his wife fired and two of the Miamis fell. James and Jack finished slamming the gates shut.

Young Eagle Claw raised his tomahawk as he sped toward Jinja. Jinja, never a man to be intimidated, swung his rifle around and caught the Miami warrior on the side of his head with the barrel of his rifle. Jinja was a strong man. The Miami toppled head over heels and lay still in the dust.

The woman and the warriors who had survived the first gunshots dashed back into the woods. Before Obie or his wife could reload, one of the fallen warriors scrambled to his feet and limped after them. Obie and his wife returned to their posts on the catwalk, while Jinja climbed up to his spot beside the gate and stared out into the woods, showing only an eye through the palisades. The Miamis had not yet fired a shot.

James summoned his wife Anna, who had been standing on the wall opposite the gate, on guard for a surprise attack from that quarter. While James slashed two long strips from Young Eagle Claw's blanket and bound the Miami's arms and legs tightly behind him, Anna approached with a gourd full of water, which James poured over the face of the prostrate Miami warrior. He opened his eyes and turned his head to look at James but did not groan, though James was sure Jinja must have given the Miami an atrocious headache.

The Miami struggled into a sitting position and stared angrily at James. For a few moments there was silence between them. Perhaps initially it had not occurred to Young Eagle Claw that James was some sort of Indian, but now it did. In ruptured Huron he spoke a few words that James thought he understood: "Who are you?" or "What are you?"

"I am Oneida," James replied in the Delaware dialect. "Come to trade with you."

The Miami missed most of that, but he did catch "Oneida," and his face distorted with rage.

"Hiroquois!" he spat. The Miamis were an Algonquian nation. It was the Algonkin language that had coined the term to describe the Longhouse confederacy. In Algonkin the word meant "real adders." It was not meant to be complimentary.

Young Eagle Claw heard some noise behind him on one of the catwalks. He turned his head and saw Jinja loading one of the swivel guns. "You think you can stop us with that?" he asked in his native tongue.

James laughed. "We've done fine with it so far." James knew how artillery terrified Indians. Jinja's grandfather Big Oak had told James that artillery terrified anybody who had any sense.

"You have built your trading place in the middle of a war, my brother," Young Eagle Claw said, suddenly assuming an intimate tone, as if James's skin were important to him. "It would be good to take your white man things and go back to the Te-non-an-at-che."

"Here they come!" Jinja shouted from the catwalk. Three Miamis had appeared in a clearing by the creek two hundred yards away. All three fired their weapons toward the stockade, and a bullet thudded into one of the stout logs that formed the wall. The Miamis were careless about concealing themselves, and Jinja said so.

"Maybe they haven't fought against any real long rifles lately," James suggested. "Maybe you ought to show them what you can do."

Jinja nodded. He had a bit of a weakness for showing off. Carefully he placed the rifle in a loophole, pulled back the hammer and sighted down the long barrel.

"This way!" shouted Anna suddenly from the back wall. Jinja pulled his rifle out of the loop and sprinted along the catwalk, followed by Obie, who had climbed the ladder at the sound of Anna's voice. Five Miamis were racing for the east wall, having figured that there were so few inside the stockade that they might have time to scale the wall while the defenders were being distracted. What they didn't count on was the other swivel gun, which was mounted in such a way that it was concealed until it was turned to face the outside. Anna had brought some fire out from the fireplace in the inn. It was ready beside the swivel when Jinja grabbed a burning splint, brought the gun to bear on the approaching Miamis, and fired.

Close as the Miamis were, Jinja had to fire fast, and he missed with all three hundred nails that had been loaded into the gun. The Miamis heard them buzz past. They stopped and retreated. "Don't worry about the rear wall!" Jinja shouted to the other defenders.

From beside the gate came the crack of a rifle, followed by a satisfied grunt from James. "Think you're the only shooter around here?" he hollered at Jinja. "I got one down by the creek."

James ran along the catwalk to the front of the stockade and peered toward the tree line. The Miamis had vanished and so had the canoe. Except for the faint lingering smell of gunpowder, and the trussed-up warrior lying in the dust below, it was as if they had never been there. For long minutes the men and women on the walls of the stockade waited for the Twightwees' next move. But except for a cold wind whistling through the cracks between the palisades, all was silent.

James jumped from the catwalk to the ground and walked over to Young Eagle Claw. His face was grim, and the warrior steeled himself for the pain and torture he knew were coming. He had heard about the fearsome Iroquois since he was a child. They had conquered dozens of tribes all around them, and claimed as their own the very lands of the Miamis, Ottawas, Chippewas, and other western tribes. Although in recent years the power and prestige of the Longhouse had waned in the eyes of the western tribes, a face-to-face encounter with a Ganonsyoni could still stir up the fearsome memories of the days when the Longhouse ruled from the Canadas to the Cumberland.

James saw through the mask of indifference on Young Eagle Claw's face. "Your brothers have left you to face your fate alone," he told the Miami.

Young Eagle Claw glared back. "You think they are gone?" he said. "The Miami has eyes that see in the night like the panther. My life is no matter. It is the life of the people that matters." He spoke quietly, yet with some emotion. James was impressed.

"My brother," James responded. "The war that has begun is a war my people would not fight. They know the English —the Americans—too well. If you could see how many they are, how many more they are every new summer, you would not think that you could save your people by fighting the Americans. Not now, not ever."

"We will see, *Hiroquois.*"

"It would be different if all the red people could forget the fights they have fought with each other, but that does not happen. The Americans are blind men in the woods, yet they always find red men who will serve as their eyes because they are fighting against the same foe that their grandfathers once fought against. These things never change. You must fight the whites with white man weapons. Where will you get them?"

"The French are our friends."

"The French are nobody anymore. Your father the French king no longer rules his land."

"What would you have us do? Come to the forts and beg for rum like all the tribes of the East? Look at you. You are like a white man. When I first saw you, that is what I thought you were. We are men. Many summers ago our people were attacked by the Nadowessioux from the country of the many lakes. There were many of them and they killed . . ." He wiggled his hands behind him, frustrated that he could not use them to show how the Sioux massacred three thousand Miamis nearly a century before. "Everybody still alive had dead friends and family to weep for. We fled to the French for protection, but we did not stay for long. We are mighty again. We are Miamis, and we are men, and we will fight those who would have our country. We remember when you too were men, *Hiroquois,* but something has happened." He was about to say more about Iroquois manhood, but he reminded himself that the Iroquois were still thought to be fierce by the Miamis, and he, not James, was the one bound by blanket strips.

"My time may be short, *Hiroquois,* but you will join me soon. It is too bad. It could have been good to fight at the side of Oneidas, Senecas, and Mohawks, killing whites until they were gone from our land."

James agreed. That surprised Young Eagle Claw. He looked around the stockade, first at Jinja. "Is that a white man?" he asked.

"Mostly," James replied.

Young Eagle Claw saw Obie watching the field beyond the east wall. "And a black white man?"

James said yes. "They are my friends. They are good friends. I have no choice if I am to have a life for myself."

"And what about your people?"

"My people are the Longhouse. Most have gone to the

Canadas to live. Some live in peace near the Te-non-an-atche. There are red men who are still free. But there is no red people. You said yourself that the Nadowessioux killed many Twightwee. Maybe we have been on this land for too long and made too many enemies of each other."

James was aware that the short winter day was nearing an end. He now understood why there were no more attacks. They were waiting till the night. "Why don't you tell your brothers to go home?" he asked. "We do not mean to harm you."

This is a soft *Hiroquois,* Young Eagle Claw thought. He is not to be feared. I will master him instead. The expression on his face suddenly turned fierce. "By sundown tomorrow," he said, "pieces of you—and them"—he looked up at the catwalk and followed it all the way around with his eyes—"will be floating down the Spay-Lay-Wi-Theepi."

"I thought you were too wise to talk like that, bound up as you are," James said, pulling his knife from his belt. "I am Ganonsyoni; we keep our knives sharp." He stuck the knife in Young Eagle Claw's left nostril, blade outward. "You will not feel this much," James said, slicing slowly upward. "You will not be as pretty." He sliced nearly to the bridge. "But if you do not say another word, I will let you keep your nose." James wiped the blade on his deerskin leggings and walked away.

"Soft," Young Eagle Claw said to himself, feeling the blood drip past his mouth. But he did not speak aloud.

Jinja felt his spirits sag as the sun sagged beneath the horizon. In the gray winter twilight he could see that the clear fields around the stockade were empty, but he knew that just beyond the first line of trees the enemy lurked, waiting for the dark. Waiting to kill.

An odd thought was making its way through his head. What made the people of the stockade the enemy of the

Miamis? It was a time when the tribes were finally getting together to drive the whites away. The stockade held two Oneidas, two blacks, several children, none of them white, and one white man who in fact was one-quarter Seneca. It was not as if they had come just to trade with the whites. They had come to supply the Indians as well.

There were no answers. It was intuitive on the part of the Miamis, and he guessed they had it right. After all, the people in the stockade were Americans, and it was the Americans who were pushing west; pushing, always pushing, with big mean shoulders. Now it was dark, with little moonlight. There was no question of sleep, not now. Three men and Anna on the walls, seeing stalking Twightwees in every faint shadow of the moon, waiting minute after endless minute for the attack that was sure to come.

Jinja was on the wall by the gate. On a dark night like this, the ears had to do a lot of the work that the eyes would do in broad daylight. He stood completely still, his eyes staring over the wall into the darkness, holding his breath, listening to the sounds of the night. There were no leaves on the trees, but the wind stirred the branches and made them rub together. There were night animals on the prowl or fleeing, little rustlings and scamperings that woodsmen could identify. And the stockade made its own little noises, a creak or a bump when a lower log feeling the weight of a building on its shoulders shifted ever so slightly, or a soft cough from one of the watchers, trying to stay warm in the path of an approaching winter.

He didn't know what made him turn his head away from the wall and look down into the center of the stockade. He could see nothing in the murky black below, but the corner of his eye caught something that made him shift his glance toward the doorway of the inn, where they had kept Young Eagle Claw, tied to a stout post. He was still there.

There was another human shape kneeling beside him.

There was no time for stealth. "Down below!" he shouted into the night, and fired quickly, just as the two Miamis straightened up and sprinted for the gate. Obie and James both fired at the faint figures, without effect, then all three jumped down from the catwalk and tried to intercept the two Miamis before they could make it to the gate. They were a step late.

No sooner had the Miamis opened the gate doors than the three bore down on them and pummeled them to the ground. But from the outside the doors were being pushed open. The scuffling men on the ground prevented the doors from swinging all the way open but the two-foot gap was enough. The Miamis on the outside started to flood through.

"Out of the way!" shouted Mary. The three male defenders knew what that meant. They scrambled to either side of the gate and let the Miamis come.

Bam-bam! Two big-barreled muskets bellowed nearly simultaneously from the doorway of the inn. The weapons, loaded with small shot, were aimed not at men, but toward the gateway where they knew the men were. The shot found targets. From the left and right of the gateway James and Jinja could see five men moaning on the ground. They and Obie drew their hatchets and bore down on the men who were still on their feet. The volley from the inn had stunned them. They retreated toward the gate, helping their five wounded companions. Jack had come down from his spot on the catwalk in time to lean against one of the doors and push it closed. Obie pushed the other, while Jinja slammed home the bolt.

"Back up on the catwalk!" James shouted. Obie, Jinja, Jack, and the women hustled up the ladder and spread out along the catwalk, while James walked around below trying to figure out how a lone Miami had managed to make his way into the compound without being detected.

None of them had any trouble staying awake now. Wide-eyed from their near disaster, they stood on the catwalk watching the dark in front of them, the walls on either side of them, and the interior of the stockade below them. They heard nothing but the usual noises of the night. No groans from the wounded. No angry whoops from the rest. Only the cold autumn wind, rubbing the branches of the trees together.

Now came the shrill sound of a bone whistle. Simultaneously from all directions a half-dozen little fires appeared from the tree lines and bounced halfway across the clearings. Men carrying fire, each of the defenders thought. The fires stopped for a moment, then arched across the sky. Four of them fell short. One of them landed harmlessly inside the stockade, and one stuck in the palisade, just about three feet below where Jinja was standing. Jinja looked down at it, but before he could reach over to pull the arrow out of the wall, he saw that the fire had just about gone out without doing any harm.

Fifteen minutes later the fires appeared again. This time the bowmen came closer to the stockade before they loosed their arrows. Jinja, James, Obie, and Anna all chose a target and fired. None of the shots hit, but they made the Indians hurry their shots. This time three fell short, two fell into the dirt in the compound and went out, while one stuck in the shakes of the roof of one of the store buildings. James jumped from the catwalk onto the roof and stomped the fire out before it could do any damage.

"We'd better put an end to this nonsense," Jinja told James, "before they get lucky and do some damage." Both had noted that each time the bowmen had approached, they used the same route. They each took a musket loaded with shot, climbed over the back wall, and headed right and left for positions about fifty yards forward from the walls of the stockade.

Jinja found a spot in line with the route of one of the bowmen and lay prone, behind a gentle swell, watching the woods line, waiting for a pinpoint of fire to appear. He wasn't very long waiting. Here it came, bouncing across the field almost directly toward him. It was impossible to gauge the distance. He would have to wait until the bowman stopped, and hope that the man had come within range of the scattergun. He started creeping forward, all the while watching the bouncing flame come closer and closer. He stopped, took aim, and waited, holding his breath while the flame bounced closer yet. By now he thought he could see the flame reflecting off the body and face of the approaching warrior.

The Miami was a little to his side, no longer directly in front of him, but still coming closer. Jinja followed him with his barrel, sighting just below the bouncing flame. He exhaled, then took a new breath, and firmed his finger pressure on the trigger as the Miami stopped running. He could see the flame being pulled back just before he pulled the trigger.

Through the smoke he could see the flame go straight up into the air. At that moment he heard a shot from the other side of the fort. Without thinking he sprinted toward the warrior, hoping to finish him off, but in the seven seconds it took him, the Miami had disappeared, leaving his bow and a smoldering arrow. Jinja did not wait any longer. Loading as he moved, he trotted back toward the stockade and found the doors cracked open for him. He made it through the gate and saw that James was back already. There was no expression on his face, but he knew that James had done what he had set out to do. Above, Jack was busy pouring water down on an arrow that had bounced off the wall but had landed close enough to the base to pose a threat to the wood below.

Still too excited to feel weary, they went back to their posts and waited for the next attack. By the time the first gray tinges of dawn arrived, they all were ready for a week's worth of rest. There had been no further incidents. Obie and the women lay down on the catwalk and slept. None of them could imagine that the Miamis were gone, unless their injuries had been worse than Jinja and James thought. But as the sun began its short journey across the autumn sky, it became clear that their attackers had departed, at least for the day. The defenders were relieved, but they also realized that their position was very weak, and that they would have to do something to make it stronger if they were to survive this war.

8

THE MIAMIS HAD INTENDED TO RESUME THEIR harassment at dawn. Although the buckshot wounds some of them carried were painful and annoying, they were not enough to stop a stalwart brave of the Twightwees. They would have this American trading post and all the people and goods within if it took them till winter to get it.

But about dawn one of them, a brave named Firemaker, spotted a canoe on the Ohio River, and when it came closer, he recognized the lone occupant as a warrior from his village. He called to the paddler, who pulled to shore.

"Come and join us," said Firemaker. "We have found a little white fort with many goods inside. The defenders are few. They are tired and the fort is weak. Join us and share our good fortune."

"That I cannot do," the canoer replied. "I come from Little Turtle. He has the American army in his grasp. Soon he will attack, and he is certain of a great victory. He wants the Wyandots, and he wants Shawnees, to share this victory. This is a war we must win, Little Turtle says. If we have the other tribes with us, we will win. This he believes. Will you come?"

"But the fort!"

"The fort will still be here when the battle is over. I tell you, all he needs to do is close his fist, and he will squeeze the life out of this big American army."

"Then why do you need us?"

"Because we do not just wish to win a victory. We must kill them all, teach them a lesson that will keep them on their side of the mountains forever. That is what Little Turtle says."

Firemaker had known Little Turtle since his childhood. Little Turtle was not simply a glory-seeking war chief with big dreams. Little Turtle was wise. What he said would happen generally came to be. If Little Turtle needed them, then it was important that they come. Firemaker climbed into the canoe. The two of them paddled from the river to the creek and then to the clearing where the raiding party had made camp. Firemaker's friend told Young Eagle Claw and the others about the coming battle. All except Young Eagle Claw wanted to go. Young Eagle Claw felt a personal stake in this raid. He had met James and Jinja and did not like either of them. His nose would heal but he would never forget the humiliation. Now that they had worn the defenders down, Young Eagle Claw wanted his revenge, and he said so, but Firemaker's friend assured him the fruits from the coming battle would be great and reminded him that the fort would not go away in the meantime.

Young Eagle Claw relented. By the time the cold morning mists had cleared from the valley, the raiding party had vanished.

Three canoes were on the water heading west. The weather stayed cold, but the paddling kept them warm. They were Miami braves. They did not mind the cold wind and the chilling spray in their faces as their canoes cleaved the waters of the Spay-Lay-Wi-Theepi. They were excited. For a century the Iroquois had made their people miserable, and thirty years ago the English had defeated their French fathers in battle. But they were Miamis. They had eyes and ears. They had seen the mighty Senecas slogging sadly westward to escape the English and then the Americans. How powerful these white men must be if they had driven the Guardians of the Western Door of the Longhouse toward where the sun sets.

These same white men had lost all their forts except Detroit to the tribes of the lakes, and yet they had in the end prevailed over the alliance built by the great Ottawa chief Pontiac. All these things the Miamis had seen and heard. Season after season they had lived their lives with dread in their hearts that the English, and then the Americans, would soon be upon them with their rifles and rum and tricks. They had hoped that among them a great leader might arise who had the medicine of the great leaders of old. That he turned out to be Little Turtle did not surprise them. He was a natural leader.

The paddles churned the windblown river. The spray flew. The spirits of the Miami braves soared.

For half a day after the night raid, James and Jinja scouted the area. They found the Miamis' camp, and assured themselves that their enemies were truly gone. Then they returned to the fort discussing what they had to do to secure the fort.

They built an additional story on the hillside tower and made sure that someone was up there at all times during the daylight, watching the Ohio River. They ripped out the floorboards of two of the warehouses and dug large secret basements. There they cached many of their goods, then they replaced the floor, leaving a cunning secret entrance in a false wall by a chimney. They found a deep ravine close to the Ohio River. In the ravine they hid two canoes stocked with useful items, and covered them with three feet of leaves. They dug a secret exit from the stockade. Their trade mission was a terribly difficult undertaking, both men now realized. Customers were few in the middle of a war. Once the war was over, they would be the most powerful traders in their area. The trick was to do what it took to survive the war.

Obie's wife Mary was not pleased with their plight. As tough as she had been during their struggle with the Miamis, she had no desire to see her family and herself wiped out by marauding warriors. Late one night, as they lay together in one of the inn's three sleeping rooms, she whispered softly in Obie's ears.

"Listen," she said.

He listened. "You hearin' Injuns out there again?" he asked.

"Not out there. Listen in here. The child."

Obie looked across the moonlit room at their daughter, barely two years of age. Her breathing was so light and even that it was barely audible.

"Nothin' wrong with her," he said.

"That's right, Obie. Now imagine how she be breathin' with a tomahawk stickin' in her head."

"Now woman, we gonna start that again? I don't understand you. You got more courage than any five women—or men—that I ever knew."

"Ain't a matter of courage. It's horse sense. People with horse sense don't go runnin' around in places where there's all sorts of people wants to kill you. Miamis 'cause you takin' their land. Fool whites so they can take your goods. Young Mingoes 'cause that's how they have a good time. Kickapoos 'cause they just feel like it. And here we are, just five of us to hold off all them crazy whites and mad Injuns in the middle of the devil's own green Hell. Look at that daughter of ours. What chance she got of livin' long enough to have children of her own?"

They lay silent for a few moments and listened to the wind whistle through the cracks in the palisades. Up on the wall they could hear the catwalk creak under the step of James.

"Listen to me Mary, please. Remember what life is like back in New York. Remember what it was like in Virginia before that. We're still somebody's property back there, remember? We go back, we'll be runnin' and hidin' again, always afraid somebody's gonna see us that knew us in Jamestown. Think about it. We're in business here."

"But Obie—"

"Mary, don't try to change my mind. Stand behind me like you always done. We are free people here. We have a chance for a good life here. We're like the Indians. Back there, we have no chance to be real people. Back there . . . back there we'll never belong to ourselves, even if they never send us back to Virginia. So help me Mary, at the moment a tomahawk splits my skull open, I will thank God for givin' us the chance."

Joanna was glad for her chance to escape her cabin in the forest, but by now her mother was having strong second thoughts. Joanna's job was to supervise a private in keeping Captain Armstrong's tent neat and looking desirable for him when he came back from his daily rounds of supervision in the field, sweaty and smelling of horse.

The captain had volunteered Joanna's mother for duty with other camp followers in the company laundry. A strong, hard woman, she could stand the hard work all day long, but it was a big step down from her life as mate to a budding country squire, then as widow to same. The captain had made it clear to her that she would not be welcome back at the tent, and Joanna said nothing. So Ruth washed dirty clothes all day long and nursed a grudge against her daughter that grew greater and greater as she spent her waking hours among the steaming kettles and lye soap.

Governor St. Clair's troops had passed the preceding months marching north from the Ohio River, building forts and leaving garrisons along the way. During this time he found out a number of things about his troops. First, he found that the militia consisted largely of men volunteered from the prisons of the northeastern cities. They weren't likely soldiers to start with, and once they found how bad and sparse the food was, they began to desert in twos and threes and dozens.

Second, he found that one Captain Armstrong did not relish building a fort as much as he did leading patrols to capture deserters. The man was a bear for volunteering when there were deserters to be found. The only thing he asked in return was the opportunity to supervise the executions of those he caught. St. Clair told him that judgments were required first, but both men understood that sometimes it was best if certain individuals were treated to field executions.

By this time Young Eagle Claw, Firemaker, and the others had taken their place as shadows silently sticking to the heels of St. Clair's army. There were more than a dozen similar parties. "No ambushes, not yet," Little Turtle had told them. "I just want to know where they are all the time, and when they stumble into just the right place, that's when we will attack. The corpses will be rotting in the woods all summer," Little Turtle promised his men, "if you keep out of sight, so we can surprise them."

But they had to watch the army, and on this day they were entertained by one of those confusing white man dramas they could never quite understand. Hiding deep in the shadows of woodland thickets, they watched a straggling group of pathetic blue-coated soldiers, four of them, dragging themselves through the woods, away from the army camp.

Firemaker tapped Young Eagle Claw on the shoulder. "We could take them and kill them all very quickly, and nobody would know."

"Little Turtle said we should not, and he is right," Young Eagle Claw whispered back.

"My brother, let us watch them and see what they intend to do."

They were astounded by what happened next. Five men on horseback came galloping down the trail and overtook the weary, careless soldiers. Before they had a chance to lift their weapons, they were surrounded by the men on horseback, who wore uniforms similar to those worn by the men on foot. The riders bayoneted two of the foot soldiers in a quick skirmish that featured some terrible language by both sides, though the Miamis did not know it. They beat the other two severely, tied their hands, tied them to long ropes, and made them run behind the horses in the direction of St. Clair's camp.

"Now why," Firemaker asked Young Eagle Claw, "would they kill their own men when they were going to need them for the next fight?"

Young Eagle Claw shook his head. "Maybe they were just practicing killing men with their musket knife. We'll know not to come close enough to let them use their musket knives."

"They must have many men if they can use them up like that," Firemaker said.

"Many who can carry a musket, not many who can fight with it," Young Eagle Claw assured him.

Captain Armstrong brought his two prisoners in and turned them over to the colonel who was in charge of making decisions. To his surprise, the colonel did not hand out a death sentence, but let them each off with a good old-fashioned, naval-style flogging. Armstrong did not mind. A flogging was almost as good as a hanging. Since the punishment was not to take place until the following day, Armstrong dismissed his patrol and headed back to his tent.

A good part of his personal stores consisted of Pennsylvania corn whiskey and rose water. When he walked into his tent, he found Joanna pouring out whiskey for him, as she always did. Only once had she poured two glasses. He had roared at her that gentlemen do not drink with sluts like her. He cuffed her around pretty fair that day, the best cuffing she had had since her father had been killed.

So now she stood in the tent with the heavy tumbler of whiskey in her hand. He grabbed it with a grunt, which she translated into a grateful "thank you," took two big swallows, and sat down on a bench that had been nailed together by one of the more competent carpenters in St. Clair's army. Now she removed his tricornered hat and his wig, pulled his cloak off his shoulders and commenced to rub rose water into his neck and hair. The strong smell of rose oil wafted through the tent and obliterated the odors of sweat and horse manure. She rubbed his blond balding scalp and his shoulders, then led him to his blankets and waited while he got comfortable on top of them, semireclining. She stepped outside for a moment and returned with a bowl of hot, savory stew. She handed it to him and he began to spoon huge quantities into his mouth until both cheeks bulged. He chewed and belched, and washed the stew down with whiskey.

She did not stare at him as he ate; he hated when she

stared at him. Instead she stood and stared at the table, watching the food she had prepared disappear. Her hands clasped demurely in front of her, she wondered how a man with such abominable manners could possibly have come from a family of Virginia aristocrats.

Having finished his stew and his tumbler of whiskey, he lay back and beckoned her to sit beside him. She obeyed, and leaned forward to kiss him, but he seized her shoulder firmly and held her away. She looked at him, wondering what she had done to displease him, half resenting the rejection that loomed ahead, and half thrilled with his power, which would lead them into a fight over nothing, and then to a rapprochement that would involve some aggressive lovemaking. Nights like this usually ended with him permitting her to sleep all night beside him, sometimes even with an arm around her, as if he really cared for her.

But no, tonight was not going to be one of those nights. There were deep furrows, both horizontal and vertical, in his forehead. He looked at her wondering if he should speak of what he and his patrol had seen that day. He decided that he must, that one of a consort's duties was to listen to the concerns of her lover and then assure him that a man of his might and power need not fear any man of any color.

"From the time I left camp this morning," he said to Joanna, "I saw signs of Indians, and once I thought I saw them. They were close, and they were watching, watching, watching. So many signs. There must be so many Indians." If she didn't know him better, she would have thought she had caught the scent of fear through the aura of whiskey and rose water.

"But I have seen your army," she said. "So many brave men, so many cannons. With an army like this, how can you be worried about Indians? I'd be more worried if I were an Indian."

"To you this may look like an army," he said. "But it isn't. Much of this army is made up of militia. They don't know how to soldier, their officers don't know how to soldier. They and the regular soldiers hate each other. And General St. Clair is sick. His sickness is making him careless."

"Do you think they would dare attack us?" she asked.

"Every day we march farther north, deeper into the territory the Miamis call their own. The Indians never attack an army in camp. They always attack an army on the march, where it is weakest. When I am away, on patrol, I want you and the horses to be where the army is strong, up toward the forward regiments but not near the high-ranking officers. The Indians will be looking for them if they attack. But I do not think they will attack yet. When they do"—he tried to look resolute—"they will die."

She gave him a quick look and was reassured. What she saw was worry, not fear. She could abide a worried man, for a while, anyway. It was a fearful man she would not stomach. Besides, he was telling her how to be safe. He was concerned for her welfare. Or maybe it was concern for the welfare of his horses and goods. She reached for his tumbler and filled it up.

The sound of the liquid against the solid glass was a good sound. It reminded him of after-dinner get-togethers in the library, without women, when the men would discuss weighty matters and make decisions that men make. "Thank you for dinner," he told her. "I enjoyed your company. Now you must leave me alone. I have some things to think about."

In the woods, scarcely three miles from where Captain Terrance Armstrong was alone in his tent thinking, the young

Shawnee chief Tecumseh was paying Little Turtle his nightly visit. Tecumseh and his men were the eyes of Little Turtle's growing army, and the eyes had seen much that day.

"These white men are not fighters," Tecumseh said. "They are men-who-go-home."

Little Turtle did not smile. These two great leaders, more than most of their braves, understood how important the next few days would be to their people.

"These men try to make their soldiers brave by making them afraid to run away. I do not believe you can do that even with white men."

"Where are the Chickasaws?" Little Turtle asked.

"They have gone away to the west. Why, I do not yet know." Little Turtle almost smiled then. More white foolishness. The Chickasaws had not been friends of the Americans, but they hated the Miamis enough to know that "the enemy of my enemy is my friend." It was the Chickasaw scouts that they feared could destroy the surprise Little Turtle had prepared for St. Clair and his army.

"Gone to the west," Little Turtle echoed. Tecumseh nodded.

"No trick?" the Miami chief asked.

"My warriors have followed them west. They are going too far too fast. Maybe the white men have them chasing something. I do not know what it could be."

"My brother," Little Turtle said, his dark eyes bright with hope. "Send men to follow the Chickasaws and do not let them back. As for the white men, they are tired. They are hungry. They are bad soldiers. And most of them do not care. Where have they camped tonight?"

Tecumseh shook his head. "On a hill without trees, behind their guns."

"Ah, then the time has not yet come. But be patient," Little Turtle advised. "I will ask you the same question tomorrow. If you are able to give me the right answer, then we will hold their lives in our fists."

9

MAJOR EBENEZER DENNY WAS NOT THE MAN Captain Armstrong wanted to see after this, his longest day in the saddle. But General St. Clair was sick, and Denny was his adjutant, so he was the man to hear what Armstrong had to say. Unfortunately, Denny had his own troubles.

"Captain." The adjutant sighed amid the swirling snow being stirred up in the wind by the horses and wagons that came and went in the endless routine that occurred when a marching army went into camp. "I know there are a lot of Indians out there. You have been telling us about your Indians for days. So have the other patrols. What do you want me to do that we haven't been doing? We have problems. It got dark early on us today. General St. Clair didn't want to make camp here, but we couldn't keep going in the dark and this was the only spot. He's got a hill that's too small for his army. He's got a swamp at the bottom of his hill, so he has to camp his militia a quarter of a mile away from the others. His men don't have enough to eat because deserters are raiding the convoys. Every day more and more of his militia are leaving because their enlistments are up. What can he do, hang them too? My commander is so sick he can't stand on his feet. He knows there are Indians out there. Tell me something that he doesn't know."

The adjutant turned around and ducked into General St. Clair's tent. Armstrong stood by the tent, his hands on the reins of his horse, and watched the men around him pitching tents, setting up artillery, and posting perimeter guards. Officers were giving orders to sergeants, and sergeants were passing them along to privates. It was just the end of another day, except that there were fewer men in camp than there had been the day before.

Armstrong picketed his horse and headed for his tent. He flipped aside the flap, walked in, threw his gloves and hat on his bed, grabbed his tumbler of whiskey and angrily waved aside the rose water.

Joanna looked at his face. Was that annoyance, or anger? Or was it fear?

"What in hell are you looking at?" he asked. This girl had a bad habit of trying to dig into a man's soul, he thought. Didn't a man have a right to his privacy? But it wasn't his privacy he wanted, it was somebody to listen. Denny would not listen. The rest of the officers and men were running around camp as if nothing were wrong. Was he losing his nerve? He had known officers who had gotten a reputation for seeing Indians behind every bush. Scalp fever, some men called it, and once you got such a reputation, you never lost it. Your fellow officers made snide comments to your face, and your men made nasty remarks behind your back.

"I could swear there was twice as many Indians out there today as there was the day before," he told Joanna.

"Did you talk to anybody about it?" she asked.

"Nobody wants to know about it. They've all got their own problems."

You sure *you're* not just thinkin' there are twice as many

Indians out there? she wanted to ask, but she didn't dare. She feared his anger too much. Besides, he was frightening her with his concerns about the Indians. She did not want him angry with her, she wanted him to calm her fears.

"Will it be all right?" she asked him, keeping her voice steady.

"I don't think so," he said. "Tomorrow, or the day after, when the army is on the march, they'll come down on us," he said. "And then somebody's gonna die. Maybe several somebodies." He threw his head back and drained the contents of the tumbler.

In the cold gray that comes just before the dawn, frozen, sleepy troops stood in formation while sergeants reported on the number of men fit for duty. The soldiers paraded before Major General Richard Butler, with lieutenants and sergeants working hard to make their men look snappy and military. The cold air brought the men to consciousness and also reminded them how hungry they were. Now they were back at attention. The wind was whistling through the ranks. They couldn't wait to get in front of a fire and a hot breakfast.

At the command "Dismissed," the men broke ranks and raced for their food. For the moment they were not soldiers, just hungry young men numbed by the cold.

Then, from the surrounding forest, fifteen hundred Indians threw a deadly fist of blazing fire into the army camp. They whooped and hollered and loaded and fired again. Dozens of soldiers tumbled into grotesque postures of death. The reactions of the surviving soldiers, most of them inexperienced, were mixed. Some dropped into a kneeling position, fired their weapons into the trees and reloaded. Others looked for their sergeants and began to follow orders. Still others looked for any piece of cover or concealment and attempted to make themselves invisible to the searching fingers of lead. And here and there was one who stood, unbelieving, paralyzed, in the middle of the parade ground, until a buzzing bullet streaked through the cold wind and cut him down.

A number of sergeants managed to get their men into firing formations and directed volleys against the invisible enemy. After the first minute or so, it seemed that they might manage to create order out of the deadly chaos. But now the militia, frightened by their separation from the regular soldiers, fled from their little hill into the camp of the regulars. Their milling, moblike invasion of the regulars' defensive positions messed up the best efforts of the organized regulars and gave the Indians more clear shots at helpless soldiers. Wounded horses were stampeding through the defenses, screaming in panic. Wounded men lay kicking their lives away, their blood coloring the snow around them. Again and again, from their tree cover, the Indians fired into the open, exposed mass of Americans. Again and again soldiers toppled to the ground and lay still.

Little Turtle had found a wooded hillock from which to watch the battle. He had been a man with a mission ever since he realized that the Americans coveted the land of the Miamis. He had assembled a tough fighting force of his own people, but did not believe at first that men from all over the lake country would come to fight under him. Yet now, besides Tecumseh and his Shawnees, there were Wyandots and Delawares, plus a smattering of Potawatamis, Mingoes, Chippewas, and others following him. There were also white men who did not wish the Americans well, English and French traders painted and scalp-locked, as well as British military officials, all ready to lend Little Turtle a hand against his hapless opposition.

There were some brave officers in St. Clair's army on this day. They organized their men for bayonet attacks and sent them hurtling at the enemy, but the warriors melted away before them and reappeared on their flanks, gunning them down, backing off and reloading, then coming forward and killing again. Soon it was the massed troops that had melted away, back into a frightened, milling army on the hill, fighting for its life. Hastily hitched teams of horses thundered forward. Artillerymen unlimbered their cannons, loaded, and fired ball and shot into the woods. The soldiers were heartened by the thunder of their guns and renewed their fighting spirit, but the artillery was hitting nothing but the trees. While the cannoneers reloaded, Miami sharpshooters picked them off one by one. The cannons roared again, and again as the gunners reloaded, then died from the well-aimed gunfire of Indians who were determined to still the weapons they feared most.

When the guns thundered again, there were fewer of them, and their volley was ragged. So many cannoneers were down that many crews were too decimated to service their pieces. One by one the cannons fell silent and cold, their crews lying dead in the snow around them.

In the heavy cold air the smoke from three thousand rifles and muskets was so dense that it closed in on the stunned soldiers like a gray shroud. Some of them may have welcomed the sulfurous fog as a curtain that would conceal them from the merciless fire of their enemy. But many of the Indians had been through battles like this before. They saw the gray shroud as cover for them. Hundreds of them crept closer to the desperate huddled mass of infantry, for a surer kill.

Young Eagle Claw was among the most forward of this group. He could feel the battle going all his way as he fired his rifle into a mass so thick he could not miss. Several men fell where he shot, perhaps one brought down by him, perhaps two, perhaps none. It didn't matter. Americans were dying, that's what mattered. He tapped Firemaker on the shoulder and waved his hand forward. Firemaker understood and nodded. Both rose to their feet and, bent double, rushed forward into the smoky gray miasma. A dozen others followed them.

Through the mist they charged, into a mass of soldiers so thick that they could not get out of each other's way. The two Miami braves cut and chopped with their tomahawks, then like spirits vanished into the mist, leaving a half-dozen terribly maimed, horribly screaming soldiers in their wake.

The brightening sky revealed a gory, horrifying tableau on the bloody hill so close to the Wabash. Hundreds of men were down. Hundreds of others, their eyes wide and haunted, continued to fire wildly at faint shapes in the mist or shadows among the distant trees. There were those who had had enough and wanted to give up, but there was nobody to surrender to, there were only remorseless killers of soldiers, firing ball after ball that thudded into flesh or smacked into bone. The soldiers had a little more elbow room now, because so many men were dead or wounded. General St. Clair, sick as he was, strode fearlessly among his men exhorting them to fight, praying for a miracle. The miracle, if there was one, was that the Indians couldn't hit him, although they had spotted and killed nearly every other high-ranking officer in his army.

Through the unspeakable, murderous horror of this battle came a merciful impulse from somewhere. They could not win, said the impulse, they could only escape to fight another day, if they made their move right then. St. Clair's surviving officers organized one last, massive, desperate bayonet charge. This charge was no aggressive attempt to break the will of their enemy. It was an attempted breakout. Down they swept on a narrow front, their bayonets held high, then forward, forward, on a quick run, through their enemy, down the new road, south toward Fort Jefferson, many miles away. At first the Indians parted before them, meaning to take them in small bunches as they flanked them, but this was a heavy, desperate bayonet attack, and before the Indians could reorganize for the final coup, most of the soldiers were gone, fleeing in utter panic from the battlefield. The Indians raced after them, pulling down stragglers, killing and scalping them. But as had happened before, many of the warriors began to conceive objectives other than wiping out the enemy. The ground the soldiers had abandoned had to be full of booty. Most of the Indians broke off their pursuit and headed instead for the American camp. There were, after all, plenty of scalps to harvest, and enough food to help some of the hard-pressed bands get through the winter.

Among those fleeing down the road, among the gleaming bayonets, was Joanna. She had spent the first half of the battle facedown in the snow, clawing at the dirt, crying and cursing Captain Armstrong, the Indians, and the army interchangeably. But as the battle went on amidst the smoke, the panic, and the death, she began to gather her wits. Thinking as hard as she could, she could find no way to get out of this battle alive. Then, in front of her, she could see soldiers coming together and heading out at the double quick, their muskets and bayonets held before them. She looked around. Behind her were only the dead, the grievously wounded, and a few men who had lost their minds in the slaughter. On impulse, she climbed to her feet and ran after the only men she could see who had any chance of surviving. She was young and she had spent her life in the open air, in the woods. She was carrying nothing but the blanket she had wrapped around her. She could keep up, and she did.

Captain Armstrong was also keeping up. Protecting their left flank, he was a one-man cavalry charge, his sword sweeping scythelike through the air, riding down Indians and ending their lives with a single stroke. But a one-man cavalry charge is no charge at all. A musket ball went deep into the chest of his horse and it sank to its knees. The captain found himself surrounded by a dozen or more furious Miamis and Shawnees. He swung his sword in wide arcs, hoping to keep them at bay or take a couple of Indians with him. A warrior fired. The bullet penetrated his thigh and broke the big bone, and suddenly all the fight went out of Captain Armstrong. Like his horse, he sank to his knees. Blood began to collect in the snow around him. A warrior grabbed hold of the captain's sword. Gently, the captain released it. He was now a prisoner.

But not for long. Strong hands tore his uniform off him. Strong hands carved strips of flesh from his body. His screams split the morning air. He felt the encircling cut on his head and felt the top part of his scalp being torn away from his skull. Kill me now, he thought through his agony.

And they did, with one cleanly aimed tomahawk chop into the top of his head. Through the trees, as she ran breathlessly along with the soldiers, Joanna heard his screams. As distorted as they were by his pain and his terror, she recognized them. For a moment she lost heart. She wanted to give up. She wanted to die. But terror is just an overload of our instinct to survive. Abruptly, she was no longer breathless. Her legs drew new strength, and she found herself passing the soldiers who were still burdened with their guns and packs. "My God, my God, my God," she cried endlessly as she hurried south with the hundreds of fleeing troops.

Joanna's mother and the other laundresses were still at the top when they saw the bayonet charge down the side of the hill. Frightened as they were, some of them thought that the bayonet charge might drive the Indians away. Ruth had spent many years on the frontier. She was the first to perceive that the charge was in fact an attempt to escape. Nearly all the men who were fit to fight were leaving the hill. From three sides Miamis, Shawnees, Wyandots, and Delawares were storming the hill, and all that were left to resist them were the dead, the dying, and the women. I can't stay here, she thought, and began to run across the top of the hill toward where the soldiers were battling their way through the Indians.

A big hand seized her coat and jerked her through the air. All around her were the screams of helpless men and women as the Indians began to slash and scalp. Her graying hair flying in the winter wind, she struggled to free herself, but the brave simply whirled her around by her coat and threw her to the ground. She lay there, stunned, and felt her clothes being ripped from her body. So this was rape, she thought through a half-conscious fog. But when she opened her eyes, the grim warrior above her was not preparing to unite with her. Far from it. He was sitting on her legs, holding a large tent peg against her abdomen. Another, standing above, was swinging a large wooden maul over his head. This can't be happening, she thought, still too foggy to react. The maul came down and drove the stake through her body, into the ground beneath her. Her agonized screeches blended with those of the men and women around her.

Young Eagle Claw and Firemaker ignored the tortures and scalpings around them. They, and some of their cohorts, were drawn to greater prizes, the cannons that lay unmanned except for the dead and wounded soldiers on the ground around them. While their friends were doing their worst to the hated cannoneers who had been too badly wounded to join the breakout, they pushed and pulled at one of the weapons until they had reached the slope. What they intended to do with it was unclear, even to themselves. All they knew was that they were in possession of a weapon so fearful that it sparked terror in even the bravest of warriors. Having a weapon like this would surely make them powerful.

As the weapon reached the slope, it began to roll. The two Miamis tried to stop it but it was too heavy; reluctantly, they let it go and jumped out of the way. The cannon rolled down the hill, gaining speed with every moment. Several of the attackers avoided it and let it race past them. It rolled over the leg of a wounded soldier who had been playing dead. He screamed with pain and tried to jump up, but his leg was broken. Firemaker finished him off with a blow to the head, and watched as the cannon continued down the hill until it hit the swamp and toppled over.

What now? There were no horses left alive to pull the weapon. Other braves had conquered other cannons and found themselves with the same dilemma. Cannons need horses. Cannons used lots of powder. Cannons fired heavy cannon balls. They could not use the cannons. Not now. But the cannons belonged to them. There was among them a brave called Red Sunset. "We will never again see these guns fire in our faces," he shouted. "Let's bury them in the swamp, where the digging is easy."

More of the weapons were pushed down the hill. The Indians were delighted to see them gain speed as they rolled down the slope, to crash at the bottom, the iron barrels rolling free of their wooden carriages. Red Sunset came running down the hill with an armload of shovels he had found in an artillery wagon. "Here!" he yelled to the braves close to him. "Where the ground is soft."

The soldiers continued south in full flight, their bayonets thrust out before them. They were harassed on their flanks by stealthy hit and run attacks, but they were too terrified to fight back. Among the warriors harassing them were Caleb, Ken, and Joshua. Deadly with their rifles, they ran through the woods until they had outrun the front ranks of the fleeing American column. Then, as the soldiers approached, they loosed a volley that brought down three soldiers and spurred the rest into even greater efforts to escape their tormentors. Not until they had bedeviled the army for ten miles did Caleb suggest that they return to the battle site. "You never can tell," he said. "Another army might be coming up from the lower forts to meet them, and we don't want to get caught between two armies." So the three half-Tuscarora sons of the patriot Big Oak turned north and loped on through the snow until they arrived on a scene more horrible than any they had ever seen. Bodies lay everywhere, often heaped one upon another, already frozen into grotesque postures.

The three young men looked at each other. They had arrived at the battlefield as red men. Now they weren't quite so sure. Half the men they had known in their young lives were American white men—like their father.

Caleb turned toward his brothers. "They didn't have a lot of fight in them, did they?" he asked.

The other two shook their heads. "I can't believe men like this licked the English, can you?"

The soldiers ran on, down the road they had recently built, mile after mile, as the sun climbed the sky. Those soldiers who kept their heads could feel the enemy thinning out as they struggled onward, and eventually the deadly, hostile gunfire stopped completely. All that saved this terrified remainder of St. Clair's army was the Indian desire to break off the battle and collect booty. The soldiers did not know this, and so they did not stop. Early in their flight many of them had flung away their packs and weapons so they could run farther and faster. Now, having outrun their would-be executioners, many of those who still had their guns dropped them because they felt too tired to carry them another step. They could not run any longer, but their fear would not let them stop. Mile after mile they dragged their weary, heaving bodies along the road. Occasionally a wounded man would collapse for loss of blood. Some men fell from outright exhaustion, to rise again after a few minutes. Among them were a few strong, valiant men, helping comrades they refused to desert.

Finally, twenty-nine miles south of the battlefield, just after the sun had ducked behind the low hills, the first of them crossed the last creek that lay between them and the safety of Fort Jefferson, a work they had completed less than a month before the battle. For two hours more the soldiers straggled into the fort, physically and emotionally spent.

It was nearly dark when Joanna made it through the gates of the fort. She did not look for a friendly face. She looked for a quiet corner of the stockade, threw her blanket around her, huddled in the corner and allowed her reason to dissolve into a series of wild, convulsive sobs. Gradually she calmed down. Her reason returned. She was cold. She was hungry. She turned her face from the wall of the fort to a low building across the parade ground with light in the windows. Without knowing a thing about it, she picked herself up and shuffled wearily toward it. There had to be somebody there who would take pity on a skinny young woman with a pretty face, who would feed her and give her a safe place to stay until she could go home. She wanted nothing further to do with soldiers, that she knew. She had been among an immense army of them, and yet had seen nothing but terror and slaughter all day. Her mother was surely dead, and so was her lover, and she had come close to sharing their fate. Her mind settled on Jinja, back in Walker Valley. He was kind, and he liked her. And he and his Indian friends were smart enough to stay sheltered behind a safe set of walls just over the hill from the Ohio River. It was close to home too.

Back to David Watley, she thought. After the cruelty she had found in the tent of Captain Armstrong, and his death at a time when he should have been protecting her, Jinja shined, way off in the distance, beyond the many miles of forest that lay between himself and this horrible catastrophe.

10

THERE IS NO WAY TO DESCRIBE THE FEELINGS of most of the men who huddled behind the walls of Fort Jefferson. Many of them had not wanted to fight in a war, they had been pressed into it, like workmen in a British seaport. Of the twenty-three hundred men who started the march north from the Ohio River, nine hundred had deserted. But the fourteen hundred who remained thought they were part of an army big enough and strong enough to whip any contingent of Indians sent up against them.

Only slowly, as patrols drifted in and out of Fort Jefferson, did the full extent of the disaster strike them. Nearly half their number lay slain, scalped and stripped of their clothing near the banks of the Wabash River. The wild animals were even now beginning the job of reducing the corpses to bare bone. Many more were terribly wounded, their groans and screams filling the days and nights of Fort Jefferson. The Indians who had attacked them had lost fewer men than might be expected to perish in a mild, peaceful winter. Huddled behind the walls of the fort, the soldiers heard daily rumors of the next battle. The Indians were preparing to descend on Fort Jefferson and wipe out everything that lived within, said the rumors. Again the desertions began, with men sneaking out in the dead of night, heading east, always east, recoiling from the deadly red menace like a deer fleeing from the sounds of wolves.

The Indians had different ideas. To most of them, a victorious battle was cause for a celebration, not another battle. Once the smoke had cleared from the battlefield, the tribes took stock of their bounty in scalps and goods and concluded they had won a victory so great that surely the Holder of the Heavens had finally turned the tide of war in their favor. They went into camp and cleared a piece of land nearly a half mile long for a celebration. They stripped the bark off many of the saplings and painted the trees red with symbols of victory. It was a special time for the assembled tribes, a time for Twightwees and Delawares to discover that Shawnees and Wyandots were truly their brothers. There were even a few Cherokees up from North Carolina to aid them in their next fight against the Americans. Red men were beginning to wake up to the threat against all of them, a threat so great that it would have to be stamped out even if it meant an end to firearms, kettles, blankets, and rum. Their celebration was more than just the celebration of a victory, more than just feasting and dancing. It was a celebration of friendship and brotherhood; a celebration of cooperation; a celebration of unity of purpose.

There was not much in the way of friendship and brotherhood or unity of purpose at Fort Jefferson. The soldiers there were plotting individually their road to survival. Those that left, fled in the dead of night. Many of those who stayed did so only because they felt that the walls of the fort were their means of salvation.

Joanna knew she could not stay for long. Although she tried to cover her face with a blanket and smudged dirt, she felt the lecherous stares of many of the men about the fort. She had been grabbed at and groped and grappled by men whose touch made her sick to her stomach. At first she had remained in the fort hoping that somehow her mother had managed to escape. But before long she understood that none of the women from the laundry group had made it through, and she had heard one man paint a terrible scene of their fate. She did not have much grief to spare for her mother, who had been hard on her since the year she had rounded into form. She also found herself resenting her mother for having encouraged her relationship with Captain Armstrong, forgetting the perverse pleasures she had experienced in his hard hands.

Once she felt certain that she would never again see her mother in this life, she began to hoard supplies for her escape. The fort had a store of hardtack, salt pork, and dried corn. She begged a canteen from a quartermaster sergeant and stole a large leather pouch from a very drunk soldier. Other items found their way to her: an extra blanket, a knife, an extra pair of moccasins, and her prize, a pistol loaded and primed, one shot for a dire emergency. It was almost winter, but the weather had turned milder since the battle. The roads and trails were easy to follow. She knew her way back home, back to Jinja. She knew how to make him care for her. He may not have been an army captain but he was a trader and he had things. He looked like a woodsman too. "Jinja." The name made her cringe, but out here among the beaten uniformed rabble in Fort Jefferson, she thought him a pretty good choice.

It was easy for her to flee from the fort. She was a white American girl with a frontier twang to her voice. She said she was going out to gather some firewood, and no sentry bothered to challenge her. She could have been a spy for all they knew. Off she went down the new road. Finding her way home would be easy. All she had to do was head south to the Ohio River then turn east and follow it until she reached familiar countryside. From there it would be no trick to find the stockade.

Young and supple as her muscles were, inured by frontier hardship to the cold and the wilderness, she made her way quickly and with sure feet over the rough road south. What she did not know was that many of the American patrols had vanished from the forests, their place taken by lurking Indian ambush parties licking their chops waiting for soldiers to show themselves. In fact, the woods were beginning to blossom with the bodies of scalped deserters who would have been better off behind the log palisades of Fort Jefferson. Had Joanna known all of this, she might never have ventured from the fort.

Off she went down the road at a rapid walking pace, her footsteps audible to anyone within a hundred yards of the path. God must watch over fools. The Indians who were watching the road for deserters must have been having lunch or washing off old war paint when she walked past, because not a one discovered her presence during the three days it took her to find her way down to the Spay-Lay-Wi-Theepi. Once or twice she wondered if the road truly led down to the river, and one time in the twilight she actually thought she might have lost the road. But toward the end of her third day she topped a rise and beheld a broad expanse of water that could only have been the Ohio River.

She had drunk her canteen empty four hours before and she was very thirsty. She hurried down from the hill and was about to jump into the river when she remembered how cold the river water must be and how cold the air would be when she came out of the water. Instead she walked to the bank of the river, leaned over and filled her canteen, then poured it down her throat.

She filled up the canteen again and adjusted the strap on

her shoulder. She was about to begin her walk east when she heard the loud bang of a long rifle in the direction she was going. The shot had been close to her, and at first she wondered if it was aimed at her. But no other shots followed, so she kept walking east until she came to a tree line near a little creek that drained into the Ohio. She knelt in the brush beneath the trees and looked toward the creek. A Shawnee brave had killed a deer. Crouched beside it, he was chanting something toward the heavens. Then he began to dress the deer with his knife, deftly, quickly, as if he realized he had better be gone from the area before an unseen enemy attracted by the single gunshot fell on him. She could see his face clearly. He was young, in his early twenties. His skin was pockmarked, but he was handsome. What she found most attractive was his look of earnest intent as he went about his chore. There was no savage anger in his face; not like the look she had seen on the faces of the attackers just a few days ago. Still, she felt certain that he had to have been among them, or else why would he have been in the area?

She thought of Captain Armstrong and the men she had seen in camp and on the march. So many lives extinguished. She thought of her mother and wondered what horrors must have befallen her in her last moments. She fingered the pistol she kept in her pouch atop her food supply. Then she looked again at his serious, handsome face. Somehow she could not make a connection between this young hunter and the fiends who had so viciously killed so many Christian men. Besides, she did not know if she could kill a man with a pistol at that distance. Fear made her wise. If she moved now, he might see her. She lay down in the brush where she could still see him. He was making ready to take most of his deer and go. Fine, she thought. If he left the area by another route, he'd live, but if he left in her direction, she would have to shoot him, otherwise he would surely kill her, or worse.

He began walking, down the creek toward the Ohio. Away from her. Good. At the river she saw him drop his deer, pull bunches of leaves and branches out of a gully, and drag a canoe from the gully to the river bank. He slid the canoe down the bank, lowered the deer to the bottom of the canoe, gave the canoe a light shove, and leaped into it just as it floated out onto the river. With the slightest of effort, he took five paddle strokes, glided toward the middle of the river, made a right turn and headed west. She gave a sigh of relief and began her trek eastward.

Young Jack peered through an opening between logs on the high tower on the hill beyond the corner of the fort. He spent many hours a day in that tower, but he did not mind. It freed him from much of the drudge work that Obie, James, and Jinja had to do all day, every day. Obie's wife Mary and James's wife Anna spent some of the daylight hours up there, but mostly it was Jack, with his exceptional eyesight.

Knowing how exposed anybody in the tower would be to those below, they had roofed it and built a wall up to waist high so that it appeared to anybody on the ground who sighted the tower through the trees that it was unmanned. But they had provided slits between the top two logs. The slits were concealed by the shadows of the half-round logs, and provided excellent fields of vision for the boy. There was a rope in the tower that led down the hill and across the compound to a small bell rigged over the door of the store. By pulling the rope, Jack could alert those below to the approach of somebody. One ring meant he spotted a deer worth chasing. Two rings meant the approach of white men. Three rings indicated that Indians had been spotted. No provisions were made for distinguishing a friendly from a hostile Indian. It was wartime, and any human being was to be treated with suspicion. On this day toward the end of November, Jack pulled the rope twice.

James opened the door of the warehouse, bolted across the compound and shouted out to the tower, "What is it?"

"Looks like it might be a woman, I'm not sure," Jack yelled back.

"We'll watch for her," Jinja replied, calling out to Obie and James. The three scattered around the catwalk and waited. Jinja saw the figure appear out of the trees opposite the clearing from the gate. The figure was familiar to him, and yet, wrapped in blankets, with a big pack protruding about belly high, he wasn't sure. She stepped out into the open and boldly walked across the clearing toward the stockade. Obie and James stood on the catwalk on either side of the gate and watched while Jinja opened the gate. "Get in here, quick!" he shouted to her, thinking again that he recognized the lean figure.

"Joanna! What are you doing here?"

"What do you think I'm doing here?" she snapped. "I'm stayin' alive out here, that's what I'm doing."

In fact, the moment she saw Jinja, her heart sank. After the dashing dragoon captain who was always the master of the moment, Jinja did not look like much. She remembered that he did not order people around with a powerful voice, and she had never seen him raise a hand to anybody in anger. It would be a mistake to believe that he would ever amount to anything in this life. How could she possibly want to share his future? He had no future. Still, he was the only prospect she had, if indeed he was a prospect.

"Where'd you come from, and where's your mother?" Jinja asked.

The look of anger on her face surprised him. "You don't know?" she growled bitterly.

How could I? he asked himself, but he said nothing, just stared at her, perplexed. Since the attack on the stockade by the Miamis, and their sudden disappearance, he and his cohorts had heard nothing from the outside world. Not a solitary human being had passed through. It was as if their piece of the Ohio River valley had left the face of the earth, taking with it only the stockade and the trees and animals around it.

"You'd better come in so we can close the gate," Jinja said. "We're very careful these days."

She walked in and he dropped the bolt behind her. She looked around the stockade. All was calm. There were no nervous, cursing soldiers; no hungry eyes and groping hands; just Jinja, James, and Obie. Her fear and anger subsided.

He led her into the inn, which felt warm and comfortable after her days in the cold woods. "Look who's here," Jinja said, watching Mary stir a huge kettle in the fireplace. "Do you have anything hot she can drink? She looks half frozen."

Mary eyed Joanna and went "mmm," as a form of greeting, but she didn't like Joanna and had no desire to cover her dislike with civility, even though Mary was usually the most civil of women. She poured a hot brew of sassafras tea into an earthenware mug and silently handed it to Joanna, who acknowledged the gift with the barest nod of her head. Jinja did not take anything to drink, but he did stand staring at her as she stood in front of the fireplace feeling her palms warm against the mug. With both hands, she tilted the mug up to her mouth and took a sip.

"You don't know, do you?" she asked. Jinja just stared back. "The Indians wiped out an army," she said. "Killed half the men that fought. Probably come here and kill you next."

"Well," Jinja replied without a lot of emotion.

"That's all you have to say?" The times she had seen him before, he had never seemed quite so dense.

"If we're next, then why are you here?" he asked without emotion.

"Why am I here? Where should I be?" Her voice was peevish, annoyed, but he refused to respond to her emotion.

"We're gonna have dinner in a little while. You look kind of thin. You need to have something to eat."

"I don't understand you," she replied. "Captain Armstrong is dead and scalped. No tellin' what mighta happened to my ma. And you're invitin' me to dinner."

"You don't want dinner?"

"'Course I want dinner. I'm starvin'. I just don't understand why you don't care about the massacre."

He looked at her as if he could see through her eyes, into her thoughts. "I'm sorry about your ma," he said. Are you? he thought. But he knew the answer. "And it sure doesn't make me feel good to know we just lost an army to the Indians."

"But you're gonna stay here anyway?"

"Well, we knew it was dangerous out here when we came out. Any men left?"

She thought about his question. "Plenty of men left," she said. "But more and more desertin' every day. David, I wanna get out of here, go east where a person can feel safer."

"Jinja, everybody calls me Jinja," he said.

"Jinja." She rolled the name around in her mind. "What in hell kinda name is that?"

"It's sorta Mohawk."

"You sorta Mohawk?"

"Sorta Seneca."

"Tell you what, sorta Seneca. You got to get out of here or all you people are gonna end up sorta dead."

"I'll talk it over tonight," he said.

"With who?" she asked, knowing that he was the only white man in the stockade.

"With my partners."

"Oh," Joanna said. "And then what?"

The bell began to ring then, continuously. Jinja ran out the gate and up the hill toward the tower. Jack was squinting at the woods to the south, where the Ohio River flowed.

"What do you see?" Jinja asked.

The boy looked abashed. "I'm not sure. I thought I saw . . ." His voice trailed off.

Jinja climbed the tower. "I trust your eyes, boy," he said when he was standing beside Jack. "If you thought you saw something, then you saw something. Point to the spot where you thought you—"

"Over there," said the boy, relieved. Jinja immediately saw what the boy saw, a lone figure crossing a gap between clumps of trees.

"Keep watching that spot," Jinja told Jack. They watched, and a minute later another figure darted through the gap, swift as a nighthawk. Patiently, but with anxiety steadily rising inside of them, they counted seventeen more, and that seemed to be all.

"Do you think you might have missed any before you saw that first one?" Jinja asked.

"No," Jack responded. "I've had my eye on that gap for days now. It's just a place where I could see someone who was coming up from the river. I saw the woman, and I believe I spotted the first of them."

"Well, there's too many of them for us to handle," Jinja observed.

"Will they attack right away?"

"They could, but I doubt it. They'll want to study us and try to figure out just how many of us there are and where the place is weak. Not all that much daylight left. I doubt they'd attack the first night either. Best time for them to attack is first light, when they figure some have been up all night on guard and the others are sleepy because they're just wakin' up. I want you to stay up here and keep a sharp lookout in case I'm wrong."

Jinja ran down the ladder from the tower, down the hill, then up to the catwalk, where he explained the situation to Obie and James. They agreed that there was no way to hold the place against so many of them. He ran to the inn and called Mary outside. He took her to the well and pretended to be talking to her about water. What he was really saying was: "We're gonna be leaving here sometime tonight. Meanwhile we're gonna cache most of our goods in their hidey-holes, but I don't want Joanna to know that. You keep her busy. Feed her, give her just a little toddy to relax her, anything so she'll leave us alone. I don't trust her."

"I'm glad to hear that," Mary said. "I thought you were gettin' all doe-eyed over her, the way you stood there starin' at her with your mouth hung open like that."

Jinja laughed. "I just don't know what to say to someone like that. She's so awful pretty, but she don't care for a soul except herself. I guess I can't help feeling a certain way about her, but I still don't trust her." He pulled up a bucket and drank a little. "See you later," he said.

11

IT WAS CLOSE TO MIDNIGHT. CLOUDS SCUDded across the moon in swift pursuit. James and Jinja would have preferred a dark night, but they were not given a choice.

They had spent the remainder of the daylight hours shifting most of their goods into the caches under the warehouse and the store, leaving just enough goods around to satisfy the raiders that they had taken all the loot there was to take. They had debated the idea of hiding themselves below, but they knew that if the Indians burned the fort, as seemed likely, they might be smoked out or found and that would surely be the end of them. On the south side of the stockade, toward the river, was a small door Obie had cut when they had built the fort. So cunning was his work that it was undetectable to anyone who was not looking for just that thing in just that place.

The cloud chases were the prelude to a solid cloud layer. James was the first one out, followed by Obie and Mary, with her hand clamped firmly over her baby's mouth. Then came Jack, Joanna, Anna, and Jinja. When they were all out, Obie secured the tiny gate and James began to lead them toward the river. The men, Joanna, and Anna all carried supplies carefully made up into packs.

There was no sense hurrying across the open field to the woods. If the Indians were nearby watching for them, they would see them crossing the open space and overtake them, no matter how fast they ran. James was counting on the raiders not expecting them to try to break out. They waited for a moment while a large cloud approached the moon, then, as the night grew suddenly darker, they began their quick walk toward the woods. James knew exactly where the path toward the river began and he carefully avoided that spot. The Indians might be watching that path.

The three men and Jack looked left and right, ahead and behind, ever cautious as they crossed the open field. Joanna stifled a nervous cough. Once they had made it into the woods, James put about twenty yards between himself and the rest of them. Slowly, he climbed the hill that stood between him and the river. He made no noise himself, but listened carefully to every sound in the night; the cool breeze in the bare branches, the rustlings of little animals, and the cry of an owl somewhere in the dark. Then there was a new noise, and the cold sensation of raindrops striking his face, light at first, but quickly growing heavier.

For a while he continued at his slow pace, but as the rain beat harder, covering all other sounds, the need for silent movement passed. He motioned to Jinja to come on, and Jinja brought everybody else up the hill at a fast walk. Now they were at the top of the hill. Through the rain, Jinja pointed southeast toward the ravine near the river, and James nodded. They made straight for that spot, through the trees, to the edge of the ravine. Jinja, Obie, Jack, and Anna leaped into the ravine and dug their arms into the piles of leaves that concealed their getaway canoes. Leaves flew left and right until finally their hands found the canoes. Jinja and Obie took the first, carried it down to the river and dropped it at the shore, followed quickly by the one James and Anna dragged. There was a third canoe, a smaller one made necessary by the quantity of supplies that had been stowed in the first two canoes and the bundles that they carried.

They were ready to shove the canoes into the river and jump in when James half whispered, half shouted, "Here they come!"

"Shove off!" Jinja said, pulling his rifle out from under his deerskin jacket. "I'll catch up in a moment."

Jinja heard the sound of canoe bottoms scraping on dirt and rocks, then the soft splashes as their bottoms met the water. Through the thick rain "they" turned out to be one Miami with his tomahawk raised above his head. Jinja pulled back the hammer on his rifle and pulled the trigger just when the Miami let fly his tomahawk. Jinja's motion of raising his rifle into firing position had hurried the Miami's toss and the tomahawk flew past his ear. But Jinja's powder was wet and his gun misfired. Quickly, as if by magic, a knife appeared in the Indian's right hand as he rushed forward to meet Jinja. Jinja flicked his weapon in a quick arc. The barrel caught the Miami under the chin with such force that it lifted him off the ground and dropped him, limp, into the pile of leaves that lay in the ravine.

Jinja waited only a moment to ascertain that there were no others, then he ran east along the river bank, raising his voice above the rain. "James! Obie!" he shouted.

He heard no answer, but thirty yards up the river he could see a canoe angling in toward the shore. He ran for the canoe. "Behind you!" Anna shouted from the canoe. Jinja looked up in time to see three more Miamis running full-tilt at him from forty yards away. Jinja did not stop, but leaped into the canoe and felt it drift away from shore on the momentum of his entry. Anna had moved up from the stern seat. There Jinja knelt, found the paddle, and along with James, took quick, powerful strokes that propelled the canoe into the rainy gloom, out of sight of the onrushing Indians on the shore. "Obie!" James shouted from the bow.

"Here! Straight ahead!" the black man cried back. James and Jinja dug in their paddles and their canoe cut the rain-swept river like a sharp knife, making hard for the canoes up ahead. Once they were in sight, James called out again.

"Keep going," he said. "We'll follow you. Head for the middle of the river and we'll come together there."

The rain poured down and the cold wind on the river made the water choppy. Visibility was so poor that it took several minutes of maneuvering for the canoes to come within sight of each other. While the men continued to paddle the canoes upriver, side by side, the women stretched big canvas cloths over themselves and the children to protect them from the horrible weather and keep the canoes from filling up with water. They then lashed the two canoes together alongside one another. The wind was sweeping downriver, blowing the rain in sheets in the faces of the paddlers and churning the water into swells that rocked the canoes as if they were toys. The paddlers kept the boats headed dead into the wind, and worked hard to make headway against the wind and the current. Sooner or later the Indians would be on the river. Getting home would be a much simpler proposition if they could somehow lose their pursuers.

The two canoes lashed together comprised a single vessel more stable than either one alone would have been. Biceps bulging with the strain, Jinja, James, Obie, Anna, and Jack stroked their canoes against the wind, against the swells, against the current. The river and the rain beat hard on the canvas covers. Sometimes, when enough water came through the openings and gathered at the bottom of the canoes, the women took pots in hand and bailed the water out. Jinja noted that the little canoe was riding a bit low in the water, but there was no time to stop and bail it out. If it dragged too much, they would just have to cut it loose.

Now the rain began to turn to sleet, and then sleet mixed with snow. Ice began to accumulate on top of the canvas. The men were working too hard to feel the cold. Only Joanna, huddled by herself under the cloth in Jinja and James's boat, got colder and colder, until she trembled like a leaf in the wind.

"Anna," shouted Jinja above the wind and rain and sleet, "are there any spare trade blankets in this canoe?"

"They're all wet, Jinja," the Oneida woman shouted back.

"Give her one of those," he said. "She'll have it warmed up soon enough."

"Look right!" shouted James. Through the frigid downpour Jinja saw the faintest outline of the shore, with some large rocks sticking out of the water nearly dead ahead. The front paddlers of both canoes dug in hard and stroked from the right while Jinja and Obie in the rear dug in their paddles on the left. The canoes veered so violently to the left that a swell caught them and tossed them high. For a moment Jinja thought they might swamp, but tied together into a single two-hulled vessel, the canoes stayed upright. A half-dozen quick, desperate strokes drove them away from the shore toward the middle of the river, and then they pointed their boats upriver again, into the current, into the wind, into the swells. The rest of the night passed in this manner.

In spite of how hard they were working, the cold wind

and driving rain in their faces was chilling them. They were terribly tired from fighting the river and the weather. But they had to outrun the Miamis if they hoped to survive. There was simply no way they could take to the woods and elude them.

Just when he thought the storm might get the best of them and sweep them downriver, back to the Miamis, Jinja felt the wind and the sleet begin to slacken. Straight ahead was the faintest seam of dawn, spreading itself across the horizon. He welcomed the dawn with all his heart. He was soaked clear through his buckskins to his skin, but beneath his deerskin coat he knew his powder was dry. He recalled his father telling him about the time when he and his grandfather and his grandfather's future wife, the Tuscarora Cilla, had outrun a fleet of Ottawas and Chippewas on Lake Huron. His father had held off the pursuers with his deadly long-range shooting. Jinja was confident that his marksmanship was up to the same task. His rifle was dry, wrapped and held by Joanna under the makeshift tent.

He continued to paddle hard, but now, as the surface of the river slowly revealed itself in the blue-gray dawn, he found himself looking back. As the day dawned brighter and brighter, he was surprised to see that no canoes followed in the churning waters behind them. Was it possible that in the horrible weather the Miamis had given up? Perhaps the storm-tossed waters had swamped a canoe or two and forced the rest to turn back. For the first time since Jack had caught his first glimpse of the Indians bounding through the leafless forest, Jinja felt a lifting of anxiety from deep in his chest.

"Here they come!" shouted James from the bow. "Better bring your rifle up here, Jinja!"

Expecting to find himself facing half the Miami warriors afloat, he grabbed his rifle, scrambled under the cloth shelter toward the bow of the canoe, and stared into the dawn at a solitary canoe with two braves, paddling toward them. As they came closer Jinja could see their war paint, washed halfway down their faces.

"Where are the rest of them?" Jinja heard Obie ask from the bow of the other canoe.

"I bet a bunch of 'em stayed back to loot the fort," Jinja said, studying the canoe.

"These must have passed us in the dark," James said. "Point your rifle at them and see what happens."

The canoe of the two warriors was a bit more than a hundred yards away and drifting toward them on the current when Jinja aimed the long barrel of his rifle at the two Miamis. They responded by putting their paddles aside and reaching for their own firearms. Jinja watched as they took their weapons and pointed them.

"You'd better pick off at least one of them birds," James suggested. Jinja held his rifle to his shoulder but did not pull the trigger.

"Come on, Jinja, you better use that rifle or—" A puff of smoke from one of their rifles drifted into the air on a breeze. "Damn it, Jinja, shoot 'em!"

Jinja sighted the front Miami dead center and pulled the trigger. To his surprise, both the Indians toppled over. One moment they were crouching in their canoe. The next moment their canoe was upside down and the two Miamis had sunk into the depths of the river.

Jinja put down his rifle, returned to the stern, picked up his paddle, and the double-hulled vessel continued its journey east. The canoe drifted by, close to them. Just behind the overturned canoe floated a single paddle. He studied the canoe as it drifted past. It was a beautifully crafted vessel covered with birch bark, made by someone who cared about the look as well as the function, so fine it might have been Chippewa.

The sun had made its appearance ahead of them and lit up the water with a million sparks on the ripples. Jinja looked over his shoulder. Behind him the mist was gone from the river. There were no signs of pursuit as far as he could see. He felt very tired, and very hungry.

And yet they continued their journey east for another hour, around numerous twists and bends, half expecting to see another hostile canoe ahead and half hoping to put more distance between themselves and their pursuers. They were nearly asleep at their paddles when Obie finally spoke up. "Boys," he said, "we're barely makin' headway against this current. I believe we ought to head for shore and make camp."

James and Jinja agreed. They untied the lashing between the two big canoes and followed the south shore until they found the mouth of a creek big enough to enter. They paddled up the creek well out of sight of the big river, and pulled the canoes half out of the water. Then they unloaded all the wet cargo and left it in the sun to dry. Jinja walked around the camp, checking on the welfare of the little party. Finding them all to be in good shape, he walked over to the creek, where Joanna was looking toward the sun, letting it warm her face, though her body was still shivering in her wet clothes.

"You could use a dry blanket," Jinja said, studying her pale features. As always happened when he got a close look at her, his heart jumped. The high cheekbones; the full mouth that almost smiled when her face was at rest; the big dark eyes and long straight dark hair; the small nose with the slightly flared nostrils.

She nodded, without a word. She was seated cross-legged on the ground, her eyes cast downward. For the first time since she had returned to the stockade he had a chance to study her a bit. Had the events out West served to subdue her, or was she just resting up for her next tantrum?

He came back with a blanket. She took it from him and felt it with her face. For several moments she said nothing, then, in a voice so low he could barely hear her, she mumbled, "Thank you.

"It's—good," she said, wrapping it around her. She lay down and folded herself up, waited for her body heat to warm the space around her, and closed her eyes.

He cleared his throat and walked in between Obie's group and James and Anna. He needed sleep, and so did everybody else. They were so tired they had been negligent about posting guards. On this day, they were lucky.

"Do you think they'll come after us when they're done looting?" Jinja asked James after half the day had passed without any further sign of their pursuers.

James shrugged and thought for a moment. "Do you remember when we were deciding which goods to leave and which to bury? I wanted to leave out more than you did."

"That's 'cause I'm the one that has to account to my grandfather for all the goods that get lost."

"Well, I know that," James replied. "Maybe if we'd left more out, they'd have too many goods to carry and chase us too."

Jinja laughed. "If you remember, I left a couple of barrels of good Pennsylvania whiskey out there for them." They had walked upstream and ducked into some old dead grass on a hill overlooking the Ohio River.

"Kind of a dirty trick to play on the Twightwees, don't you think?"

Jinja knew what James was talking about. Many of the

Miami bands had managed to avoid much contact with white men. Consequently, they had not yet acquired the alcohol habit. But they knew about it, and both Jinja and James were certain that if they found it, they would drink it, and if they drank it, they would drink more of it, and if they drank enough of it, which they would, then by the time they were fit to do anything, their prey would be halfway back to Pennsylvania.

Jinja sneezed. "I better go back and get a dry blanket," he said to James. "You want one?"

12

"I CAN'T UNDERSTAND WHY YOU'D DRAG ME back into these horrible woods!" Joanna cried. There was fire in her eye and venom in her voice. "I've lived in the woods all my life and hated every damned day of it, and I finally find myself under the roof of a nice house in a town without a single damned Indian in it, and you drag me back into the woods. I hate the woods. What in hell are we doing in the woods?"

Jinja looked at her with a crooked grin on his face. "*I'm* in the woods because I want to visit my grandfather," he replied. "*You're* in the woods because my mother, my father, my sister, and my brother-in-law couldn't put up with you and begged me to get you out of Albany before one of them killed you."

"Snooty old bunch, your family," she grumbled. Then she simmered down and stopped carrying on, though Jinja could still hear her grumbling under her breath. That was enough for him. He took three steps past her, up the trail they were walking, then turned around and got nose-to-nose with her.

"You are the most ungrateful creature I have run across in my whole life. We take you in after you run away from the army, where you did Lord knows what with who knows who, which makes you a you-know-what. In Pittsburgh I kept you from getting arrested. In Oneida you insulted James's family—"

"I was just surprised that there were still Indians up in New York! They killed my family, you know."

"The Oneidas didn't kill your family. James helped to save your miserable life. Or don't you remember anymore?"

"Well," she said, dropping an argument she could not win. "This grandfather of yours, is he an Indian?"

"He is brother to the Senecas, and brother to the Mohawks. He had a wife from each."

"At the same time?" She was aghast.

"Nooo," he said, softly, patiently. "His first wife died many years ago. She was my grandmother but I never met her. His second wife died early last fall. I want you to say nothing about it to him. You only say wrong things. It is like something is missing where you should have a heart. He is an old man now. He has a pond below his house. If you say anything to hurt him, I will see to it that you breathe your last breaths at the bottom of the pond."

"Why should I hurt an old goat?"

"That old goat is a great man. I have not seen him since long before his second wife died. I love him. I'm warning you. Keep your mouth shut."

The look he gave her was so cold and deadly that she respected it and walked on in silence. They had been walking since early the day before, and now they emerged from the woods, nearly blinded by the morning sunlight that reflected off the sheet of white covering the bare hillside. Near the top of the hill, surrounded by carefully selected shade trees, was Big Oak's fine house. There was smoke in the chimney. Good, Jinja thought. The sooner he got to talking with Big Oak, the sooner he would be spared the carping, complaining conversation of Joanna. Somehow he could not find a way to get rid of her, though he had tried to nearly a dozen times since they had left the river at Pittsburgh, put most of their goods in the company storehouse, and hired horses for the remainder of the journey home.

The snow was not deep, maybe three inches, but they slipped a little as they climbed the hill. She complained about fools who go floundering around in the snow during the winter instead of staying home by the fire. He did not respond. Jinja banged on the door, waited a few seconds, then walked over to the glazed front window and looked in.

There was a fire deep in the fireplace throwing light on the main room, but there was nobody there. Jinja looked toward the pond and saw what he expected to see, footprints leading downhill toward the water. "Come on," he said to her, stepping off the side of the porch and following the footprints. She tossed her head, annoyed, and followed him.

He was seated on a couple of blankets, wearing his deerskin coat and cap with two more blankets snugly wrapped around him and a scarf covering his cap and his chin, wrapped twice around his head. With a long stick he had broken a path of ice about three feet wide and eight feet long in front of him. A length of line with a bobber dangled off the end of a long cane pole and floated in the black water. The stem of a clay bowl pipe stuck out of his clamped jaw and he was working hard on it, sending puff after puff of smoke into the winter air.

Jinja shrugged aside the ache that hugged his heart. The great old warrior's cheeks were hollow. His beard was scraggly and his eyes sagged vacantly. His right leg was bent under his left, but the left leg stuck straight out, from a knee that could scarcely bend anymore.

"Hello, Thad," said the old man without looking up.

"It's Jinja, Grandpa."

"'Course it is," said the old man. "Your father don't bother to get up here much anymore."

"He doesn't move around like he used to, Grandpa," said Jinja, remembering a time when both his father and grandfather were deadly adversaries of the British, during the war for independence.

"Me too," said Big Oak. "I guess maybe I should go down to Albany and visit him and Katherine." He looked up. "Help me up, boy," he said.

Jinja reached down, took a gloved hand and helped Big Oak to his feet.

"You look good," Big Oak said, fixing his eyes intently on his grandson. He was wrapping the line around his pole when he spotted Joanna. "Pretty. Who is she?"

"Her name's Joanna. Her family is all dead. She lived near our stockade."

"Ah. Pretty girl. I said that, didn't I? How come you're back, boy? Miamis burn you out?"

"You heard about the Miamis?"

"Paul Derontyan told me when he came in last month." Paul Derontyan was James's father, an Oneida who was a longtime friend of Big Oak's and a key employee in the trading firm of Wendel and Watley.

They climbed slowly up the hill to the house. A cold wind had whipped up and was blowing down the hill in their faces as they walked. Jinja watched his grandfather labor up his hill, his head drooping sadly. And yet he also noticed that his grandfather was not breathing hard. His heart may have been broken, but it was not yet spent.

The interior of the house had a pleasant warm glow after

the biting cold wind outside. "Feels good," said Jinja, dropping his pack and blanket and stomping his feet in front of the big fireplace. Joanna walked over to the fire, dropped her mittens and stood beside Jinja, her hands as close to the fire as the heat would allow. Big Oak picked up a couple of big logs and threw them in the fire. He walked to a corner near the door, letting his blankets fall, unwinding his scarf, throwing off his cap and his coat. Then he picked up his blankets and wrapped them around his thin body.

"I'm sorry there's not much to eat. Plenty of dried corn from the summer. Some dried beans. Dried meat." All food that had been prepared when Cilla was still alive, Jinja noted. The old man was not going out of his way to survive. Jinja's father had told him the sad story. Cilla had gone to Albany to visit a woman she knew who kept house for one of the rich men in town. The woman was about to have a baby, and she needed help with the house. So Cilla kept house for the man for two weeks, while the woman had her baby and got back on her feet. Big Oak had spent his days visiting Thad's daughter Anne and her fourth baby, who was also Big Oak's fourth great grandchild.

In the last week of October, Big Oak and Cilla left Albany for their cabin. The first day they laughed practically from dawn to sunset, talking about babies, the newborns they had just seen, the ones they had raised from childhood to adulthood, and the dozens yet to be born that they would see come into this world. That night, for the first time in many years, they talked about the day they had met in a Huron war camp twenty-nine summers ago, when she was a slave from the hated Tuscaroras and he was a prisoner soon to be tortured and killed. They recalled their desperate escape, their long journey home, their wedding in the big Albany church and their many years of happy family life in the woods above Albany. He told her his life with her had been so happy that he would cheerfully heed the call now if it were so given. She laughed and told him he had his greatest years before him.

She awakened the next morning feeling ill, she said. In twenty-nine years she had never said that. They tried to walk the remaining ten miles home together but she weakened until she fell, so he carried her for an hour, until she begged him to make camp. Go, she said. Get some sassafras bark. Make some tea for her. Let her lay down on a blanket. Forget the tea. Bring her water to drink, a cool cloth for her head. Let her sleep, she'd be fine.

He did all she said, and sat by her till he knew that she was very ill, that she was dying, that she was dead.

Many years before, he had loved a beautiful Seneca woman, and been married to her for seven years before she died. He had thought he would never get over her, had carried his sadness in his heart for a long time, until he had met Cilla. Twenty-nine years with Cilla had seemed such an impossible dream that after the birth of their third son, every day his prayer of thanks grew longer and more heartfelt. Cilla was nearly twenty years younger, very strong and healthy. It had never occurred to him that he might someday bury her, and the day he did, he cursed himself for every day his business had taken him away from her.

For the first time in his life, life meant nothing to him. He did not seek out his friends. He did not seek out family. Alone, he spent his days walking the woods, listening for echoes of laughter—hers, the childish laughter of the boys when they were young, and his own, when he still, unbelievably, had two decades of happy family existence in front of him. Every morning he found himself looking in the mirror. The image of the old man before him satisfied him. Surely a man who looked like that did not have many moons to live. His faith in God and Jesus and heaven grew strong. He would be with Cilla once more, and this time forever.

Then came the dream. One month before Jinja arrived, he dreamed of Cilla. He dreamed of her walking away from him, never turning to face him, always her back to him, walking slowly, farther and farther away until she was a pinpoint in the darkness, and then she vanished. The people of the Longhouse believed in dreams. Big Oak had New England parents but he had spent so much time among the Seneca people that he had learned the meaning of dreams. This one was easy. He was to live a long time without her. Each day his memory of her would become dimmer and dimmer, until she would only be a pinpoint in the corner of his mind.

This he would not allow. It was one thing to lose her. He had no choice. But to forget her smile? Her scent? Her touch? The sound of her voice? Never. When Jinja approached Big Oak by the pond, puffing on his pipe and watching his bobber, the old man was thinking of a conversation she had had with him one summer afternoon as they both sat by the pond. She had told him that an Oneida in Paul's village had dreamed that an owl had come to Paul and whispered that if they moved north to one of the big lakes above Lake Ontario, then the king—meaning the king of England—would grant them their own country where the white men might never go and bother them.

He had been surprised that she had mentioned the dream. Cilla got along well with most white people, and had raised their three boys to have the white talking paper. And yet Cilla wanted to go away from the white people. He didn't say much to her about it, but the rest of the day, when she wasn't looking, he would stare at her. He could not believe that she would want to go back to the Indian villages with their hungry winters and their drafty, smoky lodges. Had he misjudged her all these years? Had she only pretended to be happy with him, all the while longing for her Tuscarora village?

"Grandpa."

Big Oak had sat down in front of the huge fireplace, stared into it, and was watching the flames race skyward. He had not heard his grandson's voice. Jinja did not speak again for several minutes, but studied his grandfather's face in the flickering orange light of the hearth fire. Mechanically the old man picked up a dry log, tossed it on the fire and watched the flames consume it. The old man's eyes and mouth sagged as if it were too much effort to hold them straight. Now, as Jinja watched, the old man began to rock, back and forth, his eyes over-brimming, a low keening sound in the back of his throat. Obviously he had forgotten that he had company.

Joanna looked at the old man and her eyes softened. There had not been much love between her mother and her father. She had heard that such feelings existed, but she had never seen a man display them before. She studied the lines on his face—stern, tough lines, and yet they led to eyes that wept without shame. She found herself straining to keep her own eyes dry. She was not about to let Jinja in on her feelings now. Surely not now.

"Grandpa!" Jinja whispered urgently. He reached over and took the old man's shoulder. He was surprised at how much muscle remained beneath the blanket.

Big Oak turned his head away from the fire, with great effort. "I'm sorry, Thad," he said, blinking.

"It's Jinja, Big Oak," Jinja said in a strong voice. His voice pulled the old man out of the mists. He took a deep breath, rose to his feet and walked away from the fire, away from the heat.

"Jinja. I know that," Big Oak said. "Excuse an old man for bein' a little crazy."

"Crazy from livin' alone with the dead, Big Oak."

"I don't want to leave her, boy. Damned if I'm gonna leave her."

"And do you think she's here with you? If she was, you wouldn't be grievin' so."

Big Oak nodded. "I know that. I just can't bear it." He noticed Joanna. "This woman has a mean look about her," he said. Then he looked ashamed. "Oh no. I am getting old. That was mean of me. That was unkind." He looked at her more closely. Her expression hadn't changed. She didn't seem to resent his comment.

"You do, you know," he said, staring hard at her. "It's a frontier look," he said. "Women in Albany don't have that look."

"You don't look so good yourself, old man," she almost growled.

Big Oak turned to Jinja. "Hope you ain't too tangled up with this one," he said. "She's too tough for any good man."

Jinja laughed. "Big Oak, I don't know what I'm doing with her. She kinda latched on to us after St. Clair's army was wiped out. She's more than I can handle. More than I'd want to handle."

Again Joanna took no offense. "A woman has to survive somehow too," she said. "I'm makin' no claims on any man. He don't owe me nothin'. I don't owe him nothin'."

"Don't owe him nothin'? Sounds to me like you owe him your life. Why didn't you leave this one out in the woods? Is she any use to you?"

"Not much," Jinja replied. "She just kind of sits around and complains while the rest of us do what's got to be done."

"Hah!" laughed Big Oak in the one-syllable chuckle that

reminded Jinja of a much younger Big Oak. "Never could understand you, boy. In a battle you were always the fiercest, most reckless boy I ever saw. I don't know how you survived. But you can be such a fool about women. I would've thrown her out of the canoe first time she opened her mouth to yowl. Middle of a war, middle of the woods. Got to all pull together. This one . . ." He shook his head.

"Grandpa, you shouldn't be alone. Will you come down to Albany with us?"

Big Oak looked sadly at his grandson. "I would, honest I would, but to tell you the truth, your mother don't make me feel too comfortable in the house."

Jinja nodded. "You know what they call her down at the warehouse?" he asked.

Big Oak shook his head. "They don't talk to me all that much down there."

"Of course not. I forget, you're a chief too. Seems I'm the only one in the whole family who ain't a chief."

"What do they call your mother?" It was Joanna who asked.

"They call her the duchess," Jinja said, and he smiled. "Tell you something, Big Oak, even Pa doesn't like to put up with her airs anymore."

"He needs to get out," Big Oak said. "Get back on the trail. On the river."

Jinja shook his head. "Don't know how far he could travel. He's not the man he was."

Big Oak laughed his single chuckle. "Hell, boy, who of us is?" He got up and threw down his blankets. He picked a kettle up from its place by the hearth and took it outside. A moment later he was back in, with a kettleful of snow that he hung over the fire. "I think Albany might not be a bad idea," he said, taking the kettle off the fire. "Would you get my rifle down? There's corn in that sack over by the window there." He gave Jinja a sharp look. "I know you've been on the trail awhile, but I don't want to spend tonight in this house."

"You mean we're goin' back in the woods?" Joanna exclaimed.

"You can stay here by yourself if you want," Big Oak responded in a tone that suggested he thought it was a good idea. She said nothing intelligible, just grumbled under her breath and gathered up her mittens and blanket.

"I'm ready if you are," said Jinja.

As he had done so many times over the past half century, Big Oak checked his pack, pouches, blankets, and rifle, slung them over his shoulders, and opened the door. "Wind at our backs, missy." He smiled.

"I'm so glad," she replied sarcastically, following Jinja and Big Oak out into the snow.

13

"OH, WE PICKED A PERFECT TIME." JINJA laughed as they arrived at his father's house the following day. It was well after dark, but all the windows on the lower floor shined with the light of many candles. A carriage pulled by matched grays stopped in front of the door. A beautifully arrayed couple alighted and sent the coachman on his way.

Just as the gentleman knocked on the door with the head of his walking stick, Jinja, Big Oak, and Joanna walked up the steps and stood behind them. The woman gave a little shriek and the man flinched as they saw the three roughly dressed strangers appear so silently and suddenly, obviously to relieve them of their purses.

"Mr. and Mrs. van Zandt, so good to see you," said Jinja, removing his hat and making a bow.

"Oh, David, we thought—" began the elderly Hans van Zandt. Then he realized that the rudely dressed old man behind the son of their hosts was the redoubtable if eccentric Sam Watley, Jinja's grandfather. "Ah, haven't seen you in a while, Sam. Very sorry about your wife. Terrible thing."

Before Big Oak could answer, the door was opened by a

tall ebony man in blue livery. Big Oak shook his head. He had never in his wildest dreams imagined his son as a socialite, and Katherine had seemed so down-to-earth when Thad had married her over the strong objections of Katherine's father, Dieter Wendel.

"Mr. and Mrs. van Zandt," the doorman announced as the elderly couple walked directly into a large chandelier-lit anteroom where wine was being served. There were at least forty ladies and gentlemen, standing around making conversation.

The doorman then noticed the three frontier-dressed people standing in the doorway. Joseph was his name, and Joseph by now knew all three of them. This did not mean he approved of them. He was not merely a fellow who opened doors, he was also chief of protocol in the house and, given Thad and Katherine's casual beginnings, definer of all that was socially graceful in their world.

"Three forest savages," he announced dryly. Katherine nearly dropped her drink when she heard the announcement, but when she looked up and saw her son and father-in-law standing at the threshold, she headed directly for the group with a smile on her face. But as much as she adored her only son, that's how much she despised Joanna. Her eyes flashed as she paid her respects to the van Zandts then walked over to her son.

"David," she purred, "how nice to see you, but why did you bring that creature in with you?" She raced right past that remark with an insincerely sad, "Hello Sam, why *have* you taken so long to come to us?"

"You sure look a sight," said Big Oak, ignoring her non-question. "I'm sorry to barge in on your entertainment. I had no idea—"

"Of course you didn't," she interjected. "Society news does not travel to Big Oak Pond." Then she looked seriously into Big Oak's gray eyes. "I am *so* sorry about Cilla." Her eyelids fluttered with emotion. "I miss her so much." In spite of her social pretensions and her artificial manners, he knew that Katherine was telling him the truth. Cilla and the children had been the biggest crack in her wall of snobbery. Cilla had possessed a mixture of toughness and kindness that attracted anybody who knew her. Katherine had treasured Big Oak's Tuscarora woman. When news of Cilla's death had reached her, she did not go into any formal period of mourning, but late in the quiet night, when the musicians were silent and the guests had gone home, Thad would feel her body shake as the tears came. Those were among the few moments when he knew that his wife could still feel.

"I will get Thad to tend to you," she told Big Oak, then gave her son Jinja a peck that must have fallen a full three inches short of his cheek. She walked across the room, followed a few moments later by Big Oak, Jinja, and Joanna.

Thad was in the kitchen supervising the help. Though he wasn't needed there, supervising in the kitchen gave him an excuse for leaving the guests to Katherine. The arrangement pleased her because in recent times Thad had acquired the bad habit of saying the strangest things to the most self-important female guests. At a sit-down dinner in honor of the Reverend Dr. Doremus Thomas, chief clergyman of the largest Episcopalian church in town, Thad had told Mrs. Thomas that he stopped drinking because wine made his Seneca ancestors rise out of his blood waving red-stained war clubs. Mrs. Thomas had had to retire from the table for several minutes, and when she returned, she found to her relief that the seating order had been changed.

Katherine summoned him from the kitchen, pointed out his guests, then returned to hers, pausing at the wine table for another glass. Thad saw his son and his father and beckoned them out the door, to the small back porch off his study.

"Big Oak, and Wild Oak—and the lovely Joanna," he said so thickly that it was clear his remark to Mrs. Thomas about abstaining was pure jest. "Sit down, please." They did, and he did. For about a minute there was a fairly comfortable silence, while Thad's brain collected itself in the cool night air. When he spoke again, most of the thickness had disappeared.

"Big Oak, I—I'm happy to see you come down here. All these months I felt you were living up there with ghosts. I believe that a man who lives with ghosts is apt to become one himself before long. I am not yet ready to lose you."

"It would seem, my son, that we've both got ghosts to give up," Big Oak responded.

Thad refused to pretend that he did not know what his father was talking about. After years of town life, taking inventory down at the warehouse, filling in at the store, playing genial host at his wife's parties, going along as reluctant guest at his wife's friends' parties, his waist had thickened as his zest for life thinned.

"I did not think it would turn out like this," he said. "Used to be the only time I felt alive was when I was on the trail or the river. I don't know if I could follow a trail in the woods anymore. I think climbing one good hill would kill me. I look like a dead pig that's laid in the sun for a week."

Jinja and Big Oak looked at each other. People had always been amazed at how the same wild spirit could inhabit the souls of Big Oak and Jinja, while the man who was the son of one and the father of the other, the one with the most Indian blood, could have turned out to be the most domesticated of the three.

"I'll admit you take a big pair of breeches these days," said Big Oak. "But a week or two on the trail would make you fit again."

"I don't know," Thad said thoughtfully. "I like the life I have in Albany."

Big Oak scoffed. "You like the life you have in Albany. The woman you've lived with all these years is not the woman you thought you had married. Your daughter is married off and become too much like your wife. What are your responsibilities, pouring wine for mincing store clerks at your wife's parties? You would give your soul for a month in the woods, and the son who is the apple of your eye would be going with you."

Thad laughed. "And what about you, my ancient father? Last year you were still running around the woods like a rutting stag. Now you look like an old crone wrapped in a tattered shawl."

"Well, son, there comes a time when a man's body gives out," Big Oak replied, surprised. "My back aches and—"

"You didn't give out, Pa, you gave up. I know that Cilla didn't think she was married to an old man. Right to the day she died she had a partner, not an invalid. I tell you what, I'll go if you go. But I'm not gonna let you lay around that cabin of yours collecting your share of the profits we bring in."

Big Oak began to chuckle, but anger rose in Jinja's throat. "Pa, how can you talk to him like this? You can't put him out on the trail in the middle of a war. There's blood runnin' down every river in the Northwest."

"He's more likely to die cooped up in his cabin than out on the trail," Thad snorted.

Big Oak was silent for a moment. For the first time in months he considered the possibility that his life was not coming to a close.

"Tell you what," he said. "Let's spend some time on the trails, the three of us, before spring. Let's see if we can shrink that belly of yours to where you will not be such a huge target for Twightwee bullets. Let's see if I can get my legs to listen to me when I tell them what to do. If we've got anything left in us, we'll teach those western tribes that it's a lot safer to trade with us than war against us."

Before their eyes most of the slack in Big Oak's face disappeared.

Joanna spoke up. "Listen to the three of you chatter along about going off to war against Indians. What do you think you're doing? They're deadly men."

Big Oak smiled patiently. "My dear, all three of us have called them our friends, and our enemies, and our brothers. We have fought against them, we have fought at their side. Each of us has escaped death at their hands by this much!" He held his thumb and forefinger a quarter of an inch apart. "We know how to fight and survive. And if it is our time to die?" He shrugged his shoulders as he had seen French Canadian traders do so many years ago. "We know how to do that too."

"Good for you. And what is to happen to me?"

Jinja looked at her more in disbelief than anger. "Why should we care what happens to you?" he asked. "Give me one good reason why we should care what happens to you."

"Then why have you taken me with you up to now? Why have you been kind to me?"

Jinja's eyebrows rose. "I didn't think you'd noticed." He thought for a moment. "I couldn't have just left you in the woods. I couldn't even have left your mother in the woods." He stopped again to think. "I am a stupid man. My father sometimes showed me that. My grandfather showed me that. I am a fool. I see a pretty face and expect something sweet to come from its mouth. Even now, after you've proved that you are not capable of sweetness, I expect something sweet to come from your mouth."

Joanna did not respond. She turned her head away from all three so they would not see her hurt expression. Nobody had ever been as kind to her as Jinja. She wanted to be kind back to him, but she had no practice. She didn't mind so much when someone returned her cruelty with his cruelty, but what if she was kind and he in turn was cruel? What would be left for her?

Big Oak was smiling, staring off the back porch, into the lone clump of trees in the backyard. The yard was small, bounded by similar small grassy yards and three-story brick houses. They reminded him how glorious it was to walk the long trail, as he had done so many times in his life. He stretched his legs, then his arms. The aches and twinges did not seem so bad. Why had he felt so old the past few months? Why had his body felt so tired and tormented? Could it be that his pain was more grief and loneliness than rheumatism?

Big Oak ignored the bickering between his grandson and the bitter creature who somehow fascinated him. "It has been a while since the Watleys went forward together and struck a blow for freedom," he said.

Thad's face registered surprise. "Since when does Big Oak regard fighting a war against the Indians as striking a blow for freedom?"

"A fight for freedom that you cannot win is not worth fighting," Big Oak continued. "The day of the tribes is done. I will weep for them and I already miss them, but I will not fight for them when I know that it is the bloody cruel English who are using the Indians for their own purposes. We are still fighting the war for independence, Thad. Decisions are still being made in Parliament, even though our enemies are wearing red skins instead of red coats."

There was a moment of silence on the porch. They could hear Katherine's musicians playing, faintly. Then Thad exploded with laughter. "You old frog-killer," he said. "You had me going for a moment. I know you. You don't for one moment think the English are gonna be back in the valley of the Te-non-an-at-che, disturbing our sleep." The smile vanished, replaced by a longing look of sadness. "The only thing that ever kept you home all these years was Cilla. And now that she's gone, there is nothing left to keep you here. Damn it, I know I said you ought to go, but you're too old for the trail and the tomahawk. They'll get you killed, you know that, don't you?"

"Maybe they will. But I promise you, if they kill me, the instrument that does the job will have been made in England."

It was one of the greenest, most beautiful pieces of flatland in the Northwest Territory, threaded through with cool, trickling streams and the wide Maumee River flowing east on its journey to Lake Erie. For days that river had been carrying scores of canoes to this spot. Assembled were men of the great nations of the Northwest: Ottawas, Mingoes, Potawatamis, Delawares, Wyandots, Shawnees, Chippewas, Sacs, Foxes; there were Conoys, Munseys, and even a smattering of Mohicans, Cherokees, and Creeks. That there were emissaries from the last two, mighty southern tribes who for so long had hated the northern tribes as well as each other, promised unity at last.

This beautiful plain was known as the Glaize. Many of the men here were representatives of tribes that had settled on the Glaize to get out of the way of American pioneers. But they knew that sooner or later the Americans would be heading their way, for the Americans never stopped coming. Others were from tribes to the north. They knew that their turn would come eventually. Best to draw the line now.

And so two Shawnees and two Twightwees walked from one representative to another, presenting the ceremonial pipe. And each representative smoked the pipe and waited, patiently, until the Shawnee Messquakenoe arose and spoke.

"My brothers, you must hear the words I say. They are important to the future of us all.

"Another summer fades, as have so many other summers before, since the white man came. Once again the white men are closer. They have more of our land. We have less. Once again we see that their words are like the softest wisps of wind, coming and vanishing as if they had not been said. They are so sincere when they say these words that I still do not know if they are liars of if they forget their own words."

As Messquakenoe's words were translated, the men made noises of agreement, for every one of them there at some time in his life had been astonished by a white's promise solemnly made and casually broken. Many of them were still sorting out the new political order, though it was generally understood that the Americans were in fact the worst of the Englishmen, unrestrained by a civilized and caring king.

"We all remember when they assured us that the lands west of the mountains and north of the Ohio River belonged to us forever. Then we all thought, surely because of the great sacrifice we have made to keep the peace, this is one promise they will not break. How foolish we were.

"But maybe it is good that we made this agreement. It was an agreement we all know took place. There were no foolish drunken men made chiefs by the whites just to put their marks on the animal skin. No, real men made this agreement, but to the whites it was just another wisp of wind. And now not only are the settlers moving in to cut down our forests and tear up our land. An army came last winter and tried to build strong houses *in the places where they said there would be no white men.*

"Remember the great victory to the west before the big snows fell? Our warriors found a pouch of talking skins there. We brought them to our English friends. They told us what the skins said. They said that the Americans did not want to have red men that lived like red men. These they would drive away. The only red men they wanted were men who would live like white men. They would have such men take hoes in their hands to plant corn. They would make them labor like beasts, their oxen and their packhorses."

One of the braves wished to speak, and though the Shawnee speaker had a good head of steam, he saw the anguish on the man's face. The man was a Delaware from the East. He arose and spoke in a choked voice.

"Hear what is being said this day," he cried. "And do not believe that by taking up the hoe and laboring like beasts, wearing white man's clothes and worshiping his God, you will find peace with them. That is what some of my people did. 'We are not Indians anymore. We are Christians,' they said. But when the white men got angry because they were attacked, and they could not avenge themselves on those who attacked them, they looked for red men, any red men they could find. The only red men they could find were the ones who hoed the corn and wore white man clothes and worshiped the crossed sticks. And when the white men found those red white men, they decided to slaughter them. Do you know what those red men did when the white men came and pointed guns at them? They got on their knees and they prayed to the white man's God, and while they were on their knees, the white men killed them —the men, the women, the children."

The men who heard this story did not cry out with surprise. Most of them had heard stories like this. They could not understand the white man, who called their own military defeats massacres, but called their massacres of red women and children great military victories. The Delaware, having unburdened himself, sat down, and the Shawnee continued.

"When the Great Spirit saw that this time we would resist the white man, he helped us to throw the Americans on their backs. In another time, our tribes would have been split, half fighting against the whites and half fighting on the side of the whites because the whites were fighting their ancient enemies. We have finally learned who the enemy is." He pointed dramatically to the west, where the last shades of pink and yellow were dissolving into black. "It is not the people who have lived beyond the river, who once had a brave who came over the river and scalped one of our women to prove he was a man." He pointed to the east, at the rising stars. "It is not the people who live beyond that hill who once many moons ago came in midwinter and stole our horses.

"Those people may have stolen our possessions, even our lives. But they never stole our dignity. Never stole our souls. And there is a good man out there from the people the Mingoes call the Twightwees. Little Turtle. We followed him and we won a great victory. So many of you who are here"—he swept his hand around the great camp —"were there. We know in our hearts that our great shame has been to lose so much to such weak fighting people. When we fought them I had no idea so many could die so quickly or flee so fast. My brothers, I must know, are they still running? Why is it they attack so slowly and run away so fast?" His audience laughed, and made noises of appreciation each according to the custom of his tribe.

"We are finally one," he said, looking from man to man as he spoke. "We can thank the white man for that. This is the day the Great Spirit has chosen to call together this meeting for the good of all nations of our color. Even our southern brothers, those mighty warriors, the Cherokee and the Creek, are here to tell us that they are with us. Today is the day that we will all remember as long as the water runs through this land."

Now arose a tall Delaware who had been fighting the English-speaking whites for so long he could not remember the last time he had shaken the hand of one. He was a Delaware named Buckangahela. He had many years on him, and yet he was still a staunch warrior, still full of fighting spirit.

"The Shawnee has spoken to you," he said, "he speaks for all of us. We are now of one mind, one head, one heart."

Others spoke of the times that the Americans had been able to set one tribe against the other, but how this time it was not to be. For the first time, when they looked at each other, they saw not Miamis or Lenni Lenape or the dreaded warriors of the Longhouse. Not Chippewa, Ottawa, Wyandot, but red man.

"We have been to the Creeks and the Chickamaugas," Messquakenoe told them. "They have agreed that we should war upon the Americans until there are none left. The time has come. After all this time, the Great Spirit has looked into our hearts. When we have defeated the Americans, we will cast away their rifles, and their kettles, and their blankets, and their rum. Never again will we make war on each other. That's why he sent them, to punish us for making war on each other."

His words went straight to the hearts of all those who heard them. When the council fires had burned out, they packed up their calumets and their medicine bundles and made ready to do battle with the hated Americans.

Among those who had come to the Glaize was the old warrior, Thad's boyhood friend, Skoiyasi. Born a Seneca on the Genesee River, he had fought beside the English against the French. But the English had abandoned their allies after the war, when they no longer had use for them. Without English ammunition for the hunt, and English blankets for the lodge, his people suffered in the wintertime. He heard from his brothers of the East, the Mohawks, that English farmers were taking the land, and their father the English king refused to stop them.

Then the Ottawa chief Pontiac had united the lake tribes. In desperation, Skoiyasi and other Senecas joined the rebellion and helped to conquer many English forts along the lakes. But the other Iroquois tribes refused to join the rebellion. Perhaps they could not stand the thought of being partners with the despised lake tribes. Perhaps they were once again bought off by the white man's promises and his goods. The rebellion failed.

Skoiyasi remembered the last time he had spoken with the great Seneca chief Kyashuta. "Remember, my brother," Kyashuta said, "we have good dreams and we have bad dreams. The white men are but a bad dream, for such evil surely could not exist for long under the Holder of the Heavens. One day, my brother, we will awaken from this terrible dream. When we do, we will be so much wiser. We are always wiser when the Holder of the Heavens speaks to us, and in this dream he has spoken many words. We must remember them all."

For many years, in the valley of the Muskingum, Skoiyasi had lived with his family, so far from the white man that he felt as if he had indeed awakened, but one day he could see them coming, and he knew they were no dream. It was time to fight again, and this time they must fight as one, with no red people on the other side to lead the blind white men into the hidden places. When he had fought in the battle against General St. Clair, their attack had been so deadly, their victory so complete, he was certain that this time, as Messquakenoe had said, the Great Spirit had once again taken them by the hand.

The morning of the day before this council was to end, Skoiyasi sat down with Little Turtle and they smoked together. Little Turtle had noted the fighting prowess of Skoiyasi and his band during the fight against St. Clair.

"My brother, I am pleased to see your face again," said the aging Seneca warrior.

Little Turtle released a fragrant cloud of kinnikinnick to float heavenward. He said nothing, but his eyes rested on Skoiyasi, knowing that Skoiyasi had a purpose for his visit.

"My brother, I speak to you not in sign but in a tongue you can understand. There was a time when most warriors of the Longhouse would not have bothered to learn the tongue of the lake tribes. 'Let them learn the tongue of the Longhouse,' they would have said.

"But times have changed. The council fire in Onondaga has long been cold. We have lost our lands to the stinking white men. It was our fault. Only our fault. We believed that we were the only real people. We believed that the lake tribes, even our cousins the Wyandot, lived only to decorate our lodges with their scalps.

"And yet there were among us those who went to the

setting sun to live among you. We left the Longhouse to do this. We were now Mingoes instead of Senecas. You chose to let go of your feelings of revenge toward the Longhouse. We have lived in peace with the Twightwees since we came to the valley of the Spay-Lay-Wi-Theepi.

"You have taught us much, my great brother. In the great days of the Longhouse, the tradition was that in time of war Seneca war chiefs would lead the Longhouse into battle. We were jealous and proud of that tradition, and would allow no chiefs from the Mohawks or the Onondagas to lead us. But today I am proud to follow a chief of the Twightwees against the white men. You and I have lived many years and we know the ways of the white men. We have punished them with a great defeat. But they will come again. We know they will come again. Even before they come, their stupid, stubborn farmers will cross the mountains to settle on our land and steal it.

"They are more dangerous even than the soldiers. If they did not come, the soldiers would not come. It will be some time before the soldiers can gather another big army to battle us with. But the others will come. I believe that we must find them and burn them out as fast as they cross the mountains. If they do not settle on the land and grow food, then the army will have no way to get food. The whites are soft. They cannot travel long distances and live on a few handfuls of corn along the way. They must have much food. If we can deny them that, then their heads will hang low when they come to meet us in battle."

"My brother Skoiyasi is wise," Little Turtle remarked. He blew another thick puff of smoke to the wind and waited to hear more.

"There are but six braves with me. It is my hope that we can spend much of the winter destroying settlers as we find them. And if you can have others doing the same, then in the spring when the soldiers come again, they will find that when their food runs out there will be none to take its place."

"What do you want of me?"

"You are a great war chief," Skoiyasi replied. "I would not do this unless you told me it was the right thing to do. I want you to tell me whether our plans fit in with yours."

14

THIS WAS AN EXPEDITION THAT NORMALLY would not have happened. There was war in the West, not only in Ohio with the lake tribes, but in the South.

Tales of carnage filtered back to Albany through Wendel and Watley's grapevine. For their own reasons, they were bound to go anyway. But not with Obie. With the same precision that made him an excellent repairer of firearms, he assessed the situation and agreed that it would be foolish to put his family in danger at this time. As for him going without his family, if he were killed or crippled, it would be the same as giving them back into slavery. Obie and his family would stay in Albany.

Nor would James be going with them. Anna was pregnant. Thad would not let him come. There was trade up the Hudson, he told them. Trade up Lake Champlain. Trade with Montreal. Trade everywhere, but not in the valley of the Spay-Lay-Wi-Theepi, where the Miamis and Shawnees were reaping scalps like a farmer harvests pumpkins.

James thought it was just as well. He had no desire to fight the whites, but neither would he let them use him against his brothers in the West. He had a job, he had a child on the way, and he still had family in Oneida. He would no longer choose sides.

The autumn colors were right on time, but after the first burst of reds and yellows, the weather turned mild. There were five in this little party: Big Oak, Thad, Jinja, Joanna, and a trusted French Canadian employee named Henri.

On a sunny October day, warm but with a promise of brisk weather ahead, they set out from Albany, over land, in high spirits. Their plan was to take the southern New York route, below the Finger Lakes, to get a feel of the trade opportunities there, then catch the Allegheny River, paddle down to Pittsburgh and finally along the Ohio the rest of the way to the stockade.

Henri was a favorite among all the Wendel and Watley employees. Big Oak had always been happy in the woods, but Henri showed it. When he was on the trail, he would do anything for anybody. He sang, he cooked, he hunted, he never ran out of energy. Thirty-five years old, he was of average height, black-bearded, and handsome, with broad shoulders, a bulky chest, and a little round belly that looked perfect on him.

In Albany he could barely hold himself together; he drank too much, got in trouble with women and got surly with his bosses, but on the trail he was the perfect partner. When night came and the campfire was warm and bright, he held no secrets from his trailmates and could pry from them the most intimate details of their lives.

The stars shined down clear and bright on this moonless night. Warm in front, crisp at their backs, they surrounded the fire and drank tea laced with rum. A breeze stirred the maples and one red leaf floated down into the fire.

"My friends," he said. "I have been on the rivers and the trails of this country since before it was a country. It is what I do. It is all I do that makes me happy. I do not know what makes other people happy. To the west the Indians are loping up and down the trails of the Northwest, killing white men wherever they find them. I cannot understand why a belle mademoiselle like Joanna, or men of substance like the Big Oak or Thad, here, would want to leave a safe bed to go west, where death lies in wait for all Americans."

He had not asked a question, and yet his statement floated in the air above the fire, waiting for somebody to reach up and grab it.

Nobody else wanted to talk, but Henri would not settle for silence.

"Big Oak, you are a great man, everybody knows that. But you have all the comforts you need. Why at your age would you chase your own death in the valley of the Ohio?"

Big Oak chuckled. He pulled out his pipe, packed it and lit up, and chuckled again, as if he had been reminded of something long ago and funny. "My French brother knows that I am a woodsman like him."

"A woodsman yes, but not like me, *mon ami.* I am a humble man of no reputation, while you are a man of great reputation who could die in bed and yet leave a legend of honor. I have watched you today. For a man of your age you move well, but the trail is not for men of your age."

Big Oak drew on his pipe and the wind carried away a cloud of kinnikinnick. "I cannot stay home now, my brother. It was a pleasure to sit by my pond and catch my fish and dream of the trails and the rivers, the trades and the warpath. There was always Cilla to go to, when the dreams grew old and the fish would not come. But Cilla is dead, my friend, and I have called for her ghost but she will not answer. She is gone and I cannot stand the silence."

A wet spot in a piece of wood crackled in the fire, belching a shower of sparks skyward. "While I waited for Cilla's ghost, I had the feeling that I was rushing to meet her halfway. I could feel my bones getting older every day."

He peered at Henri through the flames. "I believe that it is wrong to give up on life when it is not yet time. You are half my age, my friend, so you cannot feel as I do. Life is a precious gift rationed out to us by our maker. I do not judge the sick, the crippled, and those who must live alone. But as for the rest of us, we must accept His gift, and let loose of it only when it is impossible for us to hold on to it any longer. One day I realized that for me life was still possible, but that without Cilla, life meant the trails again. To my surprise, once I was back on the trail, my bones stopped complaining and my legs did as they were told. I am still sad, but I am no longer rushing so fast to meet my beloved Cilla."

The Frenchman nodded. The smoke from Big Oak's pipe made him reach into his pack for his own. "And you, Thad, boss, if I may."

"Why would you ask when you know?" Thad responded. "My home is home to a hundred guests. My wife lives to entertain them, not me. I admit it, I do not love the trail like my father and my son love the trail. I love the hearth on a quiet night, with children, or grandchildren, and a wife who would speak to me about her day, and my day. My wife is bored by such a life. She loves chatter about fashion, gobble that means little to me. I do not like her friends, and I do not like her when she is with her friends. When a man marries, there is no way for him to guess what his wife will be like thirty years later."

"But would you prefer the trail to her dress parties?" Henri asked, delighted by the turn of conversation.

"I would prefer the torture stake to her dress parties," Thad answered, to the fervent nods of his son. "It is good to be back on the trail with my son and my father. It has been so many years, that I thought I would never see it happen again. I watched my father today, watched his strong legs in motion. He is rested. His old knees are like those of the young Big Oak. On this day I am a happy man."

Big Oak looked at his son. "I didn't know you were such a sentimental old fool," he said.

"And *your* knees, Thad. Can they carry you down the long trail as they once did?"

"My knees are not the problem, but for years they had to carry too much Thad Watley. Over the summer my son has led us up and down every trail within fifty miles of Albany. You see that my body has melted away till my clothes had to be retailored. I hope I will never see ten stone again in my lifetime."

"And you, sweet Joanna," Henri said soothingly. "What would make such a beautiful woman risk her life on such a journey? I would think that the comforts of Albany might please you."

"I am not good enough for Albany," she answered bitterly. "I have lost much in my life. My father, my mother, my neighbors, my gentleman."

Jinja snickered. "You mean that captain that hauled you and your mother off to battle with him?"

"He was a gentleman," she replied. "Speak well of the dead."

"Or not at all—" Jinja said. And he went silent.

Henri looked sadly at the young woman. "You are such a beautiful woman," he said. "To have had—" here he was interrupted by an involuntary scoff from Jinja. Henri gave Jinja a sharp look and Jinja looked the other way. Joanna watched the interplay and perceived that the gregarious

Canadian's feelings for her were considerably warmer than those of her protector.

Jinja looked toward the campfire with a stony, serious expression on his face. She thought he was swallowing his pride. In fact he was desperately trying to keep from laughing. Sometimes, he thought, it seems like you can see a bullet leave the muzzle of a rifle and head straight for your head. At such times, he thought, a man ought to duck. Henri, my friend, you had better duck this one yourself. I cannot warn you. You would only get angry, and this trail is too long to travel with an angry friend.

As often happened in New York during the early autumn, the weather stayed dry and the trails easy to travel. Henri paid so much attention to the comforts of Joanna that Jinja found himself doing most of the point work. Big Oak insisted on single file with at least five-yard intervals, as if there were a war going on in western New York. But not only did they find no traces of the western war in New York, they found few traces of travelers along the old Iroquois trails.

"I don't know where they've all gone," Big Oak told Thad as they sat on a rock that looked down across the green and yellow tree canopy for miles and miles facing west.

Henri turned to the old trader. "Gone to Canada," he said. "Gone to the Ohio." He peered into Big Oak's aging, squinty eyes. "Gone."

Big Oak looked away from Henri and toward the tree canopy. He was not looking out at space, but across time, back to a day when that canopy could have been sheltering a war party of Cayugas or Senecas. He squinted his eyes almost shut, to focus if he could. How many times had he sat in this spot and stared across that space? This time the canopy was not endless. Where the hills ended, the fields began, acres and acres along the river, pale yellow with the remains of corn plants. There were smokes out there too, thick white man smokes from white man chimneys that said, "We are here now, and safe, and need hide from no one."

Big Oak did not mind the farms. His trails were still here, and it was good for a man to break up the land and plant corn. His Seneca and Mohawk sisters had done the same. And it was their presence that he missed. No, that was not true. It was Cilla that he missed. "Come on, boys," he said, "and lady. It's mostly downhill for the next ten miles."

They slung their packs, blankets, and weapons over their shoulders and continued on without a word. Even Joanna had no complaints. The chivalrous Frenchman had put her on her best behavior. Here was a man to share a cabin with. She could feel beneath his quiet joy on the trail a treacherous temper aching to come out. A deep down instinct nurtured from childhood had detected that fire. So she choked off her own anger and behaved like a lamb. Big Oak and Thad were amazed. Jinja was not. He had seen her once before like this.

A day later they crossed the Canisteo River and followed the main trail southwest. This trail ended abruptly at the edge of a pasture that held a half-dozen fine milk cows. Jinja stopped and waited for Big Oak to come up.

"Which way from here?" he asked, studying the wood fence that stood at the edge of the forest.

Big Oak looked across the field. His vision might no longer have been sharp, but his perceptions of the land and its shapes remained flawless. "See that big old elm across the field?" he asked. "I believe you'll find the trail again right about there. He climbed the fence with surprising agility, grunted as he dropped to the ground, and led the way across the pasture. Jinja followed, then Henri, Joanna, and Thad in the rear.

On the other side of the field, replacing a fence rail, was the freeholder of this property. Of medium height, he had broad shoulders and worked shirtless in the noon sun, which gleamed off his balding head.

"Hello, the fence!" cried Big Oak from halfway across the field. The farmer, who had been handling a huge log by himself, dropped the wood into place with a loud *thwunk* and turned around to face the voice, hands on hips, a grim look on his face.

As they approached, he pulled a large rag from his belt and wiped the sweat off his face. He was about forty years old. What hair he had left on his head was reddish-blond. His face and shoulders were sunburned pink, with freckled spots on his upper back. The sparse blond hair on his chest glistened with sweat.

"You people looking for me?" he asked.

A wide friendly grin split Big Oak's face. "We've been traveling some time, headin' west," he said. "Good to see a friendly face." Jinja chuckled. There was nothing friendly about the man's face.

"See this fence?" the man asked.

Big Oak nodded.

"I figure you crossed over one just like it when you trespassed onto this field," he said.

"It's a fine fence," Big Oak replied.

"Then you get yourself back to that fence and admire it as you walk around it, understand?"

Thad had stood off a few feet, admiring the cows, until he heard the farmer's angry voice. Then he moved closer, interested to see if his father still had his knack for handling rude people.

"Let me *try* to understand," was Big Oak's response. "We

have come three hundred miles, and we have more than that to go. You want us to go back to yonder fence and walk around your field because God's land belongs to you."

"I paid for this land. It belongs to me."

"Did you buy it from God? Give the money to God?"

"I cleared this land with these two hands. Maybe folks like you don't know what it's like to do a decent day's honest work with your hands."

The smile faded from Big Oak's face. "You cleared the land with your two hands, did you? How long ago did you do that?"

"Past six years, if it's any of your business."

"Mmm," Big Oak grunted. "Cleared it of trees? Stumps? rocks?"

"That's right. I did it myself."

"Let me tell you something, Mister These Two Hands. With these two hands—and those two hands"—he pointed to Thad—"and those two hands"—he pointed to Jinja—"we cleared this land of Indians so you could have it for yourself. Great God above, Thad, Jinja, is this what comes of our work? Before Sullivan's army came through here, if you had tried to clear this field, two or three Senecas might of come up behind you and instead of giving you a friendly hello like we just did, buried a tomahawk in your head."

The farmer looked at Big Oak and worked his jaws but said nothing.

"I see," Big Oak said, "that you don't even bring a gun out to the field with you. Must be pretty safe out here these days, don't you think?"

"You get yourselves back there and walk around my field or you'll pay."

"Joanna, can you go first?" said the old frontiersman. Joanna began to climb the fence rails. The farmer clamped a grip on her shoulder.

"John!" Big Oak said in dangerous tone. Thad laughed. John was the name by which some whites addressed all Indians who had taken to living like whites. "Take your hand off her or I will blow a hole in your face."

The farmer turned his head and found himself looking into the muzzle of Big Oak's Pennsylvania long rifle. The muzzle looked as big as the mouth of a cannon to him. He released his hold on Joanna. She climbed the fence and dropped over to the other side, followed by Henri and Jinja.

Thad had noticed the man's ax lying in the grass near the fence. He picked it up and brought it over to the farmer. "This ax, where did you get it?" Big Oak had lowered his rifle. The man regained his courage.

"None of your business."

"I'll tell you where you got it. You got it from us. In Albany, right?"

The man was silent.

"If we're gonna survive as a country," Thad said, "we can't get our backs up everytime someone steps on our land on the way to somewhere else. You see that old man you addressed as if he were a miserable beggar? Without him you don't have your little piece of land here."

"I want you off this land now," said the farmer, as if his ears were filled with dirt. "If you ever come back this way, I'll make you wish you hadn't."

"Any way for us to give this land back to the Senecas?" Big Oak asked Thad as he leaned his rifle against the fence, climbed over, then took the weapon in hand again. "Sure wish we could." Then he laughed and pointed his rifle at the farmer while Thad made it over the fence. Jinja found the trail easily enough. Just before they disappeared into the woods, Big Oak turned around for a last look at the farmer. He had his ax in his hands and was glowering at them from beneath his pink, freckled forehead.

The following afternoon, on the bank of a nearly dry creek, they were surprised to find a tiny Seneca village. There were three families there, living in flimsy elm-bark-covered huts. There were seven children among them, splashing naked in the cold water, for it was a warm day and the children would not be denied their last water sports of the year. Two of the men were in the village, tending to their weapons and equipment.

The women were doing the same with their cooking and gardening tools. But they were not caught unawares. The eyes of all the adults had spotted the travelers while they were still in the woods, fifty yards from the clearing. They followed the small party as it approached. Thad and Big Oak came forward boldly among them. The Senecas sat in silence, working with their hands, but their eyes never left the strangers.

"We come to the Keepers of the Western Door," said Big Oak in the Seneca tongue, holding up an empty hand. Beyond the lodges, he could see a small cleared field that had been harvested at least a month before. These people did not seem to be in want, but their heads were down. Even the sound of a white man speaking perfectly good Seneca dialect did not stir their interest.

Henri and Joanna hung back. They were the ones who heard the approach of the third warrior of the village. He stood behind them with his rifle at the ready.

"We are passing through to the valley of the Spay-Lay-Wi-Theepi," Big Oak continued. "We are traders."

The villagers looked dubious. These traders carried no goods with them. Finally, one of the men stood up and stepped forward. "Who are you that you speak our tongue so well?" he asked.

"I am Big Oak, from the village of Tonowaugh, on the Genesee River."

"I do not know of such a village," said the man.

"It was wiped out before you were born, my brother," Big Oak replied.

"I have heard of such a village," said the man behind them as he walked into their midst.

The man approaching them from the lodges extended his hand. "You are welcome, my brother," he said. "We do not have much, but we are happy to share what we have. I am called Long Hunter."

Big Oak, Thad, and Jinja joined Long Hunter in the shade of a great elm in front of his lodge. All three ate sparingly, for they did not believe their hosts had much to give them.

"Why do they not come?" asked Long Hunter, pointing to Joanna and Henri.

"Last winter she suffered much at the hands of the Miamis."

"So let her not come to the Miamis."

"She cannot tell one red man from another. He would come to you and eat all you have, but he is . . . caring for her," Big Oak said haltingly, because in truth he did not *know* what Henri was doing with Joanna.

"You are the only Ganonsyoni we have seen since we left Albany," Big Oak told Long Hunter as he reached for his pipe. The Seneca watched Big Oak pack kinnikinnick into his pipe but he did not join him. "Does my brother have no kinnikinnick?" Big Oak asked.

"We have had no tobacco in many moons, Big Oak," he said. "We are the last of the Ganonsyoni in this place. You see that we are packing, and we will soon be going west."

"Is it wise to do so when there is war?" Big Oak asked.

"We want no part of war," Long Hunter replied. "But, my brother, we can no longer stay here. Scarcely does a moon pass without a white man coming through to tell us that the Indians must live on the other side of the mountains. When we tell them that this is our land, they always say, 'No longer,' and we must be gone soon.

"Often, when we hunt, we hear the sound of the big tomahawk chopping down trees. What was forest yesterday is field today. If we go to the house of a white man and ask for food, we are driven away. They get angry when they see us, and treat us bad, yet in their eyes I see fear."

In his eyes Big Oak saw sadness. Jinja had been listening, saying nothing. Big Oak gave Long Hunter his pouch of kinnikinnick. The Seneca took a clump and filled his pipe with it. He beckoned to his wife, who was standing over a steaming kettle. She ignited a small burning stick in the fire and brought it to Long Hunter, who handed the stick to Big Oak. Soon both were puffing away, contented.

"Long Hunter," said Jinja, "I am Gingego, grandson of Big Oak." The Seneca's eyes widened in recognition of the Mohawk name. "I have been west. Is there a place there where you would go?"

"We do not know."

"Beyond the mountains, between the lake of the panther people and the Spay-Lay-Wi-Theepi, was to be red man land, so said the English and then the Americans. But the hunger for land is great among the Americans and they fly across the mountains like great flocks of pigeons. At first the American chiefs tried to stop them, but there were so many of them that now the chiefs send soldiers to fight the Twightwees and make another treaty. When you go west, go far to the west, and then to the lakes."

"The Menominees," Big Oak added. "Go to the Menominees. They are good people."

Long Hunter's face froze like stone. "The Menominees—no! I will go to the Senecas. We are still a mighty people. We have not yet been defeated and scattered. Somewhere there is still a Longhouse."

"Then go to Canada. That is where many of them are. I have heard there are those still in New York, but the white men will not let them remain."

"That is what Blue Flower says," said Long Hunter, inclining his head toward his wife. "Go to Canada. Better we be colder and away from the Americans."

"She is wise," Big Oak observed. "When are you leaving?"

"The creek is low. We must carry our canoes much of the way to the Genesee. But I can no longer bear the cruel words of the white men, and if we fight them, more white men will come to kill us. We will leave in the morning."

"Tomorrow morning we will head west to the Allegheny River," Big Oak said. "We would like to buy a canoe. Are there any Senecas left on the Allegheny?"

"I do not know. But I can tell you that we have a canoe hidden in a hollow by the river."

"I will buy it from you," Big Oak said, reaching into his pack for a piece of gold coin.

"This is good?" the Seneca asked, looking at the metal.

"It is very good," Big Oak said. "Describe to me the place where you have hidden the canoe."

15

THAT NIGHT IT BEGAN TO RAIN, HARD, AND the next morning the creek had a fine bed of water coursing between its banks. That was good, Long Hunter told his people. Perhaps they would not have to carry their canoes to the Genesee after all.

All the members of the three families said courteous good-byes to the Watleys, and launched the two canoes. Almost immediately they realized the canoes would not float far. They were too heavily loaded, and beyond the next bend the creek was not so high as they had hoped. There was no complaining. They unloaded the canoes, strapped the packs to their backs and those of the older children, and carried the canoes down the trail that led to the Genesee. Both the men and the women bore enormous burdens, but it never occurred to any of them to complain.

Big Oak watched them as they vanished silently into the forest. He turned to Thad. "Remember when General Sullivan spoke to us on the long march west," he said, "and talked about how we were clearing the Indians out of New York and making the land safe for Americans?"

Thad nodded.

Big Oak said nothing more. He didn't have to. Both he

and his oldest son were choked up on their memories. Now there were more than individuals gone who would never come again. Whole peoples were going, and there was nothing they could do about it.

Joanna walked up to them, looking ugly. Jinja braced himself for the unpleasantness he knew was about to come.

"Henri told me that you bought a canoe from the Senecas."

Big Oak nodded.

"Where is it?"

"Hidden in a hollow by the Allegheny River."

"You bought a canoe on the word of an Indian, without even seeing it?"

Big Oak saw Jinja open his mouth to say something to Joanna, but he lifted his hand and Jinja remained silent. The five of them began to walk, Joanna peppering Big Oak with choice invective and getting no response for her troubles until finally Henri smiled and said, "*Mon amie*, shut your mouth, please." And she did.

The following day they arrived at the Allegheny. It did not take them long to find the canoe, but the elm bark covering was rotten.

"I told you that you can't trust an Indian," Joanna sneered.

Big Oak just waved a hand. "We did not expect the bark to be in good shape," he said. "You stay here and don't let the canoe walk away." The four men took out their hatchets and went looking for a large, healthy elm. Within a few hours they had found one and cut it down, stripped the bark and done a good job stretching it over the framework of the canoe.

The next afternoon found them paddling down the Allegheny. All four men were stroking, more or less rhythmically, not working overly hard. This was a beautiful, colorful fall day, and in truth they were in no hurry. It was a long, winding voyage down the river to Pittsburgh. The closer they got, the more signs of settlement they found: clearings where there had been none, and fields of crops already harvested. Rarely did they see any white men, and not once did they spot an Indian.

When they finally hauled their canoe ashore just above the union of the Allegheny with the Monongahela, and walked into Pittsburgh, Big Oak could feel a sense of tension among the people on the streets. He had expected to find the frontier town he had seen nearly two decades before, the last time he and Thad had paddled west to trade with the Miamis. They left Henri with the canoe. That was fine with him; he had no desire to walk around a town teeming with strangers. He would only wind up in a fight.

Pittsburgh was swarming with people. Big Oak had survived on his ability to recognize people for what they were, and many of the people he saw walking the streets of Pittsburgh were not townspeople. "These people are frontier farmers," he said to Jinja, pointing at first to one man struggling with an ox cart, then to a family walking out of a store, then to a young boy untying a plow horse from a tree at the head of a dusty street. There was a field just across the river from the town, and in that field was a multitude of tents and shanties, dozens of them, mostly surrounded by hordes of dirty little children.

"Now what do you suppose is going on here?" he asked Thad. Thad couldn't say. Neither could Jinja, and he had no interest in Joanna's opinion, which at any rate she did not offer.

For all his experiences, Big Oak was a shy man on the streets of a strange town. He could not simply pick out a strange face and throw questions at it. People in towns sometimes said and did odd things when strangers asked questions of them. But long experiences with the military made him comfortable with men in uniform, so when he spotted a man wearing the epaulets of a U.S. Army officer, he approached him without concern.

"What is happening here, Captain?" he asked. The man was short and clean-shaven, neatly dressed, and he had an intelligent look on his face, which was more than Big Oak could say about most of the people he saw scurrying restlessly around the town. The army captain looked in a hurry himself, and he was about to give a disrespectful response. But Big Oak still had the sharp look in his eye that commanded respect, and the fine long rifle he carried as if it were a part of him reinforced the impression he made. The officer stopped, and in the dust of the crowded street the two men talked.

"Folks are comin' in here from out there, if you know what I mean," said the captain, pointing west. "The Injuns are runnin' wild out on the frontier, and these people are scared to death. To be honest, the folks livin' here ain't too comfortable either, and that's the truth of it."

"Well now, Captain, we're headin' that way, and if you could stand to be bought a pint, I'd be obliged if you'd tell me a thing or two."

"Traders, are you?" he asked, sizing the three men up immediately. The woman he couldn't tell about, but she was pretty. Wouldn't hurt to spend some time with these men and figure out where she fit in too.

He took them to the least crowded tavern. Big Oak sent Joanna back to Henri, and the four men found a table. The captain was disappointed, but at least there was no sign that any of the three traders were attached to her.

The table was raw, unfinished wood with splinters searching for unwary hands, but none of them paid any heed. The tavern owner pulled mugs of ale for them from the open keg and they brought them over to the table. "This place is nearly empty," the captain explained, "because most of the people camped in that field out yonder don't have the money to spend in a tavern."

"Are they runnin' from the Indians?" asked Big Oak.

"You can bet they're runnin' from the Injuns and that's a fact," the captain answered.

"Don't take offense by my next question, Captain, but is the army out trying to protect these folks?"

The captain scowled, then he smiled. "The army is not allowed to do a damned thing, old-timer, if you get my meanin'."

" 'Fraid not, Captain."

"It's the English," the captain explained. "Always the damned English."

Big Oak nodded. "*Always* the damned English," he agreed. "What are they doin' this time?"

"First, they're still manning the forts they should have cleared out of ten years ago. Second, they keep the Indians stirred up because they kind of think the Ohio Valley is still theirs."

"Well it isn't, and they know it," Thad interjected.

"They know it, but then you know the English. They'd like to make it so hard on us that we'd come back to them, beggin' on our knees for the king to tie a rope around our necks and put us on a leash, right?"

"That is the English," Big Oak conceded.

"The president of these United States is sending a peace mission up to the Northwest to talk to the Indians and make a new agreement. He does not want to see any fights between us and the English, or between us and the Indians, because he does not want to get them mad. So we sit scratchin' our arses in our garrisons while the Injuns set fire to the whole damned frontier."

"Are they really out there raising holy hell?" asked Jinja. The captain gave the younger man a slow smile but said nothing.

"And they get their ammunition from the English?" Thad asked.

"They get anything they want or need from the English, and that's the damned truth. What we need is another bloody war against the English to knock 'em out of Canada. Ain't a day goes by that they're not hatchin' new plans to destroy us. If they had it their way, the Injuns would be tearin' up Philadelphia right now. You know, they're fixin' to have war in Europe again, and the English are sure we'll side with France over here."

Thad laughed. "English, French, Spanish, they're all the same. They'd sell us out in a minute if they thought it'd put money in their treasury."

"Now you've got the truth of it, man," the captain replied, banging a hand on the table. "But the president can't see this. He says we are not to fight the Indians no matter what they do to our people—at least not until they have their meeting with the Indians and the English."

"The English are gonna be at these meetings?" Big Oak was aghast.

"The Indians won't come without the English. They don't trust us, you see."

"I can understand that," Big Oak said. "I just can't believe they'd trust the English."

"Gotta trust somebody," said Jinja.

Big Oak stroked his short-trimmed beard. "I don't know," he said. "Up until that last time we fought the French, the Iroquois were pretty good at playin' the French against the English. Maybe the Miamis are tryin' to do the same with us and the English."

"I don't know about that, Big Oak," Jinja said.

"Nor I," added Thad. "Too many frontier folks over the mountains, crowdin' in on the Shawnees and the Twightwees and the Mingoes. I believe they're so worried about us that every other white man looks like their friend, especially the English because they give them so much."

"Isn't polite to let a man buy you ale without at least learnin' his name," the captain said abruptly.

"My name's Sam Watley, but the Indians call me Big Oak. This is my son Thad, and this is my grandson Jinja. The wench is Joanna something, and don't let the pretty face fool you."

"Well, I *was* wonderin'—"

"We know you was wonderin'. She ain't attached to any one of us. She kind of fancies one of Thad's traders. They're back around our canoe together. No tellin' what they're planning. I know it's hard to believe when you see a girl like that, but she'll give a man a good bit of devil in the belly."

"I was just wonderin'—"

"And you're still wonderin', otherwise you wouldn't keep sayin' that. I'd say if you want her, she's yours, but I don't want to get ol' Henri mad. He'd probably want to fight you, and then either you'd kill him or he'd kill you. Either way we'd lose him, and we'd just as soon keep him."

The captain nodded and smiled. "There's no shortage of girls around here, with new folks comin' in almost every day."

"Well now, you know our name but you haven't told us yours."

"Captain Joseph Renwick, Pennsylvania militia." He finished his brew, stood up and stretched. "I wouldn't go out there if I was you," he said. "Those Injuns are powerful mad. They know that our commissioners are gonna try to get them to give up more land, at least out to the Muskingum, maybe clear out to the Wabash. And I don't think they want to give up an acre more."

"Yup," Big Oak said. "They give up enough already. Thing is, you got the Miamis, the Shawnees, the Wyandots. Then you got the lake tribes. Then you got the Iroquois that we just squeezed out. These tribes have never hung together before and I don't think they'll hang together now."

Captain Renwick hammered the table again. "That's the truth of it!" he exclaimed. "Damned if it ain't. But there's a little more to it than that. They've stirred up the Creeks and the Chickamaugas. If we don't watch out, we're gonna have Indian wars solid from the lakes down to the Gulf of Mexico."

"Look at me, Captain," said Big Oak. "What do you see?"

"Old man in deerskins."

"That's the truth of it!" Big Oak chuckled. "I've fought my share of Indian wars. Sometimes with 'em. Sometimes against 'em. Usually with 'em and against 'em in the same battle. Now I ain't sayin' that it ain't gonna happen. I'm sayin' it never happened yet. Just when you think they've finally figured out that if they don't get together we'll run 'em clear across the big river, that's when they decide—again—that they hate each other worse than they hate us."

Captain Renwick's face froze in an annoyed squint. "Just a moment here, old man," he said. "You say you used to fight on the side of Indians?"

Big Oak laughed. "I was adopted into the Senecas. I fought with the Mohawks against the French and against the Caughnawagas. The Iroquois are my brothers." He studied the captain's face and decided the man harbored hostile thoughts. "I also fought in the war for independence, and so did these two boys here."

"On whose side?"

"Tell you something, Captain. I am an American, don't doubt it. But I'd like to see us let the Indians alone for a change."

"What should we do, let 'em slaughter our frontier farmers? That's what's happening right now," growled Renwick.

"Let me ask you one thing, Captain. Did you see anyone pickin' them people up by the hind end and throwin' them across the mountains? I know them people. They pick up and go. Then they stay awhile, and they pick up and go again. You know why? Because makin' a farm pay is hard work and you gotta keep at it for years and years. They ain't got the patience. They stay for a couple of years and the land don't get on its knees and yield forth plenty, so on they go to the next river bottom just hopin' that this time it'll be easier. Why, I seen folks with fine farms in the middle of Pennsylvania sell everything and head out West just to find another piece of land to squat on. I swear, they'd rather build a cabin and clear stumps than plow a perfectly good field. I'm tellin' you, they got no more sense than a bullfrog."

"I'll tell *you* something, Watley. I'm a white man and I favor my own kind. It might be that them folks are where they ought not be, but when it comes time to take sides, I'm gonna side with my own. A savage is a savage, after all. It might be that a frontier farmer got no sense, but there's a chance his children might. A savage, on the other hand, ten generations from now, he still won't have no sense."

Big Oak wanted to argue with him, but he thought about all the generations of red men who had seen the whites push them farther and farther west, and still they hung on to their old revenge quarrels as if they were precious traditions. "Damned if you ain't right!" snapped Big Oak.

Renwick looked closely at Big Oak, trying to see if the

old man was making fun of him, but what he saw was a man perplexed.

"Nice meeting you, Captain. It seems that when the Americans meet the Indians in battle, someone gets slaughtered. I hope when your turn comes, your army will be ready to fight."

"And when that time comes, Watley, whose side will you be on?"

"I'm an American," Big Oak repeated. But there was a touch of sadness in his voice.

They bought a few provisions that afternoon, but not much. They didn't need much. The following morning the five of them shoved off and made their way into the Ohio River. Big Oak and Thad recalled their first journey down the Ohio twenty years before. They had gone with a pack train then, and scarcely saw a white face west of Pittsburgh. Now, well-established farms clung to the fertile lowlands along the Ohio.

Along the broad, winding Ohio they paddled. Four strong pairs of arms made the bow of the canoe sing as it sliced through the turbid waters. In perfect unison they stroked, never missing their time when they switched sides. Their breath came strong and easy, and their muscles rippled beneath their deerskins. The days were cool, and yet the sweat rolled in waves down their faces and sometimes soaked through to the surface of their shirts.

As a team of paddlers, the four men formed a confederacy that paid little attention to Joanna, who sat in the middle of the canoe in silence. If she marveled at the brilliant colors of the fall or took pleasure in the efforts of her strong companions, she did not show it. By night she and Henri always made their beds near each other and away from the others. They would talk in whispers until the others were asleep. Then at last they would nod off. Big Oak, who needed, and took, less sleep than anybody, often pretended to sleep, and listened hard to make out what the two might have been saying to each other. Big Oak was not nosy, he was suspicious. In his life he had felt fortunate in the women he had known, but occasionally he found one that bordered on what he called difficult, and he had concluded that Joanna was one of those. He was almost disappointed to discover that Joanna was working hard to talk Henri into a lasting relationship, and Henri was trying hard to talk Joanna into his blanket. Big Oak sensed that gradually a bargain was being struck.

Day by day Thad watched his father shake off the rust that came from years of careless, easy living followed by hollow grief. His back straightened and the black veil over his heart lifted. Big Oak checked the priming of his rifle more often now, and began to trim his beard with greater care, although there was nobody around that he was preening for.

One morning Big Oak awoke before the rest of them and shot a wild goose far enough away from camp not to alarm them. By the time they were up, he had plucked the goose, cut it in pieces, and handed it to Joanna, who began to roast it over a fire. This might be the last free day, Jinja had announced the night before. They were coming close to the end of civilization, he said. "This is where frontier people begin to get touchy because the woods just might come alive at night."

"Then this ought to be the end of our canoe journey," Big Oak declared.

"Are we gonna walk from here?" Joanna moaned, balling her hands into fists.

"Maybe," Big Oak replied. It was easier to travel in secrecy by land than by water. On the other hand, traveling on a wide river had its advantages, and it was certainly easier. Big Oak shrugged off his annoyance with this impossible woman and chewed on the stem of his pipe. "Tell you what we might do," he said. "Startin' tomorrow, we can travel mostly by night."

"In a canoe?" she asked.

"In a canoe," he replied. "Just for you, my dear. With a little bit of luck we can make it all the way down the river to the stockade before the Indians know we're there. After all, the river does not leave a trail."

In the forest the best of men is half blind. Had Big Oak known that they had already been discovered, they could have saved themselves the time they lost by being stealthy and cautious.

16

WHILE JOANNA WAS COOKING GOOSE IN what Jinja still supposed was American-dominated territory, two formidable young Mingo braves studied the party of woodsmen from across the river.

In the mix of red cultures that stewed in the Ohio Valley it was inevitable that men from other tribes would join this aggressive, rebellious strain of the Senecas. Delawares, Shawnees, and Miamis, among others, found their way to the fires of the Mingoes. And so it was not surprising that the two friends who on this day skulked in the tree line across the river were a Shawnee called Sees the Moon and a young man of Seneca parents known as Badger.

Both of these braves had fought in the great Miami defeat of St. Clair. For each it was their first great conflict. Their village high up on the Muskingum had been fortunate enough to avoid association with whites for many years, and their mutual hatred of the Americans had prevented the various tribal entities from engaging in the fratricidal raids that won honors for young warriors.

For many years the village elders had counseled caution, but recently war chiefs had arisen in the village to defy them. The young warriors had so little war experience that the old ones had their way, until one day a message had arrived from the Miamis requesting that the men of the village head west to fight the white soldiers. The old ones tried to get their restless sons and grandsons to stay home, until they heard word that men from all the Northwest tribes were coming to the Glaize in huge numbers. Then they smiled, and not only did they approve of the action, some of the old ones joined. Badger and Sees the Moon had lost their way and missed the first battle, but the second had provided them with their first scalps and a confidence they would hold on to until their dying day.

They could smell the goose cooking across the river. "They must think that the whites have already driven us west from this place," Badger said softly to Sees the Moon. The two were almost the same age, about seventeen years, but their appearances were very different. Badger was about middle height and thin as a shadow, while Sees the Moon was three inches shorter, thickly muscled around the chest and arms and thick around the middle. Badger wore the traditional Seneca scalp lock, while Sees the Moon wore his hair long and flowing. Badger's eyes and hair were dark as a moonless night. Sees the Moon had hazel eyes and a touch of brown to his hair, evidence that somewhere in his past there had been a white parent. The language they spoke to each other was closest to the Seneca dialect, though it contained bits and pieces of several tongues.

"Do you think that just the two of us could take all of them?" Badger asked.

"If we waited for the right moment, all their scalps would be ours," Sees the Moon responded with assurance.

"And yet it is something we should not try to do," Badger insisted.

They crawled away from the tree line, deeper into the woods. It made no sense to risk being seen when they knew where their enemy was without having to watch them.

"My brother," Sees the Moon said in a voice tinged with disgust. "The mighty Iroquois have been too close for too long to the white man. You remember his victories and you forget his defeats."

"Ah, there you are mistaken," Badger said. "We remember his defeats all too well. My father told me that in the war against the French and their red allies, the English were defeated again and again. And yet they were stubborn and they won the war. He told me that later, when the Americans fought against their king, almost the only battle the Americans won was the final battle."

"But never did they suffer such a loss as the battle you and I fought together, Badger," Sees the Moon said with pride.

"My father says they will not stay defeated. He says that Joseph Brant believes we should make peace with the Americans."

"Ah, yes, your Joseph Brant."

"He is not Seneca. He is Mohawk."

"He is of the Longhouse. Once a great war chief, now a peace chief. They say he is in the pay of the Americans."

"That is foolish. He lives on Grand River, in Canada, under the English. But he knows how hard it is to defeat the Americans. He has learned all about the Americans."

Sees the Moon studied the face of his lanky friend, looking for signs of insanity. "My brother," he said. "Has your father not told you that there will be no stopping place for these people? They want all the land. Brant knows that. That is why some believe the Americans pay him. Tecumseh believes that Brant is too much of a white man. He speaks their tongue and can scratch their words on skin. He has been across the big water. He follows the horse that scrapes the earth. Tecumseh says that as long as life is good for Brant, he does not care that the rest of us suffer by being made to live like white men—poor white men," Sees the Moon added.

"Still, there is supposed to be a truce now," Badger insisted. "Until the conference up on Erie Lake."

"Look at them." Sees the Moon pointed through the trees and across the river at the traders who sat breakfasting on wild goose. "Their treaty said they were not to come to this country. That was in the days of my grandfather. Why should we keep our word? This truce just gives them more time to send farmers to fill up our land."

Badger knew his friend was right. He said nothing. Sees the Moon pursued his advantage. "We are not bound by the word of our peace chiefs," he asserted.

"Still, we do not want to be the ones to start a fight. Let us follow them and see where they are bound. Perhaps they are going south. The Cherokees and the Chickasaws have not yet had their fill of the white man."

Sees the Moon agreed. "But if there is just the right moment to attack them," he added, "then we should make them ours."

Badger thought in silence for a few moments. "Have you seen their rifles?" he asked.

"I am sure that they can shoot. But can they shoot in their sleep? We will follow them. And we will see."

Big Oak and his group rested for the next five hours. It was nearly noon before they shoved their canoe out on the river. They paddled toward the middle and kept a steady, swift course downstream. In motion through the woods without a trail, far enough away from the river that they would not be noticed, the two Mingoes were hard pressed to maintain contact. For nearly five hours the paddlers continued at a rapid pace, until the twilight. The Mingoes had expected the canoers to come ashore for the night, but they continued to paddle, albeit more slowly and carefully.

With less need to conceal themselves, the Mingoes moved closer to the tree line, then stopped and listened. Only their finely tuned senses allowed them to hear the soft paddle strokes of the canoers. "Two are paddling," Sees the Moon whispered. Now they could walk at a slower pace, quietly, always listening.

Halfway through the long night the two young Mingoes came upon a succession of creeks that emptied into the river. They were not mighty cataracts, but they were noisy enough to obscure the nearly inaudible sounds of the paddlers. Big Oak heard the creeks too, on both sides of the river, and so did Jinja. Instinctively they picked up their stroke.

Sees the Moon and Badger tried to keep contact by maintaining their steady pace even though it meant slogging through streams in the dark. Each one of them fell and got wet, which was no casual matter when the cold winds blew through the trees and beneath their damp deerskin jackets. They had been walking through the woods for more than ten hours now and wanted to rest, but they dared not let the canoe go. With the dogged determination common to their tribes, they continued, until they were beyond the succession of streams.

They stopped to listen, and heard nothing but the low hiss of the wind in the trees.

"Do you think they may have come ashore?" Badger asked.

"No," answered Sees the Moon with conviction. "If you were on the water, paddling slowly to make as little noise as possible, would you not paddle faster where there was noise along the shore?"

Badger agreed that he would. The men they were trailing were experienced woodsmen. Surely they were capable of thinking that way. The two Mingoes picked up the pace and moved through the woods in an easy lope, dodging trees as they came close to them and lifting their feet to avoid tripping over roots. Their pattern was to lope about a hundred yards and listen. Then another hundred or so yards and listen again. They did this for several miles and never heard the telltale paddle strokes.

They were discouraged. Had the whites paddled ashore? Or had they awakened the others and the four paddled so hard that they were even farther down the river? They had the current with them, so such things were possible. The two young braves decided to continue their lope through the woods for another hour or two. Surely they would overtake the canoe. Then they could lie in wait for it, and when the dawn came and the whites were exhausted and careless, they could kill all of them and bring their scalps to the village. And the fine rifles—the finest they had ever seen, they could tell that, even from a distance. On they ran, carefully, following the bends and loops of the river, tired, but hardened to the rigors of long pursuit.

Badger and Sees the Moon had run into a bit of bad luck. After the long stretch of hard paddling, it occurred to Thad that there was no need to hurry down the river in the middle of an exceedingly dark night, when a canoe might catch a snag that would rip the bottom out of it. Big Oak agreed, so they decided to let the canoes drift with the current for a while, taking care only to keep the vessel from drifting toward shore. The two Mingoes had passed them in the midst of this drift.

The beginnings of dawn found Badger and Sees the Moon several miles ahead of the canoe. In their hearts they felt that they had passed the canoe somewhere in the middle of the night, but they could not be certain. The only thing they did know was that there were no rivers the whites could have turned onto along the way. Their quarry were still on the Ohio, all right. Now all they had to do was wait.

At the first fingers of dawn they found a hillside that commanded a view of at least three bends of the river. At the top of this hill they made camp, dining on cold corn and water. They found a perfect place from which to watch the river without themselves being observed. They had not slept in nearly twenty-four hours. It felt good to sit in the grass with their backs up against stout, comfortable tree trunks.

They awoke five hours later, the mid-morning sun boring its way through their eyelids, fiery like a stern war chief castigating them for their carelessness. On their first warpath in which they and no others were totally responsible for their action, they had truly messed up. Now where were the whites? Surely past them farther downriver. But how far downriver? By now they had figured out that the whites were resting in the daytime. Would they be able to spot their camp? "We'll have to try," Sees the Moon insisted. The more easygoing Badger submitted, although by now he would have been pleased just to go home and wait for the call to war that was bound to come before long. They walked along the tree line, their eyes sharp for signs of the white men across the river, walked for half the day without spotting any signs of them.

During wartime Big Oak had always traveled as if the enemy were on his trail. His caution had saved his life numerous times. On this day they had carried the canoe more than a hundred yards into the woods on the Kentucky side. Jinja knew that by now the land on the north side of the river was well into hostile territory. They lit no fires. They spoke in the softest whispers. And they posted two guards on four-hour shifts.

So sometime in the late morning the two Mingoes loping briskly along the opposite shore passed the traders again. They were out of food, and hunger was clawing at their bellies. They could not betray their presence by hunting, and they could not abandon their pursuit to forage for roots. As they crossed a cool creek, they slaked their thirst with water, but their hunger persisted. They pushed it to the back of their minds until late in the afternoon.

"We must have passed them by now," Badger declared. "We have to wait for them now."

His friend agreed. While Sees the Moon kept his eye on the river, Badger took to the woods to look for something edible. About an hour later he returned with a few walnuts and hickory nuts, a meager assortment that had somehow escaped the squirrels. The shells of the walnuts were thick, hard, and small. The hickory nuts were no better. They made do with very little, lying on the ground behind the trunk of a big old beech tree, watching the river as the sun made its last glowing appearance of the day over the hills to the southwest.

When darkness was complete, they moved to the flood plain, as close to the river as possible, so they would be able to detect any signs of the canoe. Late as the season was, the night was not too cold for the mosquitoes and gnats. It being well into fall, the two young warriors had neglected to bring their bear grease with them. Now, the insects landed and bit. The Mingoes did not scratch or slap.

They did not have to tell each other that, weary as they were, they simply could not sleep until they knew where the white men were. Over the past few days they had traveled many miles and slept little. They were so weary that sleep grabbed at them with an iron grip, and yet they shook it off again and again as the quarter moon drifted across the sky and the river remained silent and deserted.

Long after midnight Sees the Moon thought he heard a sound on the river. He peered into the deep gloom, thought he saw something upriver. At first he felt he must have been mistaken, for the object did not appear to move. But as it approached the bend it turned enough to present a broadside view. Now its outline was apparent to both of the warriors. It was not close. It was so far out on the river that only its motion made it visible to the sharp-eyed Shawnee and Seneca.

"What do we do now?" Badger asked.

Sees the Moon thought for a moment. "If we can get any kind of shot at them, we should shoot. There is no danger that they could pursue us. If they attempted to, we could wait at the trees and ambush them as they come running across the flood plain, or we could disappear deep into the woods. I have yet to see a white man who could track a red man in the clear light of day. It is the dead of night. The whites will be surprised."

They waited for the canoe to come abreast of where they lay. The boat was two hundred yards out, a hopeless shot in the light of the dim crescent moon, but Sees the Moon had been sleeping so little lately that his judgment was poor.

Big Oak and Jinja were paddling. Thad and Henri were asleep, their chins on their chests as they sat on the canoe bottom. It was Big Oak who was looking to his right when two spears of fire flashed out from the shore, followed by two explosions.

"Grab your paddles, boys," said Big Oak, digging his into the water and moving the river past the canoe. Almost immediately the four men were paddling hard, in unison, heading for the next bend. Badger and Sees the Moon scrambled to their feet and ran along the shore, trying to reload as they ran, but in the dark it was a nearly impossible chore. They got the job done, but just as they were drawing a bead on the canoe it disappeared around a bend. Sees the Moon was not about to give up. He sprinted along the flood plain, followed by his friend, until he thought he saw the canoe plainly. He fired again, and like the first time, overshot the craft by so much that none of those on board heard the bullet as it flew over them or the swift *ffft* as it hit the water and plowed itself into oblivion.

They continued to run hard alongside the river. Badger missed the pan when he tried to dump primer into it, then tripped and went sprawling. He was up instantly, following his Shawnee brother. The flood plain vanished and they found themselves climbing a bluff. The going got steep and their run slowed down to a crawl. They continued upward, then ran along the bluff, their nostrils flared, their chests rising and falling, forcing their weary legs along. They could not see the canoe now, but they were sure it was still out there. Then, abruptly, Sees the Moon came to a halt. Far below, well around the next bend, in the glow of the quarter moon on the river, he could make out the rhythmic stroke of four strong paddlers. He exhaled wearily through his mouth and stood there, wobbling, the butt of his rifle resting beside his foot.

The bluff now became a downhill slope. Down they ran until they were nearly abreast of the canoe. They stopped and tried to aim their rifles at the canoes, but their chests were heaving so after their long run that the barrels wove in circles before their eyes. They dropped to one knee and waited. By the time they had caught their breath, the canoe had disappeared around still another bend. Up they jumped, jogging slowly along the bank, trying to save their breath for better-aimed shots. By now the canoe had veered farther away from them, but if they just had a little luck, maybe they might hit one of the paddlers. If they hit one right, he might tip over the whole canoe. The whites would be defenseless then. They'd probably lose their guns and starve to death in the wilderness, if they managed to make it to shore. Badger and Sees the Moon had heard rumors that some white men could not even swim.

There was a right-hand bend next, with a spit that protruded into the river. The spit had tall grass on it, and if they could make it there before the canoe, they might have a very good chance to fire from a hidden position at short range. They broke into a sprint, leaping over fallen wood and large rocks, found the spit and laid down in the weeds. They could see the canoe rounding the bend, the bow pointed almost straight at them. They checked their priming and waited for the canoe to come closer. There was no hurry, they could wait until the moment the canoe began to veer in order to round the spit. Their fingers tightened on their triggers.

And suddenly the dim light of the moon was no more. The night had been nearly cloudless. They weren't thinking of clouds. They were thinking only of the canoe and the hated enemy it held. For a moment they lay still and hoped that the cloud would pass. Then they looked up and saw that the cloud was a front. The moon would hide for a long time. They crawled up to the edge of the spit and listened. If the canoe sounded close enough, they could fire at the sounds and trust to luck.

They listened, but they heard no sound. In the pitch-darkness the whites had stopped paddling and looked for the current to carry them downriver in the dark. They continued to listen, minute after minute. Finally, Sees the Moon breathed an exasperated sigh. "Let's head downriver," he persisted. Badger looked at him as if he were crazy.

"Here is what *I* will do," said Badger. "I will run three more bends with you. Then I will wrap my blanket around me and go to sleep. They will do the same. When I wake up, I will decide whether these whites are too smart or too lucky to pursue. I hope you will agree to do the same."

Badger, like the creature he was named for, could be very tough and stubborn. Sees the Moon had no choice. They began to trek west along the winding bank. Before they had gone a mile the rains came, very hard, very cold. There was no refuge for them. Tired, half starved, their feathers drooping in the rain, they found a rock shelf barely big enough to shelter a small part of their bodies. There they stayed, their blankets wrapped around them, nearly as wet as they were.

Meanwhile Big Oak led his party to the opposite shore. They turned the canoe over and propped the sides up with large rocks and fallen tree branches. Four of them slept, while Big Oak sat up and kept watch under the canoe. They passed the rest of the night considerably drier than their pursuers.

17

KEN WATLEY, ALSO KNOWN AS KENDEE BIG Oak, was a little of this, a little of that. The second of Big Oak and Cilla's three sons, he was the most intelligent and introspective. Big Oak had been more careless raising these three boys than he had been when he was Thad's only living parent. Consequently, the three had little formal education, which was fine for Caleb and Joshua. Those two learned to read and write a little, enough sums to do some trading, and a white man's English. But they picked up a lot more in the way of woods lore and the Longhouse view of the world.

Ken was another story. While his brothers haunted the trails of northern New York, he spent time in the warehouses of Wendel and Watley, and in the home of Jinja's grandfather, Dieter. It tickled Dieter to have this young, dark, Big Oak progeny around. His friends would make caustic remarks about Dieter's savage friend, then Dieter would ask Ken to explain to them the current trade conditions. Ken would give them a rundown on the availability of prime otter pelts, the current demand for kettles and strouds, and the temperament of the various tribes. They'd leave Dieter's house impressed with the old merchant's savage.

Everybody assumed that Ken, like Thad before him, would wind up on the white side of the blanket. What most of them did not know was that when Ken was not in Albany, he was with his brothers visiting their Tuscarora relatives south of Lake Ontario. Usually they brought plenty of food with them. Their aunts and uncles lived on poor land. After the Revolution, they tried to get decent land from what had been the land of the Mohawks—not much, just a few hundred acres that they could make a living off. But all that land went to the whites, and never mind that the Tuscaroras had been loyal to the Revolution. And so Ken's aunts and uncles continued to struggle in the summer and starve in the winter.

Ken, like his brothers, turned bitter toward the government of New York and the grasping speculators who took control of so much of that land. Several years after the end of the Revolution, he asked his grandfather to do something to help his in-laws. Big Oak thought about it for a while, and decided to buy some land for them. He inquired around and was steered to the office of land sales in Albany. It was located in a downtown office building that was a converted old residence. Behind the crumbling brick facade the interior had been newly plastered, and the furniture was beautiful English imported, probably confiscated from wealthy Tories. Unfortunately, Big Oak's fame and reputation were such that the secretary knew all too much about him.

"I'd like to buy some farmland among the Finger Lakes," he told the secretary.

"Have you grown tired of your pond, Watley?" the secretary asked him.

"You might say so, sir. It's too hilly and rocky to do any real farming up there."

"Since when have you wanted to trade your trail pack for a plow?" the secretary had asked.

Big Oak shrugged his shoulders. "I'm getting too old for the trail. I'd like to have a place that could support my family."

"You have three young sons, do you not?"

Big Oak nodded, surprised. He was always surprised how well-known he was to the people of Albany.

"Three Indian sons?"

"They are *my* sons!" Big Oak replied, feeling his neck turn warm. "No more or less Indian than my son Thad, who is the president of the largest trading company in Albany."

"I know Thad," replied the secretary, backpedaling. Big Oak waited patiently while the secretary collected his thoughts. "I must study the records to find out where land might be available for you," he said, and Big Oak believed him. "If you would come back in three days, I will be able to suggest some possibilities."

Big Oak agreed to return in three days. A half hour after the old trader left his office, the secretary dispatched a messenger to Thad, who immediately put on his coat and walked the three blocks between his office and that of the secretary.

"Have you heard," said the secretary once Thad was seated in the most comfortable chair, "that your father is planning to move west among the lakes?"

Thad clasped his hands comfortably across his belly and chuckled. "Did he give a reason?"

"Said he wanted to farm."

Now the chuckle became a laugh. "He would no more farm than would a young Mohawk war chief."

"He was in here looking for land to buy west of here—a place for his family, he said."

"His wife's family more likely."

"The Tuscaroras?"

Thad nodded. He had no use for Tuscaroras. Although he had been a patriot and fought against his Seneca forebears, after the war he had acquired their disdain for the Oneidas and Tuscaroras, who had broken up the ancient Iroquois confederacy by siding with the Americans. Especially did he despise the Tuscaroras, who had only in this century moved up from the Carolinas to join the confederacy. It was too much for him to tolerate the idea of Tuscaroras living on land that had been confiscated from Senecas and Cayugas, even if he had himself helped to dispossess them of those lands.

He shook his head. "Roger," he said, "if you sell him land out there, you'll have a Tuscarora village in the middle of hundreds of whites who survived Mohawk marauders during the Revolution. I don't think they'll stand for it."

"That's what I thought," said the secretary. "But how do I refuse to sell land to Big Oak?"

"You don't refuse. You lie to him. Tell him it's all gone. If you want, you tell him that there's still some land left up here." He walked over to a map on the wall and pointed to a spot not far from the current Tuscarora holdings. "He'll growl back at you, tell you that of course that land hasn't been bought up, it's no good for anything. But he'll believe you, and you won't get any trouble from him."

Years later Ken heard the story from Dieter. He had not told his father because it would have been wrong to stir up bad blood between Big Oak and Thad, but he had never forgiven Thad for his betrayal, even though Thad was always kind to him. As long as his mother had been alive, he did not act on his anger toward the new republic, but now that his mother was gone, he and his brothers were determined to right a few wrongs.

Ken was moving along the south bank of the Ohio River when he heard a sound he had often heard in Albany, the sound of white men arguing. At Big Oak Pond his parents and his brothers always spoke softly to each other. Even in the Longhouse villages he had never seen men stand face-to-face and shout at each other as if they were standing across the Te-non-an-at-che from one another.

He had left his brothers whiling away the bad weather in a Twightwee village on the Auglaize River and headed south to the Spay-Lay-Wi-Theepi for no very good reason. He had run into no white men on his journey, so he was frankly surprised to hear the voices rising high above the wind that blew through the poplars from the west.

The voices were so close that he lay on the forest floor and crawled toward the noise until he could see them, three men standing so close together that their frozen breaths rose as one from their midst. They were all shouting at once, their words coming in such a confused torrent that at first he could not understand anything that was being shouted. Gradually their passions subsided enough for them to listen, but they still had no love for each other.

"We'd have our bellies full at least if we'd stayed at Fort Jefferson!" screamed one in the face of another, whose ragged blue tunic he held with both hands. The three men were of a type, a little above medium height, a lot below medium weight. All three had a week's worth of scraggly beard, and all three wore uniforms so uniquely tattered that they certainly weren't uniform.

"If we stayed there they'd be sendin' us back out into the woods. Injun bait! That's what we'd be."

"Where do you think we are now? What do you think we are now?"

Now the third one spoke up. He didn't even have a hat, and one of the sleeves was completely gone from his tunic. He was wrapped in a blanket to ward off the cold. "At least we're headin' home," he said, speaking more softly than his cohorts. "Headin' away from them damned Injuns. I hope I never see another one as long as I live."

Ken would have been happy to oblige the three deserters. They had obviously had a belly full of the frontier and posed no further danger to the coalition of tribes that remained in the field. He was no natural killer. His mother had called him the most peaceable of her three sons. But then the deserter who had regretted leaving the fort had one more thing to say.

"I wish I had just one of them red devils under my nose right now," he said. "I'd cut his heart out."

This one time Ken let his emotions get the best of him. He saw only that his rifle was in his hands, loaded and primed, and that their weapons were stacked thirty yards away from where they stood. And he stepped out into the clearing, like an apparition from hell summoned by their most dreaded thoughts.

"Well what do we have here?" asked the one who wanted to perform the surgery. Ken was wearing woodsman's skins, and a floppy brimmed hat that threw his face into shadow.

"One of them red devils you were talking about," Ken replied, tilting his hat back.

They still did not get it. "You come from the fort?" asked another.

"If I had the chance, I'd burn the fort down," said Ken.

"Me too," said the third deserter. "The army can go to hell."

"You can say that again," came a voice from the west side of the clearing, and abruptly, four more men, clean-shaven and dressed in well-kept soldier uniforms, appeared in the clearing.

"Who in hell are you?" asked one of the deserters.

"Depends on what you are," replied the biggest one, who wore the uniform of a sergeant. "If you're peaceable, we're your escorts back to the fort. If you're in the mood for a quarrel, we're your executioners."

The silence hung suspended in the chill air. The three deserters stood frozen, looking as if there were already a noose around their necks.

"And who is this one?" The sergeant asked, pointing at Ken. Feeling that the question was not addressed to him, Ken was silent. But the deserters also declined to answer, since they didn't really know the answer and could not imagine how answering could save their necks.

"Ken Watley," Big Oak's son answered finally.

"And what are you doing here?"

"I'm a scout," was the only response Ken could come up with.

"You are. Speak pretty good English for an Injun."

"Half Injun," Ken said.

"Who you scout for?"

"Colonel Potter, sir," Ken responded, forcing himself to speak with respect he did not feel.

"Don't know a Colonel Potter," said the sergeant, starting to unsling his musket. In spite of himself, Ken felt ice water at the bottom of his belly.

"You will in a few weeks, sir. He's formin' a new army in Pittsburgh right now." Ken had no confidence that the sergeant would buy that, and the sergeant's eyes told him that he was right. He stood as relaxed as he could, but he knew that his life might be hanging in the balance. He measured the distance to the tree line—about four running steps. What he had going for him was that he was standing on the other side of the clearing from the three deserters. The sergeant's men had their muskets pointed at the deserters, but the sergeant now had his musket in hand, and in a moment he would be pointing it at Ken.

Ken's eyes and ears were missing nothing. The range was short, but the sergeant's musket was not cocked. Still too chancy to risk a run, not yet.

One of the deserters shifted his feet nervously. In doing so he kicked a rock, which hit a stick, which crunched a couple of leaves. The sergeant shifted his gaze for just a moment. Ken bolted.

"Damn!" shouted the sergeant, raising his musket and cocking it, but Kendee took three, four steps, put a large tree between him and the sergeant, and sprinted through the woods, dodging trees right and left. A single shot rang out, but the tree that caught the sergeant's bullet was so far behind Ken that he never heard it hit. He did hear the sergeant shout for two of his men to cover the deserters while he and Private Wirtz went after the Injun.

Ken could hear two sets of footsteps crunching the dry leaves of the woods. His strong legs, his light pack, and his moccasins easily outdistanced the ponderous, heavily laden sergeant and private. Two hundred yards led him to a creek, which he jumped without touching water. He found rock that left no trail, sprinted hard along a downhill stretch, then loped on level ground for about a mile before he stopped and lay down behind a huge old beech tree.

He could hear nothing but the wind in the bare trees. These were no woodsmen. Had they been anywhere near him, he would have heard their footfalls in the leaves, probably heard them yelling to each other or cursing the tree roots that tripped them up every other step. He knew that he had them beaten, but now that the danger was past, he felt the sting of humiliation.

He had been routed like a squirrel by a handful of uniformed soldiers. He remembered all the campfires, all the years of listening to the tales of Mohawks who had ambushed and routed Continentals, or Oneidas who had ambushed and routed English foot soldiers. And now four soldiers on the prowl for deserters had forced him to take to his heels as if he were being pursued by the entire Nadowessioux nation. He felt humiliated.

He sat and drank from an army canteen he had seized during the last great victorious battle, and chewed on a strip of dried deer meat. He could not let the matter rest. In the village on the Auglaize, beside his brothers, there was a young Twightwee girl who had shown interest in him. It would be good to bring something back to her.

He knew they had to be on the trail back to Fort Jefferson. With prisoners to guard, they wouldn't be traveling very fast. He was certain that if he started quickly, he could overtake them. And then what? Would he ambush all seven men with his lone rifle? He decided that's exactly what he would do.

Deep in the night he took off through the woods, letting the moon light his way. He knew where the trail was and he avoided it until he was certain that he had passed them by. Then he picked up his pace and loped along for another hour or two. He was sure they were taking a full night's sleep. He would be able to stop and nap for a couple of hours himself, then awaken and find a perfect ambush spot. A mile off the trail he found a soft bed of leaves. Using his pack as his pillow, he pulled his blanket around him and immediately fell asleep.

A glint of sunlight from first dawn quickly awakened him. He washed his face in a nearby creek, filled his canteen, checked his rifle load and headed for the trail. Once he found it, he walked alongside it until he discovered a place that had a long field of fire from deep within the woods. Then he hid himself and waited for them to approach.

He waited half the day, lying on the ground behind a fat old maple, occasionally dozing, occasionally wondering if they had decided on a different route. It wasn't until halfway through the afternoon that he heard what he thought were footfalls, followed by the sound of a guard scolding a prisoner.

"Sometimes they just put you in the stockade," the guard was telling the prisoner. "They don't shoot you, they just lock you up, then let you out in time to fight in some big battle or other."

The three prisoners appeared along the trail first, their hands tied behind their backs, with hobbles on their legs. Behind them came the sergeant and his three privates, all carrying muskets with fixed bayonets pointed at their prisoners.

Until this war, Kendee had lived a tranquil life. He had been too young to fight at his father's side in the Revolution, and the trading trips he had taken for his father's company had been remarkably free of violence. The St. Clair debacle had been a breathless melee, excellent experience for a warrior of the Longhouse. He had never conducted a one-man ambush before, and yet he saw clearly what he had to do. He pulled back the hammer of his long rifle, took a breath, aimed carefully and pulled the trigger.

The rifle cracked, and through the thick smoke he saw the sergeant go down kicking and grunting with the pain. The wound was not fatal; it was better than fatal because it forced one of his men to tend to him. The two others sought cover. Of the three prisoners, two of them dropped to the ground, but the third one tried to escape. He might have made it, hobbles and all, into the woods on the opposite side of the trail from Kendee, because Kendee was still going through his loading drill when one of the soldiers leveled his musket and brought the prisoner to earth. Behind the smoke from his rifle Kendee had squirmed along the ground to the cover of a fallen tree. In the confusion, none of the soldiers had spotted him as he left the immediate vicinity of his gun smoke. All three of the soldiers took aim at the tree from where Kendee had fired his shot. Their muskets cracked in rapid succession, and Kendee could hear the rounds ripping through leaves and thudding into tree trunks.

He made a quick calculation. He was close enough to them to rush at least one and kill him with his tomahawk. Or he could fade into the woods, reappear a little farther down the trail, and pick off another one. The two surviving privates might scatter, and then he could do as he pleased with the two prisoners.

But why should he? With the reality of his enterprise staring at him in the form of a wounded officer and one dead deserter, his desire for action was sated. The soldiers hadn't even rammed their charges home much less primed their pans when Kendee stood up, waved, gave a turkey gobble, and jogged away at a leisurely lope. He did not even look back, but his move was well-calculated. Five steps put the trunks of three trees between himself and the musket fire of the American soldiers. The soldiers did not even try to fire, once they had loaded their weapons, but Kendee could easily imagine the incredulous looks on their faces as they watched this arrogant lone warrior make his casual retreat. He knew that their journey back to the fort would be swift as possible and very nervous. They would see imaginary red men hidden under every bush and ambushes laid from atop each hill. He picked up the pace, pointed his body north and headed for the Maumee River.

18

THE NEW COMMANDER-IN-CHIEF OF THE United States Army was Major General Anthony Wayne, of Pennsylvania and Georgia. Gout-ridden, temperamental, sometimes prone to excessive drinking, Wayne possessed something denied General St. Clair—the innate ability to raise an army, train it, and fight a campaign with it.

He was a loyal supporter of Washington and a genuine hero of the Revolutionary War. He had failed in his efforts to become a successful Georgia planter, and had won an election to Congress only to become involved in an electioneering scandal not of his making. His leg was often so swollen and painful that he should have been back at his Pennsylvania farm swearing off rich foods, but duty called, and so did his last opportunity to repair his tarnished reputation.

It was June of 1793, and the weather in Pittsburgh was hot and sticky. Traffic along the streets, both of the two-footed and four-footed variety, moved along at a dusty crawl, and the doors of the taverns were flung wide open to let in every wisp of a breeze. In the months that had passed, the wild fears that possessed Pittsburgh had quieted down a bit, only because the marauding western tribes had decided not to carry their attacks all the way east to the confluence of the Allegheny and Monongahela. Although many in town were pleased by the arrival of such a noted fighting general, without the stress of imminent attack to persuade them, there was no flood of local volunteers rallying to Wayne's standard. And he desperately needed volunteers.

Nor were the folks on the eastern seaboard keen to go west and fight a war. The revolution they had fought more than a decade before had pushed the Indians so far west that nobody in the East felt threatened anymore, and most of them had little sympathy for the rough, lawless, obstinate frontiersmen who insisted on going over the mountains without the legal right to do so, then crying for help when the Indians objected.

Nevertheless, bit by bit the beginnings of an army of sorts began to dribble in. Some of them heard tales of horror in the West and turned tail for home, but there were those who stayed too. Almost out of habit, Wayne began to drill and train them, even though it appeared that Congress had forgotten he had an army to equip and send off against the united tribes of the Northwest. The summer dragged by, and Wayne worked his men, wondering if he was making real progress. He found out on the evening of August eighth when a buckskinned individual came riding into town on a lathered horse to report that the tribes were approaching from the West and were getting ready to burn the town down and scalp its inhabitants.

Wayne assembled his army, such as it was, and posted sentries, then led a contingent of dragoons out to gallop around the enemy's rear. Through the dark his scouts probed for the enemy and found none. They probed farther and found not a trace. Wayne boldly exposed his dragoons. They attracted no hostility greater than the annoyed shrieks of a few night creatures. Disgusted, Wayne led his men back to town, and found that a third of his sentries had departed.

Then the cold weather came. Wayne was aware of what the warm hearths of a town can do to the fighting spirits of soldiers in the dead of winter. He moved his troops out a long day's march down the Ohio River from Pittsburgh, to an encampment that he called Legionville. Legion was what he intended to call his army, if he was ever going to have an army. He kept them busy cutting trees and building huts and drilling and marching and shooting. He had them out making imaginary bayonet charges and staging mock battles against each other. They were still not an army, in numbers or spirit, but at least their bodies were gaining stamina for the grueling ordeal ahead.

Wayne invited a number of Indian chiefs to Legionville for informal council, but when they arrived they could only disagree with him on where the boundaries stood between white and red country. The officers mitigated their boredom with a series of quarrels, duels, and other mischief. Some money, not nearly enough, arrived from New York, and more volunteers dribbled in, from Maryland, New Jersey, and Virginia. Eastern Pennsylvania sent about a hundred, and western Pennsylvania four or five times as many. The real frontier finally caught the spirit. From the land between the Ohio River and Lake Erie, which was the place the trouble was all about, came a hundred and sixty-six wilderness-toughened frontier farmers.

In the meantime there was a building boom in Pittsburgh. Wayne had decided to transport his legion west on ninety-five flatboats. He put the boatwrights of Pittsburgh to work building them, and soon the town resounded with the pounding of hammers and the rasping of saws. Wayne was not yet sure that he was going to war. There were a trio of American negotiators preparing to meet with the tribes near Lake Erie, to see if they could pry the land from the Indians bloodlessly. The English also had their agents around the lakes, encouraging the tribes to hold out so the English could maintain their handhold on the Northwest, an area that they regretted ceding to the United States at the end of the Revolution.

"We will feed you, we will arm you, we will help you drive the Americans off your soil," said the English. Maybe the Indians had short memories concerning English promises. More likely they felt they had no choice. They were certainly no fools. The American carrot was that if the tribes would only move a little farther west, then the Americans would give them more goods than they had ever seen or imagined, and more money too. By this time the Indians knew perfectly well what money could buy, but they had retreated their last step. Later that summer they would suggest a better way for the Americans to spend their money.

The frontier settlers, they said, must be very poor or they would never come to live in an area that was so dangerous for them. Why not give the money to those poor settlers so they could afford to live back East with their brothers?

That was later. This was the spring. Badger and Sees the Moon, who never had regained contact with the Watleys and their canoe, were enjoying a glorious May morning stalking a deer along the banks of the Ohio, when they both heard a shout. It was a white man's shout, one of those words that white men hollered when a horse stepped on their foot or a spark from one of their wet wood fires jumped up and bit them on the cheek. The shout came from the water, around the upriver bend.

The two young braves gave up their chase and dashed

into the brush on the bank of the river. They waited patiently, and in about two minutes a small flatboat floated into view. Its decks were loaded with barrels. There was a pair of horses on board, but only a half-dozen men whom they could see, if that many. They could barely contain their excitement. While Sees the Moon remained to observe, Badger ducked into the woods and ran to seek out two of their companions who were nearby. He was back quickly with the others.

Two men were standing on either side of the square bow with poles, watching for shallows. A third man was on top of the shack, which was located astern. He was manning the long steering sweep and talking to a fourth, who was standing beside him. The fifth man was standing atop the shack, farther forward, his eyes focused downriver sometimes, and sometimes at one or the other of the banks, looking at everything, seeing nothing.

The four braves peered at the flatboat as it drifted slowly downstream. In low whispers they discussed their strategy. It would be a simple matter to pick off the steersman and his cohort in the back, and the two men with poles in the front. No, said Sees the Moon, the fifth man was the only one actually holding a rifle. They must make sure to kill him, and then take one of the men with poles on the reload. The other two agreed that the strategy was sound. They each chose a target, then spread out in the brush and waited for the boat to come abreast of them.

Badger pulled back the hammer of his rifle, his heart pounding, his hands moist. He had thought they would be hunting deer on this morning. He was not prepared for war. But the targets were too good to pass up, and the booty was irresistible, even though they had no idea what was inside the barrels. Just the personal effects of the men were bound to be dazzling to any of these four young men, all of whom were by white men's standards poverty-stricken. He heard three other hammers click into position. The sounds were so loud that surely, he thought, the white men must also hear them.

He did not know what made him look up from his gun sight, but he did and spotted another flatboat just beyond the bend, fifty yards behind the first. "Don't shoot!" he whispered to the other three, just in time. They held their fire and watched, for minute after breathless minute, as one flatboat followed the last down the river in an endless procession. All the rest were much bigger than the first, all bristled with armed men. There were dozens of men, hundreds, hundreds and hundreds, the four warriors thought as they watched the aquatic parade. This must be the army they had heard about, floating west to have another go at the Miamis and their allies.

Badger had heard his grandfather talk about the white men after the last battle. "Oh yes," he had said. "You may defeat the white men in battle. They are not that hard to beat. They will send another army. You may defeat it too. But they will only send more. Most of them have no sense and many of them have no courage, but what they never lack is men with muskets in their hands. Sooner or later, by accident, they win a battle. And when they do, we do not have the braves to replace those who fall. That is the secret of the white man's success. More than their guns, it is their numbers."

For two hours the flatboats continued to come. Once they had come to grips with the fact that there would be no ambush, no scalps, no booty, they watched the procession with all the curiosity and interest of children watching a dress parade. They saw wheeled brass cannons, men wearing a half-dozen different kinds of colorful uniforms, all manner of military supplies in many shapes of bundles and many sizes of barrels. There was livestock on board, mostly cows and horses. They saw a number of men with bulging cheeks spitting great brown gobs into the water. On one of the flatboats stood a hefty man in a fine blue uniform with red facings. He had younger men around him, and all four braves could see that this man wore the aura of command.

The sun was directly overhead by the time the last flatboat had passed. They raised their heads and watched it until it vanished.

"Little Turtle will be sending runners for us soon," Sees the Moon said. "Will you fight them?" They all said yes.

When the Watleys pulled their canoe ashore on the creek off the Ohio River, Jinja was not surprised to see that much of the stockade had been burned to the ground. Some of the buildings within had likewise been destroyed, but the floor over the storage cave they had dug was intact. The goods they had stored were in good shape, and so were the swivel guns buried the night before they had escaped.

While Big Oak and Thad began the task of cleaning up, Jinja accompanied Henri and Joanna to the homestead Joanna's father had built. There was nothing left of it but ashes and a few charred beams. Jinja watched her mouth work silently. Her eyes stayed dry. He stood by her while Henri poked among the ruins.

"I know I told you bad things about my father," she said to Jinja. "But we were a family. My mother was a strong-willed woman. She needed a tough man like my father. She would have bossed a man like you, and that would have been wrong." Her voice was unusually gentle.

Jinja removed his slouch hat and scratched his head. "I don't imagine I would have ever joined up with a woman like your mother—or one like you for that matter. I don't like for a woman to boss me, and I got no desire to boss a woman. I like for a woman to know what she's got to do in her life, and to let me alone to do what I've got to do, if you know what I mean."

The conversation ended there. Henri returned from studying the ruins.

"Don't look like too much trouble to rebuild the house, eh?" he said to Joanna. "We start right away."

Jinja shook his head. "Not right away, my friend," he said. "The stockade comes first." His dark eyes met Henri's with a steely stare that surprised Joanna. "Let's get back to it."

On the way back, Jinja studied the trail for Indian sign and found none. He mentioned the fact to his father and grandfather when they had made it back to the site of the stockade. "I don't believe they have been here since they burned down our little fortress," he said.

Over the next month they worked very hard. Jinja noticed that although his grandfather was still clever with tools, he was very careful about lifting the heavy logs that made up the palisades. Their rifles were always loaded and within reach, but during the entire time they were rebuilding, they only had one visitor, a solitary old Delaware who came to beg a few rounds of ammunition before he resumed his trek west.

"Haven't got none to spare," Big Oak growled, and sent the old Delaware on his way.

Jinja was surprised. "You're gettin' kinda crabby in your old age, don't you think?" he asked.

Big Oak smiled. "But I'll tell you, grandboy, when I talked to the soldiers in Pittsburgh, they told me that the Delawares were in this war up to their necks. And I surely want nobody shootin' my own ammunition back at me."

The last building to be finished was the watchtower on the hill, which overlooked both the fort and the Ohio River. The new stockade was almost identical to the old, except that Big Oak insisted they set up additional swivel mounts in various parts of the wall. When they were done with the main work, they stood outside the stockade and studied it, quietly congratulating themselves on their good work.

"Only thing I don't understand," said Henri, "is that if there's a war on, if the Indians are united against us and the white men have been run out of the territory, then who do we have to trade with?"

Thad and Jinja did not answer. It was the old woods brawler, Big Oak, who responded. "There's gonna be a big battle before long, monsieur. The commander is Mad Anthony Wayne, and that man knows how to win battles. If we ain't the first traders out here, we're certainly the best. I tell you, Henri, the frontier people—the ones that haven't run away—are swarming west, even in the middle of the war. They're so hungry for new land they can taste it.

"They'll trade with us. And from here we can send trading parties northwest to the Wabash, to the Illinois and the Piankashaws, and the lake tribes."

"Of course," added Thad, "that's if General Wayne beats the Indians. If he loses, we'll be lucky to get back to Albany with our hair." He smiled, a big broad smile, and Joanna decided that Thad was crazy.

Throughout most of the winter, the ground was covered with snow. But all four of the men were good hunters, and they had brought several sacks of corn with them from Pittsburgh, so nobody went hungry. Joanna was in charge of the kettle in the fireplace. Once, while she was stirring the stew, Big Oak said, "Sure wish we had a few green onions. When Cilla was alive she'd always throw a few in the kettle. Cilla was—" Big Oak stopped suddenly, as if he had discovered himself committing a social blunder. Nobody wanted to hear an old man blithering on about his dead wife. "Ah, hell," he said, turning his back on the fire and walking away.

In the early spring the snow was washed away by the rain. Day after day of rain. There were things to do. Bolstered by rumors of General Wayne's army heading west, a number of people who had settled in the area and then left had decided to return. They were delighted to see a stockade in place, a refuge just in case the Shawnees and Miamis were to resume their depredations in the area. New people came in too. They stopped at the fort and stayed at the inn, bought some goods, then moved on. "There are always new people coming across the mountains," Thad told Jinja. "That's why we're here."

There was silence for a moment. Jinja looked down at his beaded moccasins. "I am a fool," he said. "I always thought that somewhere there would be a stopping place. That the farmers and the old soldiers and all the rest would finally have enough land. That at some river or mountain they would stop, and President Washington or somebody would finally say, 'We have gone far enough.' No more. Now I believe that someday the whites will have all the land."

Thad studied his son. "When your grandfather was young, the Te-non-an-at-che was the river of the Mohawks. There were Mohawks alive then who remembered when the Hudson Valley was the land of the Mohican, and there were still Abnaki villages in New England. Think. When did you last see an Abnaki village below the St. Lawrence? In those days few questioned the right of the six nations of the Longhouse to most of New York. So quickly are the six nations gone, and the United States has barely taken a breath before they have spilled over the mountains into the land of the Mingo, the Shawnee, the Miami.

"There is a treaty that says the whites will not go beyond the Allegheny Mountains. It was made by the English after the war with the French. We should have been bound by that treaty, but so great is the tide of men and women westward over those mountains that the Congress must pretend that the treaty does not exist. Do you know why they must give in to these settlers?"

Jinja reached for his pipe and began to pack it.

"Because the settlers live a long way from Philadelphia. Congress would rather not fight wars with the Indians. War is expensive. Congress has few men and little money to fight them with. But they're afraid that if they don't support the settlers, then the settlers will choose to form their own country."

"But how could they? They have no money, no ships, no trade."

"They have the Spanish, on the Mississippi. The Spanish have agents who would like to have a nation of American farmers in the West. What they don't want is a big, strong United States."

"Why should they care?" Jinja was no fool, but life on the trails had not done much for his education on international affairs. As a merchant, it was important that Thad keep up with the doings of England, France, and Spain.

"If the settlers will not even take a breath while they push the Indians west, what makes you think they'll stop at the Mississippi River? And what is on the other side of the Mississippi River?"

"Spain," Jinja muttered.

"Spain," Thad repeated. "Now there was a time your grandfather here"—he waved his hand toward Big Oak, who was sitting on a bench by the window, quietly smoking and looking out at the rain—"your grandfather loved the Longhouse, but he knew the truth. He knew that the Longhouse had no way to save themselves, and he knew that the Indians could not resist the whites because they would never unite."

"But he was wrong," Jinja said. "They are united now."

"Are they? You saw Miamis and Delawares and Shawnees. Where is the Longhouse? Where are the Ottawa and the Chippewa? Why have the Creeks not come north? Why do the Chickasaws still scout for the whites?"

Big Oak turned from watching the rain and studied his son for a minute. He was sucking on the stem of his pipe. The tobacco had gone out and gone cold, but he had no desire to relight it. He turned back toward the rain. Thad stared at his father's thinning white. He remembered a time when the old man's scalp would have been a prize for a young Caughnawaga brave. Without the incentive of bounties, if he were killed today, his slayer probably would not even bother with his scalp.

"Pa," Thad said, walking over to the window. The rain had blown in. There were drops of rain on his father's face, but the gray eyes did not blink. They were focused on something too far away for Thad to see.

Then suddenly they did blink. They blinked because on the hill they saw Henri scrambling down from the observation tower. His legs were in motion before they hit the ground. He ran down the hill, slipped on some wet leaves, rolled over a few times, found his feet and continued running. Jinja ran out the door and opened the gate just wide enough to allow Henri to slip in, and followed him into the store. Henri entered spreading his arms as if to say "It's all right," and took two quick breaths.

"Flatboats!" he cried. "One after another! Troops!"

He didn't have to say anything more. All four of the men bounded out the door, followed by Joanna, who was not about to let them leave without bolting the gate shut after them. They ran down the slope to the swollen creek, swept the leaves and brush off the hidden canoe, turned it right side up and paddled it down the creek and into the Ohio River just as the flatboats began to appear around the nearest bend. They made straight for the first boat, and found themselves staring into the muzzles of three muskets.

"Put them things down before you hurt yourselves," said Big Oak conversationally when the canoe was nearly close enough to touch the bow of the leading flatboat.

"We've got the best brandy this side of Pittsburgh," Henri asserted, standing up and tossing a rope to one of the men standing at the bow.

"Y'all whiskey makers?" asked a soldier with a North Carolina accent standing on top of the shack.

"We are traders for Wendel and Watley of Albany," Thad responded formally.

"What in hell are you doin' out here?" asked the southerner. "This is a dangerous place to be carryin' goods to."

"Then we won't have much competition, will we?" Thad smiled. "Where's your commander?"

"Fourth boat up the river," another soldier answered.

"Would that be General Wayne?" Big Oak asked.

The two men they were talking to both nodded.

"Then that's who we'll be seein'," Big Oak continued. "If you're lucky," he said, peering through the rain, "some of you 'll be sleepin' on land tonight, under a roof that don't leak."

19

"'BOUT TIME THE PRESIDENT CHOSE A REAL general to lead the army," Big Oak said, passing a pewter goblet filled with brandy to General Wayne.

Wayne reached over from his chair and grunted as he took the vessel. "There are days, sir," he said, "when this real general can't get up on his horse without help."

"I'm sorry to see that, General," Big Oak replied. "When we were with General Sullivan we heard a powerful lot about you, and what a fighter you were."

"I had better be a fighter yet, Sam. I believe we have a lot of fighting in front of us this summer," Wayne replied. The two men had never met, but Wayne had heard of the great scout called Big Oak, and was delighted to meet him. The two hit it off immediately. Thad saw a spark in his father's eye that he had not seen since before Cilla had died. Big Oak listened quietly, puffing his pipe, as Wayne talked about Stony Point and the Battle of Yorktown. Then Wayne took a sip of brandy and his face creased with pleasure.

"This is excellent brandy," he said. "Where did you get it?"

Thad cleared his throat. "We have a good trade with

some Caughnawagas near Montreal," he said. "They know good brandy, and we pay them well for it. They never let us down."

Wayne nodded and turned back to Big Oak. "I have known of you over the years. Always like echoes of an old legend. Like King Arthur, or the Duke of Marlborough. I did not know you were still living to fight in the war for independence. To have you with me on this night is a special moment. I once heard a story about you and a certain beautiful English lady up along the St. Lawrence River. I've heard the story three different times—in fact in one of the stories it was not even you, but a Lieutenant Hawkins."

Big Oak's gray eyebrows rose on his head. A long neglected memory appeared through the mists of a time almost completely forgotten.

"Did this story have to do with Lady Lazenby?" Big Oak asked.

"Lazenby, that's the name. I would enjoy hearing the true story of how you stole her from the Mohawks."

"Ah," Big Oak sighed, packing his pipe with kinnikinnick and relighting it. He puffed away for a while, leaning his chair back against the wall, watching the smoke rise toward the ceiling. It was only respect for the old man that gave Wayne the patience to wait for Big Oak to begin. Several of Wayne's officers were sitting around the newly made oak table, along with Jinja and Thad. Joanna had been tending the stew pot. She was astonished by the respect shown by this famous general for the bent woodsman she had taken as just another useless old tramp who had had his day and ought to be resting under a headstone somewhere. She moved within hearing, a dripping wooden ladle in her right hand.

"Not Mohawks, General," he said. "Abnakis. They were Abnakis. It was maybe a year after Willow died. Willow was my first wife. Beautiful . . . Seneca woman." He went silent again for a while. More puffs of smoke rose toward the ceiling. The room was quiet and waiting.

"So very long ago," he sighed, "an English major at Fort Niagara, a Major Fairweather Lazenby, had a beautiful young wife. Her name was Sarah, and she may have been twenty years old, which was half the age of the major. She was outside the fort picking berries when a band of Abnakis stumbled upon her. Fort Niagara was Seneca country, and had the Senecas caught these Abnaki braves, they would have taken three days before they'd burned enough pieces of them to kill them, but young braves are about as dumb as young anythings. Well, they argued for a few minutes about whether to take the top of her head back home with them or take all of her. The smartest, and therefore the dumbest, since he should have known better than to be there, thought that if they took her back to the village, at the very least the French would pay them well for her. They'd be heroes in the village, that was for sure.

"So that's what they did. They took her back to their village and sent word to the French that they had the wife of the commander at Fort Niagara. Now this got the French military all stirred up, but at the time the French and the English were at peace, so they couldn't make a move without first talkin' to the governor of New France, who happened to be visiting in old France—at the time."

Big Oak's pipe went out and he paused to light a splint from the fireplace and use it to rekindle his kinnikinnick. The room waited patiently for him to continue his story, and he enjoyed the attention.

"Major Lazenby was not a very good officer, but his family had considerable wealth—I'm surprised that they did not buy him a higher commission than major. When his wife did not return to the fort that day, he sent out search parties, and when they came back empty, he called me in to track her down. At first I did not want to do it. I was not scouting for the army at that time, and I was still feelin' awful sad over the death of my first wife."

He stopped for a moment and took a deep breath. Recollection of his first grief reminded him of his second. He continued.

"I guess it was the major's grief first—and his gold second—that persuaded me. I went to the last place she had been seen and snooped around and eventually found signs of moccasin tracks and a struggle. Then I took to the woods and started asking questions among the Cayugas and the Caughnawagas and eventually found that she had been kidnapped.

"Now, the major found out that the French governor was back in old France, and he had been warned that the Abnakis might decide she was too much trouble and either roast her or let one of their braves have her for a wife. The major could not abide her bein' made the wife of a greased-up ol' Abnaki. He offered me—you won't believe how much he offered me if I would get her back. Could I do it?

"I said I would try. He offered me so much to find the village and so much if I brought her out, and so much more if I brought her out alive and unharmed. We shook on it and off I went."

"By yourself?" asked General Wayne's aide, a Captain Marlowe.

"Better that way. Quieter. So off I went to Canada, and headed east on the St. Lawrence to Abnaki country until I found a Caughnawaga who knew an Abnaki, who knew another—eventually I found the village. They were keepin' her hidden away. I laid in the grass for three days before I finally figured out what hut they were keepin' her in. By that time I knew every lodge in the village—which men and women lived in each, which one had a grandmother living there, how many children. Finally, the fifth day, I was running out of corn and deer meat, when most of the men went out on a hunt and the women went into the fields. That's when I finally saw her.

"Now I'd heard how beautiful she was, but seeing her was something different. Just for that day, I have to confess, Willow went clean out of my mind. I was still young then, and when I thought about what a sorry excuse for an officer Major Lazenby was, and what a sorry excuse for a man, for that matter, it struck me then just how much money can buy. Her hands were bound behind her back, and she had a lead around her neck. She was dirty and her hair drooped down her face like a tangled old mare's tail. But she was still a lovely creature."

Jinja looked around at the audience that sat spellbound in the flickering light of sputtering candles. He was surprised to see Joanna standing behind the general's chair, her hands clasped in front of her, as rapt as the rest. In her face was the realization that this old, dried-up woodsman had once been a dashing, adventurous army scout, stirred by the same feelings that stir other manly young men.

"I followed them out to the fields, and watched while the woman who had led her out tied her to a tree. It was early in the morning. The men were far away, and I decided to wait a while so the women might get tired doing their weeding. But they were having such a good time chatting to each other as they worked—you know how they do it—I figured they weren't paying much attention. So I thought I could cut her loose and we could cover some distance before they noticed. I crept through the woods until I was close to her tree. It was only about thirty yards away. I pulled my knife out, ran to the tree and cut her thongs, and damned if there wasn't a little girl I hadn't noticed sitting with her eyes glued to her prisoner.

"The little girl let out a shriek loud enough to wake the entire spirit world. We're off through the woods and they're coming after us, about ten, twelve of them, and they have hoes and mattocks and I don't know what-all, whooping like warriors, only shriller—I tell you it froze my blood. And Thad here'll tell you that my blood don't freeze easy.

"That's when I noticed that Sarah was wearing no shoes. And she's got these pretty, soft little feet. Well, she's scared to death and game as a racehorse, runnin' hard as she can, and I can hear her breath coming in gasps. They're gainin' on us and she is just about spent. Remember, she's been tied up for days. No exercise, and I'm sure she didn't do much more than walk a little before she was ever captured. I grabbed ahold of her arm and pulled. Her feet musta gone faster than they ever had. When she tripped, I just pulled harder, and she flew through the air behind me. They were gainin' on us, that was for sure. Then we came over a hill and there below was the St. Lawrence. I ran as hard as I could then, with her feet just kind of wheelin' and bouncin' along on the ground under her.

"The canoe was hid under some leaves and branches, you know. I dropped her and threw my rifle in the canoe, shoved the canoe out into the water, leaves and all, and here they come, over the top of the hill, waving them hoes and hatchets and whatever. I threw her into the canoe and nearly missed. The canoe almost turned over, but it didn't. Then I ran into the water and gave the canoe a push and dove into it, gave the boat just enough shove to be thirty feet out by the time they made it to the shore.

"Of course, they didn't stop just because we were in the water. They saw me flounderin' around on my belly, trying to grab a paddle and get into position to paddle out of there. They were screamin' mad, I'll tell you, and she's spread forward over the bow with her hands in the water, paddling with them, if you can imagine. And I'll bet it did some good too. So I got to my knees with the paddle in my hand just as this one woman grabs hold of the hind end of the canoe. I wanted to whale at her with the paddle, but if I broke it we were done. They would have chopped us to pieces. I poked her with the end of the blade. In the nose. She didn't scream. She didn't say a thing. She just hung on with both hands. I whanged her harder in the nose, then came down on her fingers, and this time she let go. I was facin' them, and the canoe bow was pointing the other way. Was I scared? What do you think? Two more were just a couple of steps from the canoe when I took a few backwater strokes and gained another ten feet. I turned around then and started stroking as hard as I had ever stroked in my life. Not five, not ten, not twenty, must have been thirty strokes at least before I dared to look back, and even though I heard the cries growing fainter, I wouldn't have been surprised if one of them had been hanging on the whole time.

"But none of them was. I looked back and I saw the one I'd poked in the nose kneeling down on the beach holding her hands to her face, with two others bending over her. Did I feel bad about what I did? Hell no! That woman had a tomahawk and she was trying to hack a hole in the canoe. If she'da been able to reach me, she would have hacked a hole in my head, that I'll tell you. Those women were plenty fierce. I guess I don't blame them. To them Sarah meant a whole lot of goods that would help them make it through the winter a little easier."

He halted his narrative for a moment, as if the telling of it had worn him down. There was a cup of brandy in front of him that he had been ignoring, but now he picked it up and took a good-sized swallow.

"Now comes the good part," said General Wayne, who had found that Big Oak's account thus far jibed with the story as told by others.

"I kept paddling, and I couldn't catch my breath to say anything to her, so I didn't until we were at least a mile up the river, well toward the middle and well out of sight of the Abnaki women. She was sitting in the bow of the canoe, leaning forward, holding her face, crying, very softly.

" 'Are you all right?' I asked her. She nodded her head. 'Are you thirsty?' She nodded again.

"I handed her my canteen and she drank it dry. Then she looked up into my face. 'Who are you?' she asked. 'And why—'

" 'Are you hungry?' I asked her. She shook her head. So I started paddling again. A while later she says, 'I'm *very* hungry.'

"I told her I was too, and that in a little while we'd be stopping for the day. She waited. Didn't say a word for the rest of the afternoon. Five miles east of Montreal there was a large creek I knew about. I turned into it and paddled a mile or so, then pulled up. There was still plenty of light. There had to be because I had to hunt some food for us. I killed a duck and brought it back and made a fire and dressed the duck—started it cooking. I spread my blanket for her, and she laid down and fell asleep right there.

"When the food was ready I woke her up. She had very dark hair. I don't remember her eyes—I can't exactly picture her. It's been nearly fifty years, you see. But some things I remember like they were yesterday.

"She ate. This lady ate, delicately, with very good manners, but it was duck and she only had her fingers to eat with and the grease was on her fingers. 'Wait,' I said. I filled my canteen in the creek and took a little tin cup from my pack. I filled the cup with water and put the canteen and the cup next to her. 'The canteen is to drink out of,' I told her. 'The cup, well, you can rinse your fingers in it.'

"I can't tell you the look she gave me then. So soft, so gentle. 'I am grateful to you, Mister—' I told her my name, and explained how I came to be there.

" 'So my husband paid you to come and get me.'

" 'If I had met you before, I would have done it for nothing.'

" 'And so now that you know me, would you give the money back?'

"I told her no, that I had earned my pay, and we both laughed.

" 'I am so very tired,' she said, and she tried to lay down, but she groaned.

" 'Where do you hurt?' I asked her.

" 'Head to toe,' she said. 'My feet are terribly sore.'

" 'Let me see.' I sat by her feet and looked at them, cut and bruised, but soft and pretty, and I began to rub them. I could hear her breath, coming softly.

" 'Mr. Watley—Sam,' she said. I was almost as young as she was, you see. 'You are a very kind man. Not like my husband. Brave too. Not like my husband. I cannot believe that a man would do what you did for me today, not even for money.' And then she stopped talking, while I rubbed her feet. 'It is getting cold, Sam,' she said. She was right. I took off my jacket and covered her with it."

Big Oak stopped talking then and looked out the window, at the stars. His guests waited, expecting him to resume.

"What then?" Joanna asked, and Jinja was surprised at the eagerness in her voice, and in her eyes.

"Big Oak is a gentleman," General Wayne said. "If he

does not wish to continue, I will tell you the story as I heard it."

"No," Big Oak interjected. "I'll tell the truth. So long ago. So very long ago. What would she look like today, if she were still alive? She was the most beautiful woman—and she was cold. 'Lay down by me, Sam, and keep me warm.' I laid down with her and felt her close to me. Felt her warm against me. And that's how we slept that night."

"That's all?" asked the general's aide.

"That's not all," said General Wayne. "When he brought her back to the fort, he found the major had gone west to chase some Chippewas who had been stirring up mischief. Big Oak here left her at the fort and went back to the woods."

"I left her in good hands and headed back to Tonowaugh to be with Thad."

"Where is Tonowaugh?" Joanna asked.

"It no longer exists," Big Oak answered. "It was a Seneca village on the Genesee River. Where Thad grew up."

"Thad was raised in an Indian village?"

"By a Seneca grandfather."

"Never mind all that," Thad said. "Continue the story, Pa."

"Maybe three moons later, I stopped at Fort Niagara for some supplies. That's when I heard that the major had been killed in a fight with the Chippewas. I went to her quarters, to give her my condolences. Cleaned up and dressed, she took my breath away. When she opened the door and saw me, she said, 'Come on in,' and when the door shut, she gave me a big hug and kissed my cheek. She told me she wished she could give me more than that little kiss."

General Wayne could sit still no longer. "What I heard was the poor girl fell madly in love with our young pioneer hero. That true?"

Big Oak took a sip from his cup of brandy and chewed on his pipe stem. "I held her hand for a bit. The poor girl had been having a tough time of it, and I'd be lyin' if I said I wasn't taken with her."

"The girl was worth a fortune. She wanted to take you back to England with her."

"That was later," Big Oak admitted.

"Later?" said Joanna. "You mean you saw her again?"

"Saw her again? Why, the two became—"

"I would come by and visit her from time to time."

"You old goat!" Wayne said.

"I was taken with her."

"But you wouldn't marry her."

"The differences were too great. She was a lady."

"And you were the lord of the forest. With her money and your—your name, your character—you and she could have been the masters of western New York."

"Pa," Thad said. "Were you in love with her?"

Big Oak looked into his son's face and tried his best to remember his feelings as they were at the time. "I loved your mother," he said. "I loved Cilla. I would have gladly lived forever with either one. I don't think I could have lived for a year with Lady Lazenby. She could not have been a partner, a mate, like your mother or Cilla. But . . ." He did not finish his sentence, though the entire room waited a long time in silence, hanging on the words that were bound to come after the "but."

There was another person in the room, a Captain Duff, who had said nothing during the entire telling of the story. But he, like General Wayne, had heard the legend told and retold on the frontier.

"There's more," he said suddenly, so quietly that he would not have been heard had not the room been totally silent when he spoke up.

"During their last . . . visit . . . at Fort Niagara, she told him she wanted to leave, but that she could find no one she could rely on to take her east."

"I offered to find her somebody," Big Oak continued.

"She would trust nobody to take her east except the man who had risked his life to rescue her from the Indians. She was very wealthy. She offered him a large sum of money."

"Did you go?" asked Joanna, leaning forward from where she now sat, on the bench near the window.

"He went all right," said General Wayne. "Didn't you?"

"Of course he did," said the captain.

"The question is," said Thad, smiling in the candlelight, "did you take the money?"

The room grew quiet again. No one would speak until they had their answer.

"No," Big Oak said.

"Of course not," Captain Duff said. "Man's a gentleman. The way the story goes, it took the two of you a long time to get from Niagara to New York City. How long?"

Big Oak rolled his eyes but did not answer.

"And when you got to New York City you found that it would be at least a month before a ship would be available to take her home?"

"No, no," General Wayne said. "She went down to book passage, and when she came back to her room, she told *him* that there would not be a ship available for a month."

Big Oak threw his head back and chuckled.

"You believed her, did you? Never crossed your mind that she wanted to have some time with you before she went home to boring old England."

The old man shook his head. The smile faded, but the eyes sparkled with the memory of the beautiful lie. "By then she must have known that I was right, that we were not fit for each other. But oh Lord . . ."

"Did you see her off?" Joanna asked.

"Did he see her off," snickered Captain Duff. "She got her private berth two days before the ship sailed. I'll say he saw her off."

"She was a sweet, gentle thing. Tiny face. Tiny feet." Big Oak was staring out the window now.

"A gentle woman, for a gentleman. You might have made a fine pair after all," Captain Duff said with feeling.

"Some gentleman," Joanna smirked. "I thought gentlemen don't tell."

Now the whole room laughed, including Big Oak.

"He never did," General Wayne declared.

"How do you know?" For a moment Joanna had crushed the romantic spell that the story had cast on her. "The story had to come from either him or her, and she went back to England. It had to be him."

General Wayne tilted his cup to his lips and drank. "It was not him. When she went back, her husband's family were not kind to her. Something about her not having been able to give birth to an heir before he died. They were so cruel she decided to seek revenge. She was no writer herself, and anyway, women do not write books. But she found a writer, who had a publisher. She told him the story on condition that if he used it he would use her real name, but not the name of her lover. The book was a sensation in London. I heard that there were French and Dutch translations."

"They must have thrown her out of society!" Thad exclaimed.

"On the contrary. The English upper class are different from solid American stock. For months she was at the top of everybody's guest list. I heard she eventually married a count, or a duke."

"But she never forgot her woodsman lover." Joanna's voice was not mocking. The spell had returned.

"That I don't know," Wayne answered. "Apparently she never wrote another book. Probably never came back to America. Probably lived the rest of her life with her stuffy old count, dreaming about her long ago romance with the man who sits before us, chewing on his pipe stem."

"So long ago," Big Oak said, out loud yet to himself as he stared out the window. "When I try to picture her face, it is always in shadow. I remember how beautiful she was, but for the life of me I cannot picture how she was beautiful." Now the room went silent, and stayed silent, until the officers began to file out of the room, quietly, respectfully.

20

THE FOLLOWING MORNING DAWNED CLEAR, but General Wayne wanted the opportunity to study the stockade's trade goods, in case there might be something worth purchasing. The gunpowder looked especially good, better than what they had bought in Pittsburgh, so he purchased several barrels, as well as some brandy.

Thad had a strong feeling that the general was looking for an excuse to lay over another day. His suspicion was confirmed when he found the general hefting Jinja's rifle just outside the stockade gate and talking to Big Oak about it.

"I'm an old army man," he said, "so I can't help but go for the musket. Massed fires from the ranks, that's what does the trick," he said.

"Might be true for big battles and open fields," Big Oak replied. "But for scouts and hunters, nothing beats a Pennsylvania long rifle."

"I've got some boys who can hit a mark pretty good with a musket. I'd like to have a little competition between you and them boys. I'd heard you were just about the best shot in all of New York. It would make a good test of weapons."

Big Oak looked across the open field to where some of

the smaller flatboats stood on the creek. "Rather not, General. Something like that, you get hard feelings." Big Oak walked back into the stockade.

General Wayne was about to follow, but Jinja stopped him. "May we speak, sir?" he said softly.

Wayne nodded, and the two of them began to walk down toward the creek.

"Sir," Jinja began, "Big Oak is past seventy now. Might say a few years past seventy."

"He looks strong and healthy."

"Very strong. Very healthy. He can still follow a trail. He can still paddle a canoe twenty miles, or walk it. What he can't do is see good enough to hit a far mark."

"I see. Well, can you shoot?"

Jinja took his rifle back from the general. He loaded it, measuring out the powder carefully. He primed the pan and cocked the hammer. "General," he said, "can you see that place in the trunk of that elm tree where some animal rubbin' up against it rubbed the bark off?"

He pointed to the tree, nearly three hundred yards away, but the general shook his head. "I can't see it," he said.

"Well I can. And I'm gonna put a bullet into the middle of it, then we're gonna walk down there and you're gonna dig the bullet out with your own knife."

"Point to it again, will you, please?" the general requested. Jinja pointed. "Well, I can see the tree you mean, anyway. You may fire when you're ready."

Jinja lay prone and positioned his rifle.

"That the way you always shoot?" the general asked.

"It's the steadiest position," Jinja explained. "And that's a long shot."

"I suppose it would be," the general observed. "Whenever you're—"

Jinja squeezed the trigger. The pan flashed, the rifle smoked and kicked, and Jinja rose to his feet.

"You figure you hit that bald spot on the tree, that I can't even see?"

"Felt like it," Jinja replied. They walked across the open space toward the tree, the general two steps ahead, out of habit. When they got there the general turned to Jinja with a look of surprise and suspicion on his face. "Here's the bald place you were talking about. There are *two* holes in it."

"I tried this same shot two days ago. Stick your finger in the lower hole. You'll feel the bullet is still warm. That's the one I just shot."

"I've seen some good marksmen in my life. But I did not think there were people, and weapons, that could shoot like this! Still, you can't load as fast as one of my boys can load a musket. And it's massed fires that stop an enemy regiment."

"But it's one well-aimed shot that can bring down the enemy's leader in the middle of a battle."

Wayne did not answer right away. He was also a battle leader, after all. The idea of being brought down by a lone shooter from three hundred yards away displeased him, not because he was afraid of dying, but because he thought it was a hell of a way to lose a battle.

"You said that Big Oak was still a clever scout?" Wayne asked Jinja as they walked back to the stockade.

"I think he's still the best inside a white skin."

"How about you?"

"Not bad."

"In a month or two, unless our ministers can be very persuasive, there will be a battle. Whoever wins it will win the Northwest Territory."

"Big Oak says that whoever wins that battle, the Americans will eventually conquer the Northwest Territory."

"If we lose this battle, there will be a bloodbath to the gates of Pittsburgh, my lad. What does your grandfather say about that?"

"He says we ought to go with you if you need scouts."

"But you don't know the territory."

"Big Oak says we will learn."

"I'm sure you'll have the time. I expect the Indians will keep our ministers dithering until the last minute."

Two days later Wayne's legion prepared to cast off and drift westward. Henri was not present to say good-bye. He had spent too much time working on the stockade and not enough on the house he was rebuilding for himself and Joanna. Big Oak had suggested it might be safer if they lived in the stockade, but Henri insisted that when he was done with the job, the house would be easier to defend against marauders than the stockade. The truth was, both Big Oak and Henri were certain that all the hostile tribes were camped to the northwest, waiting for yet another army they knew had been sent to destroy them.

Joanna and Jinja stood on the bank of the river, watching the flatboats parade past. It was Joanna who had wanted some final words.

There was no sign of anger or peevishness in her now. What was it he saw in her eyes? A little fear? Melancholy? Worry?

"Jinja," she said, "I just wanted you to know, I hope you make it through safely. I hope you come back. It's lonely in the wilderness without friends."

"Have you ever had friends?" he asked.

"I've always been lonely," she replied. "I know you tried to be my friend. I am sorry I have not been yours."

"You have Henri," he replied without emotion.

"Henri is my lover, not my friend."

Jinja thought for a moment. "Perhaps it would be good if you made him your friend. He is my friend, and a good one."

"But then how could he be my lover?"

"Joanna," Jinja said, patiently, "Big Oak and Cilla were lovers, and I promise you they were each other's best friends."

She opened her mouth to say more, but Jinja held up a hand. "I cannot let them drift on forever without me," he said. A canoe stood bobbing in the water a few feet from where he stood. Only the line he was holding had kept it from drifting with the flatboats. He climbed in and placed the rifle down beside him. Just as he picked up his paddle he felt a hand on his.

"Thank you, Jinja," she said. "For being gentle."

He nodded. "Look to Henri as a friend," he said. He wanted to assure her that he, Thad, and Big Oak would be back, but he felt no such assurances himself. "Henri is a good friend."

Then he took a half-dozen strokes toward the middle of the river before he turned his canoe downstream.

Her voice floated across the water one more time. "Jinja!"

He turned his head toward her.

"I am afraid of the Indians," she said, and her voice quivered.

"So am I," he answered, smiling. "And I believe I will be seeing many more of them than you." He knew those were not the words she needed to hear, but he did not know the right words. "Look to Henri," he repeated. "Henri." Then he dug his paddle into the river and labored to overtake the general's flatboat.

* * *

Wayne and his army passed the entire summer near the Ohio River waiting for word from the treating commissioners. Some of his troops were stricken down by influenza and some by smallpox, while a few others deserted. Big Oak, Thad, and Jinja knew little of what was happening with the troops back at Fort Washington, because they were in the woods, heading north. Thad had a pocket full of papers to make notes on. Every night he sat with his father and son and they exchanged thoughts about their observations: terrain, signs of passing warriors, places of possible ambush, old villages, trails, creeks, rivers.

Big Oak took notes with his senses and stored them away in his mind for further use, as he always had. Long ago, during the last war with the French, Sir William Johnson had sworn that Big Oak carried the entire map of New York, in minute detail, between his ears. Their usual method of travel in these strange woods was for one to walk along the trail while the others moved parallel, about twenty yards left and right, concealed as much as possible. They would move a few hundred yards, then stop, look around, and listen to all the sounds of the forest. After the heavy spring rains, the streams were wide and there was a considerable number of temporary lakes and ponds. As the weather warmed, the mosquitoes swarmed. The three men covered their faces, necks, and the backs of their hands with rancid bear grease.

Given the obstacles and their attention to detail, their progress was slow once they had passed the areas that the army knew well and had secured with forts. The trails followed the watercourses, winding in and out of the low rolling hills, sometimes doubling back on themselves, running any way but in straight lines. When the birds and the scurrying critters were silent, they had to stop and listen. Just one failure to note what the forest had to say to them could be fatal. Thad was heartened by his father's stamina. He was no longer young himself. If Big Oak could do it, then Little Oak could do it.

At night they kindled no campfires. They lived off the corn and dried meat in their packs, or the occasional wild edible plants they found in the fields and forests. They left no white man's trail. They spoke no more than they had to, moving silently, eating silently, sleeping silently. If they were to be found by the Indians in the woods, it would have to be by pure chance.

They did find a couple of small Miami bands, and then they studied them for a while from a safe distance before moving on. Farther north, they crossed the many creeks and streams of the Glaize. It was here that they began to feel the increased presence of the red man, in the form of new traces and numerous moccasin tracks of all sizes. Once they struck the Auglaize River, they followed it as it wound north, through magnificent stands of oak, ash, black walnut, and elm.

It was Jinja who spotted the first party of warriors. There were eight of them, shaven-skulled and stripped to the breechclout, and they were heading northeast with a pair of dressed deer quartered and divided among them.

"Wyandots!" whispered Big Oak. Obviously they were going back to their war camp. The three Watleys decided to follow them.

The Wyandots were chatting with each other as if they had not a care in the world. It was apparent they felt little concern for their safety as they walked without haste along the valley of the Auglaize. Big Oak understood the reason for their ease when they came over a swell and found the junction of the Auglaize and the Maumee. Up and down the bottomland of the Maumee River were miles and miles of cornfields. Beyond the cornfields lay a succession of villages dotted with bark-sided domed wigwams. They had discovered the chief dwelling place of the enemy.

Now they had a problem. They had done their job and found the people the army would be fighting if there was no peace treaty. But there was more to learn. Who were they? Who were their chiefs? How many warriors were there among all the women and children and old men who lived and loved and worked and played in these villages? Was it worth the risk they'd have to take to discover this information? All that they'd learned was worth nothing if they could not bring it back to the army. Nevertheless, Big Oak felt they could learn a little more without being discovered.

"You know what I think?" Thad said to his father. "I think you always liked to take just a little more risk, take another chance. You like the way it feels, don't you? Little thing it does to the bottom of your belly?"

"Makes life a little more interesting," Big Oak conceded.

"That's the way I feel," Jinja whispered. "I believe at least we can find out how many of them there are."

Thad said nothing to that, just motioned them down. He had turned around in time to see another party approaching from the south. "You suppose they found our trail?" he asked.

Big Oak shook his head in a way that indicated he didn't know. "Shawnees," he observed calmly. "Maybe we ought to depart after all."

They lay still in a patch of long grass for more than half an hour, but the Shawnee party never even approached within hearing distance. Carefully, Big Oak lifted his head so he could see through where the long grass thinned at the top. The Shawnees were gone.

"We have to get some idea of how many they might be, boys," he said.

Eagerly, Jinja agreed. Reluctantly, Thad did the same. Slowly, carefully, they began to make their way along the ridge line above the Maumee Valley. Below them they could see first one then another village coming into view, separated by gardens of watermelons and squash, or rich green cornfields. Jinja and Thad had never seen so many Indians gathered in one place. General Wayne would have his hands full with this bunch if the commissioners failed to win a peace treaty.

It was Big Oak, then, who saved their lives. While Thad and Jinja were heedlessly studying the teeming villages of the Maumee Valley, Big Oak was keeping close watch around them. He did not like the way the Shawnees had disappeared. Although his eyes were no longer keen, his mind was sharp as ever. In the blurred background on a low ridge to the south he caught a movement that could not have been a deer.

"That way, boys," he said, quietly but urgently, and they did not have to be told again. They let him lead the way, back from where they had come, in an all out sprint that might keep the Shawnees from cutting them off. Now Big Oak saw three things. First he saw that there were six Shawnees in the party that had discovered them. Next he saw five of them explode out of their place of observation, trying to cut off their path of retreat. The sixth headed directly down the slope toward the river, toward the villages, whooping. Soon there might be a hundred or more on their trail.

Big Oak did not concern himself with how they were going to dodge a whole army of warriors a hundred fifty miles north of General Wayne's legion. He was focused on the more immediate goal of getting through the gap between the braves and the river before they were cut off. The Shawnees had a lot of ground to make up, but they had a downhill run, while Big Oak, Thad, and Jinja had an up-and-down sprint along the trail that averaged out level. There were no villages on their side of the river, so Big Oak decided to leave the trail and angle down the hillside toward the river. That gained them more speed and maintained much of the distance between them and the Shawnees, though the speedy young warriors were bound to gain on the old-timer and his shopkeeper son. Soon they had reached the flood plain, on level ground. They could see their pursuers gaining on them step by step, and off in the distance behind them they began to hear the chorused whooping of an aroused red army as they launched their canoes to cross the river and join in the pursuit.

Ahead they saw the junction of the Maumee and the Auglaize, and the fields full of tall corn that lined the fertile plain of the Auglaize on both sides of the river. They redoubled their efforts and dashed for the distant cornfields, but the shouting, whooping Shawnees behind them were far too close and gaining too fast.

"I'll slow them down," Big Oak gasped, abruptly dropping to one knee. The Shawnees were a hundred fifty yards away when he cocked his rifle and somehow steadied his breathless body. The distance must have looked pretty good to them. They didn't slacken for a moment until Big Oak pulled the trigger and knocked a leg out from under their leader. That stopped them in their tracks—for the moment. Thad and Jinja had stopped fifty yards farther down the flood plain, kneeling, their rifles pointed back toward the Shawnees, who fled from the flood plain into the adjacent brush. Big Oak retreated at a trot. The whoops from downriver were getting louder. The three scouts again broke into a sprint. Directly ahead were the cornfields, and beyond the fields, just above the wooded hills to the west, hovered the big red ball of a sun.

The three did not all run down the same row. They disappeared into the cornfield at three different points and maintained their speed to keep as much distance as possible between themselves and the Shawnees, who returned to the flood plain as soon as they saw their prey enter the cornfield. As the three scouts had raced for the cornfield, at least fifty warriors running along the flood plain had come close enough to see what was happening and follow.

For just a moment Big Oak had the thought that an old man had no business trying to outrun the united Shawnee, Miami, and Wyandot nations in the northwest wilderness. But the thought vanished quickly as the warriors drew nearer. "This way," he huffed to Jinja and Thad, and he veered south, toward where the cornfield met the woods. They veered with him to the left, hoping the warriors were not trying to flank them, hoping they would not be cut off.

As they ran south, Jinja moved ahead by fifteen or twenty yards. There was a small cleared space between the field and the woods. At the edge of the cornfield Jinja stopped and looked out to see if their pursuers had covered this avenue of escape. They had not, but as Big Oak and Thad emerged from the field, so did one lone brave, a young Miami waving a huge war club. Jinja and the Miami immediately ran at each other. Jinja would not shoot, for that would give away their position to their pursuers. As the young Miami raised the club over his head, Jinja reversed his rifle, veered to the left and swung it into the belly of the Miami. The wood smacked into flesh with tremendous impact and the Miami fell as if poleaxed.

Now they were in the woods. Gratefully, they slowed down to a trot and listened to the war cries growing fainter. Below, they could see where the cornfields ended. The woods led deep into the valley, close to the river. The valley was deep in shadow. They headed for that shadow.

Soon the night would cover them. Then the only question remaining would be how far would they have to travel on this night to get beyond the clutches of their pursuers. However far they went, it would not seem like enough. And yet they had to stop now. For once in his life Big Oak could go no farther. Quietly he sank to one knee, his chest heaving uncontrollably, his legs numb with exhaustion. He did not try to talk. He did not even have the strength to tell them to go on without him.

They would not have, of course. They waited patiently in the shadow-sheltered woods while Big Oak's breathing came under his control and his heartbeat slowed down. He tilted his head back, closed his eyes and let his mouth gape open for a few more moments. Slowly, he arose from his kneeling position. "Boys," he said, "don't get old. It's a hell of a fix to put yourself in."

"There are villages up and down the valley," Big Oak explained to the hefty figure with the powdered hair. "There must be at least two thousand warriors. Wyandot, Shawnee, Miami, and Delaware."

Wayne glanced up from his meager breakfast with a look of pain on his face, but he did not complain about the gout that was making his morning hell.

"Mmm," he murmured. He chewed and swallowed. "We can't match those numbers. Not yet. But if I know my government, that commission will take its time, and the president will not let me down. We'll get more men. We're well-equipped, you see. And we're turning into a real army, you'll see that too."

"Have you seen any sign of the Miamis while we were gone?" Big Oak asked.

"Just traces," Wayne replied. "I'm glad you're back. We'll

begin the march north in three days. And if they'll not have peace, then by the Almighty we'll give them war."

"They did not seem to be in the mood for peace," Big Oak remarked. "And if I were them, I would feel the same way."

"Yes, well—you're not, old fellow, and I hope you don't forget it."

"Forget it? General, I can promise you that when the Miami-Shawnee-Wyandot legion was chasing us down the valley of the Auglaize, they did not inquire as to my sympathies or political beliefs. My allegiance is to my family and the men of the army I fight for. It's just that I have observed three score years of the white man pushing the red man toward oblivion. It is as clear as the pool of a mountain stream. I used to believe that if the Indians could unite, they could find a river bank and make their stand and stop the whites right there. I used to believe that if the Indians could only learn to make white man goods, so they did not have to depend on the white man for guns, blankets, and kettles, *then* they could guard the mountain passes and keep the white man on their side of the divide.

"But I know different now. In the end, it is not the nature of the red man that ensures his defeat. He could unite in mighty confederation from the lakes to the mouth of the big river. He could learn to make his own rifles and keep them repaired like new—he won't, but even if he could, even if he *could*, in the end it is numbers. There are too many whites willing to brave all the dangers and defy all the odds—they stream over the mountains thick as the western buffalo. And it is the numbers that will overwhelm my poor red wretches.

"The night we made our desperate escape from the Maumee Valley, there we were, at dawn, huddled together in the brush by a rock that commanded a view for miles around. We saw no signs of the warriors who pursued us. They had decided that we were not worth the effort. And I looked north toward where those thousands of Miami, Shawnee, Wyandot, and Delaware were camped, with their cornfields and their melon fields and their children and their dogs, and I thought that if I came back here in two years or five years or ten years, I would find the cabins of white farmers, living in peace and security, because the red men will have given up more land, and moved west of the Wabash, or the Illinois, or whatever river the white man claims as the new permanent boundary."

General Wayne had lived mostly in the settled areas of the nation and fought his greatest battles against white men. He was a Federalist. First on his list of national aspirations was a prosperous, secure, united States. There was not much room in that dream for thoughts of the welfare of the tribes. But the simple earnestness of this American legend who sat in a chair opposite him, sucking on his cold pipe, caught his attention.

"I know it is hard for you to understand, General. You look at their painted faces and you see savages. But I have lived with them as my brothers. I assure you that they are men. Men with faults, men with flaws. Some of those flaws are the same as ours, some of them seem different. But they have their goodnesses too—some the same, some different from ours. They leave their legacy. When they are gone, we will have lost something precious, but we will also have something grafted permanently to our national character, something fine. I only hope we will have the greatness of spirit to thank them for having put it there."

21

THE MAPLES IN FRONT OF THEM BROUGHT A crimson mix to the yellow and pale green of the walnuts and hickories. The night before had been a cold one, and Big Oak had awakened to his first stiff joints of the season. He didn't think much about it. He simply moved himself into the sun and walked around until the sweat came and the stiffness disappeared.

Over the past month, General Wayne's legion had marched north till they were about seventy miles north of Cincinnati. A hundred twenty miles or so farther north was Lake Erie, which might well be their spring destination. Before them was a wide, defensible grassland with a stream running through it. This would be winter quarters, Wayne decided, and he put his men to work building tiny log huts. Wayne was a soldier's general. The first huts were built for the rank and file, the next for the officers, and the last one for the general himself. They built blockhouses on the outer edges of the camp and connected them with walls. He named the place Fort Greenville, after his departed friend, the Revolutionary War hero Nathanael Greene.

The Shawnees did not know the name of the new fort, but they knew it was there, one more fort aimed at the heart of their country. It was time for them to exact a price. The grass on the prairie around the fort was yellow, but it was still long and straight. Big Oak and Jinja were standing on the catwalk looking over the wall at the creek winding off in the distance.

"Tell me, Jinja," Big Oak said. "Have you ever stood in the tall grass and listened to the wind move through it?"

"Many times," Jinja answered.

"It's different from the trees. Grass talks to you. Tells you things that the trees keep to themselves."

"Like what?" Jinja asked.

"Boys!" Big Oak said to a handful of dragoons who were grazing their horses beneath the walls of the fort. "I'm gonna fire a shot over your heads into the grass down toward the creek. I'd get ready for some action if I were you."

By now most of the men in the fort knew about the old scout and his fearsome reputation. They waited while he raised his rifle and cocked the hammer.

"You seein' what I'm seein' or are my eyes playing tricks on me?" Big Oak asked.

"I see all right," his grandson replied as Big Oak's rifle roared. Immediately two Shawnees jumped up from the tall grass where they were crawling and raced for the stream with the dragoons in hot pursuit, bareback on their mounts. One of the Shawnees was cut down by the sword of an officer, the other was ridden down and trampled by the hoofs of the horse of a sergeant.

Dozens of soldiers gathered at the wall, silently staring down at the sudden death of two men they had not even known existed. "They weren't there just to admire our horses," Big Oak observed. "I'll bet they've been out there every day since they found out we were here. We just never noticed them until today."

"I guess we'd better tell the general, then," Jinja suggested.

General Wayne heard the news in bad humor. He stomped around his quarters, and every time he stepped with his bad leg, pain shot through it, which intensified his profanity. "Damn it, Sam!" he growled. "I've got a convoy heading south tomorrow for supplies."

"Couldn't you delay a day?" said Wayne's adjutant. "Send the dragoons out tomorrow to sweep the area clean."

"The Indians would just vanish and come back the next day," Wayne replied. "There's no way to keep them from knowing we've got a convoy leaving. I've got to make the convoy strong enough to protect the wagons but not so strong that we're left too weak here."

The next morning the gate opened and a train of wagons left, protected by ninety foot soldiers who formed lines on both sides of the train. Down the trail they went toward Fort Jefferson. Not very far down that trail was a reception party of about fifty warriors, and with them were Badger and Sees the Moon. They were concealed in thickets on either side of the trail, thirty to fifty yards removed from the path of the convoy.

Both Badger and Sees the Moon felt dread in their bellies. There were twice as many soldiers as attackers. But as they looked to the left and right of them, they took heart from the rough confidence on the painted faces of the older warriors. They must know what they're doing, both of them thought, as they waited, motionless, their tomahawks at the ready, for the signal to charge.

A single ululating howl was drowned out by the war cries of fifty voices as they ran forward across the narrow space that separated them from their enemies. Badger saw the look on the faces of the soldiers and, slim as his battle experience was, he knew this would be a good day. Before they had crossed the space, half of the soldiers had recovered from their shock enough to start racing back up the road to Fort Greenville. Others did not take flight until the shrieking red men were almost upon them, but they took flight nevertheless. That left fewer than two dozen, some of whom managed to fire their muskets before tomahawks crashed down on their skulls.

Their death was quick and sure. When the war cries came, Badger and Sees the Moon were both a step late off the mark. By the time they reached the convoy, every soldier who had failed to run was down, either dead or dying. The two young braves turned and looked for any other white men who might have survived. All they saw was the dust rising on the trail headed north. Both took a few steps in pursuit, then realized it would only be the two of them pursuing an astounding number of soldiers. They returned to the convoy and found several horses standing in their traces. Although neither was an accomplished rider, each cut a horse free, mounted it, and attempted to bend it to his will. Both horses were unused to having riders on their backs. Both of them reared. The two warriors slid off and watched the horses go galloping through the woods.

There were more than sixty horses to be seized as spoils of war, and a number of fine wagons. Within ten minutes of the first screech, the trail was lonesome, silent and deserted, save for the scalped bodies of twenty men who had begun the morning in the ranks of General Wayne's legion.

General Wayne was furious when he was told about the rout. "Why is it," he shouted as he stomped around his quarters, "that the best men, the ones who stay at their posts, are the ones who die, while the cowards slither away?" He called a court-martial, and the evidence gathered indicated there were no more than fifty Shawnees attacking the convoy, that they were outnumbered by two to one, that they were outgunned, and that they could have been slaughtered if the soldiers had only kept their heads.

But what was he to do? Seventy men had run away. Should he shoot all seventy? You shoot a deserter to enforce discipline. If he punished these men, he would begin the deadly cycle of nightly desertion, especially once they were back on the trail. No, he would have to swallow this disaster and take it as a warning that his men were not yet the soldiers they needed to be if they were going to win a war against wily woods fighters.

The attack also served as a warning that Fort Greenville was vulnerable. He had four hundred men on sentry duty at all times, and prepared to send a large working party to build yet another fort still deeper into Miami territory. Just before Christmas, Big Oak, Thad, and Jinja started north before eight companies under the command of Major Henry Burbeck. On their flanks, so stealthy that even Big Oak and Jinja could not find them, though they assumed they were out there, were a handful of veteran Miami warriors. They were astonished to find that these soldiers made camp on the very hill where six hundred Americans had been cut down in battle only a couple of years before.

Among the warriors lurking in the woods was the old Mingo veteran Skoiyasi. In another era he had been raised alongside Thad in the Seneca village of Tonowaugh, and bested Thad in competition for the young girl Kawia. The years of privation that were a part of the red man's existence had left him with a body more like Big Oak's than Thad's.

The white man had taught him one great lesson—that he was no longer a Seneca, nor was he a Mingo. He was—he didn't even know a good word for it. He was a "not white man." He was brother to the Twightwees, brother to the Shawnees, brother to the Chippewas, brother to the

Ottawas. If they could ever throw the white man away, they might suffer without guns, or blankets, or kettles. But it would be nothing compared to the humiliation they suffered now. The past spring, he had seen the first white smokes near his village on the Muskingum.

With him was a Shawnee named Yellow Kettle, who had attached himself to the Mingoes of another village. Yellow Kettle had been here before, with the Miamis when they slaughtered the troops of St. Clair. They watched together as the companies of Major Burbeck tramped through the long grass, laying out their new encampment. They watched when the soldiers noticed that they were stepping on many objects hidden in the long grass. They watched as the soldiers bent down and began to pick bones out of the long grass.

"They cannot lay down tonight." Yellow Kettle laughed. "Until they pick up enough bones to clear a spot for their blankets." Tents were erected, and then, while a hundred men stood sentry around the camp, the rest combed the long grass on the hill and started making piles of bones, and a separate pile for the skulls.

Skoiyasi's still sharp senses caught the distant approach of a patrol. He recognized as familiar the figures of Thad and Big Oak ahead of the patrol, though for the moment he could not attach them to names and places. "Come on," he said, and he and Yellow Kettle sneaked away undetected, deep into the woods.

"White men are very foolish," Yellow Kettle said. "To camp at the place where so many of their kind were destroyed. We will pile their bones on top of the old bones, don't you think?" He was not nearly as old as Skoiyasi, but he had experience on the warpath. He should have known better, Skoiyasi thought.

* * *

The men buried the bones of their brothers in arms. Then, once again, pointed like the end of a sword at the heartland of the Miamis, they built a fort. It was compact but sturdy. To the consternation of the Miamis and Shawnees who watched the fort go up, there were four bronze six-pound cannons on the walls to defend it. These cannons were familiar to those Indians who had fought there before. During St. Clair's defeat, they were the ones the Indians had conquered and buried in a swamp. The white soldiers of Major Burbeck had stumbled upon the place where the cannons had been buried.

General Wayne named the encampment Fort Recovery. There it stood, arrogant, on the hill that had witnessed America's greatest defeat at the hands of those who had come before them. It was a simple fort, a square log stockade with blockhouses at the corners and loopholes in the walls.

Big Oak, Thad, and Jinja were just about the only souls in the legion who roamed freely outside the walls throughout the winter. There were heavily protected supply convoys between Fort Greenville and Fort Recovery, and frequent wood-cutting parties, but nearly everybody else stayed within the shadows of the walls and did drill. Neither Big Oak nor Thad were keen about running around the woods by themselves, but Wayne insisted on frequent reconnaissance. It was up to them to figure out how to stay alive.

They varied their routine, usually leaving the fort under cover of darkness. They would spend hours at a time lying still in a dark hollow, listening for the soft tread of moccasins on old leaves. They seldom crossed the Wabash River to the north. They found occasional evidence of Indian spies, but it was obvious to all three that the braves of the united tribes were observing their usual custom of saving their fighting for the good weather.

What Wayne's faithful scouts could not have known was that in February the Miami chief Little Turtle was conferring with Lord Dorchester in Canada. And Lord Dorchester was promising Little Turtle not only small arms and supplies, but also English soldiers and artillery. The English, he said, would probably be at war with the Americans before the year was over. If Little Turtle had been the old Seneca chief Kyashuta, or the Mohawk Joseph Brant, he might have known better than to take Lord Dorchester's words literally, but because he did not know the English as the Iroquois did, he regarded Lord Dorchester's words as if they had come from the mouth of an honored chief. He had to. Each time General Wayne built another fort deeper into the wilderness, he drew the united tribes closer and closer to calamity.

This general and his troops were ever alert. There would be no sneak attack at dawn such as the one that had annihilated the force of Arthur St. Clair.

Neither the scouts nor General Wayne knew that the British were building a fort along the Maumee Rapids, not far from where the scouts had nearly met their end the past fall. The fort was built on land the British had ceded to the United States by treaty in 1783. Had Washington known of the fort, he would have considered it an act of war on the part of the British. But he did not know. Buoyed by the presence of the British fort as evidence that they had a staunch white ally, the tribes began to plan an attack. In fact, many of the braves were positively thrilled by the prospects of an attack. These were Americans, they said, easy pickings, with ample supplies to ease the passage of the Indian villages from the winter into the summer months. But they were in no hurry. It was their own lives they were risking, and they would attack when they were good and ready.

The weeks went by, and the months. The leaves came back to the walnuts and hickories, and Thad was beginning to wonder how his old father-in-law was handling the business back home. The signs of tribal activity around Fort Recovery had been increasing for the past few weeks, to the point where the three scouts told Major Burbeck that it was getting too dangerous to be scouting anymore. The Indians were out there, all right. The major agreed to give them the freedom to stay or leave, according to when they thought it might be safe. He armed his supply convoys well. The men were very careful. It was summer, the war season. They knew that soon the bullets would sing.

Major William McMahon was one of the tallest men in North America. Six-foot-six, with whipcord muscles stretched across his big-boned frame, he rode out the gate of Fort Recovery at the head of a convoy bound for Fort Greenville in the pale glow of the early morning sun as it peeped over the treetops. The empty wagons creaked and the harness leather squeaked. The day before, the convoy had arrived carrying goods from Fort Greenville. They had seen no sign of hostile activity along the previous day's journey. Still, the men were anxious to get out of the closed-in little fort and back to what they considered the safer environs of Fort Greenville.

They would never make it—at least, not this day.

As they moved through the stretch of prairie between the fort and the trail heading south, McMahon and those with him at the front of the convoy saw the grass across their front oscillating violently.

Damn! McMahon thought. "Indians!" he shouted, a brief moment before a barrage of musket fire plowed into the column. The range was short and several officers immediately slid from their saddles. Horses turned and headed through the column back to the gate, followed by men on foot who had fallen off their mounts or abandoned their wagons.

Suddenly the fort was surrounded by Miamis and Shawnees, hundreds of them, shooting from behind trees and stumps or racing toward the stockade. The big gates were swung forward and the men of the convoy raced for the opening. The gunfire from the Indians boomed and crackled, and more soldiers outside the fort fell. The Indians closed in, running after the shying, terrified horses while gunfire found some of them from the loopholes of the fort.

Just before he reached the gate, McMahon turned around to get a glimpse of his pursuers. A single bullet pierced his forehead. His eyes rolled back and his mouth gaped open as he toppled from his horse. Others around him also fell. Their more fortunate comrades made it through the opening, and frightened men pushed the gates closed just in time to shut out a howling gaggle of Miamis. From the blockhouses a blazing cross fire brought down a number of the invaders in the shadow of the walls of the fort. The rest of them retreated quickly toward the tall grass and then to the tree line, where they reloaded their weapons and helped their companions keep up a continuous deadly fire aimed at the loopholes of the fort.

Their aim was not bad. Within the fort, men were beginning to tumble from the catwalk with ghastly wounds in their faces.

The Mingo Skoiyasi was not among those who searched for glory beneath the walls of the fort. He had no family or village left to hear his songs of prowess in battle. He was out there in the warm morning sun with no purpose other than to kill as many whites as he could, from behind a stout tree with his deadly rifle.

But it was the men in the fort who had the best position. Once they realized it was a bad idea to stand in front of the loopholes loading their weapons, they were a hard target to find. Big Oak found tiny crevices between the logs with which to seek out targets. Once he had sighted a scalp lock that looked good to him, he appeared at the appropriate loophole, rifle loaded and cocked, for no more than two seconds, pulled the trigger and withdrew to reload. Jinja, also a seasoned veteran, used a similar technique. Nor did they appear at the same loophole for every shot.

Two men in succession lingered too long at the loophole next to Jinja and fell dead, each with his face a mask of blood. Another came up to take their place. Throughout the morning and into the afternoon the united tribes kept up a withering barrage. There seemed to be no end to their supply of ammunition. That was odd. Indians generally had to make do with scanty supplies of lead and powder. Big Oak, Jinja, and Thad blazed away at the painted faces as they appeared from behind the trees to continue their deadly fire. Big Oak found that he was not all that concerned for Jinja, whose instincts for fire and cover were every bit as good as his own. It was Thad who concerned him, Thad who had spent so much time among the counters and warehouses of Wendel and Watley and so little in the woods, especially in times of war. A man can lose his edge, Big Oak thought as he poured just the right amount of powder down the barrel then rammed the bullet and wad home. All it took was one lost moment of exposure, and a bullet would destroy your body.

He dumped primer in the pan, took a quick look over the wall and spotted a Shawnee kneeling by a buckeye tree. He ducked his head and pulled back the hammer of his rifle. Then he sighted quickly through the loophole. The Shawnee was gone. He pulled back immediately, just as a bullet tore a splinter out of the side of the loophole. He looked again, spotted his man and fired. Maybe he hit him, maybe he didn't. He did not linger at the loophole long enough to find out. Well away from the loophole, he was loading again, then peering out through the tiny gap between the logs.

He heard Jinja's rifle explode beside him, and saw a man who thought himself concealed jerked backward by Jinja's bullet.

"Good shot, boy!" he said.

"I got him?"

"Got him good," Big Oak assured him.

"Mmm," Jinja grunted, and proceeded to reload.

To Jinja's right, Thad clutched at his right hand. He groaned, and climbed down from the catwalk with blood streaming down his fingers.

"You all right?" Big Oak asked, looking down toward his son.

"You better get someone else up there, Sergeant," Thad said to a stout soldier below who was carrying ammunition from place to place. "I don't think I can hold a rifle steady with this." He held up his bloody hand. "Damn!" He looked up at Jinja and Big Oak. "I'll be back when I find out if I've still got a hand left."

There was a lot of language coming from within the fort, and screaming and moaning from the wounded. The only drug was whiskey, no help for those dying of belly wounds and not much help for anybody else who was wounded. But as the sun continued its pitiless journey across the sky, Big Oak began to wonder if he was just wishing or were there actually fewer red men behind the trees blasting shots through the loopholes?

Skoiyasi was among the last to slink away into the deep gathering shadows of the coming night. Although he and his cohorts had not conquered the fort, he counted his successes in the number of American lives he had shortened. Two for certain, and probably more. He was not discouraged, he was exhilarated. Fighting the Americans was all he lived for, and he knew that there would be more fighting in the days to come. As he ran through the woods with the last of the fighters, he took a deep breath of the sweet warm forest air and decided that in spite of the death of some fine young warriors, it had been a good day.

He ran through the woods until it was completely dark, then slowed to a walk. Ahead he spotted the flicker of a campfire. It drew him like a moth, and there he was pleased to see the Shawnee war chief Blue Jacket gathering hundreds of braves around him. When he had their attention, he began to speak.

"The men in the fort," Blue Jacket said, "must believe that we have done enough fighting for the day. You know how white men are. They will be in deep sleep on this night. And this night we will sneak through the tall grass up to the walls of the fort." He pointed through the leaves of the oaks, elms, and ashes around him. "Look. The moon hides its face for us. If we are quiet, they will not discover us until we have climbed the wall and opened the gate. And then, my brothers, they will wake, just in time to see the faces of their killers."

22

ACROSS THE FIELD OF LONG GRASS LOOMED the dark, solid mass of Fort Recovery. Skoiyasi stood with Blue Jacket and his Shawnee warriors at the tree line. Then they all dropped down and began to crawl through the long grass.

Perfectly confident that they could move across the field to the foot of the stockade wall, they crawled slowly, silently, carefully, arm by arm, knee by knee, toe by toe.

Captain Gibson knew the value of his scouts. Once it was certain that the daytime attack was over, he sent the two men to their quarters, and they slept for several hours. When Big Oak awoke, he was pleased to see Thad sleeping close by, his hand bandaged but otherwise unharmed. He awakened his grandson and the two men walked from their darkened quarters into the darkened out-of-doors. They were not pleased to see a black sky with neither stars nor moon to give them a clue.

They mounted the catwalk of the front wall of the fort. Below, the grassy field was deepest black. They stuck their faces out the loopholes. And they listened.

The minutes crawled by in sluggish procession. There was no wind to stir the trees or the grass. That was good.

They listened with patience. They knew that the attackers had not been licked yet. A night attack was not at all out of the question, given the enemies' disrespect for the skills and senses of the Americans. Nighttime was a good time for fear war.

More minutes went by, then an hour, and more. Still they listened and heard nothing.

And then Jinja heard something. He wasn't sure. He tapped his grandfather on the shoulder and saw him nod. Big Oak looked across the gate. On cat feet Jinja moved down the ladder, crossed in front of the gate, then up the ladder to the other side.

Still Big Oak waited, to be certain of what he had heard. It could have been an animal, and yet he did not think so.

And then he was sure. The noise was the same, clothes on grass, closer this time. There was no question. He pointed his rifle down into the blackness and fired. The roar of the Pennsylvania rifle echoed in the night. Jinja answered with fire from the other side of the gate, followed by a score or more of shots across the front wall, then a few seconds later a few shots fired by those who were a little late, and then more shots from the fast reloaders. In the night they could hear the swish-swish-swish of men fleeing through the long grass, back to the shelter of the woods. The men on the wall fired a blind fusillade at them. Then there was silence, except for the faint crunching of dry leaves as the warriors fled deep into the woods.

The suddenness of the attack put nerves on edge for the rest of the night, in spite of the fact that the Indians had not fired a shot. Sleep was hard to come by for the men of Fort Recovery, until the sun glowed pale yellow over the hills to the east, and then the men could scarcely keep awake. Instead of the usual routine of drill and busywork, Captain Gibson allowed the men to sleep in shifts, while those on the wall kept a sharp eye for any activity in the nearby woods. With the dawn, he dispatched one very nervous messenger on a swift horse bound for Fort Greenville to inform General Wayne of the attack. He then made his rounds to visit the many wounded and to order a burial party out to a spot so close to the fort that they could inter the dead without fear of yet another attack.

General Wayne was not thrilled about the casualties at Fort Recovery, but he was encouraged by the news that his old comrade in arms, Colonel Charles Scott, was coming up from Kentucky with close to a thousand tough, Kentucky militia, many of them mounted. There, Wayne thought, were some men to fight alongside.

What pleased him less was the role of the British in this whole affair. After Big Oak, Thad, and Jinja had brought General Wayne news of the huge encampments on the Auglaize and Maumee rivers, the general sent out two riders, Captain William Wells and Lieutenant Robert McLellan, to find out more about the warriors of this encampment and their intentions. What they found out was that the tribes were camped there to be close to the new British fort below the rapids of the Maumee River.

When Captain Wells brought him that news, Wayne stomped around his quarters so hard that his swollen leg throbbed in agony. "Damn them all anyway!" he cried. "Why did they bother signing a peace treaty if they were going to be so damned treacherous about it!" He had been sipping brandy that day—or maybe gulping it. The brandy and the bad news brought his talent for profane invective to new heights as he damned the English for dastardly caitiffs, and swore that if he caught any of them with the Indians, their remaining lives would be short and unpleasant. He knew from his meetings with Shawnee chiefs that the English had been telling the Indians the Northwest Territory was theirs and that therefore they had the right to keep it. Damn them, they knew what the treaty said. What conscienceless liars! How many good American citizens would lose their lives on account of these lies? How many soldiers and Indians would die on account of these lies? "Arrrgh!" His fury displayed itself in an inarticulate growl as he walked from his quarters into the hot sunshine.

Soldiers in faraway posts do not like to live like stone-age savages. They enjoy amenities that remind them of their civilized roots. When Wayne walked out of his cabin, he walked into a beautiful garden lovingly tended by a pair of green-thumbed privates. The garden was surrounded by a very English-looking picket fence. The setting served to calm the general down a degree or two. His mind began to work in more orderly fashion. Standing in that garden, he started to plan the expedition that would decide the fate of the Northwest Territory for this generation.

When the Kentuckians arrived, Wayne resolved to move quickly, before these new militiamen had a chance to get restless and worried about the future. On July 28, just two days later, the four sub-legions of Wayne's legion, plus the mounted Kentuckians, marched out into the breezeless heat, bound north for Fort Recovery. Wells and McLellan had gone on ahead of the legion, picked up Big Oak, Thad, and Jinja at Fort Recovery, and then continued north. By the time the legion had camped on grounds north of Fort Recovery, Jinja had discovered signs of red spies on the right flank, warriors taking big steps northward toward the Maumee, to tell the united tribes that the Americans were on the march in force. These spies would be back, reporting to their leaders about every movement of the legion.

As he had done all along his string of forts, Wayne put his men to work building roads and bridges to ease the way for supply wagons. Up ahead of these pioneers were the scouts, searching restlessly for Indian scouts or ambushes, forever keeping themselves between the enemy and their army, knowing how little the main forces suffered if their scouts were ambushed, and how much they all would suffer if a large Indian force were to slip by the scouts and surprise the main body.

Big Oak, Thad, and Jinja were together on the right flank on the second of August when they heard the sound of horses to their right. They ran in the direction of the sound and made it just close enough to see four Shawnees on horseback. Across the back of one of the horses, trussed tight and gagged, lay a white man in civilian clothes that Big Oak recognized as Newman, the deputy quartermaster. They were close enough to hear a high-pitched, strangled keening from the terrified clerk. The three bolted into a run, cocking their rifles as they sprinted through the forest after the horsemen, but the Shawnees had seen them and pointed their horses north at a gallop. By nightfall they would be in their village, torturing Newman until he had told them everything there was to be told about the strength and destination of the legion.

The legion continued its march north, but the scouts were way ahead of them, more and more cautious with each day. They had reached the Auglaize River and knew that the following morning they would be nearing the first of the long succession of villages along the Auglaize and the Maumee. There was no shortage of Indian sign now, the question was, how long had it been since they last passed, and what did they have in mind to surprise the army of General Anthony Wayne?

The long series of adventures was wearing Big Oak down, but he knew that as long as he stayed healthy, he would have the strength to make it through. Their contact with the first villages made him believe the battle was near. His experience told him that if Wayne could give the tribes one decent beating, they would consider themselves defeated and make a treaty. On the other hand, he had taken the measure of General Wayne, and he knew that it would take a defeat the size of St. Clair's to send him back to the Ohio. Only a great surprise attack by the tribes could possibly attain such a victory, and he doubted that Wayne would ever allow himself to be surprised.

So he wasn't surprised when he heard what Thad and Jinja had to tell him the next day. While Big Oak had remained in the field watching and listening from high in a big old elm tree, his son and grandson had loped on back to General Wayne to tell him about discovering the first of the villages on the Auglaize. Captain William Clark, who was with him at the time, and General Wilkinson, his second in command, thought the mounted Kentuckians ought to ride down on the village and annihilate it. Jinja laughed later when he told Big Oak what Wayne had to say to Wilkinson. "Sir," Wayne had said with cool courtesy, "while they're tearing through that little village looting it, the rest of the valley will be on us like bad on Lucifer. I tell you, I want to meet most of theirs with all of ours."

"Big Oak," Jinja said, "the air went right out of Wilkinson and he stuck out his lip as if to tell Wayne, You *never* do what I wanna do. Then he stomped out of General Wayne's tent without even saluting."

Big Oak nodded. This was one tough general. He had drilled his troops day after day behind the walls of the successive forts he had built, and he had continued to drill them on the march north. He did not treat his scouts as if they were fools or scoundrels or both, but listened to their reports carefully and always seemed to ask the right questions. He was the kind of general who could make a winner out of any army.

By August eighth they had made it to where the waters of the Auglaize flowed into the Maumee River. Sitting astride his horse, staring down from the military crest of the nearest hill, Wayne could see the Maumee sparkling in the late afternoon sun like a diamond necklace. He could see the endless cornfields, with pumpkin plants growing between the rows. He could hear the birds and the bullfrogs. Among the cornfields stood a village of elm-barked wigwams. He studied them for a while with his telescope and said with certainty, "Gentlemen, there is nobody left in that village."

His aides and commanders were silent, listening.

"And yet we are in the heart of them," General Wayne declared. Nobody could argue with so obvious a declaration. Then he did what he always did during a deep foray into Indian country. He commanded that another fort be built. Across the river, close to the empty village and the cornfields, the site was perfect. There would be water on three sides, and a narrow field of attack on the fourth. The Indians had thoughtfully planted plenty of vegetables adjacent to the cornfields, and there was all sorts of forage for the precious mounts of the Kentucky horsemen. Like other previous forts he had built, it would be a simple affair of heavy logs, square, with a blockhouse on all four corners. With food plentiful and the strength of the position evident to even the most inexperienced private, morale was high as the men traipsed into the woods with ropes, horse teams, and axes. Let's see them attack us while we're building this fort. Let's see if they can swim faster than the bullet of a musket can fly. We're building a fort so close to them that they could reach out and touch us. We dare them to try.

This fort was more secure than the previous ones, with massive earthworks outside the walls, and a ditch that was both deep and wide, with a drawbridge that could only be raised and lowered by ropes controlled from within the fort. Confident as his men in the strength of this fortification, he named it Fort Defiance.

Still, it was Wayne's hope not to fight a battle if he did not have to. It was experience, not fear, that made him reluctant to fight. He had been a warrior long enough to know that in battle nothing is certain. He was too old and covered with glory to need another great victory. Results were what counted. He would be happy to return to civilian life as the peacemaker.

So in the middle of August he sent one of his scouts, Christopher Miller, to the tribes under a flag of truce. He carried letters for the Shawnees, Miamis, Delawares, and Wyandots, explaining to them that the English would not be there when they needed them, and that for the sake of their families, General Wayne begged them to send representatives to him for new treaty discussions.

Three days later the scout had not returned, and General Wayne did not wish to wait. The gates opened, the drawbridge descended, and the legion marched out, accompanied by Colonel Scott's mounted Kentuckians. Their destination was the enemy.

Nineteen miles east along the Maumee they saw three scouts emerge from the woods. They were Thad, Jinja, and Miller. Miller had a message for General Wayne, not on paper, but in his head. The leaders of the united tribes were considering his offer, and they would appreciate it if the captain of the white soldiers would wait there for ten days before he marched forward any farther. If he came any sooner, then they would fight.

Big Oak stood close by, leaning on his rifle. It was one

of the few liberties he took as a famous scout. He did not stand at attention in front of anybody, much less a general. It was not his way of being insolent. Rather, it was his way of reminding officers that he was a civilian, that he would fight willingly, but that he would not be ordered into ranks to charge into the mouth of a cannon. He had impressed this thinking on both Thad and Jinja.

Wayne and his officers listened to Miller as he conveyed the Indians' reply. Big Oak was also listening, curious whether General Wayne would understand the message hidden in Miller's words. Big Oak was a patient man. He almost never interrupted in conversation, and seldom volunteered advice until the officer involved was treading dangerously close to the precipice.

He need not have worried about Wayne. The general stood with his hands behind his back, staring at the route east along the north bank of the Maumee River. It was a hot day, but there was a light breeze blowing west from Lake Erie. For three long minutes the men in the camp who were close enough to see watched as the general stood still while the breeze blew in his face.

"Gentlemen," he said, "the miscreants expect us to wait for ten days while they make ready for battle. They want us to wait while they summon every savage who lives within a hundred miles of here. They want us to wait while they dredge up every envious Englishman and Frenchman to join them. But we will not wait!"

Then he turned to his adjutant. "We will continue the march tomorrow," he announced.

"That's it, then," Big Oak said to Thad. "All I can say is, it's gonna be one hell of a fight."

23

SKOIYASI WAS TIRED. FOR SEVERAL YEARS HE had lived in his village as an old bigbelly. He did a little fishing and a little hunting, but he had no young children to support, and when Kawia died there was only himself. Over the past two years his efforts on the trails had helped to beat him back into fighting shape. But he had too many years on him, and recently his old war injuries had come back to haunt him. He ran with a severe limp, when he could run at all. His joints were stiff, and his hearing was no longer what it once had been. He was wondering where his sons were. Why had they not heard of the coming battle, and if they had, then why had they not come?

He lay wrapped in his blanket, trying to sleep, knowing that the following morning there would be a big battle, possibly a decisive battle. He thought about the many battles he had been in, first against the Canadian Indians, then against the French, then against the English during what he had heard the white men call Pontiac's rebellion.

Three young men who had come, and were on the other side of the camp from Skoiyasi, were Caleb Big Oak, Kendee Big Oak, and Joshua Big Oak. They sat by the fire talking of home in the Tuscarora dialect that was their mother's.

"Do you think that Big Oak might be out there?" Joshua asked.

"Why would he make this war his war?" Caleb responded.

Ken, the middle child, the reflective one, sat and listened.

"Do you think Jinja might be out there?"

"Why ask me, Joshua?" Caleb shot back. "If Jinja is here, he should be fighting with us, not against us."

"With Jinja you can never tell, my brother," Ken said. "He wanted to be with us in the forest, and yet he worked for his father in the warehouse. And our father, do not forget, is an old man. He loves his life at home now, fishing, hunting, having visitors like the Oneida Paul Derontyan, or mother's family. I hope none of them are out there with the American army. We know where they are. We know where they are going. Blue Jacket has found the place to fight. When they come up tomorrow, we will be ready for them."

There was silence for a while. They stared into the heart of the flames and the glowing coals beneath them. Then Joshua spoke again.

"Big Oak always told us that no matter how many battles we won, in the end the whites would win the wars."

"Big Oak always was right about things like that," Ken responded. "And yet we must try, and hope that time and a life of ease will make them soft, so they will think it costs them too much to continue to fight us."

"Do you think that will happen?" Joshua persisted.

"I will fight this battle," Ken replied. "If we lose, and we survive, I will go to where the sun sets until I think I will not see the white men again in my lifetime."

The fire crackled. Neither Joshua nor Caleb wanted to share their thoughts. Not yet. Caleb threw some good dry wood on the fire and they watched it as it quickly ignited.

"If we lose this battle and I survive," Joshua said at last, "I will go home."

Not far from where Big Oak's three boys sat, Badger and Sees the Moon were talking about how hungry they were. They had eaten nothing, customary to many warriors the night before a great battle. For a long time they said nothing, but looked forward to the morning. It would be a great battle, Blue Jacket had told them. They were nervous, but not frightened.

Sees the Moon looked up at his young friend. "Can you see us going home after a victorious battle, entering our village with the scalps of many white men, being the ones to bring the news of the great victory?" he asked.

"If we do not win," Badger reminded his friend, "we will have no village to go home to."

"We will win," Sees the Moon insisted. "We must win."

"We have beaten them before," Badger agreed. "But this time they have a very great army."

"So have we," Sees the Moon reminded him. "We have four mighty peoples of one heart. This has not happened much. And our scouts say there are no Indians scouting for the Fifteen Fires. So they have no eyes."

Early the next morning, just as the mist was lifting from the valley of the Maumee River, Jinja, Thad, and Big Oak crept to the edge of thick forest growth and found themselves looking out on an area that had been partially opened up by a big wind many years before. Everywhere, there were huge uprooted trees, acres of them, resting on each other in great tangles, a natural fortress, easy to defend, almost impossible to penetrate.

"Uh," Big Oak grunted, his economical way of saying, "Here it is." Both Thad and Jinja also realized they had found the battleground as soon as they saw it. The question was, were the Indians already on the field? They lay quiet behind their tree trunks, watching and waiting for the men they knew had to be out there.

Jinja had eyes like telescopes. The leaves on the trees two hundred yards away appeared to him in sharp focus. And so did the movement of a single arm behind a large fallen maple tree.

"They're out there," he said, pointing to the spot. For Big Oak to spot anything at that distance was impossible, but Thad's eyesight was still strong enough to spot other indications of occupation.

"I don't know what the general can do about this," Thad said. "It would be hard to get through that if no one was there. Maybe we should head north and look for a route around their flank."

"The general said he wanted us to bring word as soon as we found them," Big Oak pointed out. "We found them, all right. Let's head on back."

It was already muggy and warm. Old Big Oak felt the strain as the three men loped the ten miles back from the field of fallen trees. Big Oak could not keep up. "Boys," he said, "I'll be along directly. You two get moving and I'll meet you somewhere along the march."

As soon as they left Big Oak, they picked up the pace. As he watched them lope away from him, he realized he'd been slowing them down, perhaps every day since they left Fort Hamilton so many months ago. Once they had left him, he did not continue to make his way after them, but sat down in a thick grove of black walnut trees and drank sparingly from his canteen. He might as well wait for them to come up. This was one battle he did not want to miss, and he did not wish to go into it bone-weary. Feeling well-hidden, he found a depression between the roots of a beech tree and lay down in it. He did not sleep, but his body rested until it had healed itself enough to get through the rest of this rugged day. Slowly, he continued the long walk back to Wayne's legion.

If Jinja and Thad thought the general would swing his troops into action as soon as the enemy had deployed, they were soon cured of that notion. This aggressive, temperamental man who had a reputation for winning battles with rash tactics was taking no chances. He had men and he had shovels. He used both to construct an earthwork. What supplies the men did not carry into battle they would leave here, and if they were forced to retreat, here is where they would assemble to defend themselves. That was a nice bit of psychology for the experienced general. With a good place to go, if the men found themselves in a tough spot, they would not drop their weapons and flee willy-nilly as St. Clair's men had.

The general explained it the following way to his officers the night before the attack: "I fully expect us either to run them out of the Maumee Valley or crush them. Either way they will be finished as a threat to us. But I will allow for every contingency. If there are more of them than we thought, if a group of men we are depending on panics and leaves us exposed, if our scouts have missed a force of enemy and we get surrounded or separated, if we must retreat, we will know where to retreat to.

"When one enemy defeats another, the greatest casualties occur when the defeated foe is fleeing in terror, with the enemy chasing them, slashing them to the ground. This will not happen to us. If we retreat to this fortress, and they pursue us, we will cut them up from behind these walls. Captain Pike," he concluded, "it'll be your job to guard whatever we leave behind when we march tomorrow."

Up to this point he had been haranguing them. Now he lowered his voice, and his officers leaned in to hear his message. "But I tell you, boys, just among us here. I believe that tomorrow we're gonna put an end to these meddling Englishmen and their Indians. In a short time there won't be a one of them left this side of the lakes."

As he lay on top of his blankets that hot, humid night, Wayne felt more relief than anxiety. He wondered how he had ever put up with two years of pussyfooting by the Federal government in Philadelphia. He was not a patient man. He had been forced to assemble his men gradually and keep them by promises and politics. He had trained them, and slowly, carefully, moved them north into the heart of the enemy, leaving forts like droppings all along the way. He had lost a few soldiers to desertion, a few to fear and cowardliness, and a few to legitimate battle, but in the process he had forged an army. Tomorrow, finally, would tell the story. And Wayne had confidence that he knew the ending.

The following morning, as the mist slowly rose from the valley, a shaved and powdered General Wayne inspected the troops in formation on his charger. He couldn't have walked if he had wanted to. His leg was aching like a mouthful of abscessed teeth.

The men had been stripped down to bare necessities. They wore linen shirts but no jackets, packs, or blankets. They carried their cartridge boxes, muskets, and canteens. They had eaten, and would not eat again until after the battle. Long, tapered bayonets had been fixed to the end of every musket barrel. They shined like torches in the morning sunlight. To the cadence of the drums, the legion stepped off in a long line anchored on the right flank by the Maumee River. Ahead of them was Major Benjamin Price's cavalry. It was their job to make first contact with the enemy. The legion marched over open ground. To their left, through the woods, marched the Kentucky militia, with mounted Kentuckians skirmishing in front of them. Advancing behind them were the shock troops, Captain Robert MisCampbell's legion cavalry.

The long line moved forward at a steady pace, one mile after the next. The men had little idea what to expect as they marched over the rolling terrain. They topped each rise expecting to meet heavy gunfire, then descended, only to rise again to the top of the next swell.

Big Oak had returned to the troops late the previous afternoon. He, Thad, and Jinja were with the Kentuckians, who reminded the old man of Daniel Morgan's rugged riflemen during the war for independence. Although the going through the woods was rougher than the open ground over which the legion marched, the militiamen had to keep up the pace in order to keep their flanks joined. At the same time, they were the ones most vulnerable to ambush in the woods, so they had to keep a sharp eye. That was the job of their horsemen who combed the woods ahead of them.

Onward they went over the rolling terrain until their shirts were soaked and their eyes stung from the perspiration. Along the bottomland and in the woods, the mosquitoes swarmed and bit. The men scratched and swatted and wiped the sweat from their eyes but they did not slacken their pace as they marched eastward, toward the waiting tribes. Major Price and his mounted troops were moving through tall grass in front of the legion foot soldiers. From their vantage point atop their horses they could see a stretch of woods before them, but once they had made it to the woods, they saw sunlight between the trunks. Must be a short stretch of woods, they thought. Perhaps another cornfield. No, when they got close they knew it was the field of fallen trees that they had been told about. There must have been some moans when they saw it. They had heard about it, and they were certain that the enemy *must* be in there.

Some of them wanted to turn around and ride back to the infantry and tell them, yup, they had found their enemy, now their job was done and good luck boys, go get 'em.

But part of their job was to draw fire from the concealed red men. They stepped out of the woods on their fine lean mounts and drew a blazing, smoking, deadly, blistering fusillade from the Shawnees and Miamis securely fortified within the massive tangle of fallen and uprooted trees.

That was enough for Price. Entrenched infantry can decimate a troop of men on horseback. The horses reared and shied. Their riders wheeled them about and headed back into the woods. General Wayne heard the gunfire and gave the orders for the men on foot to charge. Across the front, both militia and legion burst out of the woods, toward the fallen timber. On the left, with the Kentuckians, Big Oak, Thad, and Jinja found themselves rushing forward toward the toppled trees, listening to the bullets buzz past them, ignoring the danger. While the rest continued their charge, the three were close enough to drop to the ground, pick a target, and fire a deadly round. They quickly reloaded, then were up again, behind their cohorts now, but looking for the next exposed scalp lock.

Between the river and the forest of fallen timbers was a long green field of corn. Now that the enemy's attention was drawn to their front, Wayne ordered Captain Mis-Campbell's cavalry to charge into the cornfield then wheel left and strike the enemy hard on his left flank. The way the trees lay made that flank more accessible than Little Turtle had anticipated.

Sees the Moon had gotten separated from Badger when the legion charged into the forest of fallen trees. The two young braves were among the Shawnees holding the left against the legion. Confidently he braced his body against the uprooted poplar tree in front of him and took aim at Peter McLanahan, one of Anthony Wayne's privates who had been with him since he first started forming his legion in Pittsburgh. McLanahan had ridden out with him on the flatboats, had drilled for months at Fort Washington, had helped to build Fort Greenville, Fort Recovery, and Fort Defiance, and had never slacked a day. Sees the Moon sighted over his rifle barrel at the husky private as he ran across the deadly open space of ground with his companions, his bayonet-tipped musket at the ready. McLanahan fired his musket and did not stop to reload, but ran shoulder to shoulder with his mates as they looked for red flesh to provide a home for their bayonets. At one hundred yards Sees the Moon cocked his rifle. At seventy yards he squeezed the trigger. At sixty-eight yards McLanahan's body stopped in midair, fell to the ground, twitched twice, and lay still in a growing pool of blood.

Others fell around him, but most charged intact into the forest of fallen trees, leaping and climbing over the rotting wood, looking for warriors to kill. But the warriors were no longer there. They were showing their backs, climbing over tree trunks themselves as they retreated through the woods, then uphill toward the British fort behind them. And that's when Captain MisCampbell's cavalry galloped out of the cornfield.

Sees the Moon had reloaded as he retreated. And now he stopped, went down on one knee and took aim at Captain MisCampbell himself. He was close, only fifty yards away, when he fired and knocked the captain out of his saddle. There was no question of Sees the Moon's escaping, and he knew it. MisCampbell's second in command, Lieutenant Leonard Covington, spotted the young warrior struggling up the hill. The warrior heard the hoofbeats coming toward him. He dumped some powder into the barrel of his rifle and reached for his bullet pouch, then decided there was no time. He grabbed his tomahawk and turned to fling it at the charging lieutenant, but it was too late. Before he could pull his arm back, the horse was on top of him, and on top of the horse was Lieutenant Covington. Covington's sword sliced diagonally down and into Sees the Moon's neck. Blood sluiced out in a torrent. Sees the Moon's last war cry dissolved into a gurgle as the darkness of eternity closed in on him.

Many of the warriors here had done their share to annihilate St. Clair's army three years back, and some of them had also defeated Josiah Harmar's forces before that. Others had staged successful hit and run attacks on Wayne's forces, like the convoy ambush that had killed twenty men and driven the rest away in round-eyed panic. They had never come up against Americans who had taken their best and kept on coming. The hard-charging Americans gave them no chance to reload their weapons. Strong, well-conditioned, lightly burdened, Wayne's legionnaires pressed hard on the backs of the Shawnees and their allies. Their gleaming bayonets sent the Indians into headlong retreat, and Covington's cavalry drove them up the hill toward the English fort.

Among the hundreds of warriors racing for the gates of the fort were Caleb, Joshua, and Ken. Lagging behind them, his body struggling in a shambling, gimpy dogtrot, was a spent, crippled old Skoiyasi. Still, as some of his companions turned to fire down the hill at the pursuing horsemen, Skoiyasi willed himself ever closer to the gates of the fort. But the gates were shut. Surely they would open up to give succor to their fleeing allies. It was these English who had convinced them to take up arms against the Americans. "We will support you," they had said. "With your father the king you will keep your land. The king loves his Indians. The Americans despise you." In desperate flight, the king's red allies closed in on the fort, but the gates remained shut. Perhaps they were just waiting for their friends to get closer, then they would open up just enough to let them slip through before slamming them in the face of the enemy.

Only fifty yards from the gate now. Already there were younger braves at the gate, shouting, whooping, demanding, begging for admittance. And yet, unbelievably, the gates remained shut. Now Skoiyasi could hear the hoofbeats of the horse of Lieutenant Covington. He turned to face the white man, with a loaded rifle which he raised to his shoulder. But Skoiyasi rushed his shot, and his heaving chest and shaking hands sent the bullet wide. The lieutenant raised his bloody sword and brought it down hard. His stroke struck true. Skoiyasi felt little pain as he sank to the ground and knelt there, stunned, while his life's blood flowed out through a great gash between his shoulder and his neck. His eyes turned glassy, then closed against the bright sunshine. Slowly, like a man going to sleep for the night, Skoiyasi stretched out full length and died, facedown, in the shadow of the English fort.

The legion had marched into battle in fine order. The tribes facing them had understood exactly the positions they were defending and what they were to do when the Americans fled, as they were certain the Americans would. But now all sense of order was gone. The Americans had chased the warriors of the united tribes for two miles to the gates of the fort. Sweeping forward triumphantly, they had simply run over those Indians who were still fighting as they retreated. In the heat and the excitement, Big Oak lagged behind his attacking comrades.

Thad and Jinja would not leave him. They moved forward well behind their comrades, at a walk, through the fallen timbers and then into a dark stretch of forest on the way to the British fort. Ahead continued the crackling of gunfire and the war cries of both red and white men. The three Watleys passed a succession of bodies as they advanced, most of them stripped to the breechclout and painted from head to toe.

But they stopped for a moment at two bodies with painted faces and leather hunting shirts. Their heads were shaved except for their scalp locks. They were unmistakably white.

They moved on past three more dead Shawnees, then to another white Indian, sitting with his back up against a tree. His eyelids fluttered feebly as they bent over him, and he cried out for water. Big Oak let him drink a little from his canteen. The man had a chest wound. His time was short.

"Who are you?" Big Oak asked.

The man took a labored breath and gave a hoarse croak. Pink froth flowed from between his lips. "Graham," the man whispered. "Graham."

"Are you English?" Big Oak asked, opening the man's shirt at the neck.

"Canadian. Graham. Where are you?" said the Canadian.

A shot rang out from a nearby tree. Jinja turned toward the sound, saw the rising smoke, and ran toward it, his rifle at the ready. He fired once at a shadowy fleeing figure, then dropped his rifle and drew his tomahawk. The man he pursued may have been wounded. He was not running very fast. The swift Jinja overtook him quickly and showed no mercy. His tomahawk cleaved his prey's skull and the man fell heavily. Jinja did not take a scalp. He did not even linger long enough to make sure his man was dead. Instead he retraced his steps, picked up his rifle and returned to his father and his grandfather. There must have been a reason, he knew, why they had not backed him up in his pursuit.

Big Oak had taken a bullet in his thigh and was laying down next to the Canadian, who had lost consciousness and was drawing his final breaths unobserved while Thad and Jinja worked on the old man. They cut off the pant leg. There were wounds front and back, and blood was flowing freely from both. They did everything they knew how to do to stanch the flow of blood, and gave him water to drink, but as the minutes passed they could see Big Oak growing weaker. Thad looked at Jinja and shook his head. Jinja blinked back the tears, clenched his teeth and pressed rags against both wounds with all the pressure his powerful hands could muster. Big Oak lay quietly, not groaning or complaining, looking from his son to his grandson. "It's a good way for a man to die, boys," he said. He took three difficult breaths. His face had lost all its color. "I believe we've got 'em beat on this day." He cleared his throat and took another breath. "But damn," he concluded, "if I don't believe we were fighting on the wrong side."

24

CALEB, KEN, AND JOSHUA RAN TO THE GATES, hollering in English for the English to let them in. It was a defining moment in the history of the English in North America. If the gates did not open, it would mark the end of hope for the red men of the Northwest Territory. If the gates did open, it might very well mean war between England and the Fifteen Fires.

The three young men demanded entrance, but not for long. Over the years, they had heard many tales from their father Big Oak about the faithlessness of the English toward their red allies. And now, as they stood before the English fort, with deadly Americans climbing the hill, they knew that they had better not give the English too much time to make up their minds.

Fortunately for them, the Americans were tired after the long chase. As they labored up the hill, their gait slowed from a run to a jog to a walk. But there were hundreds of them, and very few red men on the hill near the fort. Desperately, the three sons of Big Oak took advantage of their pursuers' weariness and sprinted away from the gate, toward the north wall, around to the rear of the fort, through the open field, and into the woods, where they joined other warriors in swift retreat. The Americans fired a parting volley, kicking up the dust around them, then gave heavy-legged chase. On this day, Big Oak's sons outraced the bullets as well as the feet of their pursuers.

General Wayne was pleased with his victory, although he was not yet certain just how big a victory it might be. Maybe it was the evil disposition brought on by his aching leg, but mostly he was furious with the British for having the nerve to plant a fort well in what by treaty was clearly American territory. Wayne had fought a bitter war against them once before. He was determined to exact a price from them, for he was now positive that it was the English who had spurred the Shawnees, Miamis, Delawares, and Wyandots into this hopeless war.

That night he camped his forces on the hill within rifle shot of the fort, daring the English to start a fight. The fort held its peace. The next day he took a detachment of infantry into the field. Almost within spitting distance of the walls of the fort, he rode around the perimeter, studying the architecture and the armament, daring the English to make a hostile move. A few of his men walked down the hill on the other side to the trading post of Alexander McKee. They burned it to the ground and then proceeded to the cornfields of the allied tribes. It was summer, it was dry, and the cornfields burned like kindling, filling the Maumee Valley with gray smoke and announcing to the hiding Indians that the winter would be a long and hungry one for them and their families. Wayne decided that since the enemy had not counterattacked, it could be presumed they had scattered as a force. He decided that was the day to do some real damage to the valley. His men torched every field, every village, anything they could find near the rapids of the Maumee River that appeared to have been put there by any man, red or white.

Jinja and Thad were in a quandary. Even though the Americans had won a great victory and decimated the valley, they needed to continue their course of destruction before their return to Fort Defiance to nurse their wounded and recover from a difficult battle. They had humiliated the British and forced them to betray their red allies, but the British fort was still on the rapids of the Maumee, and the Indians might be back. They would carry with them a thirst for revenge. Woe be to any Americans who might fall in their way over the next few days or weeks.

But Jinja and Thad would have to go their own way if they were to care for Big Oak. A number of mounted officers and men had fallen in this battle. Thad, who was the better horseman of the two, decided to go looking for a roaming horse and bring it back as transportation for his father. He walked forward up the hill toward the fort, where he spotted a number of horses grazing on the green grass within range of the fort's guns.

But there was a parley going on between the commander of the fort and one of Wayne's officers. He felt it would be safe to climb the hill and catch a horse so long as he didn't come so close that he might tempt one of the redcoats manning the walls. He walked past a number of bodies on the way up the hill. There were two fine-looking horses standing together, chewing on tufts of grass, their reins dragging along the ground. They did not object as he came close to them and caught the bigger of the two, a chestnut mare. He turned his back on the fort and began to lead her down the hill, keeping the horse between him and the fort just in case one of the English soldiers could not resist taking a shot at him.

It was then that he saw the body of his boyhood friend. He was lying on his back, unscalped but stripped of his possessions by a soldier who had admired the beadworked bullet pouch that Kawia had made for him long ago. Holding tightly to the reins of the mare, Thad knelt down by Skoiyasi and studied the peaceful face. For a moment his mind returned to the early years on the Genesee River, when he, Skoiyasi, and Kawia shared the endless summers of their childhood. His throat knotted up as he thought about a world that was gone forever, a world he had run from many years before. Now he would give his soul for one more day, one more hour, with his childhood friends. He forced himself to turn away from the still form of Skoiyasi.

They rigged up a sort of a travois, placed Big Oak upon it and slowly brought him to the woods along the north bank of the Maumee. Then Jinja loped up the valley to the earthworks where General Wayne had his temporary headquarters. He asked permission to see the general and came forward.

"I heard your father was wounded," Wayne said. "I am terribly sorry. How bad off is he?"

Jinja shook his head. "He's still a strong man, sir," he replied, "but he's lost a lot of blood."

"Have him brought to our surgeon. We'll give him the best of care. They will pull him through."

Jinja had seen the work of battlefield surgeons. He had seen infection spread like wildfire through a field hospital. He would have none of the army's tender brand of care. "We'll take care of him, sir," he said. "That's why I'm here, to tell you we won't be joining you in the march back to Fort Defiance."

"You can't do this, Watley," replied the general, coloring a little. "We need you. You have no right."

Jinja smiled. "Sir, we are civilians. We have signed no papers. Received no pay. You do not need us anymore. You know the land well now. Any skirmishers will do as good a job as we could."

"I can make you stay," the general said.

Jinja fastened Wayne with a steady gaze. "You honor my grandfather. He fought for you at an age when he should have been sitting by his pond catching perch. Give him his fading hours with his family. You owe that to him."

If Wayne had been more alert that morning he might have realized that if Big Oak had been fading that fast, Jinja would not have left him to come to Wayne and take his formal leave. But Wayne had an army to think about, so he did not critique Jinja's reasoning. And Jinja was right. They had signed nothing. They were civilians who had just devoted some valuable time to the cause of his legion. "I am grateful for what you men did," he said. "You have been valuable to me, and that's why I would rather you not leave me. But you have that right."

Jinja made his way quickly down to the woods by the river. Big Oak lay on a blanket, saying nothing but following his grandson's movements with his eyes. "How is he doing?" Jinja asked his father.

"I don't know," Thad answered. "He's been asleep the whole time."

"He's not asleep now," Jinja noted. "His eyes are wide open."

Thad walked over to the blanket where his father lay. "Can you hear me, Pa?" he asked.

Big Oak turned his colorless face to his son. "Thad," he said. "How in hell are we gonna get across the river so we can head on south to Jinja's stockade?"

"My God," Thad responded, turning pale himself. "I kind of thought you were dying."

"I kinda thought that way myself, son. Someone must of plugged up my holes pretty good, now, don't you think?

While I'm figurin' out a way to get across this here river, will you get me some water to drink?"

"Sure, Pa," Thad said, and he walked down to the river to fill up his canteen and that of his father.

"Here is what we're gonna do, boys, and you should have thought of it yourselves. You're gonna lead this horse you've got here along the Maumee. We've got all these villages whose inhabitants have fled so, you see, I figure there has got to be at least one canoe left behind in the villages. We'll take it."

That's what they did, and sure enough they found not one, but three canoes left behind in the second village they came to. They chose one and laid the stoic, uncomplaining Big Oak on the bottom. They tied the horse to the stern of the canoe and let her swim across the river as they paddled the canoe toward the south shore. Once they had made it to the other side, Thad rode the horse along the shore and Jinja paddled the canoe until they spotted an opening in the forest that seemed to head south. They shoved the canoe into the middle of the river so the current would take it downstream, away from where they were. Then they again hitched up the travois to the horse and tenderly laid Big Oak down on it. Jinja smacked the horse a couple of times on the rump. She tugged at the travois and it headed into the forest with Thad ahead and Jinja behind.

The trail they found was old, and it petered out just a dozen miles south of the river. The way was rough for the wounded Big Oak, but he did not groan or complain when the travois bumped over a rock or hit a tree.

Having suffered a number of wounds in his life, Big Oak knew the feeling of infection, and so far he wasn't having any of it—no fever, and none of that particular type of soreness that makes you wish you had chosen to be a cobbler instead of a soldier or a scout. The first clearing they found in the woods, they halted for the day to give Big Oak time to rest.

It was late in August. The trees were still full of green, but there were a few yellow leaves blowing around the forest floor, and Big Oak could sense autumn around the corner. There was a time when he had loved autumn. It was a time a man could take stock of what he had and decide what else he needed to get through the winter. But since the boys had left, autumn had become the time of wondering: How many good autumns did he have left? When would he see the boys again? And then Cilla died and autumn turned neutral because he didn't much care how many autumns he had left.

In spite of his wound, this campaign had brought back a little of his old hunger for life. Watching his son and his grandson facing danger reminded him that he still had a lot left to lose.

The warm, humid, late summer afternoon had lulled him into a stupor on his bouncing travois when he was awakened by the faint smell of smoke in his nostrils. He turned and began to say something, but Thad cut him short.

"We caught a trace of it about a half mile back," his son said softly. "Jinja is skulking on up ahead. He oughta be back any minute." So they waited. Big Oak lay on his travois, but in his hands was his rifle, loaded and primed, while Thad knelt on one knee in front of the horse, his eyes scanning every direction except the one guarded by his father. After about five minutes the old man heard the snap of a twig, but it was Thad who first saw Jinja approaching. The look on his face was that of a man who had seen too much.

"They're gone," he said. "Six, seven Twightwees. It's a cabin, and it's bad."

It was less than a mile to the source of the smoke, a

pathetically tiny cabin in the midst of a small clearing, only about three acres. The cleared area was surrounded by woods, bordered on the south side by a creek, planted in corn on the east side from the shadows of the cabin almost to the beginning of the woods. The other half was a fenced grassy pasture that held three cows. There could not have been nearly enough grazing in the pasture for three cows, they must have grazed the cows along the banks of the creek. Now it no longer mattered. The cows lay on their sides, butchered by the raiders who had burned the cabin.

They stopped the horse by the creek bank and tied it up to a tree. Thad and Jinja left Big Oak lying on his travois while they walked carefully up to the cabin, which had by now burned nearly to the ground. Jinja found a young man in the doorway, his skull crushed, his scalp bare and bloody. Thirty yards away from the house lay a young woman, shot once in the back and scalped, otherwise untouched. Were there others? If so, there was no evidence. They found a horse grazing in the woods west of the little homestead. The warriors must have been in a hurry. They had not noticed the horse during their rampage.

This was a quick hit-and-run raid. There was no torture, total destruction, and, as far as Jinja could see, very little booty carried off. Thad and Jinja carried the two bodies to a ravine by the creek, lowered them into the ravine and filled it with rocks. Jinja found a bridle of sorts in a small outbuilding that the raiders had not bothered with, and suggested that Thad ride for a while on their newly acquired steed. Jinja started to lead the other horse, but Big Oak suggested that he might be ready to ride.

Jinja didn't believe it, but he knew how stubborn his grandfather could be, so he spread his blanket on the back of the animal and gave Big Oak a lift. With a harsh grunt,

Big Oak eased his wounded leg over the back of the animal and found himself a seat.

"I wonder what brought them this way," Jinja said after they had been on the trail for an hour, silently studying the footprints in front of them and judging that the Twightwees were running along at a pretty swift clip.

Thad shook his head, but Big Oak thought he knew. "They had to have fled from the battle," he said. "This was a fight none of the warriors wanted to miss. I believe they're headin' due south for the Ohio. Once they get there, they will find or make a canoe and take the river west as fast as their paddle blades can take them."

Jinja stopped walking for a moment and looked up at his father and his grandfather. "What I been thinkin'," he said, "is that if they take a beeline south, they'll come right near the stockade, and right near Henri and Joanna's cabin. I'm thinking we ought to try to beat them there."

Thad laughed. "We can't beat them there and you know it. Maybe you could, by yourself, but who says we're safe? Besides, if they're in such a hurry to catch the river west, as your grandpa says, what makes you think they're gonna run dead into the stockade?"

"Because this little trace we're on now leads directly to the fort."

"But Henri and Joanna are not at the fort. Besides, Henri can take care of himself. It isn't Henri you're worried about. It's that girl. You're partial to that girl, aren't you?"

Jinja did not immediately offer a rebuttal. They walked about a mile farther before Jinja replied. "It ain't like you think it is," he said to his father. "I don't feel that way about her."

"What is it, then?" Thad asked.

Jinja was silent.

"I think he feels sorry for the girl," Big Oak said through clenched teeth.

"She's not what you think she is," Jinja insisted.

Big Oak looked down at his grandson from atop the big army horse he was riding. "Tell you what, Jinja. I've been watching you for more than thirty years now and you always liked to live dangerously. When things get calm, you get bored. Whatever things that girl is, boring ain't one of them." He shook his head. "But bein' around her is too big a price to pay for not being bored."

The furrows dissolved into a smile that took in Jinja's entire face while he weighed his grandfather's words. "I know what you say is true," he said. "You have to believe me. I don't get sad thinkin' about her, and Lord knows, I don't want her tendin' my cabin for me. I just think about her a lot."

"You know me, boy," Big Oak continued. "I don't judge. But life's too short, and thinkin' about a woman can do funny things to you. You let a woman make a home in your mind and soon she'll be makin' a home in your wigwam. You know what I mean?"

"You mean like you and that woman in the story the general told us?"

"Jinja," he said, "it took me two years to get that woman off my mind."

"Did you really consider goin' to England with her?"

Now it was Big Oak's turn to take plenty of time while he weighed his words.

"Never," he replied finally.

25

THE TRACE THEY WERE TRAVELING WOULD reach the Ohio River at least a mile west of the company stockade. But two miles before it hit the river, the footprints turned onto another trail that headed east. All three agreed that before they could check on the stockade they would have to follow the raiders along the trail, which meandered close to Joanna's cabin.

They traveled about a mile. Thad had had enough of riding without a saddle to suit him for the rest of his life, so he was leading his horse, walking beside Jinja. His son came to an abrupt halt, like a hound on the point, his nostrils flared.

"They've been here and gone," he told his father and Big Oak. He said nothing more and his voice was flat, but Thad could guess what he meant. They picked up the pace and arrived at the compound Joanna's father had built years before. The main cabin was half burned, as if the raiders had tired of pillaging before they had been able to finish the job. At first the area seemed entirely deserted, but while Jinja and Thad were going through the charred buildings, Big Oak looked around and spotted Henri, or what was left of him, stripped naked.

He was bound tightly to a hackberry tree, his bloody-skulled head leaning forward in stillness. His hands lacked fingers and his feet lacked toes. He was surrounded by charred piles of wood that had sizzled him like a barbecued steer. Cooked strips of skin had been flayed from his body. A part of him had been cut off and stuffed in his mouth. This happy French Canadian who begrudged nothing to any man had ended his life in indescribable torment, and Big Oak knew why.

"They had expected an easy massacre," he explained. "I found a whole lot of blood near a tree at the tree line. I think he shot one of them. And look. Here's his knife. Blood on it. They probably charged him after he fired his rifle, and he fought them off for a while with that knife. He might have gotten more than one with it. You know how they are. They hated him for what he did to them and respected him for his bravery. God rest his soul." Jinja looked shaken as Big Oak spoke. He liked Henri very much, and it didn't seem to bother him that Joanna preferred Henri to himself. As for Joanna, there was no sign of her until they found tracks that led toward the river. There were six sets of tracks. Five of them wore moccasins. The sixth was a pair of smaller, bare feet. They followed the tracks along the flood plain. Eventually they reached the creek that led to the stockade, and then the place where Jinja had hidden the two canoes.

Both canoes were gone.

"We've got to go after them," Jinja insisted.

Thad shook his head. "Your grandfather can't travel and we can't leave him here alone. They have a big head start on us and we're not even sure which way they're going."

Jinja scowled. "You know very well which way they're going. They're going west."

"West . . ." Thad mused. "And then where? Licking

Creek? Miami River? Ohio River how far? Tell me, my son, how do you follow a cold trail on a river? And why would you want to? This woman who was so cruel to you, who had no respect for you. To care for someone who does not care for you—that is a terrible weakness. I have never seen that in you before. And for such as her. Why?"

"It's not like you say. That's not how I feel about her."

"If she was an old crone, would you be so eager to put our lives on the line by chasing her into a country where the enemy has fled, where the enemy hates us so that our lives would be worth nothing? Old crone, my son. Would you chase an old crone?"

"No—no, I wouldn't, but I have never touched her, never tried to make love to her, never showed—"

"Because you were afraid she would say something that would make you feel small. Your mother could never make you feel that way, not at her worst, nor me, nor your grandfather Dieter, nor any of the girls in Albany nor anybody else I ever knew. *Why her?*"

"I don't know why her—no, it's not like you think. How she hated and feared the Indians above anything else on this earth. After what they did to her father and the people in Walker Valley—after what they did to her mother. I can't stand to see her in the wigwam of some warrior who will use her like a slave."

Thad squelched a laugh. "I don't envy that warrior. A tongue like that—within a week he'll be back on the warpath just to get away from her." They stopped their conversation at the front gate of the Wendel and Watley stockade. They were relieved to see that it was intact. Big Oak and Thad had dismounted and stood beside Jinja while he fished into his pack.

The stockade gates had a large padlock on the outside. There were two keys to that lock, one of which Jinja carried, the other one buried near the southwest corner of the stockade. Jinja took the key from his pack and turned it in the lock. The tumblers would not budge. He put more muscle into turning the key. It yielded a little but not much. Now he jiggled the key in the lock and turned it again, and this time it opened. He was about to push the gate forward when he felt a hand on his shoulder. It was Big Oak.

"Don't open the gate," he said quietly.

"Why?"

"They're in there."

Jinja did not have to ask who was inside the fort. He knew.

"What do we do, then?"

"Keep fiddling with the lock and we'll talk about it. They're hidin' on the walls, ready to hit us as soon as we open the gate. They're not where they can shoot us now. Rattle that lock and cuss a little."

Jinja rattled the lock and cussed a lot. Meanwhile Big Oak presented his plan. "What we're gonna do is pretend to give up on the lock. We need an excuse to rush away from the stockade suddenly, without them figurin' out that they know we're in there."

Thad had an idea. "I'm gonna lose control of this horse right here, get him running, and then we'll chase him. If we can just make it twenty or thirty yards we'll be in the tall grass and brush and we'll make tougher targets in case they decide to shoot."

Big Oak remounted his horse, as if making ready to enter the stockade on horseback. Meanwhile Thad took his knife from his belt and pretended to try it on the lock. After a minute or two he turned his back on the stockade and surreptitiously stuck the horse in the abdomen just hard enough to make the animal bolt and run. Thad and

Jinja ran after the horse and Big Oak rode close behind. They all zigzagged through the field just in case the warriors in the stockade decided to shoot, and fortunately the horse galloped across the creek and out of sight of the fort. When they caught it they led it farther into the woods, then tied the horses up and sat down to talk about what they were going to do to get their stockade back.

"You sure there's somebody in there?" Jinja asked his grandfather, who was stepping gingerly on his wounded leg and finding it still capable of only limited service.

"There's a loophole up there that should have had sky showing through it, and instead it showed dark. Moving dark."

"All right, we've got warriors up there. How are we gonna get our stockade back from them?" Thad asked.

"Beats me," Big Oak replied. "Unless we can come back in a night or two, open the gate, sneak in and take care of them while they're asleep."

Jinja smiled. "It's a noisy lock, but I did get it open, and I didn't *quite* relock it."

"I don't know," Big Oak mused. "They might have the gate guarded, and anyway, I remember how bad those gate hinges creak."

They took out a little parboiled corn and chewed on it. The scanty meal must have helped Jinja's memory. "You know," he said, "we do have a secret gate."

Thad looked at his son in disgust. "You finally remembered, hey? Any chance they might have found it?"

Jinja shrugged his shoulders. "I don't see how," he said. "It comes in under the floor of the warehouse, behind a row of barrels."

"Well then," Big Oak said, "I suggest we get a little rest now and do a little raiding of our own tonight."

They rode the horses farther into the woods northwest

of the stockade and made camp two miles away. They kindled no fire, and they talked in hushed voices.

"How do you suppose they knew we were here?" Thad asked.

Big Oak thought for a moment. He was very tired. "Maybe they knew they were being followed."

"But they were ready for us," Thad persisted. "Don't tell me they were standing ready for us the past two days, night and day."

It was Jinja who had the answer. "It's not hard to figure out," he said. "Don't you remember? There's a lookout tower outside the fort. Overlooks the valley. They could see us from the tower long before we were close enough to the fort to see them."

The air was growing cooler as the sun vanished, leaving a red blush on the western horizon. Beyond the blush were the layers of blue that blended to black, with an early star winking.

"I have been chewin' on our problem," Big Oak said softly.

"It's no problem," his grandson responded. "We sneak on in there, kill the Indians while they sleep, free Joanna, and get the stockade in shape for the tradin' business."

Big Oak shook his head. "It's the girl you want, I know that. But what makes you think she's in the stockade? The canoes are gone. I think the group might have split in two. One took over the stockade and the other paddled west. In that group was a warrior looking for peace, looking to find a home far away from the white men, and he thought it might be a good idea to have a woman to go with him."

"Looking for peace, eh?" Thad snorted. "I don't think that woman'll last a month with a Twightwee warrior."

"We gotta find out if she's in there," Jinja insisted.

"If I had it my way," Big Oak said, "I'd head for home

right now and to hell with her. I've lived through two peaceable marriages and I can't for the life of me figure out why you would want to have anything to do with her. But if it's something you have to do, I would suggest you go in tonight and don't kill anybody unless they spot you. Go on in and look around and see if she's there and how many of them there are. Just you. You leave your father out of it. Two'll just make more noise and"—he looked at his son—"Thad is past his prime as a sneakin' spy."

It was well past midnight when Jinja made his way down the creek, then up the hill that stood between the fort and the Ohio River. While they were building the stockade, Jinja had discovered the tiny entrance to a cave that extended deep into the side of the slope on which they had built the stockade. To his surprise, the rear of the cave turned out to be clay, and he had started to dig toward the fort in his spare time. After the stockade had been rebuilt, Thad and Big Oak helped him dig the tunnel the rest of the way to the fort. They then spent considerable time camouflaging the opening, first narrowing the entrance even further, then corking it with a large flat rock and hiding the rock under a natural-looking pile of fallen wood.

Jinja heard the hoot of an owl as he arrived at the spot and began to unpile the wood. Moving the rock was no chore for a man of his great strength. Big Oak had convinced him to leave his rifle behind, that under the circumstances his knife and hatchet would be more effective.

He crawled along the floor of the cave, through spiderwebs, sniffing at the dank clay and listening for any noises that might spell danger. The exit inside the stockade was well-hidden, but there was always a chance that the Indians inside might have found it, and if so, they would expect the owners of the stockade—the people with the key to the lock—to use it. So there was always the chance that someone might be squatting at the other end of the tunnel with a smile on his face and a tomahawk in his hand, waiting.

He could feel the floor of the tunnel slanting up now. He continued to crawl until his hand touched a big old tree root that told him he was only a few feet from the exit. He lay in the dark, holding his breath and listening for any signs that he had been discovered. He thought he may have heard a rat gnawing somewhere, but that was all he heard. He began to move forward again, reached out his hand above him in the darkness and found the floor of the warehouse.

It was just one plank of the floor that moved. So cunningly fitted that you could walk on it without it feeling loose, it was easy to push up and lay aside. It took a thin man to squeeze through, but Jinja had no spare fat on his frame. He pushed himself up through the opening and found himself behind a row of barrels, as he knew he would be. Softly, he crawled past the boxes and to the entrance. There were no windows in the warehouse. If he wanted to find out what was going on outside, he had to open the door. First he lay down by the door, which was a crude affair with leather thongs for hinges and another leather thong outside that tied the door shut. The door did not fit any too snugly either.

He listened and at first heard nothing, then heard what sounded like steps on the catwalk—soft, moccasined steps, one set. When the steps stopped, they stopped toward the back of the stockade. The warehouse was in the front.

With his knife, he cut the thong, opened the door and crept out. He picked up a pair of rocks from the ground and placed them to hold the door shut, then looked around. His eyes were used to the dark by this time. He saw the dim shapes of two young men on the catwalk, one toward the rear and one by the gate. Both of them were peering earnestly into the night.

He was about to crawl toward the store when he saw something that nearly made his heart stop. Out of the corner of his eye he spotted another shape, a human shape. He turned his head and saw that the shape was no more than ten feet from him and that the man was sleeping, sitting on the bare dirt ground and leaning back against the logs of the warehouse. Here was an opportunity, he thought, and hardly had the thought come to his mind when the man stirred and stared straight at him. He was an older warrior, a Shawnee, not as old as Big Oak but nevertheless too old to be on the warpath. Jinja did not think. He reacted, drawing his hatchet as he sprang silently toward the old warrior. The man opened his mouth to cry out, but he was groggy and his reaction was slow. The flat of Jinja's hatchet connected with the side of the old man's head with a flat *click* sound, and the old man went limp.

He could hear one of the sentries on the catwalk walking toward them and he knew he had no chance to hide. He simply sat next to the old warrior, propped him up, and prayed. The sentry looked down from his post and saw two vague figures in the deep moon-shadow of the warehouse. Perhaps if he had paused in his rounds to look just a little closer, he might have thought the two figures were a little too close together, or that one of them was heavily clothed and missing a blanket. But the night had been a long one. The sentry was tired. He saw what he wanted to see.

Jinja held his breath while the footsteps went past on the catwalk above. He waited until the sentry had returned and was well along the catwalk to the back side of the stockade. Then he lifted the unconscious Shawnee and carried him through the doorway into the warehouse. He placed his captive gently on the floor, braced the door closed with rocks, dropped the old man down into the hole, went down after him and replaced the board. He crawled over the old warrior and started to drag him through the tunnel. About halfway along the captive started to groan softly.

Damn, Jinja thought. He took the old man's arm and pulled him along through the tunnel as fast as he could. It was cool in the tunnel, but it was also damp. Jinja's effort made him sweat furiously. His hand got slippery and started to lose its grip. To make things worse, the old man started to resist even though he was not yet conscious. Jinja pulled the old warrior along on his back, his moccasins digging into the clay floor of the tunnel. It was hard work, especially when the prisoner was digging in his heels. Then Jinja would shake him, jerk him forward, and continue to drag him.

He could feel the tunnel rising up to meet the surface of the earth. Between the sweat and the slick coating of bear grease, it became almost impossible to pull the old man forward. Nevertheless, Jinja managed. With a last great effort Jinja dragged him through the mouth of the cave, and they both rested on the floor of the forest. Jinja waited a few moments to catch his breath, then picked the old Indian up and bore him toward their tiny encampment. He ran through the woods carrying his prisoner across his shoulders. There was no time to lose. It would not do for the warrior to awaken enough to be aware of what was happening to him. He would cry out and then all hell would break loose. So Jinja ran as hard as he could. The old man was skinny and dried up, but he still seemed heavy and unwieldy to Jinja as he ran with his unconscious captive bouncing up and down on his shoulders along the woods path.

Halfway back to the camp, weary and breathless, Jinja

tripped and fell headlong to the ground. The old Shawnee went sprawling, his body bouncing off several roots and slamming into a big old hickory tree. Jinja lay there for a moment, catching his breath and watching the old man carefully, to see if the fall had brought him back to consciousness or killed him. He heard a groan from the gray warrior but did not see the man move. With great effort, Jinja arose to his feet, squatted and picked up his captive and continued his laboring way back to their camp.

He heard the click of two hammers as he approached camp, and recognized the second click as that of Big Oak's rifle. Gently he lowered the old Shawnee to the ground and knelt down beside him. The old man's breathing was regular. His hands were opening and closing. There was a swelling above his right eye. A soft groan escaped from his mouth.

"What did you do to this man and why is he here?" Thad asked matter-of-factly.

"Only way I could think of findin' out where Joanna is was to get him out of the stockade," Jinja answered.

"That makes a lot of sense," Big Oak said, "but it looks like he caught a severe beating somewhere along the way."

They could see Jinja's look of embarrassment in the moonlight.

"We . . . we fell . . . you see," Jinja replied.

"You did," Big Oak observed. "How many times?"

"Just once."

Thad had wet a piece of old shirting with water from his canteen and was wiping the Shawnee's face with it. They watched the Indian's eyelids flicker and then open, first blinking, then fixing on narrow slits as he grasped his situation.

Big Oak knew four of the six Iroquois dialects and a

smattering of at least seven others. Now he attempted to engage the old warrior with his smattering of Shawnee.

"I am Big Oak," he said. "How are you called?"

The Shawnee did not respond. The eyes remained slits.

"We will not harm you. We are of the Longhouse."

That might not have been the right thing to say. The Shawnee did not have a fond history of relations with the Iroquois. The older ones remembered them as fierce warriors with fiendish tortures. The old man's face twitched and his body stiffened.

"Sit him up and give him some water to drink," Big Oak said. Jinja did as he was told. The old man groaned as his body assumed the new position. "His body probably wasn't all that great *before* you got to work on him," Big Oak told Jinja. "Now he can't figure out when and how he got all beat up."

"I know," Jinja said irritably. "But I got us a prisoner."

Big Oak nodded and returned his attention to the Shawnee.

"You are old to be out on the warpath, Grandfather," Big Oak said. This time the Shawnee's face curled into a grim smile, for he could see that Big Oak had plenty of years on him.

"Ah yes, Grandfather," Big Oak continued. "You and me both, we should be in our lodge, near our fire, with our pipe and our grandchildren. But my wife is gone, and the lodge holds only sadness for me."

The old Shawnee's head must have cleared during Big Oak's speech. "Water," the old man requested, and Jinja complied. He drank slowly, sparingly, and when he was done his face was more severe. He knew that Big Oak was struggling with the Shawnee tongue, so he spoke slowly, as if to a backward child.

"Like you, I no longer have a wife," he said sadly. "But

not like you, there is no longer a place for my lodge. My home is the warpath because my villages are gone. Now, Longhouse," he said sarcastically, for he knew that Big Oak was a white man. "Do what you will with me. I do not wish to be alive in your company."

Big Oak shook his head. "We do not wish to harm you. It was my grandson who took you, because he wanted to know where your warriors took the woman."

"Your woman?" the Shawnee asked in surprise.

"Not our woman," Big Oak replied.

"That is good for you!" the old man said. "But then what would you want with such a woman?"

Big Oak rolled his eyes. "Not me," he said, pointing. "Him. And I still don't know what he wants with her."

"That woman," the Shawnee said with such a depth of dismay that Big Oak had to laugh.

"I am Big Oak," the old hunter repeated. "What are you called?"

"I am called Hidden Heart," the old man answered, signing as he spoke, in case Big Oak missed the words. Indeed, Big Oak had not known the Shawnee word for heart. "Did you fight in the battle of the fallen trees?" he asked.

"We were there, and you?"

In response, Hidden Heart pulled a blond-haired scalp from his waistband.

There was light in the forest now, first dawn, and in the new light Big Oak could see the deep wrinkles and the wispy gray hair of Hidden Heart. His chest was sunken in and his belly stuck out, although not very far. The lump above his eye was colored a deep purple.

"Would you like something to eat, Grandfather?" Big Oak asked him. The old man did not answer. With the coming of dawn, he expected to be killed or tortured. "Tell us where the girl is. We will let you go."

"There is a warrior who wanted the woman. He took her—" He pointed away from the new sun, west along the Ohio River. "That was when we first came here."

"After you killed the Frenchman?"

"A Frenchman?" The Shawnee looked surprised. "We did not know, or we would not have killed him. It is too bad our young brave cut his tongue out in the beginning. I do not know where he took that woman, but he will be sorry he took her."

"One brave took her west," Big Oak told Jinja. "But he does not know where." Big Oak caught a glint in his grandson's eyes. "Do not think of following. The farther west you go, the more Shawnees. They will slice you up like a beef cow."

Jinja did not reply. "Would you like something to eat?" Big Oak asked Hidden Heart. The old Shawnee did not answer. In the dawn light, he was certain that his time had finally come.

26

THE CHILL WIND BLEW THE RIPPLES IN COLD wavelets across the surface of Big Oak Pond. They blew the leaves in a golden shower onto the shore and into the lake. Along the shore, unheeding, wrapped in a blanket to seal out the October cold, sat a melancholy Big Oak.

In the twilight, watching the feeble sun sink toward the horizon, he tasted the bitterness of being alone late in life.

On the long trek home, Big Oak's leg had gotten better and better, until he could climb down from the discomfort of his horse's back and continue home on his own feet. As long as he walked in the company of Jinja and Thad, his spirit stayed strong, but when they came within sight of Albany, the trail forked. Although both his son and grandson pleaded with him to spend some time in Albany, Big Oak took the north fork of the trail. Thad and Jinja watched with a terrible ache in their hearts as the once mighty hunter and scout vanished into the forest of tall oaks and maples. Big Oak could not bear to go with them to Albany. Katherine would be socially embarrassed by his presence and would attempt to make him stay in his room. Thad would resume the social calendar he could barely tolerate in order to preserve the domestic peace. And Jinja had already decided to go west again, this time by himself, chasing after Joanna. Big Oak was certain that one day soon Katherine would come to Thad shrieking that her one and only son had disappeared the night before and did Thad know where he had gone? Thad would know, all right, but he would not dare to tell her.

So Big Oak had gone alone to his house on Big Oak Pond. Still resilient, his tears no longer flowed over the loss of Cilla, but there was an empty space inside him that needed to be filled. The second day after he had arrived home, he cleaned up the house. As he worked, his memory marveled at the thought that this woman, who had fought with such deadly effect to free him from the lake tribes, could take such great pride in the modest arts of housekeeping and raising children.

The memory of his three Tuscarora sons made him realize that much of his heartache was fear that they might be lost to him forever. He had dreaded the thought of seeing them in his sights at Fallen Timbers. Of course, he would not have pulled a trigger on one of them, they were his sons, with their own convictions. Still, he was concerned for their safety, and in the absence of Cilla, he missed them terribly.

On this, the third night after his arrival, he ate trail corn and drank water from the well, then wrapped his blanket around him and went to sleep before the fireplace, in which he had kindled a roaring fire. In the morning he awoke with a dream of Cilla fresh in his mind. Maybe, he thought, he could sustain life in the warmth of these nightly dreams. In the bleak early morning he made his way out of the house, down the hill, to the shore of the pond. He had no kinnikinnick to smoke, and probably would have ignored it had it been present. Pleasures meant little to him. Only the will to survive made him eat at all.

He sat huddled in his blankets, his back pressed up against the sycamore tree, and thought about Hidden Heart. When Hidden Heart realized that the three strange white men were not going to torture him, his spirit crumbled. Old, crippled, tired, and sore from his unconscious encounter with Jinja, he felt he was no longer a warrior, that the only thing he could still do was withstand the tortures like a real man should. But there would be no tortures. His captors must have felt he was so withered and useless that they neither feared him nor respected him enough to test him and kill him.

These men were so strange to him. The old one with the red man name, Big Oak, was obviously no red man, yet spoke his language. The one called T'ad did not speak his tongue and he acted like the white men in the towns, and yet he looked more like a red man. The youngest they called by the strange name that was maybe a Longhouse name, and he looked a little like a red man, yet he did not act like one.

The man Big Oak was a friendly man, and the hatred that Hidden Heart had carried through the years of strife with the whites faded before Big Oak's kindness and his own weakness. Big Oak knew that something had happened to the old man when Jinja had knocked him unconscious and then fallen with him. He thought that the old man might be dying.

"Let me give you food, Grandfather," he had said again to Hidden Heart.

"A little water now, food maybe later," Hidden Heart replied. "What is it you want from me? White man always wants something from an Indian in return."

"I want your time, Grandfather. I have a message to you for your people."

"I will listen," the old man said. Big Oak was not so

foolish as to believe that Hidden Heart would take his words and spread them among the scattered Shawnee. Big Oak seldom felt compelled to open his heart to anyone, but as he felt his own death closing in on him, there were thoughts he needed to share.

"Hidden Heart," he said, "I have lived among the Senecas and the Mohawks and the Oneidas most of my life. But I am a white man, and I know the white man. There is a choice for the Indians."

"Indians," Hidden Heart repeated. He knew the word. He knew what it meant, yet after all the years of fighting against other Indian tribes, it was still hard for him to grasp the idea that the Shawnees and, say, the Mohawks were the same people. He still did not believe it was so. Only the whites really believed it was so.

"You must go west. Go far west, far away from the white man. Tell them that the white men's guns, and kettles, and metal knives are good but they are not worth the price you must pay for them. Tell them to go far away."

Hidden Heart raised his hand and waved away Big Oak's idea as if it were a dandelion seed in the wind. "Easy to say. Wherever we go we will find an enemy—the Sioux, or the Osage, or the Chickasaw. They will not share their land with us. We have spent too many moons too close to the whites. Those who have not been close to the whites are still strong and will drive us away."

"The Shawnee must find a way to live in peace with the Sioux or the Chickasaws," Big Oak replied.

"Live in peace like the Fifteen Fires and the English? Like the English and the French?" Hidden Heart asked, ironically.

"There are so many Englishmen," replied Big Oak, "so many Frenchmen, that they may fight their wars forever and still there will be an England and a France and plenty of people for another war. It is not so with the Shawnees."

Sipping his water, slowly, made the old man stronger. His thoughts were clear and his words honest.

"In the East is a place you call Wyoming Valley," he said.

"I have been there," Big Oak recalled. "Jinja nearly died there."

"Long, long ago," Hidden Heart continued, "when I was very young, we lived in peace with the Lenni Lenape in that valley. One day, when the men of the Lenni Lenape were out hunting, the women of the Lenni Lenape went down to the river where the wild plums grew and they began to gather plums. Some of the women and children of the Shawanoes had crossed the river in canoes and were also there gathering plums and berries. They greeted each other as friends and each group continued their search for the fruit, for there was plenty of it, enough for everybody.

"One of the children of the Shawanoes caught the biggest grasshopper anyone there had ever seen. The child was a little fellow, but he was a fighter. One of the bigger boys from the Lenni Lenape demanded to see it, and then would not give it back. They began to shout at each other and a fight began that was so noisy the mothers came over to quiet them down.

"Among our mothers, their child cannot be the evil one in an argument."

"It is so among the white men also," Big Oak observed.

"And soon the women had taken up the argument started by their children, over who the grasshopper belonged to. Some of the women of the Lenni Lenape said the grasshopper belonged to them because the Shawanoes had no right to be on that side of the river. They told the Shawanoe women to leave, and when they did not, the women of the Lenni Lenape forced them back to their canoes, for they were many compared to the Shawanoe women. The women of the Shawanoes went back to their own side of the river. But when their husbands returned from the hunt, the women told them about what happened. The men were angry. They picked up their rifles and their bows and their tomahawks and they crossed the river to seek vengeance.

"But in the meantime, the Lenni Lenape women had told their men what had happened. When the Shawanoes arrived at the other side of the river, the men of the Lenni Lenape were waiting in ambush. They began to shoot when the Shawanoes were still in their canoes. Many good young men died on the river that day. The Shawanoes landed and fought hard but so many had been killed on the river that they were driven back to their canoes by the men of the Lenni Lenape, not before they had fought bravely and killed many of them.

"That battle, over a grasshopper, so weakened our people that they had to move to where the sun hides. If we can go to war over a grasshopper, then how can we live in peace together or unite against the white man?"

The image faded over the pond. Big Oak pulled his blanket closer around him. Hidden Heart had not died after all. He had the spirit to survive. Jinja had tried to persuade Big Oak and Thad to help him take Hidden Heart west and trade him for Joanna.

"Why do you want her?" Thad asked.

Jinja would not answer.

"I will not help you find that harridan so you can be miserable for the rest of your life," Thad said.

"Like you and Ma?" Jinja asked.

Thad laughed. "Your mother isn't half as bad as that one. She just likes to be around mincing gentlemen in silk slippers. She likes little orchestras and big party rooms and rich, gossipy women. She doesn't beat down on a man like he was a war drum—like that woman you want to snatch from the jaws of the Shawnee nation. Tell you what, son. I love your mother. I just need to get away from her now and then. But you—and that woman—that Joanna . . ."

Jinja did not reply, and Thad let the matter drop. They never spoke of it again, but one gray dawn after they returned to Albany, Jinja slipped out of the house, leaving a note that said he'd be back in a month or two.

Big Oak reached out from under his blanket and tossed a single pebble into the pond. A small fish surfaced and bit at a ripple. If Jinja hadn't gone off to chase the woman, he'd probably be visiting him on this day. Big Oak thought about his grandson, so much more like him than Thad. It's a good thing for him to rescue his damsel. He knew Jinja. He would not put up with her bad disposition forever. Either he would gentle her down or he would throw her out. Jinja was his own man, like himself.

He barely heard the twig snap ten yards away from where he sat wrapped in his blanket. A few short years before a sudden sound like that would have brought him to his feet with his rifle cocked and leveled. Now the first clue he had that he was not alone was a gentle hand on his shoulder.

He turned quickly and found himself looking into the dark eyes of Caleb and Joshua.

With great effort he climbed to his feet, threw off his blanket and hugged them both. "Where have you been?" he asked.

"In the West, fighting Americans."

"In the field of the fallen trees?" he asked with wonder. They both nodded. "We beat the tar out of you, didn't we?"

They nodded, solemnly, and Big Oak was suddenly struck with fear.

"Where is Ken?" he asked with dread.

"Somewhere," Caleb replied.

"Went north to Canada to visit the Mohawks," Joshua added.

"He's all right, you're sure?" Big Oak demanded to know.

"Last we saw," Joshua answered. His gaze was steady. Joshua was telling the truth. "Were you there?" the young man asked with amazement.

"I did my part," Big Oak said. "My last warpath, I am sure. You gonna stay with me a spell?" he asked, and refused to let the tears fill his eyes.

Caleb studied his father's face. "Seems like a good place to be, these times," he said. "We have to decide," he added, and Big Oak knew that he meant they had to decide on what side of the blanket they would live.

"I wish Kendee had come back with you," Big Oak said.

"He will rejoin us soon," Caleb promised. "We all saw the future in the blood that flowed on the Maumee River. It is hard to see your people going away before your eyes."

All three looked across the pond, toward the wooded hills. "Is it not odd," Big Oak asked, "that the leaves are most beautiful when they are dying? And yet the tree lives on, dropping seeds for new trees. I knew the Senecas when they were still a great people. And the Mohawks. Their greatness shone bright like the autumn leaves, and yet they were soon to enter a long cold winter.

"You can defeat a people, but their greatness will live on, like that tree. One day spring will return to the Longhouse. Stay with me for now. But always watch for the new leaves to come. And when they do, go to them. You are Ganonsyoni."